M D Matthews has a background in social sciences and is a semi-retired professional driver. Now with a grown family, he lives and works close to the Lake District, England. These days, countryside is preferred over the clamour or glamour of a city.

M D Matthews

COMFORTING MELANCHOLY

A Whitches Story

AUSTIN MACAULEY PUBLISHERS™

LONDON • CAMBRIDGE • NEW YORK • SHARJAH

A CIP catalogue record for this title is available from the British Library.

ISBN 9781528995276 (Paperback)
ISBN 9781528995283 (ePub e-book)

www.austinmacauley.com

First Published (2020)
Austin Macauley Publishers Ltd
25 Canada Square
Canary Wharf
London
E14 5LQ

A thank you to my sponsor, Audrey.

Chapter One

A few years ago now, so far enough away for telling in comfort. The evening of the first Friday in November 1992. The beginning at a traditional grey industrial town in northern England. Not Manchester, Newcastle or Sheffield, you may appreciate, nor was the place anywhere remotely similar. The above are cities, you will understand. Indeed, Whitches is not a city, but a town. If you look closely, Whitches can be found on the map. Good for you, if able to find it. Maybe you even know the town, perhaps not otherwise. To be honest with you, it does not matter, whether located or not. Just identify with enough of that Whitches does exist and, of course, people live there.

Here in Whitches is the story. The day was a normal one. For me, despite the customary unfathomable depths of life, there was really nothing of special interest to look forward to and little of note to reflect upon. A pointer to five or six on a scale from one to ten for general happiness would have indicated this. Hundreds, just like me, myself included (obviously), had worked in the day and were looking forward with a kind of grim satisfaction from the week just passed. In rapidly fading light, most hurried on as the day surrendered to an arresting wintry grip. At the onset of this particular gloomy evening, I recognised freedom from the Monday to Friday shackles of paid employment. It was a kind of content welcome setting in.

Darkness grew thicker by the November air signalling a temporary end to the grind. The descended night had gradually depressed the drab day and begun to support a clammy acidic mist. In the dragging rush hour, cars and pedestrians floundered on between whiles as the weekend beckoned ahead once again for most. As vehicles made slow, all around headlights shone bright through the eye smarting atmosphere. In the flared rays, tiny droplets glinted like celestial dust caught in moonlight. I walked in relentless urgency, the only accompaniment an ambiguous escort of expectation and dread. The minutes clicked clockwise, effortless toward my six o'clock appearance. All around, citizens of Whitches walked collectively separate, moving together with nobody in all directions on disconnected missions inside their individual bubbles.

Having filtered away from the many commuters, my arrival alone before the old door was an instant comfort. I, at last, stood right there in perverse eagerness and fumbled clumsily for the key. Turning the lock became a luxurious moment, for away from dark and chilled night this time of six was a sudden relief. I stepped forward and inward with definite purpose into the foyer. Wet mist began to pervade the interior, seeking out every vulnerable niche. Inside, an assembled company of two had already dressed to leave. They were instantly aware of damp coldness as I shuffled in to occupy the restricted space. With such dimensions there, it meant we moved in avoidant circles of each other. The two people, one female elderly, the other male a little younger seemed mentally weary and were thus anxious to escape. With a fresh glow, but now of ceased exertion, I greeted them on their departure as they facilitated my beginning. Their melancholy appearance, now bore heavily on my mind, left there to float around in my dreamy head. I spoke to reply in an orderly reserved mechanical way. Inevitably I assumed, what had worn them out that afternoon would lag behind and equally fatigue me into the evening. The enthusiastic vocal "hello, goodbye" was a mildly amusing note to begin on. My first duty was to kettle and to coffee.

Over an hour passed, time was sinking again, so it was back to a reverie which haunted my life. Why am I doing this? I wondered. Why for heaven's sake, thinking again and again. Looking deep into the vessel, the mug, the pitcher, the receptacle. No, it is simply a mug! Why do I, or indeed why do we or even why do you and me – why do some people over analyse the everyday? Profoundly Crazy! Me? Sombrely anxious!

Coffee cascaded downward as the stainless steel, yet grubby teaspoon tilted. I held the spoon between thumb and forefinger. Too tight I held it! It betrayed an otherwise nonchalant action. A tiny uncontrolled motion at the small end, exaggerated to a seemingly great shake at the tip of the spoon. Those volatile bitter coffee granules plunged down disturbing the calm and shallow sample of taupe milk contained inside the mug. Uncanny it was, that noise. A clatter almost. Oh so amplified! It was a sound which I could not in honesty remember previously. Though sight of freeze dried coffee hitting milk, then reacting with the liquid as I enthusiastically poured boiling water had a familiar resonance.

It was as if, I at that instant was beginning to develop a new perception of the everyday. The subject of the everyday or commonplace is after all what we (that is you, me and others) take for granted. Yet we still may have different ideas about this, that and the other. The concept of our understanding, such as the ordinary being taken for granted does not hang too well with inquisitive thought and discovery. Actually, one contradicts the other… The day-to-day, the ordinary or mundane, against unusual, abnormal or exciting.

"Robert," it was a shrill female. "What are you doing?"
With that I spilled the boiling water all over the worktop. "Ow, you made me jump," I replied, reaching toward the sink for something to mop up quickly.

"Sorry, dear," came back the disapproving female voice. It was Stella. Stella did not look like a 'Stella'. No, she was more of a Juliet. I had the impression that Stella with her soft appealing features and usual warm tone ought to be a Juliet. I do not know why I felt like that. It was not as if I knew or had known a Juliet. Perhaps it had a little to do with all that Shakespeare she is so keen on, but Stella was hardly an adolescent nymph. "Never mind, would you like some coffee?"

"Really, Robert. No thank you. You drink far too much coffee. You have been in here ages. What are you doing?"

I decided the question rhetorical, looking back at her with an apologetic smile. No answer required, only the showing of imperfect teeth. Conscious of this and feeling a slight embarrassment, I put the coffee mug to my lips. For a fraction of a second our eyes engaged. At that moment, I felt some implausible invitation, a miniature contrived arrow perhaps. With that she retreated to the next room. Through the inconceivability, I sipped coffee which was far too hot and the shock of it brought reality back to me.

On that day, Stella was wearing a vivid green blouse, it was similar in colour to lush summer grass following hours of rain. The top really was not very flattering. It was of a woolly looking material which clung unforgiving to her undersized underwear. Nestling below Stella's arms were a series of stretches and creases in the cloth. A seemingly collarless neck offered an open area exposing tanned freckly skin from the chin and neck to the top of her breasts. The cloth rippled again as it stretched at an affectionate spare tyre. The blouse was tucked unfortunately into charcoal jeans of unknowable fabric that was smooth and shiny. The wide leather belt, plain, worn, and a large buckle, emphasised her womanly hips. She had a pleasing and faultless pelvic form as the legs tapered away shapely to reveal tops of tanned feet and flattering caramel pointed shoes with sensible heels.

It was the eyes, though, which so enthralled me. Her spectacles partially veiled enchanting eyes. Through the glass, they were dark and alluring. A flicker of the lids, a quiver of the lashes and a smudge of mascara was captivating. Her hair was coloured blonde, highlighted or something. Obviously the colour could not have been natural for a woman of her forty-plus years. However, its lustre and gentle swirl adorned her intriguing head. It cushioned and curled upon the shoulders – it was both glossy and matt as it turned and absorbed the uneven light. Her ear looked dainty, cradled by long strands of hair behind it from the parting to her shoulder. An earring of gold decorated her neck and chin that was firm and youthful for her age. The wrinkles around the eyes and forehead gave away her years, but were a congruent token of her beauty. Make-up was as usual in evidence, the eyes were given attention. The lips were a bright crimson to match her impossibly red fingernails.

The image I had at that moment and the click clack of the plastic wall clock was interrupted. It was that familiar sound and rationale – the rhythmic noise from the next room along with the reason or the supposed reason for me being there. Yes, that telephone ring. A summon felt in the stomach which gave a heightened state of alert. I counted each ring, one. I could feel my heart beating suddenly. Two, even more it pounded. Three, anxiety, then four, the ringing stopped – composure was gradually restored.

I felt relieved, knowing it was very likely that Stella had answered the telephone. Questioning myself, wondering why each time the phone would ring, why did I get that very same anxious sensation? A concise answer would be the fear of the unknown. This, however, is inadequate to describe a notion of endless possibilities overlaid by the likelihood of making mistakes. By some conscientious miracle, I had learned to overcome the nervy 'butterflies in the stomach scenario'. I had developed a strict routine to use repeatedly in an hour of need. The method is probably exclusive to me, I thought. And then stupidly, I know, I think that if I tell anyone about this secret device – its effectiveness would be diminished.

In my head, I rehearsed this very routine as I opened the glass panel door into the main room. Gracefully and steadily, I quietly stepped inwards. Phone number two stared back at me, nestled in the left-hand corner of the desk. It was a daunting object, portal to a range of frightening possibilities. Beside the desk to the left a construction which was host to number one phone. To all intents and purposes, the phone was also placed to the left of a desk chair – this housed within glass of a wood framed booth. At this point, so embraced by the rehearsal routine I saw the call room in pure terms. Two phones, two desks, two office chairs, one booth and two easy chairs – merely a clinical observation of pragmatic consequence. In fact, beyond this level of consideration the small room had a homely appeal. The long windows were cloaked by thick beige curtains which comfortably muted noise of traffic from the road directly outside. Heat from the new gas fire and gentle lighting provided a cosy ambience. Imperfect were the walls. Cracks in the plaster had been filled, refilled, painted over and cracked again.

Of course there was Stella sat to the desk with the receiver to that dainty ear. The ear was a pivotal point of her flirtatious look and the subject of my gaze earlier. Now she leaned forward emphasising the spine curvature, where at the bottom her buttocks pressed firmly upon the office chair. With elbows on desk looking chic, cuffs were turned back to reveal attractive wrists. This and her feminine posture served to fuel my imagination. I even thought that the way that she adjusted her glasses and twirled her hair around her fingers was a habit deployed for my benefit.

Looking again at phone number two, I knew it was not going to ring somehow. "A watched pot never boils," my mother used to say. My eyes moved to the left automatically to see Stella through the glass door of the booth. She was deep in conversation with head nodding and probably oblivious to my presence. Her toes and heels seemed to caress the splay-footed chair. Oh my imagination again feeling a definite tingle! This was surely a cue to make some more coffee. The mug I was holding was half-full of cold coffee. I must have been daydreaming. I walked with soft footsteps in the direction of the kettle.

I was there again making coffee at the coffee-making station. With kettle switched on, I searched several cupboards for the nicest cleanest mug. Having found it and examined it, I began the coffee ritual. Two mugs kissed each other on the worktop as I pushed them together like his and hers. How would it be, I thought, if Stella were to drink from my mug and I from hers? Then I felt guilty by this perverse representation. The rim of my mug would be against her lips. The beauty of the plot would unfold before me without her knowledge. No, I really could not do that, it would be a contrary action to trust and doing such a thing is definitely not normal behaviour. Reassured of normality, but gripping the spoon harder than necessary, I tilted and spilled the dried granules again. Smudged was the worktop as coffee stained and leeched on the damp surface. I wiped again in that typical casual fashion. On this occasion, I had not listened to the associated sounds of sprinkles, plunges and stirs. Instead I was wetted by steam due to the lazy switch off of the kettle.

Job done, I began to think about the telephone. Picking up her mug, I proceeded into the booth as quickly as possible. Stella was still there on the phone sat in the same position. I hovered behind her a little, looking for a mat to place her mug upon. There was no mat on the desk, so leaning forward almost touching Stella I grabbed three tissues. With left hand, I made a tissue triangle against my chest and placed it under the mug to her right. Stella gestured with open hand and wriggling fingers to thank me. At that instant, I responded by placing my hand upon her shoulder feeling

11

the seam at the top of the sleeve. The hand had dwelt stroking the fibre beneath. Only a second it was there but I could sense the soft flesh below like an emotion. In that moment of realisation, I released my hand immediately.

As I exited the booth, I felt an ambiguous itching at my fingertips. Still sensing a softness at my palm, I promptly rubbed my open hand above the knee of my jeans. Conveniently, this erased the sensation to my hand, but conspicuously emblazoned a sense of sin within. Stella with her back still turned to me was rubbing her shoulder just where my hand had been. Reaching out spontaneously in that second had tainted what seemed to be our special relationship. From now on, things could get worse between us. All the previous engagements of our eyes were now a depleted ruin.

Now I was embarrassed by the feelings of desire I had felt for Stella. Up until this point, the admiration had been non-sexual. A first kiss could be reciprocated, but touching a shoulder in such a fashion must surely have been tantamount to rape. Oh no, I thought. How do I behave when she comes off the phone? Do I apologise? But she would probably say, "What for." I would say, well, I do not know what I'd say. I would certainly have some explaining to do. Or would I carry on as normal. Then she would know something was wrong and ask me what the matter was. My heart was beating quicker now. Oh that coffee, I need a pee.

I took the second phone off the hook while I went upstairs. Whilst stood I caught sight of my haggard face in the mirror. What a sight! How could I possibly imagine that a woman would give me a second look – especially Stella, so sophisticated and worldly? Obviously I look like this because I am exhausted. Too much of what, I do not know. Perhaps all that was needed is just to take it easy. Not take things to heart. Chill out. Relax. Do not worry.

A little later in the call room after making more coffee, I was looking at the phone hoping it might ring. All was peaceful. Stella, still on the phone was doodling then twiddling the pen. Her doodles were usually circles and loops. I did not suppose that she had written 'I love Robert' then doodled over it so I would never know.

Ring-ring broke the silence. My heart thumped again. Ring-ring, two, I counted. Three, ring-ring, it went, relax and listen, I told myself. Ring-ring, four, deep breath, relax and listen. Ring for the fifth time. Remember the routine. Answer! With an expert pause I impeccably in a very relaxed unintimidating manner said, "Hello," pause, "Samaritans, can I help you." This was met with silence. In my head counting one two three, "You are through to Samaritans, how may I help you." Silence. One, two, three, four, five, six, "How may I help you?" No response and the line went dead.

I remained waiting, deluded in hoping it would ring again. However, it stared at me in punishment with the tangled umbilical line twisted and tormented. Perhaps the phrase "how may I help you" is too cheesy. Then I gave a sigh swivelling on pivotal toes right, left, right. My eyes moved skyward not seeing. Another sigh. Eventually, I left the chair wondering and hoping pointlessly. Stella was gesturing to someone who could not see and I absorbed her body language to that someone who was invisible. Stella was in my heart, but I was sinking.

The call to me, the four and a half rings, perhaps not a call to me? It could have been a sincere silent cry for help to anyone that might listen with care and empathy. The likely alternative could have been a man seeking a sexual thrill from Stella's voice. Maybe that is too cynical, what could possibly be wrong with the spiritual support of a woman? The call could just purely have been something very innocent. It simply could be anyone. Really, I should not under or overestimate, because apathy was beginning to take purpose.

The voluntary organisation to which I had been proud to be a member had lost its appeal to me. No longer did I bask in the ethos of 'doing good' or trying to do good through a sympathetic stance in a non-judgemental humanistic way. Unfortunately, I had elevated myself dangerously into the optimisation of an amateurish client centred therapist. Maybe it was time to give the work up. Of course giving it up would mean closing the door on a social outlet to people of the kind I would not otherwise meet. No longer could I claim to give my time willingly to help others. The truth was that my motive had swung into self-indulgence from a previously genuine and sincere altruistic dedication.

My mouth was feeling dry, but I decided not to have coffee again until the night was out. I just sat to wonder as time trickled by. The intention was to empty the mind of all the experiences in feeling which had overwhelmed the evening. The tragedy of the night was that Stella's phone call had meant I was relatively insignificant. Yet Stella was so significant and I was left thinking that our non-relationship could go nowhere but backwards. I wished the night never happened. I wished it could begin again at six o'clock. That way I could have got the call, had a sense of purpose and consumed less coffee. That way, Stella could have arrived, assessed the evening by pondering me and the damage in my face.

The lock at the outer rear door clunked as I heard the sound of a key move. The draught attracted the kitchen door toward it slightly as the outer door opened. Acknowledging the event, I rose to greet the person as then unknown. "Hi," I said with an embracing tone, almost American.

"Hello, it's bloody cold out there," he said as I quickly closed the door to the call room.

"Mmm," I replied processing his face to come up with a name – buying time. "How are you, Chris?" Recalling it by a persistent endeavour and feeling proud of myself. "I haven't seen you for ages."

"No, Robert, no," conjuring up my name impressively like a rabbit from a hat. "I won't bore you with the details. I have been back a month or so. Visited my sister in Canada for three months. Do you know it is absolutely beautiful over there?" he said intensely and rhetorically.

"Lovely," I said being envious, but trying not to show it. Then I thought that is not such a big deal, compensating the envy. His sister is probably shallow anyway.

"Gorgeous," came his repost, smiling as if he could read my thoughts.

This was followed an unusual pause for ordinary conversation. We could hear the murmur of a large vehicle passing by from the road and then the tick-tock of the clock. Chris hung up his coat on the peg while I felt the cold invade the kitchen from outside.

"Busy?" said Chris questioningly through the silence raising the tone of his voice to get my attention again.

"Yes, well, no not really. I have had a few silent calls."

"Masturbatory?" Chris replied with a tone neither comment nor question, but half-intellectual and half-dismissive.

"Perhaps," said I taken aback, thinking did he really say that, a new word, an amusing new word, but in such a context a serious word nonetheless. Chris made it serious delivered with such conviction.

"Masturbatory," he had said it again, but this time the delivery was wholly more dismissive. He sounded like a pompous sergeant major.

I hesitated, for it was challenging almost as if to test my resolve. Not rising to it, I invalidated the challenge and offered a smile. "Stella has a call, I do not know who it is, but I expect that they are not suicidal."

"Stella," said Chris sounding a little confused and furrowing his brow, Stella?"

"Yes, Stella."

"No, no," he said knowingly looking upon layers of glass, through the door and into the booth at the subject. Cupping his hands like binoculars against the pane to shield reflecting light, he said, "That's not her real name. No, no, her real name is Janet or Jane or something."

With this knowledge, I was utterly taken aback again at this point. How dare he be privy to such information when I had no idea of it! In fact, I was more concerned that no one and particularly Stella herself had not seen fit to tell me. Feeling affronted, I proceeded to make exaggerated movements straightening clothes and reaching for my jacket preparing for my time to leave.

14

Still engaged in a conversation with Chris, I was awash with new ignorance. Over and over I kept thinking, how could this be possible, to be in the dark about Stella's real name! The overwhelming feeling was irrational, for doubtless I was quite low on her list even though she was high on mine.

Looking at Chris and cutting the small talk of about ten minutes' duration, I said, "I expect your colleague will be here shortly."

"Yes," replied Chris, "Maureen, finishes work early to get here, but is often late. You can go if you like. I'm sure she will be here soon."

"Okay," I said in resignation. "See you. Oh say goodbye to Stella – I mean Janet or Jane or whatever her name is for me."

"Okay, bye."

Another night wasted. The back door closed behind as Chris saw me out. There I was in the town, in the dark. In view were backs of terraced houses lit by the odd bedroom window or downstairs at the kitchen. To the side, a minor road converged with another out of sight, yet moon and stars still pierced infinite mist. Barking dogs exchanged claims in the distance. Maureen arrived in her smart new car as I made my journey to the front of the building toward the main road. I nodded in the misty night, but from behind the windscreen, Maureen looked not knowing that it was me silhouetted against a street lamp. In the darkness, I deliberated that I ought to make an effort to declare my presence, but was host to a waning enthusiasm.

I walked on, hearing my footsteps plant and scrape upon the wet pavement. Maureen must surely have been well behind by now and moving in the opposite direction. Conveniently, I excused myself due to a personal lack of interest. I did not need to communicate with any other person that night unless it was absolutely necessary. Roaring in the distance through the mist a car could be heard revving excessively. I listened as it appeared to gasp as the driver obviously changed up into the next gear. The engine cried again as the revs changed and the car accelerated away further into the dark. Soon there was silence except for the crisp footsteps and the faint buzzing of the streetlights above.

I thought about Maureen and Chris. I wondered would I be the subject of their conversation at that very moment? If they had dispensed with the small talk? Would they have been discussing the extortionate price of carrots these days in Marks and Spencer's following the exceptionally wet autumn? Does Maureen really get double time for working Sunday? Was Chris really trapped in such a good-looking body or is he just an ordinary-looking fellow? How is it that Chris can bask in retirement without a care for anyone else but himself and promote an outward persona of sincere concern for others? Was I the only one who could see it – that is seeing

15

Chris in his archangelic egocentric middle-class pompousness? Then there was Maureen striving forever working and working living in a continual disorder. What a pair, natter natter it would have been at that moment. I could no longer think to flatter myself anymore as being the centre of their twitter. Actually, I could not be the subject of their ramblings right then for I was after all a minion of a part which they were so familiar. I should not pretend to compliment myself anyway. Why should I be so important, especially with my haggard face? All I could think to do while walking briskly was to listen to the pattern of footsteps beneath. Some night it had been.

It was easier to think of Stella, so I thought of her. My love, I dreamed. Stella my love that is, but unrequited. She is so charming and I the charmed recipient. Stella casually enchants, all sorts and all ages. If Stella was the witch I was surely caught in her spell. I thought of those eyes, the allurement drawing me in. Behind those spectacles there are questions. I wondered was she aware of her influence over me? Did she know how I felt? Is it actually harder for me, I thought in contemplation, to think of her because the power she had over me. It would be easier not to think of her if it were possible, then I could just go on living my life. That way one thing would follow another. More prepared I would be. More prepared! Only I could not have needed to be because if I forgot her, I would be empowered, ready for anything. The sensible thing had to be to embrace the contradictions, digest them, consider them and reject them.

Then there is her name. Stella is not her name at all. Why? Why after all this time did she not tell me her name? I am still confounded, not knowing, aggrieved feeling a mixture of love and contempt. Why should middle-class, middle-weight, shallow Chris be so privileged to know? Not to remember. That is the worst part – not caring enough when gifted with the knowledge not fit for the likes of me.

Chapter Two

Sunday morning, the room cold, there I was in it alone, but warmed and reassured. Bells rang from the nearby church to remind the reluctant listeners that it was indeed Sunday, the Sabbath day. The message tolled and told of the proximity to civilisation – a definite society. I convinced myself of it, not alone after all and labelled it a paradox – though be it a tenuous one. Thank god for the warm and comforting bells.

Whilst lain there on the day of rest, I wondered who actually goes to church now in our secular society. The curious thing was that most people I knew believed in god or a god of a sort, but none of them attended church. What had become of England? Going to church could even be viewed as abnormal. I likely knew more about pervasion of crime than of redeemers, but a society without crime could also be abnormal. Imagine our society, all saints, and a perfect cloister of exemplary individuals where crime would be unknown – such a possibility – impossible! I from this flexing of grey cells on the matter upon waking eventually concluded – crime and religion were part of normal society.

I blamed the bells for the wake up. How inconsiderate of the church on a Sunday morning and every Sunday morning. Others must have been woken too. I suppose no one dare complain to the church – so righteous. Louder the noise became. Yes, it was a 'noise', yes it had become just that as time passed on – a sizeable annoyance. No longer was it a welcome rhythmic drone as a link to a wider world beyond my bedroom, but a claxon doing its bidding to every entity. I buried my head and bent the pillow around the ears to drown the commotion of bells. But therefore being overwhelmingly defeated, it only served to bring a reeling back of the morning. There was no way then I could get back to sleep.

I thought about where all the clothes were in relation to the room. How many layers could I wear in order to keep warm and not look ridiculous? I lay there in bed, all snug, challenging. Without using words, I talked to myself, "Get up now, get out of bed. Now come on, Robert!" I quivered and curled an enormous embryo beneath the quilt. I thought I will have to think some more before leaping and dressing in a frenzy to avoid the cold.

At last I had to get out of bed through fear. Fearing when hearing flushing and washing from below – I worried that there would not be any hot water left. With a guess that the bathroom was now empty I grabbed the toilet roll from the windowsill. Unfortunately, when I reached the important room, it was engaged. So not to waste the journey, I descended to the kitchen clutching the toilet roll like gold.

On reaching the kitchen, I presumed with ninety-nine percent certainty that the bastards had been at it again. I had only the previous day spent a good hour washing up and generally cleaning the kitchen. Now I had found dirty crockery piled high, surfaces lashed with grease and rubbish abounding. To top it all, the cupboards were empty and therefore nothing to drink from – clean or otherwise. I struggled to make coffee tripping over the cat in the process.

It seemed that the bastards who were DJ from the ground floor, his layabout crony from the first floor and associated guests had made a great extending mess as usual. Habitual and inconsiderate as ever, because they repeatedly made it, but also because they never cleared the mess. I despaired at myself living alongside such people. In the kitchen stood alone, examining condensation dribbling down the window I wished for better days.

I detected a sound of the bathroom door opening above. In immediate response armed with mug and toilet roll, I climbed the stairs only to find before me a figure coughing her way down. I could not help but look for there was a seventeen-year-old rosebud coming towards me wearing white stained pants and a black push-up bra. I had no idea who she was, except doubtless to be one of DJ's triumphs. "Good morning," I said with raised eyebrows in a tone comparable to a stand-up comedian. She returned a glance condescendingly with eyes decorated with the artistry of *Titian.* Conscious of her own young body, she must have viewed me as a dirty old man, almost twice her age and an old boot face to boot.

As I opened the bathroom door, she disappeared into DJ's room. In the mirror was an ashamed look, the image looking back humiliated. Almost half my age young enough to be my daughter, I felt weird at the tainted desire. Whatever possessed me to look at her propped breasts bordered in black, the skinny ribs, a navel and those knickers? She was not even attractive or sexy, just half-naked and female. I had looked at the girl out of curiosity rather than a lustrous yearning. I was not envious of the DJ. No, those numerous fragile encounters of girl after girl after girl must have diluted the meaning of sex to him. Yes, it was a concern that I was not having sex. Celibacy was Hobson's choice as I was not having meaningful relationships with available women.

18

In the mirror, my nose carried a red pimple complete with yellow head. It must have been festering overnight while I dreamt of love and romance. My haggard face was itchy too. I wondered could I get a razor from my room without giving up my rights of possession to the bathroom. With stealth I examined the landing, then up and down stairs. I shot up the stairs and down again like some mad superhero. I so dislike shaving. Well, it was either shaving, thinking back to prepubescent anxieties, or periods. There was never any choice in the matter but if there were I would have plumbed for the preferred option. There is nothing quite so quenching as a shave that feeling of losing hair, irritation and the refreshing relief.

Once again I found myself staring out of the window of my room with mug of coffee in hand. At thirty-two years of age and counting at an alarming rate, I was captivated with fixed eyes on row upon row of terraced houses. In sombre consideration, the focus was yet again switched on, as if triggered by some engaging association with some obscure book I had read. It had been repeated numerous times from that same passage and view of that very scene I had many times concluded the very same thing – 'every person there was constituted as the profound secret of every other'. The manifestation was born from the reading of the expanded town in view, where each individual in each discrete home was enclosed in their very own secret never to be written of. Each room had its story unwritten, every beating heart belonging within in their very own spoken words and yet unspoken pages of mystery. The pattern developed as a resounding repetition as I once again transformed my thoughts ever onward, this was always the case. It was extraordinary, opposite were the rows of houses neatly arranged as books on a shelf, just like one and other. Each home, every interior, a unique narrative. All these houses were like the one I was standing in, three storeys, terraced, similar level and height. In my room on the top floor, one appeared to be looking down on the rooftops – another tale within a tale. It was all very well losing myself in the loop and gazing inquiringly at this apparent optical anomaly, but what should I do next?

I chose to lie on the bed with eyes closed and listen to *Abbey Road* back to back. During the third hearing of *Sun King,* I decided I was bored and considered the next course of action. I toyed with the idea of *Sergeant Pepper's Lonely Hearts Club Band* for a moment. However, I automatically put on my late grandfather's vivid green jacket and soon I was walking into town on Sunday lunchtime.

The air was filled with drizzle. It was neither rain nor fine. It was that kind of stuff that wets easily. While walking, the smooth chin felt chilled. Then some gorilla-looking chap walked toward me. He looked imposing, so I crossed the road. For an inexplicable reason, my stride seemed longer than necessary. The more I adjusted it, the more awkward it became. Suddenly, an image came to mind. Due to the stretchy stride, I saw myself moving up and down. Perhaps I was bobbing down while my legs were at full stretch. I must have looked like one of those lanky informal guys raising and falling as they walk. Yielding to developing a stoop because they are freakishly tall and prefer to give the impression of being shorter to be more ordinary in appearance. Then I thought about the belt, was it fastened tight enough and was it through the loops of my jeans? It felt cold down there so I checked my zip. Must be gaping, I thought, exposing my penis to all the town. Fortunately I was overreacting – no such display. There were just a few people and the occasional car – all of which were unconcerned about who I was – even if the jacket was silly.

Of course it was Sunday and the shops were closed. That was fine, I could look in the windows without been tempted to go inside. The problem now was that there was a moron looking at me with a bright green jacket. My refection was something to avoid for I became increasingly more aware of me. Luckily, I was saved, no longer did I have to squint into windows of closed shops. At least one place was open, the biggest, the best, the supermarket.

Manned and womaned by workers on single time there was just a skeleton presence of staff. Being there, I supposed I would have to buy something, but what? I ambled around giving little attention to shelves and what was on them. It might have been useful to find something to eat before nightfall as I was hungry. I arrived at the cabinet of exotic sounding pies: chicken and mushroom, cheese and onion, apple and pork, mince and onion. Eventually, I found an appropriate plain pie, but it was too big so I found another which was too small. I stood there scratching my head to make a decision. A world of shoppers passed by, seemingly unaware that I was there with such a dilemma.

"Try getting two small ones, Robert." It was Stella with the warmest voice.

"Hello," I said surprised.

She smiled. Her hands fondled the handle of the shopping trolley. "Fancy meeting you here. Shouldn't you be drinking beer at the pub somewhere?"

"No," my brilliant mind deduced that she was teasing. "I prefer to shop, you never know who you might bump into."

"Quite," she replied mildly with another smile. "Listen, I never really had the chance to have much of a conversation with you the other night. I'm sorry."

"Oh, don't be. You were busy. That is what we do, it's a job."
Conversation became easier again, although being so strangely in love is
an obstacle to coherent speech.

"Robert, I would like to chat with you. How about the café?"

Taken aback I said, "All right, but what about your shopping?"

"I have more or less finished. Perhaps you could help me, but what
about your shopping?"

"Well, I do not have a trolley, I don't have a basket. In fact, I don't
know why I came here. I was feeling hungry, but I don't anymore."

By now I had observed the healthy colour of her cheeks and her face.
Faint lines on her forehead bore a few traces of anxiety. Perhaps her
thoughts were not immediately with me. Maybe she was principally
occupied with the cares of others. Yet I was there and Stella's focus was
on me. She smiled dropping into a comfortable attitude surveying my
being, knowingly. At that moment I guessed hazardously of a reciprocal
attraction. Realising unaccountably a remarkable appearance of
satisfaction I smiled back. Unaware I was displaying the state of my teeth,
haggard face and lurid green jacket. Our eyes met again, only this time
something was different, there was meaning in the colour, the blueness
radiated through the glass of her spectacles signalling a message –
mysterious vulnerability perhaps. As she blinked, I was diverted to her
eyebrows and a line to her feminine nose. Her lips appeared to throb
slightly as if to begin speech, but no words were required. It was her turn
to speak, but I think she knew the onus was on me to say something
foolish. I duly obliged. "Oh, I am hungry after all." It was not for food
though as she probably guessed. My appetite was more akin to the
consequence of a resigned celibacy. "Perhaps we could eat in the café," I
said trying to correct the earlier mistake clumsily, but only compounding
the issue with confusion.

"Yes," came a honey reply, a smile and a tiny-cloaked laugh afforded
to indicate a meeting of minds. Infected, I laughed, quietly smiled unable
to straighten my face.

"Okay then," with a deliberate sideways glance as if to hide a yet
undetermined motive associated with such an infection.

Past pies and pastries, toward wines and spirits – I led Stella with a
finger hooked around the wire front corner of her trolley. The destination
was the checkout. Before us stood a short fat man with arms open. He
occupied the wide aisle with his presence, seemingly unaware he was
blocking our pathway. Much to our relief he made room, then knelt
picking pieces of glass off the floor from a puddle of liquid. Someone had
dropped a bottle, such an event had attracted an audience, so breaking the
tedium of shopping for several witnesses. The man rose, looked towards

me, shaking his bald head set neckless on broad shoulders. In a fashion not dissimilar to that of an excited schoolboy I steered the trolley left towards cereal. School girlish, Stella followed swishing her open coat flirtatiously. "Where are you taking me?" she giggled.

"To cereal, biscuits and beyond."

"Ooo, I can't wait."

I was beginning to feel cramped within my jeans which were tight anyway. I hoped she had no knowledge of my predicament as I strode awkwardly on. However, her manner became more enticing as I responded with equal encouragement. At the checkout I put the bought items in bags after she had methodically placed them before the assistant. At this juncture we said nothing, I looked continually at her as she occasionally saw me looking. First tins, then vegetables. I struggled with fingers and thumbs filling. Stella had her lips now compressed with a pensive expression of thoughtfulness. She glanced at me, raised her eyes more, then on to groceries anew, flushed a little with expectation and embarrassment. She was more beautiful than ever, I momentarily and conveniently dispensed of feelings of love – substituting to lust. Like a purring panther on a pre-murder mission, I absorbed the passion-confining craving to a prowl. She knew, she really knew she was the object of my desire. My body and heart were absolutely to be toyed with under her control. Vegetables, tissues, toothpaste made their way in my direction. Finally she lifted bought flowers, but first Stella with feminine nose and eyes in my direction embraced the fragrance. Instantly, at that moment romance engulfed my heart with reminders of love again. Her eyes and lashes moved flirtingly and emotional.

"Thank you, Robert," with a passionate kiss in her voice. "Here are my car keys. My car is the dinky yellow one just to the left of the main door. Take the stuff and put it in the boot. I will meet you in the café." She pinched my hand playfully passing the keys. The softness of her hand embraced my knuckles in an exquisite command. There was nothing to do but obey.

Walking more comfortably now, I proudly pushed the trolley under an eternal glare from the shining lights above and uninterested people looking on. In a uniform fashion, shoppers exited on the left and entered on the right. It was a perfect illustration of how individuals consciously conform to expected behaviour. My advance was slowed to a near halt as an exiting shopper stopped abruptly to avoid two children jumping up and down. Negotiating such hazards enabled a brief unwelcome escape from the importance of the situation unfolding with Stella. Steering a shopping trolley through a crowded foyer of shoppers to a dinky yellow car was an

22

automatic action almost. My real attention being for Stella and the gush of our very own private encounter in public.

Having left Stella in the supermarket at her request, gave a breather to help take stock of a new level of our relationship. Clearly it was bound to develop beyond its current state fairly soon. Strangely, but without a definite plan – what was happening was linked to elements I had mentally rehearsed. Yet it all seemed spontaneous – the feeling exceeded the uncanny. My mind was curious as to what Stella was thinking and feeling – whether she knew what she was doing or even what I was doing. For me, the story unwinding for Stella and I had no bounds – consequences were insignificant with nothing to lose. For Stella, however, such actions to come bore the hallmark of complexity which could in the end have a detrimental effect. In a selfish way, so far my behaviour could be excused or at least explained. Her circumstances were quite different especially because she was married. Now Stella was making the running and I being flattered gladly followed.

A withered and worn-looking old man leant against a 5 mph sign close to the car. As I opened the boot, he gave a steadfast vacant gaze. He had a short raggedly cut white beard, a hollow face and exceedingly bright eyes. The hollowness and thinness of his face made his eyes unusual and unlifelike. The eyebrows were dark and bushy. He scratched his forehead with a skeletal hand drawing attention to a confused mop of white hair. His gaze of stare pierced and burned into my back. Like an incredible inexplicable ogre, his look taunted, though it was impossible for him to know my affairs. The reasons were unclear, but I felt guilty, it was not due to him or his bright staring eyes. To rid myself of such a feeling, I manufactured a notion of contempt for the old man, albeit his only crime was to stare vacantly toward me and at the dinky yellow car. To suppress this attitude I had to hastily scurry inside to meet Stella.

Once back in the hive of the foyer, guilt had dispersed and the cold outside had alerted me to the coffee I drank earlier. The imminent renewal of our meeting and the build-up of liquid meant the next prudent option was to pee. The 'Gents' was a crowded place. Strong lights, smell of urine and sound of driers was reassuring. Men orderly used the facilities. Nothing is usually spoken there, the men all strangers, not knowing another present. The pause allowed a collection of thoughts with an opportunity to establish composure for the café and Stella. The bright light was unflattering, exposing a haggard face again in the mirror. I convinced myself that the café lighting would be less cruel. Making sure that no one was looking, I smiled at the mirror. Smiling back, I experimented with expressions in order to delight my love. The teeth, clean, white but messy in their configuration playfully beckoned for her mouth. Next move, out into the corridor.

A dimly lit shared corridor for males and females had several doors. It was essentially a functionless room between respective toilets and the main body of the supermarket. Each door was uniform to the next in its colour, but displayed different symbols to its neighbour. This passage was an unfortunate junction which by its design created an awkward bottleneck for the users. Before me was the neckless gentleman who had been present at the alcoholic spillage earlier. With bald head perched he charmingly gave way to an even larger lady than himself entering the corridor. The presentation and exchange of glances between them did nothing to alleviate the bottleneck. I was compelled to wait with forced patience immovable and restricted by people all around in close proximity. To stand frozen was the best course in this environment. The fat lady wobbled past and I was pleased to be moving forward again as the gentleman ahead negotiated the crowded pathway back into the supermarket.

Escaping the confinement of that unnecessary room and into the great hall of retail paradise was refreshing. A buzz from a swarm of shoppers immediately met the ears, but gradually quietened as I listened to my thoughts once more. A large piece of the shop floor was annexed for the purpose of the café. I stood at the tail of the queue looking out over a swollen collection of seated diners and across at shoppers buzzing. It was some time before I spotted Stella. She was not in the café, but only a few metres away talking with a tall woman of about sixty years. Whilst weaving through the swarm, I must have passed close to them without realising they were there. This further pause served to provide yet another breather.

I had the good fortune to capture an empty table for two. Unfortunately that haven was surrounded by other tables of two, four and six which were full. From where I was sitting I had a good view of Stella and her talking partner. Stella had her back to me and slightly beyond her stood the tall woman draped in a white raincoat. The woman was pale and about her head was a canopy of grey hair. Her face was like a fine covered web of transparent paleness with every feature clearly defined, for make-up had been applied with precision. She had a perfect, beautifully formed nose slightly pinched at the top of each nostril. She had one set expression embodied peculiarly by her thin lips coupled red to the horizontal and by the meticulous eye make-up. Suddenly, she saw my observation evidenced by a noticeable stare. Remarkable, nonchalant and by a small degree I looked elsewhere without causing alarm. At least I assumed, distracted so, I recognised that the two cups before me might look

24

suspicious to the viewer of such a pale complexion and rigid expression. There was nothing revealed in the view of watchful attentiveness and no visible clue behind her pale mask. She ran her painted eyes on my position, but I saw nothing in them to half suppose the woman knew anything of me.

Conspicuous I caressed the coffee cup and saw a world of life teeming at the tables nearby. Conversations were punctuated by chewing and reinforced by a nod, a smile and moments of laughter. Children splashed, crunched and played through meals. Daughters, sons, mums, dads, grandmas and granddads all played out their roles. While sipping again, I looked in solitude at people all around. Then I looked in the direction of the two women again, but they were gone – disappeared.

There was a primitive surge of adrenalin as my heart fired at the notion that Stella had left. Comfort was restored just as quickly, however, with the reminder of her car keys in the pocket next to my leg. Just then I sensed her approaching from behind. As I turned to look, I was stroked on the upper arm with a gentle hand.

"Sorry, Robert. I went to freshen up and was accosted on my return." Her hand lingered like a lost longing to pause and embrace. "You saw?" ruffling my hair in a graceful gesture with the same gentle hand.

"Yes, your coffee is going cold," I said searching for a reasonable reply. Then with an almost remote action and seeing her eyes I curled her hair deliberately around her ear touching her cheek ever so gently. She tilted her head towards my hand and lifted her shoulder. This was the first time we touched with such mutual affection. Her eyes danced with complicity at our wrongdoing destined for tears, but the momentum was sown by the love to be made. My hand reached and caught hers across the coffee cups.

"Robert, really, my husband?"

"I'm sorry," withdrawing my hand.

"My husband is out this afternoon," she paused with a precise calmness. She stared into my eyes with a fearful look grabbing my wrist. Her lips began to form the beginning of words, but no sound proceeded from them. With laboured breathing she began, but with quick pauses between separate words. "My – husband, my – husband, is seventy-four years old." Then speaking more fluently she continued, "He cannot play golf anymore, but spends much of his time at the gentlemen's' golf club." She paused to think again.

"I see," I said deciphering.

"My husband does not mind. I love him. He is a gentleman. He is old but understanding."

"Stella stop," I said quietly putting a finger to her lips and one to mine. "I, I understand, you don't have to say anymore."

"No, no, no, you must listen. My name is not Stella," she said in frustration.

"I know."

"That woman I spoke to. She is a neighbour. I don't want to. Oh shit, oh shit." Tears were apparent in her eyes as she scratched about for a handkerchief then she held my hands and squeezed hard. "Oh shit," another sniffle. I smiled an understanding smile showing the usual array of imperfect teeth. I lifted my eyebrows for empathic affection and then later again for comic value. Slowly, she wiped her eyes at the corners and lifted her eyebrows in repost. Tears turned to giggles, back to tears then giggles again.

"You know there really, really is so much too much of you," I replied with restraint. Instantly, I knew I had said it (I love you) in manner disguised in her own language.

"What do you mean?" she replied with a quizzical and suppressed tone.

"I, I, I," lost momentarily for words. "You know."

"Do I, no, know what?" she replied with a snigger. She was justified in asking such a question to explain such a vague comment.

If ever there was a time to make my feelings known to Stella, this was it. However, since I was embroiled in the chase and all so exposed the complexity of the situation called for politic. "I want to say, 'Something Stupid, but I don't want to spoil it all."

"Like the song?"

"Yes, like the song."

"Really."

"Yes, really."

"Really, really," laughing.

"Yes really, really, really," laughing.

"Oh, Robert, that is a lot of reallies." Her watery eyes reddened at the edges and gave a dangerous appeal of desire. She stood gracefully with her throat flushed and pulled my arm upwards.

"Please sit, I have known you about half a year." With a curious look, she returned to her seat. "We know very little about each other. I just know how I feel and I think I know how you feel."

"Yes!"

"What are we undertaking?"

"Robert, I don't know and I don't care. Come on with me, I need some help with shopping and things." With that she got to her feet. "Come on."

With a particular combination of perplexity, wonder and satisfaction, I strode after her. She burst in a full-blown way jostling through the swarm of people to the exit and like some faithful obedient dog, I followed in weaving haste. As I chased, she turned to sow an eagerness for her attention. She stopped to be grabbed and I grabbed and held. Together we marched away naively devoted.

Chapter Three

A prolonged afternoon was recalled as we lay together in her bed. The ceiling looked devoid of colour and pattern. A notion of eyes from above making judgements seemed peculiar as our destiny outstretched by each passing minute. As the daylight shaded into night, those eyes became closer and oppressive. Stella with her splendour and elegance had wrapped her body around my body. We lay bathed in a fountain of intoxication, soaked in a temporary madness. She spoke, her warm breath pulsed against my skin. Her eyes were stark and naked in the half light. The blueness was unseen, yet the measure of the conveyance remained. The texture of her hair upon my shoulder tickled delightfully while she rested soothingly on it.

"Robert," as she played with the hairs on my chest and fingertips adorned with those impossibly red nails melting into black.

"Mmm."

"What are you thinking?"

Uncloaked, I recognised the language of lovers. I knew that I had to consider my answer very carefully. It was unspoken female convention, women can demand an answer and know instinctively if a reply is genuine or not. Men know that an honest answer is the only true course to sustain the relationship. Yet the opportunity for a man to give an honest reply is tainted by his own frailty. A statement of truth in order to promote the interests of a relationship is weakened by his disguise and effort to make that very truth more acceptable to her.

"Robert, what are you thinking?"

"I am thinking about you and us."

"What about me and us? Do you mean, me and you and him?"

Thankfully, she was attuned with almost a telepathy which is so rare. "Mmm. I am wondering," I said with cheerful conviction. "I have fancied you for a while now, but I never imagined we would be here like this now. And especially so because you are married." Then I paused expecting her to reply, but she only laid her face upon my chest. She moved her chin as if to say something, but thought better of it and said nothing. I cradled her head in my open hand and kissed her forehead tenderly. In the tradition of pillow talk, I thought of something romantic to say – though said nothing.

She raised her head looking through the darkness at me. "What?" she sighed.

"I thought you were going to say something."

"I thought you were," she returned.

"Well, there is something."

"What?"

Silently, I wet the tip of her nose with my tongue and stroked her lips with my lips. Meanwhile, I toyed with the idea of asking an inappropriate question for the mood. If I asked it, then it would test the resolve in the newfound level of our relationship. However, if I were to ask it at a later time, then that could have been even more inappropriate. Finally, I decided, for now and the future that moment would encode her name. "What is your name anyway?"

An uncomfortable silence met those words, as the point of inference was clear. The uneasy knowledge of knowing my words were in her ears was taken with grace. I observed from her manner that she pondered them inwardly. We both knew that such a question would be remembered for long afterwards.

Suddenly, Stella gave an indeterminate shriek. Instantly, I was taken aback, because the nature of it was so foreign. To my relief the ambiguous initial response became uncontrollable laughter shrieking to a height of a previously unknown possibility. "Guess, guess, guess," she replied with a progressively increasing shrill tone. All I could do was laugh at our condition. We laughed together, as she lovingly thumped me with an open fist then picked a pillow and whacked me with it.

"Bathsheba," I cried.

"No, no."

"Cleopatra."

"Don't be silly. That's a cats' name," she clawed dramatically.

Laughing, I realised I could not make a sensible guess or guesses, because I could accidentally and eventually arrive at a name which did not belong to Stella but to me. "Rumplestiltskin?"

"That's a boy's name, Robert."

"Is it, what about Stella?"

Boisterous play between lovers developed into a rolling romp which soon came abruptly to a halt. "Stop, Robert, I can hear Adam!"

"Adam?"

"Yes, my husband." She looked at me for a moment as we both fell silent, listening half inquiringly and half as if angry that her husband was back. She sat up naked in the darkness. Light through the window intersected her torso like a frozen strobe highlighting her womanly physique. There was no colour to be seen as light and dark danced upon her frame as she stood quickly to dress. In her manner was composure unaltered except for a shrewd glance in my direction. The look disclosed a shadowy indication, perhaps avoidance or dread like a cold wind had passed over us. At such an impracticable time, she touched me on the chin with a sorrowful sense of peace. At her fingertips was a foundation to a greater emotion unspoken.

Now dressed, she sat on the bed in a perplexed state. I sat up as she switched on the light. "I cannot hear anything."

"Rest assured, he is here," she said. "Wait here." Outwardly, she appeared restored to calm and collection, but after replacing her jewellery looked with a disturbed sense of sight. With a long intake of breath, she stood once more the devoted wife in one miraculous transformation. With an outstretched arm in my direction, the flat palm of her hand restrained me. "Stay there and don't move," she said with diplomatic assertiveness. "I will deal with this." The hand with pointed fingers in all directions eclipsed the light from the lamp. The command had struck me with fervent admiration and I was helpless to obey. I trusted her firmness of purpose and resolution in her words. A plan was afoot of her contrivance, but whatever that was I knew little of. It may have been easier to guess her name correctly.

She closed the door behind as she left the room. I remained there constrained by a manifest unwillingness to question anything further than that moment. I lay there alone, naked, waiting and quietly listening in her bed. All that I could hear were her footsteps disappearing in the descent of the stairs. The emptiness of the silence rang loud and clear. The void of no sound had a fuzzy deplorable peculiarity of weakness in my confinement there. The hint of a tick from the bedroom clock was a merciful relief from the silence below. I listened, only to hear nothing. I listened more intently to imagine a squeak, a murmur, the tread of a foot, anything, but there was nothing to be heard.

The head, my head, lay alone on the Adam's wife's pillow, not severed at the neck, but broken at it. Numbed I was, eyes open staring into darkness, thoughts open, body closed and paralysed. No feeling anywhere as I heard moaning music and skeleton dances on naked branches of trees without leaves. The brisk chill was unfelt, but an angry breeze moved curiously across my shoulders. Spellbound, hypnotised almost in my own idle company. The breeze sighed in a respectable tyranny of a small wind. Giddy leaves scatter and fall to decorate the floor – a blanket for the dead.

"Robert, Robert, wake up, wake up." I woke to find Stella kneeling beside me. "You do snore," she giggled, and, "you fell asleep. You must

30

go. Listen carefully. I am going back down to Adam. Creep downstairs and make a quick exit through the front door – it's open."

"Okay," I said with a cumbersome yawn.

"I will see you here tomorrow at half past two. Don't be late."

"Okay, I won't. I mean I'll be here but not late."

Stella leaned forward to kiss, so I clasped her head with both hands to oblige. Stella's hair ruffled at the touch as I held her fair face to look at the well-remembered expression on her forehead. We kissed and she pulled away, I touched her cheek with delicacy. "Go on, Robert, go on," she whispered. "I will see you tomorrow. Remember you have to go – I have to go." She twirled again, skirt swishing about her legs flirtingly and disappeared gracefully out on to the landing.

Without a thought, except for that of the moment, I rapidly dressed. The actions were interrupted suddenly as I caught the reflection in the bedroom mirror. The paleness of my body and the faded surface of my haggard face impressed familiarness. This caused a pause which divided my attention. I stopped to think. Looking back at me from the shining glass was a face of silent protest. Although I looked on attentively, there was something absent from the perception. An attempt to absorb as little of the appearance as possible was a feature of my gaze. I could see all before me, but much of what I saw did not register. One thing was certain, I had fallen or was falling in love with Stella. However, the vivid but featureless expression of the face in the mirror exposed an inducement of doubt. How could I reconcile the previous routine of yesterday and further back from yesterday with the events of that day – the next day and beyond? Was I living in a delusion, just for a moment confusedly wrapped in a libidinous arrangement? A critic might consider such a convenience as a foolish escapade doomed to failure. Did someone once say 'fortune favours the foolish', or was it 'fortune favours the brave' – either way no heed regardless of origin.

When dressed, I decided to emerge out from the indulgent analysis, instead there was a determination to look forward to the next day and our meeting at two thirty. With that I crept downstairs as quietly as possible to exact her instructions. On leaving, I saw no one in the house, though I was aware of the couples' presence. The television was on, the lights were lit and the warmth of the house made a departure a reluctant one. Indeed, the door had closed softly and silently – yet with a noiseless extraordinary jarring. Leaving Stella to him and finding myself alone again was not easy. Never before had another person used the word 'Robert' so frequently and spoken it with such affection.

***

While rubbing eyes, I doubted whether I was still asleep. By now an effort to arrive at work in reasonable time would have been engineered. Usually, the plan of action would unravel exponentially as the reality of Monday morning took a hold. That Monday, however, was altogether different, for the day before, life had taken on a new meaning. It was about time I took the day off. Now was a good time I thought. There was no particular plan to follow except of course to meet Stella again later. The clock read eight thirty two. Depending upon my allocation, I would ordinarily have been at work by that time.

The honourable thing to do would be to phone them. Tell them what though? "Oh I'm sick, love sick." Whatever reason I gave would be dishonourable. They would be no better informed for the merits of the case anyway. To be ill is quite sufficient information to tell them and such a worthy cause for missing work. Maybe, I do not phone, what an idea – for all they knew, I could be dead. For all they would care, I could be dead, it might be the talking point for a few minutes, but of little importance. No, I am not dead, in fact very much alive indeed – indeed. Other people are in love or fall in love. They go to work. Other people break the no sex continuum. They go to work. Eventually, I decided to tell them. To tell them – "I am sick," but with amazing evasive skill. Phone them! Speak to them! Tell them nothing and that is what I intended.

There was something tediously familiar about standing in the kitchen with mug in hand, where all about were menacing spreads and piles of dirty crockery. Those inconsiderate bastards, I am sure they make the taste of coffee even bitterer because of the disgraceful state of the kitchen. The glass on the window had a liquid surface anointing the air with a bewildering aroma of damp and a redolence of surrounding dirt. From tea-stained spoon to crusty saucepan each piece displayed an individual fury to taint. The odour and composition of all parts threatened in a whole conglomerate of grime. Armed with luxury toilet roll, I climbed to the bathroom in despairing surrender at the kitchen.

Leaving the hideous doors behind and out of mind, I walked outside with the perkiest of steps. The air seemed heady with oxygen abundant, despite a disquieting tinge of smoke from a source unknown. Moving on, towering above, bare branches of trees beckoned forward – "Walk on, Robert, walk on." I enthused at the new moment that Monday morning. The daunting necessary phone call was only a small obstacle to the business of the day.

The supermarket which had been so instrumental in recent events was the immediate destination. There I found a telephone and a daily rag of a sort. To the right as I left was the so familiar in-store café. Clanks of cups and plates accompanied a noise of incoherencies from the busy swarm. Home was the new destination now as time ventured on with each step and stride. My watch which showed a quarter past eleven was a reminder that the contents of the newspaper were now history. Nevertheless, such information of print could narrow the day and broaden the mind.

The journey home was taken with a profound sense of anticipation as the time of pleasure drew nearer. Above, the same trees bestowed an inquisitive impatience with bare branches and twigs extending. In slight agitation, the newspaper was removed from hand to arm then back to hand as fingers conferred. More floating than walking the view ahead was disturbed. Amid the buildings, two men moved and with marvellous quickness ran in front at a distance. Their motive was an unknown mystery as they crossed, then both climbed hazardous architecture of a high pre-war stone house. As each disappeared through an open window, I looked on caught in curiosity and suspicion.

A very short while passed before I was surprised by a police car which sped in the direction of the scene. It drove past that location and was soon followed by a second car. The latter made haste only to stop in the vicinity of the event. Much closer, and several officers could be witnessed milling around in the street. Amused at their aimless manner, I saw one talk on his personal radio. It was a matter of wonderment to me – why do they appear to talk into their lapel? Why do they not remove their radio when in use? Peak cap posed, neck craned and tilted he appeared to speak forcefully to his own chest. Another whose face was fresh questioned me. Transfixed by his weak moustache, I floundered to answer. Looking up at the particular building in question I wondered at each alleged culprit and their exercise of agility. Still in marvelling at his faint ginger moustache incongruent with glimpses of beige hair defying his black helmet I told him what I saw and no more. He returned a young ugly look of disbelief and told me to remain a while.

Soon I was joined by several others who seemingly emerged from nowhere. The faces shared a mutual contagion of curiousness. We looked on expectantly at the scene of nothing in particular. I reluctantly tried to answer incoherent questions with equal adhesion to sense. Then without fail gossip abounded and conversations around bombarded with local accounts. Stories were prolific of robbery, vandalism and numerous unspeakable acts of deviance. The interest inspired by the event further swelled the knot to a group and that to a crowd. I sneaked away unpursued but in a hint of perspiration.

On entering the shared house which I humbly refer to as my home, I met my second-floor neighbour. Jim was afflicted with an unfortunate black mist which over-clouded his manner that was overtly evident in his spectral face. All the residents of my humble home were acquainted with the story. Involved in a motorbike accident – he was. His head was clamped in a vice-like grip as his crash helmet compressed giving way under the wheel and tyre of a huge lorry. That was years ago, but Jim was still plagued by a gloomy abstraction of mind.

I regret that I had often taken perverse comfort from Jim by mentally comparing him to myself. The keystone of my thoughts alluded that his terrible enchantment in life was worse than my condition of reality. Such a phenomenon surmised a hypothesis that Jim was even less appreciated in the world than I and thus not at all wanted. Otherwise, I saw Jim in the hallowed non-judgemental light or at least tried to. It was clear, however, that others saw him by pitiful eyes. They knew his thrown casting in the world was due to unfortunate consequence and subsequent misfortune. The same people also reasonably assumed that he lived exclusively by State income maintenance and therefore was despised. A manifestation to pity and resent in others meant an ignorance of Jim for them, and for Jim was persistent isolation. For Jim it was a life, suspended and besieged in a bad hour overflowing into years. "Hello, Jim," I said as if to identify by announcement of his Christian name an inference to his poor fortune against my fortune renewed. Then I remembered the maxim: *'Do not eat in front of the poor'*. I compelled myself with great difficulty to focus entirely on our exchanges without the variety of baggage.

"Morning," he replied with a compromising seize to my attention.

"All right?" I quizzed.

All of Jim's spoken words were behindhand – it were as if each proposed sentence was deconstructed and reassembled in a long pause before he spoke. This proved a chore for the listener which usually meant conversation was limited to the rudimentary sort. A verbal stimulus for him was confined to restricted exchanges of a clumsy fashion. "Yeah," came a delayed reply.

"There is a bit of a commotion down the road. I don't know what it's about, but there are coppers everywhere."

Jim angled slightly away from me, but then almost facing afforded a glance. He moved his head bit by bit. "Coppers?"

"Yes, they are all over the place. You will probably see them if you are going that way." Jim looked at me again and I wondered if I had said too much in one go for his comprehension. He looked confused with a latent uneasiness of mind and I felt ill at ease with him. I refrained from breaking his processing by not speaking.

"Yeah, I'm going into town. I will take a look. See if I can find anything out."

34

Now I felt pleased with myself for allowing him the dignity to reply in his own time and mindful of this I waited a little longer than usual before I spoke. "There was a bit of a crowd gathering – trying to figure out what's going on."

"Yeah," came a much quicker response from Jim who blinked a number of times in succession. His eyes had a curious appearance, always part closed, but opened a little wider each time he spoke and reduced when restored to quiet. The nose was a near perfect feature in shape and size. It was of a sort one might choose if given a choice for one's own. I hated what I thought then. I thought that nose was wasted on such an individual of dullness. His hair was thin and greasy – probably unwashed for weeks. The beard had a grotesque abandon and a likely host to contamination. Hair around the mouth was discoloured and bore the contents of breakfast or even meals of weeks past. Such an assemblage of unknown content was cause for distraction from the conversation and I returned again to speak with a certain aversion.

"Were you going anywhere in particular?"

"No, just into town," he replied unabashed and not knowing I was scrutinising his unsightly appearance.

By then, I ought to have been ashamed of my drifting attention of Jim. I began to feel a pity and resentfulness that others thought of him. We stood facing each other. We were both ill adapted to such a polite exchange. It was strangely awkward. His look was that of vacant awe as if transferring a blotting out of words to me. He looked composed as his eyes shrunk relinquishing his responsibility to speak and direct the onus to me. There was a painful space which I was obligated to fill. It would have been easier to say 'see ya' and shoulder on but I had this misplaced inward resolution to do good. It was probably more of a to and froing of a vision to do good. Somehow, I did say something by completely switching the conversation to angling. I thought that I should spare some time for Jim out of good will. I knew he was once a keen angler and had an exact knowledge of fishing which he was always fearless to impart. However, after several long minutes about the importance of specific bait I said "see ya" and shouldered on.

While ascending the stairs and on into my room, I was roused again into vigorous life. The good deed of giving my time to Jim was a drain, but escaping was a relief. The clock acted perfectly, always actively employed. Each hand signalled written instructions as I watched time – then time for action. I had struggled for some minutes to trust my judgement to look my best for Stella. This had included presenting the very best underwear for her approval and scrutiny. Despite efforts to relax,

I was encumbered with an aggravated sharpness, so I remembered and employed the routine; one two three.

Out of the house, I went to my car; it was a sorry but reliable-looking faded red thing. So frequent was the moving from house to car that the performance took an incompleteness of action. Unimportant details were discarded. There was no need to listen because I could see. There was no need to look when I could feel. Almost automatically, I drove on in a tunnel of only thoughts for Stella and the destination. The trees, almost leafless looked on, they could not summon my attention. The gestures of branches and twigs were lost fearfully wild in the breeze. Buildings looked down disinterested, windows were closed and doors were shut in capricious fancy.

On arrival, my haggard face was hidden from the passer-by and resident neighbours by sympathetic evergreens. A curious empty watchfulness had commenced from windows of local buildings guided unseen eyes. I fell quiet as the engine fell silent and the imagined audience noisily commented in judgemental anticipation. The ghostly faces at windows haunted with knives drawn. Each spirit whispered disapprovingly in religious observance of our sinfulness. The faded but reliable red thing was now only a useless capsule nothing more than a marker to infidelity of our individual case. But headlong was the motive which was now bereft of discretion in the game of fervour and forfeit.

It was two thirty, so undeterred with precise deliberate footsteps I stepped onward. The tarmac underfoot bore a peculiar feel against polished shoes and super poly wotsit soles. Stella appeared suddenly at the door as if to whirl life to another dimension. In a colourful way she presented in a dreamlike procession moving forward to embrace. For a moment, we turned together in a sea of caresses like some mad scene on the shore with the sea crashing in a symphony from some romantic film from the 1950s.

"Robert, stop, stop, stop," her voice echoed forcefulness and reluctance combined, but was disguised in a loud whisper as if to hide the volume and the act. "Listen," she implored with a positive assertiveness – "listen."

Taken a little aback, I began to listen impatiently for we were entwined in desire. Her eyes offered a new message as we stood apart slightly. She held my wrists to push away, but I clasped her elbows in a powerful grip. Though her head remained fixed her eyes darted to the side. Eyes were front again then quick and to the side. Her focus relaxed on me as impatience abated. Still holding in a demeanour of calmness she spoke to my eyes. Stella tilted her head in customary communication to procure an undivided attention. "What?" I said tinged with anxiety. "Tell me!"

She stood before me, collecting herself like a delicate flower looking skyward to the sun. Again the eyes moved signalling, the eyelids were dressed in a silvery blue with full dark lashes which shouted conspicuously. From a temporary abstraction she adjusted the tone of her voice. The comfort she applied to the conveyance was received with a heightened sense of curiosity. "My husband, Adam. He is upstairs. He often sleeps in the afternoon and wakes at about three." She released her hold. "Come inside."

I had surmised that he, Adam that is, would be elsewhere. It had been a matter of convenience for me to allow Stella to formulate the plans for the deceit and carry the burden of responsibility. Now I was beginning with tunnel behind to see a broader vista. "Come on," she repeated as I hesitated. In we went with cautious feet and a shared fate. Dim shadows were subtly cast about the kitchen on that overcast afternoon. With lowered voices, we spoke among the running tap and heating of the kettle. She faced the window whilst making coffee. I the amorous lover clasped her wrist and playfully licked the back of her neck. With difficulty she attempted to avert attention and explain the execution of her elaborate plan. "Stop it, stop it," she whispered. "Listen, you must trust me. I have spoken to Adam. He would like to speak to you. You do trust me don't you?"

"Of course," I said automatically, but doubted those two words as soon as they were uttered. It seemed as though someone else had said them. I was so surprised by the hatching. "Yes, why should I not trust you? I love you." Even more surprised was I by those three little words spurting out as if to lighten the load on our hearts. We were not alone. It was a surely a naked cherub moment, an angelic child wearing nothing but wings whom carried arrow and bow hovered above us both.

"Oh do you, do you, Robert?" she replied turning to embrace. "Do you?"

"Yes, of course," I replied between kisses.

Coolly and lightly, she continued. "This may sound strange, but Adam is looking forward to meeting you. We have spoken at length about what I want. I have told him about you, what you can offer – which he cannot. Do you get my meaning?"

It seemed very extraordinary. She had spoken in an eloquent way to clearly state the position. I knowingly acknowledged what she had said and was then not totally sure of the meaning. Like the fool that I was, I repeated yet another, "Yes, of course." She wanted to hear just that, but I would have said anything to please her and she knew it as I did.

I had to remind myself that that moment was not another dream from which I had come back from – I was really there. It was a real situation I felt a divisible superiority between that moment and forty-eight hours earlier. Stella clung to me, her pretty head rested warm on my shoulder. Approvingly, she said, "You love me so sweetly." In response, I dabbed her lips with my own and lovingly stroked lightly the forehead. "Robert?"

"Mmm."

"It is nearly three. I am going shopping, but you are to stay here and wait for Adam."

"But –"

"No buts. Do not worry. Adam is an old gentleman. He is very understanding. He is intelligent. I have told him – you will be here. Just introduce yourself. He will do all the talking. Just be the charming guest." She smiled an impossible smile. "I am going now." She touched my nose with a forefinger and kissed with a taste of coffee. The gentle hands pressed against my arm to brace. With an imploring look up to my face her eyes conveyed a kind inspiration. I observed affectionate reassurance by her light manner and the saying of the words, "See you later, love."

Almost speechless and in impeccable conduct, I returned, "All right, bye."

The dinky yellow car pulled away and nervously unprotected I was alone waiting for Adam.

I stood by the hearth of their lounge. The mirror gave a receiving look which did not inspire confidence. Nervously, I gave a peculiar short cough which caused the mirror to momentarily cloud over. I began to change rest from leg to leg as if I had a hundred of them, but then on wiping my head with an arm, I moved away from the fire to sit by it. While leaning forward, my eyes gradually sought the fire for sympathy and strength. The mirror had an ominous appearance. It was the fire which offered a returning image of comfort.

I was unprepared for this contrived arrangement. The anticipation of meeting Adam for the first time in the lounge of his house was like a diabolic sentence. I questioned Stella and her plan. If I did not love Stella I would surely hate her for it. Then it struck me. I could have been waiting there to see Adam only to meet some terrible fate. He could have been forgiven for blowing my brains out with some explosive firearm. After all I was 'shagging his wife', or at least that may have been the expression others might have used. He could have shot me and then claimed anything that came to his mind to defend his actions. My defence would have been implausible, particularly so if I were no longer alive.

I could have thought a thousand things as the flame from the fire was touching a light in my head. The light was constantly occupied and could be switched at will, but not so easily turned off with any amount of determination. Like a beacon, the light was lit with an extinguishable flame but an overriding spark proposed that I left there and then. Leaving would mean an escape and a relief from the anxiety that I was experiencing. To go and leave nothing behind did appeal. The push, however, did not exceed the pull. To exit and close the door behind would have eventually led into regret and back again into tedium. If I stayed to meet and listen to Adam, it would prepare the way into the next day and towards a chain of associations for tomorrow.

To stay or go was no longer an option to ponder as the old man silently entered the room. Though expected, it was still a shock to see him before me, so my thoughts were instantly extracted. The blank face had been softened by years and was the colour of a dead leaf. Automatically from good manners, I stood to introduce myself, but the embarrassment of the unusual situation was beyond any disguise. The boldness was not lost, however, as it utilized a beginning.

"Hello, Robert. You have been the subject or part of the subject of Miranda's appeals to me." He paused with a sustained blank expression with eyes focussed on mine. "Miranda is my wife and I naturally her husband."

"Yes." It was prudent to speak little and listen a lot in such circumstances. Although I heard what he said, I struggled to process all the things relevant to that moment. Like an obsolete computer overwhelmed with information I stalled in perseverance. I recalled what she had said. *'He will do all the talking, just be the charming guest'*. Such an odd guest I was though, the adulterous male to the adulterous wife, a charming impostor of lecherous concealment. The name too, was actually no surprise, Stella superseded by Miranda. I could have conceivably guessed at that in time with confidence. It was more difficult then to associate feeling to the name Miranda than emotions consigned to the name Stella.

I was hypnotised a little by his voice which was almost moribund in its delivery and weakness. There was an idiosyncratic deplorability to it that was pitiable and dreadful. Like his face, the resonance was so affected as if a once beautiful colour had faded away into a hopeless and lost creature. The creature, a feeble old man that stood before me. His strength of past years experienced was only evident in the honour attached to his words. "I have had a good life you know. I fear that my days are numbered now and Miranda will live on a good while yet. In my twilight I aim to give her anything she wants. Miranda is not backward at coming forward. You understand?"

"Yes," was my immediate reply as if I were condemned to speak somehow.

39

I endured a prickly pause has he poured himself a brandy, quaffed and exacted himself another. While holding the glass precariously in his bony hand he gave that sustained look again and half turning his head he said, "Drink?"

Now I felt condemned and compelled by his curious tone and nodded to the affirmative. I trod forward with an extended gait to receive the glass of generous proportion and making sure not to touch any part of his hand in the exchange I said, "Thank you."

The alcohol seemed to galvanise him as he continued, "Now where was I?"

"Miranda, not the sort to hold back. I mean, I mean you mean she is not backwards at coming forwards as you aptly put it."

"Yes, I remember. I am not senile you know. I still have all my marbles."

"No. Yes, of course," realising I had said it again. I thought I really ought to stop saying it, because it was becoming irritating.

"I was twice her age – you know – when we married. She was twenty-five years old. Now she is as old I as I was then. Fifty is young when you reach my years." Next followed a pause for thought. It was one of those natural silences. He wore a thinking look as he sipped brandy then sipped a lesser amount. My only thoughts were that I was capable of working out his age of seventy-five and self-congratulation at the feat of doing so, but then remembered cautiously it could easily be seventy-four. Sitting by the fire he placed the glass upon the hearth. Likewise, I found a suitable place to sit, but held the glass out of comfort. Before speaking again he moved forward awkwardly to reach and put the glass to his lips. "Yes, fifty is young and you are a boy."

Feeling insulted, I said "yes" to hide my disapproval.

"Anyway, boy," he exclaimed with an incongruent vigour. "It seems you have taken her fancy. Miranda, she has these fancies. I give her everything she wants. Money is no object. If she wants to go to Australia – she goes to Australia. If she wants a diamond necklace – she gets a diamond necklace with matching earrings. If she wants to go there – she goes there. Money is no object." He emptied his glass. "I like to think she wants for nothing. She does want for nothing. We live very different lives, but we are together still, and will be. Do you see?"

"Yes."

He saw that his glass was empty and asked me to fill it. Like a perfect guest I obliged, recharging the glass by his own generous measure. A sip became a gulp and he continued. "Yes, we have three children – grown-up now and flown. Boy and two girls you know – well – young man and young ladies – grown-up now and flown."

40

"Yes, yes."

"She has had affairs – several. I was a bookmaker for fifty odd years. Stayed away a lot I did. Anyway – change of subject. I can't perform like I did – lost interest anyway. We don't sleep together anyway – very inconvenient – I mean convenient you know."

"Yes."

"This is where you come in. She has always had the appetite. Well, enough said I think. She looks after me you know, not that I need looking after, but she does it and I love her for it. Have I made myself clear?"

"Crystal."

"I make sure she gets everything she wants you know." He downed the brandy again in a remarkable quick movement. His face adopted an outrageous appearance as he swallowed, white head at one with glass.

A steadfast voice said, "More brandy"; it was mine, delivered as a sort of assumed consensus between us than a question to him. His arm was part extended, a support to a wobbly glass as he remained seated. I took the gesture to indicate that the expectation was for me to refill for him. I complied possessed by a strange eagerness to ply him with drink for no reason other than to please him. It was another exceptional measure, a double or treble perhaps. I was content to sip and let the liquid tingle the tongue and not absorb the liquor wholesale. This conservative strategy tended to assert an advantage which afforded me an aid to superiority.

Still very much part of reality and with more of the perception of it than he – I felt able to speak freely. It was Adam though which utilized the time by his ramblings. Even at such an age he found it necessary to impress upon me his curriculum vitae. Time passed amazingly slowly as he went on and on. I sat, I listened and I sipped. He sat, he spoke and he drank. I wondered is such a potent life and high proof breakfast was directly related to impotency. The matter would remain a mystery as the darkness pawed at the day.

Nightfall was illuminated by the return of Miranda. She impressed her tender needs to the relic through the delightful feminine tone of her voice. "How have you men got on?" She ventured the question toward Adam while kissing his pruney cheek. He stroked her loving arm with his bony fingertips, "all right," he declared – eyes scornfully to me.

Miranda noticing his look and influenced condition gave me a subtle wink. "You have been drinking you two, haven't you?" she playfully said condemning. He continued to look at me raising his white eyebrows to socially register a shared affinity. Such a notion had missed the mark, but I returned him a wry smile. My response was probably so ambiguous that it had a few meanings. Safely, I thought it meant one thing to him, but something else to me. In a triangle of recognition, three pairs of eyes settled on their own story. It was enough for my satisfaction that Miranda's eyes saw me perfectly. And lost in love land complete with brandy I watched her with an earthy lust.

She sexed around the room, doing this, doing that. Arousal first began as she slowly button by button undid her single-breasted long gown of a coat. She stood and faced me as I sat. On opening her coat, she revealed the front of her white blouse open at the collar three top buttons undone. Through the sleekly ironed white cotton was a hint of lacy lingerie. An 'A' line skirt which finished just below the knee defined the form of her thighs. The shoes were bright, shiny, cut away at the tops and with bold two-inch heels. The affect gave the feet and ankle a narrow appearance to flatter the legs. With coat removed and put away, she went about her business. First adjusting this and that. Again to the window she went lighting a perpendicular lamp on the way. Up on her toes she reached to the head of each curtain to close. A fine grey black mesh creased across her calves slightly, then stretched tight again as she lowered. I imagined she might be wearing stockings strung from suspenders for my benefit. She knew I was watching. She moved so gracefully glancing occasionally toward me, fully comprehending. I was quite certain that Adam was wholly oblivious in this moving about. Miranda's attraction and my pricked senses, were to him lost by his over indulgence.

At this juncture, Miranda abided a little distance remote from Adam. In her mediation, she knew that he was greatly overpowered by the potent spirit. He shook his head without reason which confirmed for us a dubious attention. His indifference and temporary departure from reality afforded me a new confidence. Possessed with such a license I took the opportunity to pursue a fruitful course. "Do you have a plan, my darling?"

She began with an exaggerated whisper, "Yes," and a form of betrayal about her. Miranda looked at me with strength, as he related with weakness. Whilst still devoted in his presence, her eyes and lips reluctantly protested at my hungry mouth. As if to reassign the moment to the ordinary, she said quietly, "He is not entirely unaware of our words. Come on, into the kitchen."

As if muted by a cruel finger of deception, Adam was not required to speak. I stood paused to look at him and saw his perception was without doubt dulled. He did not respond. I think he chose not to participate in the conversation or respond to the obvious signals between Miranda and myself. I left him there while I joined Miranda in the kitchen.

Miranda had begun to prepare bread and soup for the three of us and on seeing me enter enquired, "What is he doing?" Her voice carried a concern for Adam which she may have thought I shared. However, even with justice and generosity, my sympathy was not for him, but for her.

That and a smouldering desire for Miranda was countered by a contemptuous pity for Adam. I delayed my answer. Instead in the instinct of the moment rested my palms on her warm hips then kissed her forehead. "He has switched the television on. He is looking through it at 'The News'."

She rotated a quarter of a circle to face the cooker and gently stir the soup. I adjusted accordingly, right hand on the cant of her hip and the left to her thigh. Miranda swayed appreciative of the fondling exhibiting a holding back with additional slowness. I discovered for practical purposes – she was not wearing suspenders. Miranda lifted her wrist and hand to remove mine with the supple soft feeling of a woman. She had this tendency to demonstrate a stop start freedom of womanhood. "Behave, naughty boy…tomato?"

"Fine."

"Tell me what you and Adam have spoken about this afternoon?"

"Well, briefly, he said, he was to let you have anything your heart desires. He said he loves you and needs you for his sake. As I am part of what you desire. No, actually he said, as I am part of what you want… he said he could no longer perform the function of a man any longer – so he said he is happy for me to do that. And as you know, I am more than happy to oblige him."

Her face creased attractively at my attempt to amuse as she poured the soup. "Is that all he said?"

"Well, I must confess my attention did wander. He did sort of peter out, but he does not want you or I to go out anywhere together."

Her amused face had become contemplative as she listened. I continued, but I heard his words echo in my head as I summarised. The strange scenario seemed so improbable that I had to mentally check throughout before delivering the words. "He more or less said – my role was to please you in the bedroom but nowhere else." I must have made all manner of doubting gestures as I spoke, but such signals only served to reveal the true diverse nature of his words. "He sees you always by his side at his convenience. I do not think he is comfortable with the sex idea, but he concedes it is part of keeping you happy."

Miranda had occupied an intense attention as I spoke. Never before had I seen her with such a look of concentration and she said, "Oh I see. Did he say anything else of note?"

"He rambled on about the past, but little else."

"Okay," she said smoothing her skirt under herself, sitting to the table. "Could you ask him to come and eat please?"

I obeyed, only to find Adam half way from his chair to the kitchen. "Hello," I said stupidly. He gave me a glance to expose a ropey white throat. Silent, he was not acknowledging. He shuffled wobbly to the kitchen. I let him sit first waiting business like before taking the other seat.

The task of eating soup in such circumstances was a difficult one. Firstly, I was not particularly keen on tomato soup. Secondly, I usually ate by using a spoon like a garden implement to prod, dig and shovel. Finally, each one of us was so unaccustomed to such a three-cornered table of extraordinary difficulty. Again, I thought it best to adopt a passive mode – let the triangle unfurl and keep a low profile. The worry concerning the use of the spoon dissipated as Adam grabbed his. He used all of a bony hand to hold. The spoon stem was crowed by every one of his four fingers, the equally skinny thumb protruded comically into the air. I found his use of it objectionable for it was like that of an excavator. Of course I would think something like that to make me feel better. The way I saw him too, those netted wrinkles upon the cheek made my face handsome in comparison. The strong florescent light of the kitchen made Adam seem paler than he was. The contrast though, of the soup to his skin made the face appear so unwholesomely deficient in natural colour. If he were to have been cut, I am sure he would have bled sour milk against the red soup. Miranda, beautifully pink, displayed a taste for the soup by licking her top lip ever so subtly. She dipped the spoon to the liquid and continued eating in the manner of an accomplished debutante.

It was Miranda who took the lead to commence the conversation. Though her words were directed to Adam, I was caught by her contemplative intensity of calm, strength and knowledge. I listened to learn that it was he who was governed and regulated – not her. Yes, Miranda was the governor and regulator by this demonstration. She leaned toward Adam until hugging the table almost, and then placed a gentle hand to his wrist. "Now dear, eat up, because you have to get ready for the dogs. Clerk will be here to collect you soon." Adam nodded and swallowed a little bread without chewing. "Adam always goes to the greyhound racing on Monday nights. Was a bookie once, wasn't you, dear. Most bookmakers go to their graves still at their pitch, but Adam retired years ago. I thought you could keep me company while he goes out." She gave me a reassuring look as if to condone our betrayal by somehow projecting it on Adam for his outing. I nodded welcoming approval. Momentarily, Miranda gave endorsement with intelligent eyes, lips devoid of words yet set in a knowing smile. Notwithstanding our subtle exchanges she continued as if to compound her scheme by talking on in a matter-of-fact way. "Oh, Adam and Clerk go back years. Clerk is still a bookie. Adam still does the odd private transaction – all illegal of course."

Adam interrupted with his pitiable voice, "The lays are not illegal. They are all perfectly above board. You know that."

44

"Yes, Adam – but you have retired – remember." Then cautiously to me, "It's a grey area." Miranda retreated into a gentle smile and gave me a sideways glance at the little joke that evaded the notice of Adam. "Hurry up," she said like one of those actors you see on television – speaking and eating simultaneously without dropping a crumb – something one seldom sees in real life.

I was for a moment thinking about Adam being hard on four score and really unconcerned by bets or lays. I had a suspicion about the nature of the wagers and had to remind myself again of reality when Clerk arrived. I was introduced as a work colleague. All of us in our different capacities played along with the half lie. Name was not Clerk, of course – he informed. Amos, actually. Adam left with Clerk (I mean Amos of course).

A quiet followed, then Miranda slid the soup bowl to the table centre and said boldly, "I would not call it courtship. What would you call it?"

"I don't know," I replied surprised. "It is not like a proper affair is it. Love and romance without the outings."

She unfastened the fourth and fifth buttons of her blouse mischievously. "No, I'm just going to the bedroom to dress for dinner." Miranda ventured a self-possessed calm and a gaze agog. She pulled away gracefully from the table as if sanctioning me to follow. I watched her walk as if through flowers leaving each retreating door in her wake.

Chapter Four

Usually following the voluptuary happenings and associated tenderness, I would sleep soundly. Having been fed and freed, I would ordinarily in ease and rest be oblivious to the demeanour of my partner. Though it wore me out, there was no time to recover. We were going out to dinner. I took a shower, the shower which belonged to Adam and Miranda. It was an odd feeling I thought, to be there where he had stood – standing there naked. Thankfully, he was not standing there then, but Adam had gone to the dogs. She, the woman in my life, was wrapped in a fluffy white bath towel, scented and seated before the ornate dressing table enhancing her beauty.

Unaccustomed as I was to the fountain of such luxury, I embraced thousands of cascading droplets against the skin. How remote we are I thought. Men are so physically different from women. Men are more apelike, characterised so with superfluous hair primitively arranged. Yes, unlike women, men have features of little interest and only one feature of little interest.

"Robert, are you going to be long? I have made some coffee."

Surprised I drew back the shower curtain to see Miranda all dressed and ready in the bathroom. This action had unwittingly exposed my torso and etcetera.

"Hurry up, coffee boy."

Confused, I questioned, "Coffee boy?"

With a giggle she noted, "Yes demijohn to demitasse."

My surprised glance at her appearance was fixed in the direction of Miranda's blinking eyes. Then her focus and mine fell together on the same object. We then locked eye to eye and laughed in unison. She turned with her customary swish, "Come on, hurry up, dear." Miranda still laughing disembarked by way of descent to the stairs.

I made haste and then we quickly resumed a lover's acquaintance in the kitchen. While I drank the coffee, she said, "Actually, it is quite a large cup and very strong." I nearly choked as I began to laugh again. Miranda laughed too as I struggled to breathe, laugh and drink all at once. Then recovered but with watery eyes I focussed again on Miranda. When the laughter ceased, she displayed a sensitive concern and consolingly asked if I was 'okay'. She was still fuzzy in my vision and as if to recognise this in a kind way of feeling Miranda touched my upper arm. The delicate hand for once felt non-sexual as if to designate a kind of loving beyond anything ever experienced. It was as if the ingenuity of the gentle hand were an extension of the heart. The instant seemed to bring a higher chemistry to bear as if the inner-most working of our minds converged at that simple moment, so clear almost telepathic. Appreciative of the perplexity understood, I moved to hold her close, she placed a gentle palm to my heart and her head to my shoulder.

Cutting through the moment I ventured to ask if I were under dressed for dinner. She said, "Yes, naked in not recommended. Go dress. Your attire is perfect."

Ready in minutes and only minutes later I took her hand. Taking the comfort of her palm in mine was like being the wearer of a perfectly tailored suit. "You look lovely," I said. "Where are we going?"

She giggled again, allowing her hand so soft and passive to be enveloped by my long fingers. "I don't know. You are the boss."

"I thought you were," I said with genuine sincerity. "You are the one in control. You are the one with the assertive command."

For a split second, Miranda's aspect beheld that of a spoilt child. As I had led by the hand, she had halted by it with a tug. I realised instantly as I spoke that my attempt to amuse had not worked. The modulation of my voice had the quality of indeterminate inflection. I had unwittingly conveyed an ambiguity which had momentarily found her affronted. It was relief then to see her recognise the afterglow of humour from my words.

She replied changing with a repost which I heard with an ear for flattery and amusement. "Oh yeh," in an affected husky voice. "Who was the boss when you pinned me to the mattress?"

I was compelled to laugh by her kinder form of allurement to amuse than mine. But as I recalled, it was she who drew me through human truth to her. It was Miranda who was in control and I was the one out of it.

As we were in mutual dispute with regard to who exactly was the boss, I decided to assume command. We both knew this was really a temporary assumption, for it was clear to both of us that Miranda was actually in charge.

To return to the subject, she asked, "Where are we going?"

I did not know, but I was of course aware that she had served a light meal at tea time. I also knew we had burned off the calories and very recently. It was the next bit that was so contrary to the wishes of Adam.

47

"Out to dinner," I said boldly, "onward." I pointed forward into air with fist clenched and forefinger erect.

"But, where?" Miranda questioned.

We moved out; marching, side by side, to the back arms around each other's waist and to the front arms across with hands clasped together in the middle. We laughed as we marched on. It was comforting to feel the female hip against mine, the warmth of another person so defined and satisfying. "To the left," I shouted immaturely and inclined to the left pushing Miranda with a rub of hips. I steered at her waist with a firm wrist. We zigzagged along like two teenagers consumed in a first love, but laughing like 'Darby and Joan'.

Hidden away in a seemingly sacred part of town, I knew vaguely of this obscure restaurant – candlelit – plain food. I could not really venture to impress her because of my incomplete knowledge or ignorance of such venues. My definition of eating out had literally been eating out, fish and chips in the street was an example. Despite the limited experience, thoughtful expedience meant it was not the time to relate it.

The waiter was a tall and slender fellow with a stoop. His ill-fitting trousers, long in leg and short in width covered two props. His upper limbs swung loose as I was reminded again of man's affiliation to the chimpanzee. We were escorted or rather we were ushered forward to a corner table set for two. He followed with a youthful enthusiasm which was not contrary to his young face peppered with acne at a generous level. We were certainly aware of him as Miranda sauntered forward. He must have specially applied there to be admitted, his presence was so incomprehensible – not regularly belonging to the town. Miranda stopped at the table and he with impeccable manners notwithstanding his appearance approached. His bony hands attached to limp arms held and pulled the chair back allowing her to display an utmost grace in order to sit. She seemed so agreeable and entirely satisfied while smoothing the skirt against her leg and underneath. A turn of a head of nonchalance implied a thank you to the waiter. He offered a menu to each of us. Miranda took hers first by turning a wrist as if to move a door handle lever. The menu was given to me with strong conviction, like the offering of a ripe banana and I received it as a mutual sacrifice of food to a kindred spirit.

"Thank you," I said in a tone dismissive, not naturally comprehending to be anything close to the literal meaning of the words 'thank you'. The hint was far too subtle for my fellow primate, so he just hovered. He held a tiny pencil poised to write in a cupped and clumsy hand. I was perplexed by the discontent the arrangement of fingers of such a waiting pose. The giantness of his thumb was an unfathomable mystery to behold, but his fingers on the whole were complimentary digits. I found his proximity disagreeable while I tried to make choices of choice. "Could you leave us a minute to think," I said with a sledgehammer hint. He bowed slightly in obedience as he turned to walk a little distance. This made me feel guilty, for I had transgressed some unwritten etiquette.

"Robert, there was no need to send him away like that."

"I am sorry, my love. It is just that all that hovering is so oppressive. I can't think straight when pestered. I would be bound to make the wrong choice." Using 'sorry' and 'love' together in such a way had the result of restraining any further criticism. She smiled a pretty smile. The subdued light fell in such a fashion as to iron out wrinkles on our faces. Her smile was youthful and fresh.

"I don't know anything at all about wine," she said unconvincingly. Our combined knowledge, however, made house red the absolute choice of reason. Easy it was, not to dwell on our ignorance moving swiftly to choosing the main course.

"Are you ready to order now, sir?"

Still a little rushed, I dared not say anything other than the affirmative. "Err… Yes," I ventured. Miranda looked uncertain and then assured herself of an opinion which was evident in her expression.

"Madam?"

Miranda appeared a little uncertain again, so I immediately interrupted the weak transparency, "I'll have the chicken, and what would you like, dear?"

"Well, I was going to have the fish, the trout, but I am unsure now." There followed a pause, her soft hand began to touch the table's edge. She became more thoughtful than usual and seemed much engrossed by the subject. Miranda looked at me again and smiled in a peculiar manner. At that moment, a handful of patrons arrived. The waiter looked in the direction of the door and I followed his glance to see them.

"Perhaps you could give us a few minutes," I said. The waiter nodded and saw me in a kinder way. He left to attend the new company.

I drew on my development of reasoning power. "You look in a muddle."

"Sorry. Yes. Oh dear. I seem to be unable to decide. What do you suggest?"

It was difficult to give my opinion without seeming to place myself unfavourably by making a suggestion. While torn in such a view, I did the unlikely thing of standing by my chair. Being stood I placed my body in the light. Conspicuously and inexplicably, I held the table's corners at my palms. Miranda saw me in an unusual focus raising her head and eyes in a quirky glee. The slight astonishment faded to a look of curiousness as I moved to crouch beside her. Facing the menu which she held before her I rested my head against her arm below the shoulder. The comfort was a mutual one. Feminine softness was so stimulating. She had a distinct natural gentleness which I knew to be exclusive to Miranda. We read the menu together and mutually accepted the other's unconditional attention. "You can never be certain of fish in a restaurant," I said.

"What do you mean?"

"It's a notion I have that's all. My dad always used to say. He was a chef. He always said fish is not as fresh as it ought to be sometimes. Therefore, eating fish out can sometimes be a dodgy business. Mind you, chicken is not necessarily a good bet either, I suppose." I kissed her cheek and then to my surprise, I was conspicuous again having caught the searchingly interested attention of several others in the restaurant. I stopped, reddened and returned a half smile to the room.

Now again in my seat she said, "What about the wine?"

Confused I said, "What about it?"

"Well, Robert, I am not sure but. But, I am not sure whether you can have red wine with fish. Or even with chicken for that matter."

"Oh I see, well perhaps we could have white," thoughtfully.

The menu, though inanimate, was the site of much deliberation. The nature or art of it and the importance was a graft of circumstance. We decided eventually, with naïve but original cleverness to summon the waiter once again. I had now instead chosen oxtail. She had considered oxtail, but was wary of the idea of it, although she did like the famous soup. Miranda assumed that I was only having oxtail because it was different. Oxtail was novel I thought, but chicken was common enough to be safe. Miranda resigned herself to chicken for reasons of her own. We chose to stay with red because it was doubtless complementary to my choice and we had thought of it first anyway.

As the waiter attended with his huge thumbs, I noticed the large proportions of his feet. Although his toes were of course confined wholly within his size twelves I imagined them to be of an unsightly form. Toes of his must have been surely elongated designed especially for narrow branches, bark and general undergrowth.

In keeping with shrubbery, we discussed the importance of vegetables and of particular interest the benefits of broccoli in the scheme of things. "So many people make the mistake of over cooking them. It destroys the vitamin C. It is no wonder that children dislike them so. All that boiling." Women, I thought, they have this superb capacity to talk about anything. Women can even make the subject of vegetables interesting.

"I like vegetables. I like eating vegetables."

"Yes, isn't that the same thing?" she returned.

"What?"

Miranda explained, "Vegetables – you like eating vegetables because you like the taste, texture or whatever – therefore you like vegetables."

"Well yes I suppose so," I replied, not entirely sure what she was trying to convey. The meaning was obvious, but what the meaning of it meant was infinitely more complex. Suddenly, I thought of something and blurted out, "My darling, think of a vegetable!"

"What?"

"Think of a vegetable."

"Okay," she said looking confused.

"Right, the vegetable you thought of is a carrot. Am I right?"

"No, broccoli."

"Oh," I said disappointed. "Perhaps I have done it wrong."

"Done what? What are you talking about?"

"Perhaps I should have asked you to name a vegetable and you would have said carrot."

"Would I. I don't think I would. I would have said broccoli."

"No I doubt it," I said with unproven confidence. "You would probably have said carrot or carrots."

Miranda with one elbow on the table, a hand to the elbow and another to the chin, laughed. Of course the amusement was not unmerited. I looked over my glass to indulge the observation by making a wry face and shutting one eye. I was so disposed to admire her, I was knowingly the entertainer although she was laughing at me it was graciously professed. The lady was a fair fortune who captivated my admiration. I had the urge to take her there and then in a proud and rampant way. However, with considerable restraint I fought to quell the flourish. She was the sort who caused men to sing.

"All right then," recovering from the laugh and filling herself a second glass, "name a vegetable." She pointed an insistent finger.

"That's no good – I know the answer. It won't work."

"Name a vegetable."

"Cabbage," I rebounded.

"Cabbage? You are supposed to say carrots – silly."

"No, I'm not. I know what the answer is anyway. Boys, men say cabbage. Girls, women say carrots."

Miranda looked at me fixedly. I leaned back in my chair as if to establish an assured fact governed by a specific law. "I do not understand, she exclaimed."

"I do not know why that it is the case, but most of the time it does work."

"I don't believe it," she pursued.

I moved forward to hold her hand, to concentrate my attention on her again. Shifting her eyes to me she looked silently at length. There was a perplexing or unfinished chord which needed to be completed. A slight motion of her hand indicated that this ridiculous subject had foolishly interposed on our affair. I knew while holding a matter of fact face that then was a wavering moment. I resolved to find a solution quickly by some cunning abstract application. Still held in her disapproval I had to release her hand to allow the waiter to serve our meal.

"Thank you," we both said in turn to break the silence has he placed the plates before us. Then eureka, the discovery was announced to myself as if some inner voice saved the moment by the invention of algebra. "Ask the waiter, my love."

"What do you mean ask the waiter – you ask him!"

"I would, my love, but for it to work, it has to be asked by someone of the opposite sex to the opposite sex."

By now the ears of the waiter were almost at a flop, seldom could one witness a look so curious. Miranda gave me an indefinite look and in a voice affected slightly by the wine began. "All right then," she said facing me. Then facing the waiter, "waiter, could you help us." He nodded with a little embarrassment and adolescent affectations. "Please, could you name a vegetable?"

He immediately displayed a stance of a human being in hesitation. He assumed a sideways subtle look towards me and I responded equally with a tribal nod. Then as if to extricate himself from a jungle monkey puzzle climbed to the treetop and announced a definite "cabbage". I could have kissed him, but preferred to supply him simply with a year's supply of bananas. Miranda's expression took on that of astonishment and she was barely able to preserve her composure. The confusion of the waiter was the shiest, but had brightness from my comradely wink. I was happy to receive a beaming smile from Miranda aided by the unremarkable wine. There was not a thing to explain to the waiter as he retreated out of a splendid picture.

"You paid him a fiver, didn't you – to say that."

"No, I didn't, honestly it really does work."

"Actually, Robert, I have a confession, I thought of carrots before I said broccoli." I broke into a good-humoured laugh out of politeness and we found ourselves laughing for no reason. Then it was said, "Robert, I love you."

"So do I," said I and paused not deliberately for effect, but it appeared to be so as her words were felt sinking in. I resumed speech again as if wounded into confusion, "I mean, you, I mean."

"I know what you mean, Robert. So tell me about this vegetable theory."

"Honestly, I don't know. I just know that it works for some reason. We obviously have some ideas about vegetables which probably overlap with assumptions we have about male and female."

"Perhaps then for some Freudian reason we choose vegetables which we think represent the opposite sex thingy. A carrot is a phallic thing for a male thingy and cabbage is a female thingy."

"Possibly," I said finding the whole idea difficult to keep serious about. "I had thought more about boys hating cabbage as boys always do and girls with penis envy – carrots are probably more like a willy than any other vegetable. That really does not explain anything, does it?"

"Robert, I think we ought to change the subject."

"Yes, sorry, I think you are right."

"How is the oxtail?"

"It is nice, it tastes just as the soup does. There is a lot of bone. It is quite a feat to separate the meat from it. How is the chicken?"

"It is nice, it tastes just as chicken does," she replied in a mood of quizzicality. Then we laughed at the ordinary conversation. We ate, paused then ate and paused again. "The waiter looks out of place here doesn't he? He has an extraordinary appearance don't you think? But he is so accommodating and polite for one so young."

"Yes, he is very tall, isn't he? He looks young enough to grow another six inches yet. Tell me Miranda," I delayed to speak while seeking the right words, "you the wife of Adam are very much his junior. What did you see in him? You must have seen something or you would not have married him I suppose."

Miranda was very willing to answer. "For a short time before we married, I worked for him as his secretary. He had an unsuccessful business trying to sell conservatories. He was good looking and had a rough appealing charm about him. I was young and foolish when he asked me to marry him. I have been a widow for the duration of our marriage. He played golf, went to the races, stayed away and kept me a lady of leisure. I have been his trophy to be paraded as necessary and have looked after him in my wonderful middle-class way. I can have anything I want as you know, within reason, of course. He is rich really." She paused to see the waiter rushing about and being reinforced with another of equal youth. "It is an art. I love him in a way, but I am utterly indifferent to our marriage. I am not young and foolish anymore. Not young anyway. I am the perfect self-reliant, never at a loss but never at ease fanciful wife. Without you Robert I am cheerless and comfortless."

"Would you care for dessert, sir?" the waiter enquired with a conscientious air. The choices did not grab Miranda or me so we concluded with coffee.

"I have bought you something," she proclaimed and moved her soft hand for her fingers to close upon mine. There was no misconception at the close beating of our hearts and the free and easy state of our minds at the end of the meal. Her words were portrayed instinctively like a question, but disguised by an expressive face and yet impassive smile.

"You bought me something?" I returned bewildered.

"Yes, I bought you something."

"Oh thank you, what is it?"

"It's a surprise. It's at home. I bought it this afternoon while you spoke with Adam."

"Well, we better leave then. Is it stockings and suspenders?"

"Of course not, you would look silly wearing those."

It occurred to me that the process of time was very rapid. Miranda and I had gone from individuals who were trapped in a stagnant pool to lovers drenched in a munificent sea in the short passing of a few days. It was not a monotonously crashing foaming sea. With good humour and communion of spirit it was a sea so generous given to the lapping at the shore and the swimming about of fish.

Chapter Five

The seemingly unalterable fixed position which I had once occupied only days earlier was now but a distant memory. We had been swept by a tide of incredulity. I felt as if I had arrived in a new world. Naturally trepidation gnawed at tolerance of the unknown as I struggled to reconcile the potency of only the previous day and now what seemed unimportant days of just a week ago.

With December ahead and now plunged into autumn, I felt drawn to the comfort and passion that our relationship conveniently provided. Indeed the munificent sea had proved its worth by two shoals the previous night. I had to leave early as Miranda attended my reluctant departure. Adam had slept, oblivious to my presence with his wife in our loving entanglement. I returned to my own home to change for work, I had to visit the old world out of necessity.

The morning outstretched like a wilderness and seemed daunting. I felt the urge to escape by undressing, then huddling beneath worn blankets to somehow shut out the confusion in the old world and the knowledge in the new. Such a breakaway was no longer a possibility then as I sat at the nerve centre or 'headquarters' as it was better known. The hub-hub at the hive of synapses declared that I was first reserve. My situation meant that because I had previously deemed myself sick I had effectively lost my position for automatic employment that day. I decided to hang around, however, because there was a high probability that I would be required at some stage. Lo and behold, the call came. The length of time spent waiting was vague but I had only one cup of bitter instant coffee from the vending machine in that period.

I was given orders by a senior manager who was ten years my junior. She was a power dressed 'five foot nothing, have a nice day, missing you already', frail figure. "Right, Robert, have you worked at the Flour Mill before?"

"Yes."

"Right, arrive there for ten o' clock and report to Mr Kenworthy. The pay is three thirty an hour and travel expenses are fifteen pence per mile. Five miles there – five miles back – ten miles – one pound fifty – okay."

"Okay." I am sure she thought I was dim-witted, but I was not in a talkative mood that morning.

The mill was situated out in the country, it could have been the perfect site for a village school for it nestled in the valley sheltered from an outside world. It was a huge building of five storeys and full high with windows. All the machinery on that modern day worked from electricity, yet the mill and its mechanisms still trembled as it did in days long gone. It had one peculiar large generator and a single tall chimney of red brick which trailed a smoking snake into the air to make an interminable scar across the sky. The spiralling mix of toxic fumes triumphantly asserted a signpost to that location. 'Here I am,' the snake of vile breath it seemed to say, 'enter you at your own peril.' The serpent was a caustic reminder of Adam and Miranda – snaking out and unfurling the coils which freed them but also held them together.

Within the cavernous rooms were dozens of employees occupying their sober senses at monotonous tasks. These were a race of men with developed muscles far beyond the human norm. Much of their work required an acquaintance with weights, the lifting and the setting down of large bags filled to capacity with flour. Each man there, young and old alike had a solid torso set at a V. Narrow waists and broad shoulders attuned to operate sequentially with bulging arms that burned calories by the thousand. The grinding of the mill and the filling was completely a labour confined to mechanisation. The conveying and the packing though assisted by machine was the eternal quest of the man.

Unconditioned to the heaving and the shifting – my assistance was very much restricted by physical limitations assigned to the standard human. Just for me to approach their industry and strength would have been a remarkable thing, indeed it would be a feat for anyone outside the race. I reassured myself that my personal deficit was attributed undoubtedly to being normal and thus proud to be part of the global mix. Further, although the application and effort in the expenditure of calories which I gave was to an absolute maximum, my rate of pay for the task via the agency was less than theirs for the firm.

I reminded Mr Kenworthy that my name was still Robert, as it was last time and the time before. "Right, Bob, what I want you to do is…" his square jaw appeared to move restlessly as he spoke, I began to get dissatisfied as I watched it, up and down. The instructions he gave were just a repeat of those of my last visit. "Lift each bag off the conveyor; place it just so on the pallet. Continue until relieved." His Groucho moustache clearly appeared a mischief in my concentration. I regretted that I viewed him in such unimaginable contempt. With a controlled compromise without condemnation, I politely informed him that I understood. It was a relief to walk to the conveyor belt, but not one of great liberation to begin.

I was lucky. The hard labour only lasted two hours, then I was relieved for a break. The exhaustion dissipated at lunch, but any willingness I may have had to engage in conversation was countered by weariness. Good fortune was realised again that afternoon as the mill ground to a halt due to a major bearing failure and damaged pulley deep within – somewhere in the system. In the remainder of my day there, energy was channelled into sweeping spilt flour over acres of wooden flooring to no end.

Among the witterings of that afternoon, I thought of Miranda. Her face so clear was then looking at me. I remembered how all her wildness and passion had subsided – I recalled how then as I softly moved her scattered hair from her forehead with responsive fingers. She had looked unreservedly at me to kiss and be kissed. We had smouldered in fulfilment with heads and hearts together. I had understood ourselves to have fallen asleep together that night like being imprisoned in heaven.

The stoppage of machinery was sufficient to make men with hard-looking heads restless. The informal conscientious drive of all hands to the deck was lost from the ceasing tremble to an eerie echoey void. Groups of men of the particular race armed with brushes carried debates in the emptiness. Among the little speeches and the chattering it was difficult adhering to a respectful patient conviction of sweeping. It was easier mastering a pure science than putting together broken intervals of leisure into an appearance of a continuous working shift. They, the workmates had tried to communicate cheerfulness – if only they knew, so I quietly expressed a blank nothing. If they did know it would have been of little or no concern to them. Any knowledge of me to them beyond my role there was of little consequence. I carried on sweep, sweep – seemingly endless, brush, brush, sweep brush, sweeping invisible dust into a pile of invisible debris. At a little before five o'clock I stumbled against something in puzzlement – gone! Some minutes earlier all the staff had wandered off to prepare to go home on the stroke of five. There was nothing to do but break off also and prepare to leave.

There were rushes of extremes to leave the car park. Being a late comer, I found myself restrained from quick escape, and all that could be done was wait. It was peculiarly dark then in that cranny where the mill stood. The overcast day had delivered a premature night like a drooping head. The red brick chimney was now a lit beacon squat in the valley. An array of twin lights sat bright upon that pinnacle to shine as one clear fire into the distance. It was fascinating to see how each escaping employee in their vehicles waited patiently as part of a continuous system. Steadily, steadily they left and then it was my turn. At the moment of opportunity to join the tail of the leaving throng, I suddenly remembered. In defiance of all calculation, it had completely gone out of my mind. Miranda had bought such a precious gift; how could I have been so distracted not to think of it? Something then had sparked my memory. I leant over to retrieve the gift from the glove compartment, it was that new wonder of modern technology, a mobile telephone, I had left it there that morning. While looking, I turned my wrist slightly to view the display screen. The phone was switched on but no signature of a previous call could be seen. At first, I felt comfortable with the knowledge that she had not phoned, because I had not been present to answer it. Having considered this, however, I then felt silly. Subsequently, I occasioned to feel thwarted due to her not calling which also seemed ridiculous. The confusion I experienced in those short anxious moments confirmed like a crush. Shriek, the doubtless conclusion, I was run over and completely smitten.

The journey back to town required the utmost care and precision. The winding road ahead, narrow and undulating was slippery with the litter of fallen leaves. At a different time, I might have been concerned at the decaying damp surface of the road, for my old Ford Escort had worn almost slick tyres. The speed of each vehicle was restricted by the slowness of the one before it. There would have been nothing sensible in overtaking, in fact darn right dangerous. I cursed as I changed down fourth, third, second. All that laboured driving, all the revving, the braking, the accelerating would all have been unnecessary if granted freedom of the trafficless open road. Fine, I conceded, just have to think calm thoughts. Endure the tedium into the painless anxiety I thought whilst climbing and revving in second gear up an incline only worthy of third. The cars ahead slowly advanced upon the journey. It was suddenly essential to brake as the next person in front braked harshly. The line of twinned red lights did not seem to reduce as a few cars peeled off to their destinations. Like paired patterned spots on the back of a snake the lights wound on spiralling at the steep hill ahead. I was inconvenienced by the slithering and coiled remonstrance, but drove on with compunction. I toiled to scratch myself here and there as my skin felt prickly. To remedy I opened the window and turned off the heater. The fresher air soothed the sweaty irritation. It was the grey white looking ash to blame, the finest grains of flour white and pure had impregnated my clothes. The fusion of sweat and flour produced a sticky explosive combination – I longed to undress and wash.

Eventually the line of cars joined the all-important next string of vehicles at the habitual roundabout. Bumper to bumper, we sat patiently, though I waited afflicted by the itching still. I looked around to observe various faces placed in cars peering outward to consult other opposite faces and view with questioning eyes. The junction of the roundabout split the unbending line of traffic. We all each sat at some length before mingling again to arrive at the next composite line of vehicles to repeat the ritual. The capillary action eventually ceased for those who reached their home.

Newtown Street was at my feet as I stepped out of the car. It was the street where my so-called home was situated. Newtown Street was one of several parallel extensions which spanned away and out to the east of the town centre gently curving beyond sight in both directions. Cars were parked only down one side, although house upon house bordered either side. Into the neighbourhood I briskly walked inspecting each vehicle as it came into view. Light reflected back from dark windows as I looked on to see the material point where my home stood. While closing the gate behind I caught sight of the pavement where I had trod at the end of a day's labour, it was a realisation of relief. The main door complete with flaking paint had been left ajar. Chips of flaked dried paint had broken away and fallen onto the step. After toeing the bits with the tip of my shoe I entered in at a swivel. The frowning walls of ancient wallpaper truly welcomed me back into the old world. Glancing at the inside of the door I wondered at the reason for it being left open. Though slightly baffled, my attention switched to the kitchen and the possible circumstance regarding its condition. Still in the hall engaged in ponderation, a noise emanated from above. A natural instinct caused me to look and turn in the area of interference. Two gents, one my age, one older by at least ten years were descending the staircase. Their murmuring remarks to each other grew louder as they reached the foot. The old steps had squeaked as if to endeavour to warn me from above of the human voices.

"Ah, you must be Mr Robert Oakley."

Still in thought, I was negligent to the words by what seemed like several consecutive seconds, "yes" was my curious reply.

The same man, the younger of the two continued, "Sorry to inconvenience you, but I understand you are just one of a few occupants who live here. I am Detective Sergeant Thompson and this is Police Constable Wolsey. This is a shared house I understand?" The speaker flashed a small card to identify himself as the same and returned it to a hidden pocket inside his coat.

"Yes."

They each adopted a posture as if to steady themselves sufficiently to observe a reaction which I was about to provide them with. Each man steadied and fixed their eyes to witness an instantaneous effect. So unacquainted I was with such a fluttering attitude, it became rapidly unnerving.

"Mr Oakley, do you know a Winston James Butler?"

Very confused by the question, I thought deeply 'Butler' and returned "no".

They looked surprised as if I were supposed to say the opposite. I became the subject of their blinking attention. "Mr Oakley, please think again. Do you know Winston James Butler?"

There was an unnatural quietness about them as I thought again in a nervy silence. Then realising who they meant I was overcome by a curious menace. I was compelled to answer to the affirmative. "Do you mean Jim, James from upstairs next to me?"

"Our information states that Mr Butler lives here. Yes."

"Well, that must be him then, sorry I mean yes. Yes, I know him."

"Mr Oakley, Mr Butler's body was found earlier today below the Freeman Railway Viaduct. We are not treating his death as suspicious. My colleague and I are very sorry. We have asked for his mother to formally identify the body, but she is too ill and therefore is unable to travel. He has a brother in the Middle East and will not be here until a few days yet. In these circumstances, it would be helpful to us if you can confirm, later today for us, that the body we have is that of Mr Butler." D.S. Thompson delivered the news and request hardly pausing in the most tranquil manner possible. I received the news with stunned affability. I agreed to his request although I was unsure why it was necessary. Also it seemed beyond belief that Jim could be dead, and nigh on impossible that he would have deliberately killed himself.

After they had left, I plodded to the kitchen, looked about, saw the usual mess and plodded out again. I had no recollection of how I eventually reached my room. My head was turned with face buried in the pillow and the mattress contoured unsympathetically into fragmented dimensions against my body. There was disbelief as I looked to the suffocating darkness, into the black I inquired, but the reading of it could not be plainly interpreted. Nothing could be sensibly written upon my mind as I wondered beyond belief in the sight of the facts. I numbed at the unmanageable thoughts. An image of Jim at the blanking out of everything else appeared offensive. That stupid distracted invalid succumbing to the shadows of death to such a lamentable end! It was a tragic finale of a whimper to a selfish self-imposed defiant act. I had no faith, but even less than nothing at all at that moment. I felt compelled to cling to an imagined wretched ignorance as a consolation – it was a superior comfort of knowing.

Once possessed with the general idea and without faith, I rendered myself to remaining where I was. In the silence I listened, nothing could be heard. The vivid image of Jim's face disappeared into a pore of no satisfaction. I took a deep breath while removing the out turned wrist as a blind from my eyes. Once again I could see familiar shapes lit by the moon at the window, these were now remarkable things of affection in the greyness. I sat up then kicked a way to the door. Here the switching on of the light was like a sharp spark to resurrect the persevering question over and over again. But then as if to reason with a hope from my discontented state, the phone rang. "Hello," I said with contradictory cheerfulness.

"Hi, Robert, it's me, who else," she said it with a particularly savouring interest. "Do you like your present?"

"Yes, thank you, it's lovely."

"How was work today – okay?"

"Wonderful," I said as something in my voice betrayed my attempt at cheerful concealment.

"Robert, is everything all right, you don't seem very enthusiastic?"

"Yes, of course. I nodded off. Sorry, I am just recharging my batteries."

"Oh yes, I don't want you out of action because you have a flat battery. Do you fancy going to see that play you mentioned tonight – tonight?"

"Yes, if you like. I would love to, my love. Would you mind coming here first?"

"No, yes all right, but you must not mess up my hair before the theatre," then added jocosely, "you can tangle it afterwards."

"Right, I will look out for you."

"Okay, see you –"

I quickly interrupted, "Miranda," then there came a pause. I wanted to tell her about Jim's misfortune but could not say for I foolishly thought it might taint our relationship.

"What?" this time it was she that interrupted as I was about to speak.

"Miranda," we were both seemingly silenced by a shared knowledge of my next words. "I love you."

"Aww, yes I know. I will see you soon. Bye."

I rested supporting myself against the wall dangling the phone in one hand. Of course I should have said 'Miranda, I love you but …'

Several consecutive minutes elapsed before I could sensibly take full account of the situation. Burdened with the needless apprehension as Miranda was driving in my direction I decided to extricate myself from the immediate attention of D.S. Thompson. He was unavailable when I phoned to tell him that it was I that was unavailable that evening. His apparent incommunicado served to dampen any further manifestation of conscience that I held and enabled a free rein for a continued romance. The gentleman to whom I spoke on the phone had a sombre, matter of fact voice which was delivered with conservative economy. "All right, Mr

Oakley. Do you have a telephone number? Someone will contact you in due course, sir."

The words were hardly excessive, I thought, following the horrible event. It was as if Jim had already been forgotten. And finally, his epitaph might read *'someone will contact you in due course sir'*. I expanded my interpretation of the officer – an unjust scrutiny;

'I am merely a constable of the law who is governed by laws which govern our lives; in particular my policeman's lot is not a happy one; while the shift lasts I wish to do as little as I can; the little that I do is as little as I am fit for and what does it matter as long as I get paid.'

The cynical view which I expressed inwardly was said outwardly almost as I gave a definite frown at the life carrying on regardless of his death. Now I did speak aloud, "Poor James, poor, poor James." There was no one to listen to those audible words. Although there was no one there to hear the words, I still felt stupid saying them. I could hear them as if said by another, by a hippy priest perhaps like an exclusive prayer to non-believers for non-believers. Shall I bring him unto thee, I thought – an empty message to no one to nothing.

He had never been known as James anyway, no person ever said 'poor James,' the usual concoction of limited words to describe him was something like 'Jim is Jim', as if by saying so little meant so much. There had been a clear understanding in the intonation and expression which lacked verbal clarity – it was assumed that one understood.

In a moment of petite madness I kept hearing the words that I had said to him. It was my voice I could hear in a combination of little pieces such as *'oh yes'*, perhaps or *'of course'* maybe or even *'mm absolutely'*. Also, I recalled an extensive assortment of facts about him which I tussled to come to terms with. It was I who was the only other person that knew exactly how he lived. A tangle of them, these inconsequential facts, were merely trivial bits of information of no importance. I felt an inappropriate and illogical anger which I attributed to this knowledge. The news of his suicide was so shockingly overwhelming. The only way for me to deal with it was to acknowledge and consign the action of suicide to an act of obstinate cunning. The balance of his mind was so disturbed as to be mischievous to the cruel world. I attributed no cause of his death to a depression. I tried to convince myself that he had thought the grass was greener on the other side, so he had rejected a desolate life in this world for a happier one in the next.

I had rapidly conducted the operation of washing, shaving and dressing while thinking all the while of Jim. The estimated time to the arrival of Miranda was another five minutes. In the meantime I found my eyes focussing on the bedroom wall, it was a textureless blank screen. I was able to consider a cinema where the mystery came back to usual life. It was an image of the past with condemnation upon it. Jim appeared shown only as in the recognition of his miserable existence. All the people he encountered had such a memory etched upon them, but their image of Jim had been a humour to behold with proportions been there for all to see – yet in life his character had been one to pity.

I had seen him clearly. Only a couple of months previously, September I think although it could have been August. On returning home one evening and entering the hall I observed a teaspoon hung plumb by a line which extended upwards. My eyes followed the line to quickly realise it was a fishing line and looking up between various balustrades I followed the track slowly skyward. On the journey higher my feet trod each successive step on the stair with quiet only to be betrayed occasionally by a creek. As I drew nearer the top floor, a faint childlike flirtation of laughter could be heard. On getting almost to the top, I guessed with confidence at its origin. Jim was to be found there in a state of sudden excitement transferring the ridiculous concept of pointless indoor fishing in a shared notion of surprise. This certainly was to all appearance unusual behaviour and as if to exaggerate the moment, the friction of the line rubbed smoothly against the balustrade while the fishing reel clicked gleefully as Jim turned the reel. That must have been the only time I had seen him smile in amusement. The sight was so surreal we just had to laugh. I gesticulated loudly, accompanying the sight with a giant unnatural parting of the arms to exaggerate the absurdity. "Going fishhhing," 'fishhhing' I actually said. Jim had assembled a large fishing rod from his bedroom across the landing then had carefully lowered the line down to entrap the attention of any unsuspecting visitor.

He was able to speak extensively about fishing, but for some reason failed to pursue his hobby of yesteryear – I wished he had. Although I did not condone blood sports I had tried to encourage him to go fishing. There was no river in the town but it was only a matter of minutes to find it from the bus and… As if hit by something I unaccountably and abruptly stopped the reminiscing. There was little point now in regretting, doubting and despising. It was a dismal resource to think back hoping to misbelieve when the deadened state of Jim was now irrevocable. There was nothing to be gained by dwelling on that memory. Each reflective hint of Jim left me increasingly bewildered. I would be visited by that reoccurring theme if I thought if only – done this or done that.

The moving around of people downstairs was in evidence as I heard muffled noises filtering up through the floor and open door. I realised I was sat perched on the bed surrounded by night with only the moon illuminating the room. The same absence of mind caused me to neglect the arrival of Miranda which I was alerted as I heard a loud knock at the front door. With the presence of mind to reach the door before any other person I used considerable agility to descend the stairs at a great speed. The sudden effort had the effect of galvanising my attention and during my rapid approach to the door I noticed my knees as bare as hands.

"I hope you don't answer the door to everyone without trousers on, Robert. Nice legs anyway."

"Hello, sorry I was just getting ready." She looked a vision with a beautiful smile, trustful and worldly wise. I kissed her forehead, stroked her arm and clasped her soft hand in mine. "I've missed you," I said as she stepped in gracefully. Somehow that was an automatic thing to say. She returned an earnest move to kiss my lips ever so gently. Undefended, I melted with surprise and was happy to reciprocate the affection. The distress in the earlier solitude now seemed ludicrous as I was restored again to the new world like an inflated pillow. I savoured the moment, but then was hit again overwhelmed as if pricked by a ghostly acquaintance and pointing finger to remind. It was as if the comfort of holding Miranda could only provide limited satisfaction against the wicked reality.

In her womanly worldly way, she sensed the difference in me. "What's the matter?" I held her in the hall tightly. "What's the matter?" she repeated. Miranda drew a short breath as I squeezed her tighter. "Robert, stop it, I can't breathe," she spluttered. "Stop it."

The repetition of her words struck a chord eventually and I released the grip. "Sorry," I said, "come up."

I led. She followed. As if to dismiss my peculiar manner, Miranda became silent momentarily. She kept close behind as we climbed. Our feet nursed each successive step precisely in order. Aware of the moment and of people in other rooms she cautiously spoke, "Robert?"

"Yes."

Miranda placed a warm hand on my bottom. "I read the other day in a magazine that women judge how attractive a man is by his firm rounded buttocks. Do you believe that – women influenced by such trifles?"

"Well, I have never heard anyone call them that before. Welcome to my humble home." I began to revert to a clichéd conversation which seemed so hollow in its delivery. It was as if I were trying to fill the empty space in the ascent. "You may need oxygen as we reach the top." It seemed so foolish but still I kept doing it. "This is it," I exclaimed opening the door.

There was a period of disconcertion for both of us. I was boastful to depreciate the worth of the room and its contents. Miranda seemed so preoccupied with the occasion and the surroundings so did not speak. It was an awkward moment. It is strange how lovers can be possessed by such suspended breaths and the abandonment of rapport. I gave a beaming smile, but her mind looked over and beyond me so the smile was thrown away.

I said sarcastically in order to make a joke, "I don't suppose you are used to such luxuriance."

"No," she replied with an enduring look. Then with her stunning appearance which quite belied the moment gave the kindest smile. "Robert, I love you." She clung to me, arms wrapped around my back and head pressed tenderly upon my chest. "Tell me what the matter is. I know something is wrong. We women can tell these things. Tell me, tell me!"

The irony was clear, because of Miranda and our relationship, I was probably less able to cope with Jim's suicide than I otherwise would have been. Now I had a heightened state of emotional responses due to the open heart. My temper was ill sorted and needed pretty comfort as an antidote – but the act of making love presented like a perverse remedy for grief. I wondered how could I articulate feelings of anger for his death and express sorrow because of it.

Chapter Six

Miranda and I had afforded consideration to my mood, and following much deliberation decided to carry on regardless. Part of a favourable consent was to depart Newtown Street quickly and arrive in the vicinity of the theatre early. That is what happened and for practical simplicity nothing could be plainer. We thought it perfectly reasonable to undertake this to escape at least temporarily from the place where Jim had lived in life. All she knew of his life was from what I had told her. Doubtless by her curiosity there were questions and only I could yield the answers. The answers seemed so important at that time and I had a great unsuitability to the questions. Ultimately her sincere inquisitiveness won over my reluctance to properly respect and talk about Jim.

Miranda drove her dinky yellow car and parked precisely with confidence. Our journey had been short and quiet. I had been locked in thoughtfulness and she had equipped herself skilfully in silence driving on unfamiliar roads. With the switching off of the engine she looked fixedly at me through the illuminating light in the cold of the town. The penetration of the electric lights and earnestness in her face were complementary reassurances against the dark of the night. I touched her warm hand as if to thank and grant permission to speak. "Are you okay?" she said in a gentle feminine way.

I returned with a compassionate nod, "Yes, thank you. We are very early, let's have a drink first."

Fearless of onlookers, we strolled hand in hand to the most convenient public house. The sign above the door was that of something often portrayed in art but never in nature 'The Unicorn'. The head and neck of a beast dramatised by a spiral horn extended an artful welcome to the thirsty patron. We had to release our hands on reaching the door and then ascended two white steps inside. Miranda quickened her step at my side as we jointly listened to the prodigious noise and approached the bar. She attentively looked at me and I acquired a concentrated look as if unable to hear her words above the volume of every other person present. People, that is everyone else there, talked in sets of twos, threes and fours. Each group and each member therefore spoke loudly to the point of shouting to lift themselves over the noise to be heard above the others. They crowded and crammed close to the bar, yet tables with requisite chairs were numerous and empty in the adjoining lounge. It was a matter of necessity to find a pair of seats as remote as possible to begin our conversation. We found our haven and were a little fatigued by the loud suffering at the bar. "That's better," I remarked now being gallant at finding space after feeling responsible for entering the noisy assembly of 'The Unicorn'. "Where were we?"

"I don't know, Robert, but tell me about Jim. What exactly happened?"

"I returned home from work to find the police there. They informed me, Jim had been found at the base of the railway viaduct. They seem to think he jumped. I am sorry but I cannot get my head round it. I hate it that he's dead. I feel guilty. I should have known. Of all people, I should have noticed something wrong, surely, shouldn't I?"

"You mean because of our work at Samaritans. You would imagine if anyone should know, we should. It does not work like that Robert. Even those who suffer the loss of someone close are often completely shocked and exasperated – without any kind of indication – absolutely unaware of their intention to kill themselves. Especially men, they do not always seek to confide in anyone. Yes, some who are suicidal cry for help, but few who do cry seldom do it in the end. It is the ones who don't ask for help that end up killing themselves. There is no way that you could have known Robert. You do not have anything to reproach yourself for – honestly."

"My feelings have taken a particular shape which is awful, indescribable. It's like anger, a sort of disbelief, and then I am also just inconvenienced by the whole thing with fluctuating proportions. I did not even like him, not especially anyway. It was a responsibility taken up with little thought for why, as if I had a natural duty to listen and speak to him – I hated it – really."

Her eyes fastened on my face. Miranda was more perceptive than anyone I had ever known, but even she could not see something that I could not see myself. The table between us marked a point of an obstacle and her reflection on the polished surface showed the stillness of Miranda as I bent my eyes upon it. The loud noise from the bar could be heard in our silence. "Sorry, Miranda. I must not burden you with all this. I think I have left you speechless. It is good advice, if you don't know what to say, just say nothing. Jim's suicide and all my stupid feelings about it should not put on us or how I feel about you. I hope you have not changed your opinion of me."

"Robert, I feel that I have never felt happier. This unusual occurrence has thrown me a bit." She unconsciously closed her open hand then slowly opened it and leaned forward to take her glass from the table. Miranda paused to sip and her grasp was set upon the glass. Now the table reflected an indistinguishable pattern of colour as she held the object still. "Throughout the day, I have thought of seeing you tonight, I seem to think of little else. I feel guilty because I deceive Adam. Oh yes, I know Adam wants me to have a sex life because I'm a woman and he is impotent. Adam can't do anything for me that way, so he approves of us fucking. But, Robert, Adam does not approve of us making love and I do not approve of deceiving him." Miranda had said the 'f 'word in such a whisper that I doubted that I heard her say it. Then she said the latter sentence in a higher key which served to ensure that I understood the meaning of it. I realised that I had been so wrapped up with my own interests I had neglected Miranda's position. It was very probable that I was from Mars after all.

Miranda had applied glass to mouth as if to quench her honesty, excuse the delivery and extinguish the crude information. I found myself apologising again… "Another drink perhaps?" Swiftly, I took her glass and ploughed through the adverse party at the bar.

The barman seemed to give his limited attention to preparing the small order, I imagined this was due to the probability of his moralising within. Would he have been judging at the disparity in our respective years – Miranda much older but much more attractive – her beauty undeniable – overwhelming though were our very unequal ages. Or could he have been thinking in a place better informed than my imagination would allow, at a point where the disparity ceases in importance so it virtually disappears? In that case, he would know the extent of the adultery, the extent of the deceit and the point where honesty evaporates. The reality probably was that he held no such information and he had no idea or notion to consider who I was with. The barman was sinking to the floor as the throng of people demanded drinks with impetuosity. Of course our affairs were insignificant to any person who did not know us. Why should I have supposed, albeit briefly such ridiculous contemplations.

I shuffled out carrying the drinks in both hands, doing wonderfully well to avoid those who were sober and those less so. The company at the bar appeared so cheerful and reliant on the presence of alcohol that a little rubbed off on me. I wore a broad smile to the approach of our table. The beam was wiped away when I discovered that Miranda had left. The impact took the form of immediate plunging within my chest, and then I assumed she had gone to powder her nose, but the original supposition was confirmed by the absence of her car.

Standing located in the empty space vacated by her car did nothing at all for one's self esteem. The distinct impossibility became an instant reality. Things were turning out worse by the hour.

As so often happens at these desperate times, you are reminded of the world that you are not a part of. At that moment several youths, all male, successfully negotiated the white steps and made a succession of humorous footsteps into the street. Sequences of the blandest and benevolent smiles were directed at me without any discernible provocation. "You are my best mate you are mate," said the first while applying a trustful hand to my shoulder. A second presented himself with difficulty against a wall shaking his head in all manner of contortions to no effect. "You're all right you are," said the first again as he moved on unable to avoid a stationary car by clouting it heavily with an oxblood upper. The largest of the party not unaffected by the beverage decided to conduct himself as a body bearer. With super strength the large youth lifted the second to assist his transit onwards. Unfortunately while the second was carried like a bride to cross the road, the groom collapsed in a heap with partner in arms. Both were only narrowly spared by a passing motorist who exercised extreme caution on seeing them. In another condition of another day, I would have viewed the scene with comic eyes, but in the state of mind at that time it served only to compound the sadness.

The drunks moved out of sight, but were still in earshot when I went back inside. I looked as a fool at the table, its highly polished surface no longer reflected the colours of Miranda. Only a recalled brightness of her and dull echo remained as a mirror to the vodka and orange not consumed. The half of bitter was isolated too, standing unmatched by the lady's glass. Blank faces of the comeliest women had observed her leaving departure and my return to the scene. These women looked at me absorbing my extreme perplexity in the relative situation. About half a dozen of them, some seated, some who were stood saw me see them, so they part turned away. They could not disguise their unveiling as the women conversed in their sisterhood and then suddenly engaged in a paroxysm of laughter. I was of course embarrassed, suspended with eyes switching from the group of women to the table of glasses and back again. I imagined I was their subject of much ridicule with the greatest of inclines to prejudice that my presumption was correct. It took a door to open and close nearby to remind me of myself again. The women looked at me again as their jollity subsided, perhaps then I recognised some benevolence in their explicit attention. Then to cut through my contemplation their laughter renewed at the roar of a petite lady shaking her arms comically to her female friends in a mysterious manner. This was a remark and illustration outside my comprehension, but I supposed then that I might not be the subject of their boisterous merriment any longer.

I could have advanced at them with rapid pace and executed an unprovoked assault – throw drinks at them or something – maybe shout to a disproportionate degree. Of course, it would have all have been in vain. That would have not made me feel any better – just compound everything. This alluring band of females were dressed smartly and actually appeared sexy even though their behaviour was repugnant to me in my crestfallen state. Perhaps unconsciously I was urged into a variety of considerations by the drunken men and boisterous women. The actions of both groups had been of an inoffensive nature, yet I had witnessed them in a raw state without amusement. I looked at the vodka mix and bitter again. I looked at the women again, remembered Jim and thought of Miranda. The women looked back with a collective glow depicting authoritative expression of female commonality. I shrunk inside, yet still wanted to transmit language or relate intelligence in order to explain. However, the only communication was toward me and conducted without fear. I was disposed to walk out and leave the drinks untouched.

Descending those white steps to the exit for a second time was torturous, I imagined eyes impaling on leaving. In the street I was free from 'The Unicorn' hordes, but it was little consolation. With increasing melancholy, I moved along quite despondently. To the path ahead, I complied automatically and soon arrived home for my hurrying. In the room I recollected the evening down to every moment. The measure of misery knew few bounds as I lay committed to the concept of sleep. The church clock struck ten but when the bell ceased the stillness was unsupportable. The body felt weary and the inability to sleep further was entirely due to the disagreeable state of mind. I tried in vain to coax slumber by closing eyes; however, the greater perseverance led to becoming alert. The longer the time to the next moment, the more uncomfortable and unsatisfactory result. In the end I got up. There was no necessity to dress as I had actually lain clothed.

The object which struck poignant at my heart sat motionless on the television. It lay there in repose and rest – not the slightest murmur from it for my attention. The mobile phone had been a token of our romance, but without a call it was useless. The affair which had lasted a few days had gone so quickly and contrasted to the tireless minutes passing slow in the dark. The noiseless night was respectful of the memory of Jim and mourning to his dismal life. I wished I could hear him, but no life was silent in the empty adjacent room. His so familiar steps which dragged heels to that final bedtime drink made in the kitchen were lost forever.

It was the truth, but I could scarcely believe the new misfortune. Only a few hours ago we had walked hand in hand as besotted lovers. We had spoken lovingly for she had softened the anger which possessed me. It was of some relief to take her warm affection of such a natural and touching way. But she was gone, I was eluded and she had escaped. He

70

was gone. Perhaps I was so embroiled by the Jim affair, I had so disregarded our own. Miranda had opened my heart, pleased me with her pleasure and filled me with pride. What a different man I might have been that night, contentment was now all in pieces. I was certain by all events to have no understanding of women, it was far beyond simple comprehension. I did not know or begin to unravel the complexity. Our shadows were defined upon the wall. Then eventually it occurred to me through all the stupidity which I seemed to possess in abundance. That device, that token, the thing so bestowed, it was given for a reason. It was not for her to phone me, but for me to phone her. Women can be so incalculable.

'Sorry,' I would say, 'I love you,' I would say. I would listen, and 'sorry' I would say again, 'I love you, love you.' It was easy, the practical solution to an emotional problem, then I commenced thinking and thinking again. Logic would dictate that there is no simple answer to a complex problem. The old maxim which had served so well in the past would apply in this case:

(Always apologise to women, no matter what, even if it is not your fault and even when you do not understand.)

Men can be so fickle!

I adopted a sitting posture, scratched my head and grabbed the phone – I had decided. Having been so intimate meant there was little point in rehearsing a conversation. I adopted a patient demeanour to subjugate the anticipation. In control I listened whilst feebly throbbing. It rang and rang and rang, but there was no answer. The wait allowed the heart to beat steadily. I waited more, and nothing. Clumsily and in a shade of melancholy the phone was returned to its former state. I was disturbed by her absence to answer or failure to quell the anxiety. In the silence I listened for the call to be returned – nothing. I was gradually overcome by a delayed exhaustion. Reflections in the blank television screen revealed my shameful figure heavy on the bed lying still to hear nothing. I dialled again – no answer – nothing – I waited – nothing. Sometime later, I was roused by the church clock striking eleven and momentarily my heart grated larger as it sprung to the false alarm. The stimulus served to operate the feeling of fatigue once more and I succumbed to drowsy tendencies into dreamless sleep.

The next morning, I languidly opened my eyes to see objects familiar to the old world and the telephone a symptom of the new one. At first the modern device occupied inattention as I stared possessed sleepy to the ceiling. The clock ticked away notching minutes in an unending procession, a reminder which made clear the event and passing of that previous night. The importance of the telephone was recalled as I sat wrapped in a duvet, and then reached out to discover that it needed a recharge. While sat perfectly still, I surveyed the particular shape of the telephone and assigned condemnation upon it. My view was probably misplaced because I really knew the key to the immediate future was held there. Could it be the saving for the fire which may not yet be extinguished?

It seemed useless to deal with important things that morning. Perhaps I needed space to see the shape that everything took. Matters are often seen with different eyes on the next morning and again on each successive day. On that morning, the possibility implied by an expedient delay of my own making did not necessarily mean that contacting Miranda again was remote. It was actually a relief to know (or to think I knew) I was doing the right thing by taking time to formulate a strategy.

I put the telephone on charge and made haste to work. The journey of that morning rekindled forgotten thoughts of days long gone, they rushed upon my mind as I hurried. Bitterness encroached as I was overcome by a sense of helplessness and desolation. Then in a surge, I hardened, made a barrier and nourished an unbending enthusiasm to a life ahead. However, a moment later, I was human again and shot away to a plumbless depth which served to confirm the position. The mental to and fro continued throughout the day. Like a man made from coarse material and indeed supplemented by a performance-enhancing drug of no limits, I assumed the entity of a solid-headed creature to suppress the facts of my life. It was a self-pitying masochistic ruse which bore no relation to common sense. Throwing drinks at mocking women in a lively manner would have been more agreeable. A ruined battlement I was on the journey home which dogged like a diseased fatigue. Once home again, I collapsed prostrate on the bed broken and tearful.

About three hours had passed before I awoke as if from a torpor. It was a curious sense of wretched helplessness. Any kind of reasoning was absent. I could trust myself usually, but now the events of that day had deserted anything resembling reality. In fact I knew the full extent of the day had passed almost and yet it was as if it all were a dream. The day had gone by, I was part of it, but deceived by it. I had gazed about in every direction except to the way of Miranda. Out of the mystery I came gradually back to usual life, that time was over and now I had come around to focus on her. The long day which had passed by seemed so short, almost expunged and had not lent itself to a solution. I timidly approached the telephone, the small screen indicated that it was now fully charged, but no one had ventured to call. Unabashed I dialled the number of Miranda.

Patiently I waited and there was no reply. Again and again I tried, but nothing. Although the explanation was missing the message was clear – the end of it. With all possible respect for her, it was quite worthless to me. I had fallen victim and admit to taking a refuge in tears.

While bound in self-pity a noise upon the landing commanded my attention, the sound of shoes upon the steps (perhaps those of two people). A double walk could be heard which had apparently become stationed outside my door. One voice was familiar, it was that of D.S. Thompson. The other was also masculine, but unrecognisable. I listened, not moving at the noise of undecipherable words which accompanied the loud knocking on the door. I began to try and compose myself to answer, but then realised my condition was by no means suitable to meet them. I had not the intention to speak, so held fast and continued to listen. The light was off so I understood them to be convinced of an empty room. Disappearing voices could be heard as they descended first to even louder footsteps which then faded into nothing as the outside door closed with a thud.

I continued to lay on the bed for several unresolved minutes burdened with questions. Why on earth would he visit at such a late hour? Why doesn't she answer? Why did he kill himself? What were I to do, being filled with agitation and anxiety?

I sat up in bed and vainly endeavoured to recall whether I had eaten anything at all during that day. Carefully I scrutinised any scraps of information which could be brought to mind. White teeth could be felt with the tongue and there was a hint – a mint flavour of yesterday's toothpaste. At least I could still taste through the numbness. It was hard to recognise that I had actually not eaten for at least twenty-four hours, although it was more of disbelief than a definite conclusion. But surely if I had not ingested anything for such a time I would be hungry. Maybe that was the missing cue, as if by some primitive law borrowed from the animal kingdom I was functioning normally without sustenance. Some biological delaying device must have kicked in throughout the ludicrous distress. Nevertheless, like an innate alarm almost as ancient as the primeval soup, all else was temporarily discarded on that very realisation for the want of food.

Fish maybe good for the brain and it might even cure the headache. An appetite I did not have, but there was recognition to eat fried fish because that was so conveniently available. Dreary enough I scrabbled along the pavement with the pelting rain slanting down into my face, such a journey seemed foolish in any circumstance. Cold I was, utterly drenched on reaching the establishment and a glance of ridicule was in evidence from the assistant. "There seems to be a little moisture in the air," the spotty-faced assistant said archly.

"Mmm, fish and chips please," with asperity. I paid and had to wait a little for the fish to fry. There was no hurry especially as the shop provided welcome shelter from the rain. The large window to the shop provided a secure viewing point to see the town and curious vehicles moving about carefully in the rain. Various headlights were a blur as they gradually moved. Red taillights distorted against the falling droplets on the pane. This marvellous feature was so hypnotic for one so inclined by it. If only I could smooth it out, manage what was there to be seen and blend all together with a fanciful imagination. The influence of it all so engrossed mesmeric like the red and yellow embers contained within a smouldering fire. As the rain still fell and ascribed upon the glass, I could feel the welling up – I succumbed to the self-imposed defiance of all calculation.

"There you go, mate! Fish and chips?"

"Thank you," I grabbed the bundle wrapped in newspaper and shot out into the night once more. The picture scene from the shop window had been vivid enough to be understood. The rain began to stop too in its gradual way as if to give emphasis to the revelation. It was a turning point to a subtle but striking disclosure which filled me with ardour. Even the first bite was food for thought. The air was clean again washed by the rain and everything seemed to begin anew. As I ate, my step quickened and stride lengthened. There was no sense in dithering when issues needed to be addressed. Not a thing could be gained by dwelling. I had another proposal which involved a frank evaluation of events; it was inspired by the visual display at the large window. The repetition of feet clonking like a giant clock seemed to strike a scornful rhythm to mock the time of earlier when I could not think straight. Now revitalised and nourished I could demonstrate a positive return to reality.

I must have looked a strange specimen of the human race that night. The time of confusion and turmoil was over. My face had taken on a philosophical expression of placidness, yet flushed with the exertion of the walk. With impetuosity and passion, I marched on without any slackening of pace towards the conclusion of the journey.

Headlong into the night, dark shade seemed to envelope hedges, trees and fields. However, it was the railway which was my guide. I joined the track by identifying the rails half a mile away from the station. With the station to the rear, most of the light was at my back as I walked on towards the viaduct. A quick determined step shortened rapidly as thick mud was encountered underfoot. As the condition of the ground deteriorated, I could feel an acute awareness of aching calves. Nevertheless, the town faded away representing a reasonable distance covered and then at last I was there 'The Freeman Railway Viaduct' where Jim had been just a few days before meeting his end.

The enormity of the viaduct was difficult to appreciate in the darkness. It evidently spanned the same river valley and the road to where the flourmill was situated only a little further away. There seemed to be plenty of room at either side of the track for a person to stand without injury in the event of a train arriving at full career. Guardrails were mounted on low walls on either side. I looked over the edge to see the meandering river to the right and winding road to the left. It was quite a drop to the bottom and I soon decided that no one could survive a fall unless blessed by a miracle. The rails disappeared into darkness in both directions. I began to feel the breeze and the coldness of it as I thought of Jim standing there. A shiver was unnecessary to allow me to think of him and what had happened there. Nothing came to me out of the night to explain. There was no extended hand to show me from where he had escaped the mortal coil. I decided to walk on a little further to see if there was a broken guardrail, or at least to find something which should not have been there. Small gravel like stones underfoot ended abruptly and the ground became slippy. I assumed that there was mud again which immediately was confirmed as I slipped. I decided to turn back as I picked myself up for there was nothing present which I perceived as out of the ordinary. The cold bit deeper too and gnawed after I had rested. There was no natural remonstrance to detain, with such a mind made up I was also roused to return.

Each succeeding minute placed more and more distance from the viaduct and less to the town. Mentally though my head was still there at the viaduct recalling the road and the river beneath – seeing the image of Jim despatched to the earth and then from the earth. The disappearance of the track into darkness like Jacob's ladder to the heavens was an allegoric addition to an imperfect knowledge to the event which caused his final demise. It seemed incredible that I, the casual acquaintance, probably knew more about him than any other person. That very likely fact had placed a peculiar cloud of grief upon me, yet the lamentation had only occupied a secondary and fragmented piece to the cause of my misery.

Aside from the shocking truth of his death and obvious influences which hitherto impacted on my judgement – I felt a reasonable and educated guess could be made about the circumstances of his death. Perhaps I flattered myself supposing I was better qualified than any other one person to arrive at a critical conclusion of opinion. My gut feeling was and probably it always was that he did not commit suicide. No, surely he was not the type. For one he was too stupid, not because he did not have the where with all to do it, but because he could not experience the depth of feeling that normal people have or have the potential to have. Maybe that view is a little naïve or even discriminating to the undistinguished of us. For two, he had lived a dismal life for years, not unlike my own in fact. Surely living from day to day, month after month, year after year conditions a person to the ordinary and to be tolerant of life.

Jim did not jump, he was capable of that reasoning. Yes his position in the world or place on the monkey bar of life may have been hopeless. In a rudimentary fashion he understood the obstacles, accepted them more than other people, for he was often oblivious to some absurdities that most of us recognise. He may even have been better able to cope with things because of certain emptiness. There was no simple horror or loathing about him or anything remotely complicated. He was good humoured and unassuming.

I stopped to look back at the line which had been the track way to the viaduct. On motioning around, I twitched a little then quivered before hesitating to take the unmarked path into town. In contrast to the viaduct covered in darkness, the town was positively coruscate, brightening and comforting my weariness. On drawing nearer to civilisation once more I could make out the position of the hands on my watch again. The time, well after midnight and the town was relatively quiet. The familiarity of buildings and streets was a reassurance to pamper my tired head through the final yards to my door.

As the clock ticked on into the early hours, the darkness kept nagging to constantly remind me of Jim. The unusual expedition had left me with aching legs which served to keep me awake through the fatigue. The long walk had also stimulated the brain that could not stop thinking of him or more specifically how his death could have happened. The second visit from DS Thompson may have been part of the on-going investigation still not concluded. I wondered if he did not jump, maybe they thought he may have been pushed, but that was more improbable than suicide. Who would murder him, why would anyone want to? He did not know anyone enough, like he would have known them sufficiently for cause of any wrongdoing. He never offended a soul. Could anyone ever have had any motive to kill him? Then I thought, for the first time I had to wonder whether the police suspected me of some dastardly deed. After all I knew him better than anyone else, if that was what knowing Jim was. Could I be their prime suspect?

The solution was plain, as indicated by all the circumstantial information which I had at my disposal. Indeed it had been revealed almost as a tangible fact, the conclusion – Jim had not killed himself. Perhaps I did understand him better than anyone, but actually the only fact to my awareness was that he was now dead. No particular clues had presented themselves, so really the only thing I could be confident about was the revelation at the takeaway. It was as if I had been engaged by some unseen force which had pulled me from near delirium. I had to persuade myself that the concept of an unseen force was of no importance or nonsense anyway and it was just my own application of common sense which had eventually revived me from emotional turmoil. The walk to the viaduct had simply served as a therapeutic mental aid for my sake.

Chapter Seven

The next day, I was feeling effects of the previous night, overhung by aching legs with an attachment of sniffles, thus signalling onset of a cold. Although the physical symptoms were in so much evidence, there were little remains of the mental feverishness. The sanity of daylight had dispelled most of the anguish recently experienced. Notwithstanding a new revived outlook, I looked anxiously to the phone, she had not called though I had phoned several times to receive only an empty ring. Although still confused by her, my feelings had not changed and not to hear from Miranda was scarcely endurable. Nevertheless has one often does I carried on regardless.

While en route to work, the mobile phone rang. The anticipation as the shrill notes toyed with my ears opened a table of possibility, only then to benumb the senses as I realised it was my supervisor. The broken signal in the valley made it difficult to communicate, but having stopped the car to stand on an elevated mound and to insert a finger cautiously into my right ear she spoke. There had been a change of plan. After dispensing of the usual niceties, she gave the orders in an authoritative voice. "Robert, I am sorry but one of our girls has been taken ill, so we have an important gap to fill and we have no one else available for this job. Do you mind stepping into the breech?"

So cornered I could not say a thing but "no". Shortly afterwards I was heading forty miles in the opposite direction. 'Miss Power Dress' had fooled me into feeling so important, so I willingly said, "…how could I possibly refuse?"

When reaching the destination never before encountered, at a poor excuse for a car park, I was immediately met by an amusing looking young man with a great beaming smile. "Good morning, good morning a thousand good mornings to you," he said epigrammatically and offering his hand to shake mine. "How are you sir? What a lovely morning. Are you well, I trust?" So overburdened I was with the prolonged and hearty welcome that I assumed a cordial and substantial expression which so removed any words to utter. On offering my hand in the firmest of holds, I was overtaken by his need to speak with the most hurried urgency. "Are you any good at filing? Whether you are, or whether you are not, you are stuck with it my friend. I have to go now," he said busily. "Very busy you know, like a busy buzzy bee. Come this way. Kate will show you what to do." The amusing man ushered me to the annex, a green portacabin mounted on probably a dozen red oxide coloured metal props of dubious strength. We entered the annex with the assistance of an upside down beer crate which doubled as a permanent step as it had partially sunk into the drying mud beneath it. "Oh, she is not here. Never mind. I am sure she will be here in a few ticks. Please be seated – introduce yourself – got to go – to the main building – her name is Kate – time waits for no man – got to go to the main building – toodle pip."

As I was seated on the inferior comfort of a plastic chair, there were large boxes upon even larger ones confusedly stacked all around. There were two extensive rows of filing cabinets before me, also a desk, a telephone and a second chair. Piled high on top of the desk was a formless stack of white and yellow sheets which looked formidable. The whole assembly was very suggestive of itself and I was in the thick of it – a sulky blotch all alone. It was less interesting than extracting the meaning from the raindrops on the window glass, but I guessed my versatile repertoire would be ill used on this assignment. The vigour appropriated to these droplets had been my exclusive treasure, but whatever these precious papers scattered about had as a secret was of limited consequence.

Several minutes passed and my curiosity only waned for I was sure that sooner or later Kate would arrive from the main building with specific instructions. Eventually, the silence was broken by a trill sound emanating from the office telephone. The alerted notice led me to believe momentarily that it was my own mobile phone housed precariously in my shirt pocket. The office phone was, however, completely different like an alien voice summoning. At first, I left it to trill on. Then a second time being so successfully confronted left it again. A minute later it commenced another trill for a long period, so I felt obliged to answer. "Hello. Is that the annex?" ventured a surprised female voice.

Thinking quickly, "Ah yeah, I think so."

"You do not seem too sure," was the same but even more surprised female voice.

"I am sorry, I'm a virgin."

"Are you? Me too! Is Kate there?"

"No sorry."

"Okay, thank you, never mind," said the resigned virgin dismissively.

As one often does on these occasions when one spontaneously behaves foolishly or says something foolish, I felt silly. However, the embarrassment was short-lived as I found the face and figure of Kate very agreeable. "I am so pleased that you are here at last. There is such a mountain of work to get through," she said releasing further papers to the desk from her delicate arms.

"Someone female has just been asking for you on the telephone. I told them you were not here. I assume you must be Kate. Hi, I'm Robert."

"Hi, thanks, Robert. Yes, I am Kate. Sorry I was not here. What did Funny Foot tell you?"

I engaged my powers of deduction, correctly assuming that Funny Foot was the amusing man. "Funny Foot said, Kate is very kind and helpful and will tell you, (me that is), what to do."

Kate smiled with a pause letting me notice her dark blue eyes before speaking. "Okay then. He is the boss, the boss of Sillitoe and Sillitoe. We process credit card applications for various banks. The papers you see here are rejected application forms. The yellow ones are just duplicates, so don't worry if you manage to find two the same, just file both. Your job is to file all of them away, in order, in their respective filing cabinets. The cabinets are numbered," she stalled to think, "I mean labelled A to Z. Any questions?"

"Do I get any assistance?"

She smiled again with a pause of a similar duration to the last one. "Well, no, Robert, you are supposed to be assisting me, but I have to help out in the main…"

"The main building," I interrupted.

"Yes, the main building, I am sorry but I will have to leave you to it. I'll come back later to see how you are getting along. Start where you like. It is probably best to begin with these on the desk and then work your way through the boxes. Just take it steady. No rush," she said with a smile. I raised my eyebrows with a sigh.

As she left, I kept my gaze carefully upon her. It was a deliberate play of light madness. It was very likely that Kate, who moved swiftly, had the knowledge of this purposeful observation. At no point in her retreat to the main building did she return a glance. I adjusted my position accordingly to enable the exquisite figure to remain in view for as long as possible. While quite contorted on tiptoes and craning of the neck to an extraordinary point of possibility Kate could still be seen through the misty window. Kate now at a slowed walk came quickly to a halt. Still looking through the haze I saw her linger in the doorway with an unnatural pause as if forgetting herself by delaying even more. The bewitching motion of her head could not have been employed with more cunning or be less ostentatious as she moved for my admiration. On the surveying eyes being discovered, I experienced an unexpected surge of blood and the automatic response was to wave with temerity. To my great astonishment Kate returned the wave like half a surrender before entering. Once inside the building of numerous windows, her now fuzzy form could be seen moving along the corridor within, at one window then at the next. I filed and filed to the heart's content forgetting for the while a discontented heart. I ventured to speculate upon, as a leisurely pursuit, the return of Kate, the countdown had begun. It is not uncommon for men to think favourably of particular women when possessed with re-occurring melancholy and I was no exception to the masculine norm. Although my hormones sought the new niche, their allegiance was still to Miranda. I felt guilty still of course and only really wanted the former lover.

Kate was younger, mid-twenties perhaps, younger than Miranda, younger than me. Kate had the smoothest skin with short, jet-black hair, well-defined pink lips and large, dark-blue eyes. She was wearing a knee length dress of fine wool which hugged a figure of perfect proportions. I was dressed accordingly as a rogue, all geared up for sweaty labours at the mill. Not donned or equipped for knee to thigh high-scattered papers and desk piled to ceiling in rejected application forms. I was thinking all the while of Kate and looking hopefully at the misty glass for her return.

The phone rang, not mine unfortunately, but the one that I had moved to allow more room for the carrying out of the task. Answering it was an inconvenience because I had just nicely developed an efficient method of filing, or rather it was of a less energetic form. "Hello, is that Robert?" I recognised the voice instantly as 'Miss Power Dress' the supervisor from the agency. "How are you getting on?" Further were numerous other questions which I answered to her satisfaction. "I would like you to hold the fort until the end of the week, all right?" She had this quality to instantly mollify, making a person feel so important as if the sterling work was imperative to the cohesion of the planet and without it who knows what. That particular job was not too bad, but it was clear that with each mounted spin the next revolution into monotony would scream.

I needed a break and wanted to leave. Back to now selfish reverie, I had to stay on a while at least, the reason Kate, we could even work weekends together, just Kate and me. Oh but maybe she is married or has a boyfriend or something, I hope she is not a lesbian. Jeez, I am hungry.

It was approaching noon and the stomach indicated an appreciation of the onset. Kate arrived as if out of nowhere, "…how are you getting on?" The voice and question struck a familiar note. One could not help but notice her cleavage as she opened the door to the desk and pulled out a bottle of painkillers. "You can break for lunch at twelve. There is a canteen over there," she pointed to the main building with her forehead and a nod while holding the drawer handle and bottle. "Through the door, first right, second left," closing the drawer removing the lid. "After lunch at one I will be here. Perhaps we can reduce some of these boxes before the desk disappears or turns into a mountain."

I smiled with a shameful dilemma, trying desperately to avert my eyes from her breasts but wanting to see. The more I looked away the more I could not take my eyes from them. "Do you have a headache?" trying to divert those obvious attentions of mine.

"Oh, the tablets, no, it's a bad back, you can help me with that after lunch. It is twelve almost so I will see you at one." What did Kate mean?

During the whole time of the lunch hour I satisfied the curiosity of several women employees who had asked; what are you doing? Where have you come from? Why are you dressed so? The unceasing unwearied questions of the women summoned me to respond in the politest way possible. It was extremely fortunate at that time to have limited conversations to an inexhaustible supply of questions. It took my mind off Miranda, Jim and the licentious imaginings with Kate.

The afternoon came along. I occupied the same seat as the morning while considering how poorly dressed I was for the particular job. Jeans, T-shirt and trainers hardly fitted the bill. There was ample opportunity to think and wonder. I did not suppose Kate would be happy with my attire. As one o'clock became two and then three o'clock I rendered my situation negatively uncomfortable rather than pleasing or desirable. Where was the object of my desire anyway? Her unaccountable absence had not gone without notice. An agreeable yawn and deep sigh were met by a touch on the shoulder. Somehow she had sneaked in noiselessly and I could not hide a momentary excitement as I reacted with an ever-brightening smile. "That was a big sigh," she said. "Sorry, I got dragged into something and I have only just got away, but I am all yours for the rest of the day." Her words rhymed in my ears as the beautiful song of the sirens and I was melting like wax. Kate had made considerable progress in my opinion by almost disappearing and reappearing with the briefest of encounters. Now to great approval she was to stay to provide touchingly and convincingly of the estimation – a visionary of the most romantic kind had roused my high regard. With my feeling so excited it was easy to become immediately connected by her perfume that imitated a combination of fragrant flowers which I knew little of their identity. Kate moved to the desk drawer again to rattle and shuffle the contents to find the bottle of paracetamol tablets once more. I feigned the stance of filing with the awareness that she was displaying the cleavage again, but I dared not look for fear of drawing her flesh to my eyes for this would alert her disapproval.

"How is your back?" I said automatically to express concern and artfully find a legitimate excuse to look at her with caring and admiring eyes.

"Oh, not much better," she returned and finding three paracetamols to consume. Kate placed them on an area near to the corner of the desk and put the bottle gracefully back into the draw which closed to the desk with a squeak. She was now seated at the desk looking at the tablets which she moved individually with the forefinger of her right hand. The prod of each tablet was done with ponderousness and every touching was a feature of our mutual attention.

I stood. She sat. We looked at one and other. "I think you are only supposed to take as many as two paracetamols at a time." I made the point with only a hint of questioning.

"I know," she said with a resignative tone. "This will be my third lot today, but if you do not take enough, they do not work."

"Goodness," I said trying to be cool and casual but not succeeding. "How many have you taken?"

Kate paused, looked at the tablets then back at me again. "This will be seven today but some days I take as many as fifteen, five at a time often." Astonished by this declaration, I recognised that whatever I said next could influence whether she would or not view me with approving eyes.

I did not want to comment and appear critical. I wished to create a favourable impression so ventured onward with caution. "Couldn't you be harming yourself by taking so many in a short space of time? Perhaps you could take a different painkiller or something?"

Kate seemed surprised at the reply, looked around as if searching in a short moment between words. The chair squeaked out of the silence as she stood up and moved to engage me with her penetrating blue eyes. She patted my left elbow with an open hand. "You poor dear. I'll be all right. Don't worry." With that she turned to pick up the three isolated tablets, carried them in a loose fist to then release them into her mouth and with an experienced swallow took them undaunted. It was as if I had given her power over me. My response was to try to be unperturbed and appear calm. Kate had not done anything unreasonable, but it was as if something of an ambiguous nature had occurred as if a new door had been hastily thrown open. The returning look of Kate was to compose herself at my calmness; however, it was clear that this was not my true demeanour. Kate's perception likely and rightly identified a look of surprise which was subtlety depicted upon my face.

Several minutes passed while we each continued the work without speaking. Kate returned to the chair and seated herself slowly. "I have an unusual request…" she began. I immediately stopped filing being welcome of an excuse to rest. "Did I mention it this morning? It's to do with my back actually and I need some assistance. In fact, it cannot be done without you."

"No, I don't think you mentioned it this morning," I wondered with zealous anticipation, guessing what it might be and implored a look of mischief. I also reserved a painful doubt in concealment of any outrageous proposal to be revealed. I waited while beginning to file again, seemingly afraid to speak as a misplaced word might have meant Kate's disapproval.

At last she spoke again following a silence brought about by her boldness and my reaction. "I know we are little more than strangers and this may seem very unusual. My back is so painful and as the day goes by, it gets worse. I want you to stand on my back. It sort of disperses the pain. Will you do it?"

I stopped doing what I had recommenced and following a pause at the sight of her longing eyes recovered the power of speech. "Of course I will, but won't it hurt? I am not exactly familiar with the art of foot massage."

"It's all right," she said. "I will tell you what to do and how to do it. It is not difficult."

"Are you sure about this, I…" I exclaimed with a perfectly reserved composure.

Before I could finish, Kate was face down on the carpet, so exquisitely vulnerable and beautifully desirable. I had to remind myself of my senses at the curious scene so improbable. She appeared so remarkably relaxed for a woman with an aching back and I felt guilty at my eagerness to partake in the exhibition of absurdity. I crutched down beside her to undo my shoes while she looked towards me resting her head on the back of her hand. Although Kate's hair was short, it fell over one eye and I instinctively moved to touch her forehead with a whispering hand then only to recoil. She smiled to repay the compliment. I stood up like an embarrassed schoolboy, missing the perfect romantic moment and against a manly urge to kiss her cheek. However, somewhere I had read that women often find sheepishness in men appealing.

"Okay, right, now place your foot on the middle part of my back along the backbone." I did as she requested putting the left to it while the right remained on the floor. "Now transfer your weight to it." Her back was warm and I could feel the contours of her backbone under my feet as I applied more and more pressure. Kate remained still and absorbed the weight, and then I released the pressure thinking that it may have hurt. "Don't stop," she exclaimed. "Don't be afraid. This time use both feet so that you are standing on my back."

"Are you sure?" I replied in the midst of the extraordinary circumstance.

"Yes, I am sure," she persevered as to compel me to be brutal. My better instincts wanted to reject her demands to a less, much less hurtful form of therapy. "Go on," she commanded, "go on." I was compelled to obey. The next bit was tricky. I had to literally apply all of my weight to one foot onto her back while I lifted the other from the carpet before placing that on her back also. The manoeuvre was accompanied by a feminine groan of relief which I could not help but be aroused at. I stabilised by placing my hands upon the wall. "That feels much better. Now move your foot towards the bottom of my back, then move the foot outward to the top of my hips." I did exactly as she instructed clinging to the wall throughout, all the while doubting the morality and medical worth of it. The saga continued for further five minutes. It was so strangely congenial. Kate gained a mysterious relief and I acquired a sympathetic pleasure by applying it. "Oh thank you, oh thank you," she said repeatedly. "That has made a world of difference."

Kate with the aid of my strong hand and arm was brought to her feet showing a miraculous suppleness. On display of an erect posture and stable footing Kate had something beautiful about her as eyes flushed. She moved one step forward to seize me around the waist with both arms and held tight. Though surprised by the vigorous tenacity I did not protest at my encircled body by her fair hands. As Kate clung to my torso, she repeated, "Thank you, thank you," then laughed. I was suspended hearing her dear voice against my chest.

"It was nothing," I returned with a fragment of laughter as she drew away.

"I am sorry," she replied with an uncommon capacity to giggle on. "It may seem strange but it is so exhilarating when the pain goes away like that. Has anyone ever told you – you have healing feet?" she concluded rhetorically.

"Do you usually embrace men who have known you only a few hours? I assure you it is a very pleasant experience," I added as she appeared to blink in a delayed embarrassment.

"I like being held," she said in a teasing submissive way.

My immediate reaction was to take her in my arms, but her arms fell limp. I kissed her, but she simply looked back. I held and kissed but she failed to react positively. The encounter was misshapen as again she drew away. Now I was the one embarrassed. "I am sorry."

"We have work to do," she said mechanically. An emptiness followed, but then she said, "Don't be sorry," brightening up a little. "It's my fault. I am not without strong impulses and can be a bit crazy. You know," she paused to collect herself, "I am very malleable. I am sorry. I am in a relationship. I feel so foolish. Truth is – I just get carried away at times. It is as if I'm possessed – I cannot help myself." Kate offered a smile that I could feel comfortable with as if to allay fears and promote a reassurance. "What about you, Robert?"

I had been quite taken in by her bright expression and was appreciative of how she asked the question. It kind of dampened the rejection and she kept her eyes very wide as if to let me back in. It was not so difficult to answer following the bizarre affinity. "I am easily sucked into things. Only a few days ago, I was involved with someone. It was a very short affair. It's over. I keep phoning her but it's useless. It's over, I think."

"Robert, I am sorry." Her eyes were still wide and curious. "You are not married then or divorced?"

"No," I replied and looked on to apply hands to the monotony once more. "Hey, perhaps we can empty this desk before five o'clock and tomorrow we will be on to the boxes."

Kate applied herself with an interesting smile and a ladylike deportment to the business. "Tomorrow is another day," she muttered sagely.

Off both we went on our separate ways at five. Each of us spending the evening in our own way, or so one might have thought. I was only twenty minutes at home before visited by Detective Sergeant Thompson and Detective Inspector Ridley. They explained their enquiries into the death of James were continuing for the time being and his brother was arriving the next day to identify the body. Having been introduced to the Inspector by DS. Thompson the sergeant said little else.

Ridley appeared to be dressed as a nineteen fifties stereotype detective, complete with trilby and light brown raincoat. I was prepared to dislike him even before he spoke. Before he commenced, on display was a row of flashing teeth and his slight frame – weasel-like – gave a suggestion of a little man well short of a shirt button. He opened, "Mr Oakley, Mr Oakley, think, think, when did you last see James?"

Immediately, I felt pain. Why could he not refer to him as Jim? Anyway there was not any difficulty in recalling. I explained. "It was the time of the commotion down the street when the police were in pursuit of two lads who had agility second to none as they remained elusive. Jim had gone in the direction of the scene shortly after I had left it – or so I understand."

"So you understand, so you did not see in which direction he actually went?"

"No, he just said he was going to have a look. He was on his way out anyway and he nearly always goes in that direction."

"And what day was this?"

"Monday."

"You were not at work on Monday then?"

"No, I work for an agency where the work is flexible and intermittent."

"Mr Oakley, consider, consider, was he acting any differently to normal? Did you notice and difference in him?

"What's normal? I noticed only what was normal for Jim. He was not doing anything out of the ordinary. Jim was not the kind of person who would throw himself from the Freeman Railway Viaduct. Yes, he lived a solitary life. Jim was so accustomed and resigned to it. He was a bit of a misfit, but that was probably due to his predicament."

"Predicament, predicament?"

"Jim was a bit of a strange-looking chap. He had no natural incentive to do anything. I even think he was resigned to being unemployable. He seemed to live almost exclusively on coffee and pot noodles."

"Why, why, why, Mr Oakley, do you think he did not kill himself?"

"I think I have already more or less said it. Jim, although he may have lived a miserable life by most standards – he was conditioned to it. He may have been miserable, but never was he depressed to such an extent."

"Do you think – Mr Oakley – that something else happened to him?"

This was a moment when one thinks that all the facts are known based on one's own intuition. To me the answer to his question was plain and very obvious. The short answer to his question did not require some brilliant deduction. If Jim had not killed himself and his body had been recovered lifeless then without doubt it had to be 'yes'. Of course the answer was affirmative, what else could it be? However, just by saying 'yes' on this occasion would inform as if the word had ten times its meaning. I accompanied the answer with a nod which conversely did not reduce in any way the impact of it, but amplified it. I had innocently, without thinking, yielded to their inquisition and planted a seed of a notion to suspicion of my involvement in the affair. The inspector looked a thinking blank at the sergeant and the sergeant returned similar to the inspector. The inspector raised his eyebrows and the sergeant shrugged his shoulders making his suit jacket move as one.

"Yes," the sergeant repeated my word in a sort of condemning way. Then he repeated the same word again as if it were is his exclusive property, but this time a question, "Yes?" Before Thompson could speak further, he was stayed by Ridley's gesture of an open hand to block his attempts to question. In any other circumstance, the swinging of the arm with an open hand may have appeared a jest; however, at this point accompanying my look, the stroke was like a razor cutting a bloody gash into the interrogation. It was at that point I became reluctant to say anything further. The inspector now made a gesture at me with the same hand, but now it was deployed in a deliberate shaky and circular motion. "Mr Oakley, please elaborate, elaborate."

A prolonged quiet followed. The more that I delayed the reply, the more of a burden the silence became. Irrationally, I hated them for speaking so of Jim and I hated the loss too. The void was like a thumping hammer. I had to say something quickly to alleviate the torment. I realised, that now they may very well have suspected foul play in the circumstances of his death. My suppositional knowledge of their suspicion was no longer a dormant thought. I blurted out as if prey to their questions. "Just a minute, you think he was murdered, don't you? You think somebody pushed him off the viaduct, don't you?"

"We are trying to get establish the facts. Get a picture of the deceased, that is all," said the inspector half-dejected, half-alarmed. Then following another silence the inspector looked at the sergeant and together they looked at me.

"Shouldn't you be cautioning me or something – telling me my rights?"

A sense of experienced police thinking unselfishly appeared to aid the inspector. "Mr Oakley, it is very likely that you knew the deceased better than anyone. At the same time, it is for us to reasonably conclude that although you knew him and because of his disposition – you hardly knew him at all. Therefore despite your claim to having an insight into his personality, we, that are the police, we can either rule out or not rule out various possibilities. The facts are, Mr Oakley, that James was found dead at the bottom of the viaduct. All the indications so far suggest that he died from the fall, the broken neck for instance. The obvious solution to the problem, if you forgive the description, is that he threw himself off in order to kill himself." He stopped speaking and probably hoped that I might hazard something in reply because I had been at the point of interjecting while he spoke. The inspector now had the propensity to look to his assistant for guidance.

"Mr Oakley," the sergeant began, only this time not restrained by his senior, "we came here tonight for all intents and purposes to wrap up the case as suicide. Now you tell us that he could not have killed himself. We have spoken to other people. These people, all of these people do not seem surprised. Yes shocked, very shocked, but not surprised. His death seemed of little consequence to anybody. Tell me. Tell the inspector. What are we to believe and conclude from this?"

At that moment I was further confused, unable to reconcile their notion that he had killed himself alongside the apparent investigation into the circumstances of his death. I was rendered speechless by his question and required time to collect my thoughts. Yet another period of silence followed, then the inspector reiterated with more detail. "We came here tonight just in the process of wrapping up, that is all. The overwhelming assumption is that he jumped off the viaduct. Now if, and it's a big if – if he was murdered – why was he murdered – who murdered him – who would want to murder him? If he was murdered, we would hardly suspect you, Mr Oakley, as the murderer, because it was you who raised the question when you already knew we had settled on suicide."

"Forgive me, but I am in disbelief at the very idea he would kill himself. The suggestion that he was murdered makes me angry. Only a deranged lunatic would kill him. Jim was such an unassuming man. He never did anyone any harm. He would just mind his own business and get on with it. I did not suggest for one moment that he was murdered. I thought because of your inquires that you had a strong suspicion that he had been pushed off," I finished frustrated and beheld a sardonic smile in the face of the inspector.

The inspector begun again, "Mr Oakley, it is I who is in disbelief, especially because of the absence of a deranged lunatic. The facts are these: he is dead, he killed himself and that is the end of it."

Now I was beginning to doubt their commitment. The latter words of Ridley were quite at odds with his earlier assertion which I heard him say about not ruling out various possibilities. It would have been prudent to let things go, for they were about to leave anyway. However, for some reason quite inexplicable I had to extend the natural course of the conversation. The need was beyond a vain selfishness to demonstrate eloquence in order raise their opinion of me. Perhaps I needed to exorcize a kind of guilt feeling which lingered following Jim's death. "Look, inspector, I do not for a moment believe that he killed himself. I think, however, that you attribute his death to suicide because it is the easiest option and ultimately it is the least expensive alternative. More likely than, but almost as remote as the notion of suicide is the assertion that he was murdered. I cannot imagine how anyone could have the slightest inclination to harm him, let alone kill him. Jim was the most inoffensive person you could ever wish to meet."

The inspector responded with a great deal of sharpness in the defiance of my assertion and struggled to utter my name in a lowered tone. "Mr Oakley, the sergeant and I are fully acquainted with these points that you have been endeavouring to make. I understand and therefore make allowances for that you are doubtless suffering at the loss of the deceased. I suggest you let the matter rest and leave the thinking to the police."

There was nothing neat about our conversation, it had become ragged and uncomfortable. One did not have to be a genius to work it out, but hey had to move beyond their limited viewpoint in order to make positive progress – I could see that. I could also see that the pursuit of truth could be lost during the interrogation. I had to appear more amiable. "Gentlemen, I am sorry, but I think you are missing the obvious. It must surely have been a tragic accident, with the responsibility for his death diffused."

"Diffused?" said the sergeant.

"Just a minute," interrupted the inspector. "Just a minute, if his death was an accident, tell me, tell me what on earth was he doing on the viaduct in the first place? It is so out of the way. No one in their right mind would go there by choice," he seethed.

"Oh really," I replied losing the amiable stance, "it just so happens that I was there last night. There on the viaduct." Both Thompson and Ridley looked astonished at the admission which had been ejaculated so proudly. They were bereft of speech momentarily, so I spoke for them. "Yes, I was there. The reason? It was because I could not get my head around his death. Obviously, he was not there in the next room last night, I was dictated to by that very awareness. I went out with no particular destination in mind and ended up on the viaduct. It was dark cold and eerie, but it was worth it. Perhaps last night I found the answer and only at this moment do I understand it."

"Understand, understand what exactly, Mr Oakley?" The inspector's tone was that of undisguised condescension.

"Last night, below the viaduct, I could make out the road and the river. He used to wander off all over the place. Usually wandering off, just meant around the town. Although he had little interest in most things, he loved to fish. Often he seemed to get excited with a sudden energy at the mention of it. Often I was at a loss to know what to say to him, so I encouraged him to talk about fishing. I think he had gone off to view the river where he used to fish. Maybe a train came along, hit him and knocked him over the edge. Or perhaps he moved out of the way as quickly as he could, only to fall over the railings."

"Come now, Mr Oakley. You will know, if you have been down there, that there is plenty of room for a train and a man," said the inspector dismissively.

"Inspector, I agree with you, but it's the most probable of the three, surely, and I have explained why he was there – I am convinced of it."

Both had the appearance of profound meditation as if calculating mentally a complex equation. "Well," said inspector Ridley, "it's possible of course but unlikely. We are ninety-nine percent certain. It was suicide – ninety nine percent certain!"

"Inspector, he wasn't exactly nimble footed, even sprightly kids have been killed on the railway, so why not James."

"Really, Mr Oakley, really," said the inspector with contempt.

As he spoke, I could feel blood pulsing and frustration welling up inside along with the guilty pain. I could hardly control myself as I exploded at them. "That's the easy way isn't it? No loose ends – cheap – easy. An assumption of murder would be complicated, untidy and expensive. An accident, you cannot entertain the idea, can you?"

"Facts, Mr Oakley, facts, we only deal in facts. Goodnight to you, sir."
I hated it, the thought suicide, murder and them.

I got through the remainder of the day to as little to my own satisfaction as was possible under such unusual circumstances. The visit from the police had been painstakingly instrumental in reaffirming my own conclusion. I regretted the argument, but I was now more agitated and uncomfortable with regard to their restricted view. Shouting had been futile and made no difference. Pointless, like polishing firewood nothing could change their minds, the end result would still be the same. It seemed clear beyond reasonable doubt that his death had been an accident. My feeling was that somebody should take responsibility. If the viaduct is potentially dangerous then it should be fenced off with warning signs. Culpability should be laid at the door of someone, but who, there is such a diffusion of responsibility. Perhaps Thompson and Ridley knew that, but were too apathetic to do anything about it. Maybe that is why they convinced themselves so emphatically that it was a case of suicide. Or perhaps they half believed that I was right and rejected it by realising it is hopeless to apportion blame to the railway.

All was useless for nothing could bring him back.

Chapter Eight

A very cold dark morning saw a light fall of snow before breakfast. A look through my upstairs window revealed an elderly woman below negotiating a pile of discarded wood in order to reach a wet topped dustbin. The scene reminded me of him, a comforting melancholy, nostalgic somehow like vintage footage mournfully captured on a reel of celluloid. The woman was often there, she probably lived a humdrum life brightened only by the visits of her children and grandchildren. My eyes were compelled to follow as she dragged her heels scraping the white surface which melted away to black, then while still watching feet she disappeared out of sight back into the morning.

Breakfast was often a non-event, simply because I seldom had anything to eat in the morning. The meaning of breakfast was more of a space in time surplus to requirements between waking and leaving for work. The interval in question, however, was frequently blurred if I was particularly late. That morning I was not late and gave considerable consideration to my dress. An unusual item for me, a tie (seemingly appropriate), a clean shirt (a must) and jeans (due to lack of trousers). Who knows, I could appeal to Kate through the clothes, I thought optimistically. Miranda had not returned my calls, I phoned during the imaginary breakfast, but nothing.

It took a while to disentangle my car, the trusty (but with near slick tyres and faulty windscreen wipers) Ford Escort. Two neighbours had parked their vehicles quite independently with selfish complementary individual thought almost flush against bonnet and boot of the Escort. There were several curses as I tacked a gentle release. The business of car extraction however so skilful in effort though long in consumption of minutes meant I was no longer early but late. I hit the traffic wrong for my escape from town, traffic lights at morning rush hour favoured vehicles coming into Whitches at the expense of those such as me who were attempting to leave it. While sat in traffic, I looked blank at the mobile phone placed expectant on the passenger seat. A horn sounded to indicate that I was sat on green, a queue in the mirror was testament to it. Subsequently as is usually a feature of lateness, every traffic light was met at red, but now the sun shone cutting through the cold and the only reminder of snow was the wet pavement. Soon paths were no longer to be seen as the town was behind. The surface of the river glistened in the sunlight and I thought of Jim sitting on the frozen bank staring at the water in search for fish. Then I thought of Miranda sat warm beside me and smelling of roses. The phone was there but she was not.

Kate waved from the window as I approached, her smile was radiant, it was the most satisfying hospitality a man could hope for. It was brave music that could transport me back to happiness perhaps, not a stony silence which I could hide away in. "Good morning, young man, I was beginning to think that you would not arrive," she said so pleasantly with a beaming smile to accompany.

"Hello, I am sorry, a few problems extricating the car from town."

"Oh, you are wearing a tie and a shirt."

"Yeah I thought the tie might look a bit silly without the shirt. You are wearing a different dress, it is very nice."

"Why, thank you."

"Listen, Kate, I'm sorry about yesterday."

"Oh, I've forgotten about it. There is nothing to apologise for, really. It was so amiable with very good intention."

"How is your back?"

"My back, oh much better thank you. You are going to be on your own again this morning. Sorry. If the telephone rings it will probably be someone wanting a rejection form. If you can find it, just put it to one side. If the phone becomes a nuisance, just pull it out. Okay, see you later. Oh clear the desk first dear. Bye."

"Bye," I uttered in the pleasantest way possible.

I watched her walk away even more attentively than before. She turned to look back and I smiled. She walked and turned again and I smiled. At the door of the main building a little distance away she turned completely around to face me. Her smile transformed into a big grin, then her fists were placed to hips and she twisted slightly from side to side before vanishing backwards through the door.

The morning then moved ever so slowly despite efforts to briskly stride on. After Kate had been gone a little time I lazily crossed my legs to consider the bludgeon of the previous night meeting with Ridley and Thompson. I suffered still to be nettled and discomposed by their infernal intrusion and the unbridled proclamation which I finally made to them. It seems absurd to assume that they caused havoc by the simplicity of asking questions. Now I felt as a fool might, yet knew it did not matter. A fresher and quicker form of conscientious filing continued while trying steadily in earnest not to imagine their turned-up faces at every opening of the cabinet. I had to release myself somehow, detaching the mind perhaps by act of closing a dusty file. The answer was surely to be found by confining them and the incident of last night to history in a file never again to be opened.

I placed the personal telephone high upon a cabinet which had been lifted to be placed on top of another. Doing this served two purposes, removing the inconvenience from the shirt pocket and also maybe amplify a call with metallic resonance should it ring. Perhaps I believed a reverberating ring had more impact to be invigorating and thus attach more meaning. I pondered the influence of the device on our lives. The object in question was something of which I had an imperfect knowledge and at the time was more akin to be owned by dynamic young executives, teenagers or drug dealers. To admit to be the owner of a mobile phone in nineteen ninety-two did little for one's *street cred*. The phone had a practical purpose but so too did a shoulder bag for men. I remember being very taken as a child by *Star Trek*. Captain Kirk and his immediate crew all had personal communicators with which they could contact the spaceship or each other. It was science fiction, especially when a signal was blocked or scrambled by some foreign force. Now part of that fiction was becoming fact as an ever-increasing number were acquiring mobile telephones.

I felt ill equipped for the world without certain portable items such as a pen or wallet, they were like crutches to aid living. Without my keys I was totally naked. I conjectured of how in the past a knife had been an indispensable item and was carried by many. Gulliver defended himself by producing his *hanger* to great effect against giant rats and wasps in *Brobdingnog*. I guessed that in the twenty first century a mobile phone would become another item to hang a life upon. I was hanging on for Miranda in a sense, imprisoned at the enormous portacabin, in the twentieth century, waiting for the murmur of my phone to develop a resonating din.

Kirk and his crew could beam down, beam here, there, beam up. It was a focus of fantastic imagination that somehow a person could dematerialise in a cylindrical haze of spots and sparks – then moments later re-emerge at another but usually alien location specified by accurate co-ordinates – the process of re-materialising would buzz and hiss in a laboured way before producing the crew intact. The whole concept of deconstructing matter into energy which travelled through space to be reformed back into matter had been beyond the bounds of my weak imagination. To a child, surely as I once was, beaming through space was something impossible though suddenly very believable like automatic doors which closed with a swish inside walls or 'down' escalators in

94

department stores that were ferociously claimed by floors. The knowledge of the reality of things was also in flux, whether to believe in, not believe in or simultaneously believe and not believe in. As a young boy, I had fluctuating ideas about the exact existence of Santa, dinosaurs, x-rays and laser beams – always continually changing loud but unclear.

Eventually, it dawned upon me, the realisation though gradual, in my peculiar adulthood was received at a frenzy. For the abiding theme of particular relevance now, no longer were there blurred edges between science fact and science fiction. There was not anything to prevent me from beaming over there to Miranda's house. By embracing the laws of physics and locomotion, I simply would drive there. It was obvious, my telephone was not about to resonate into song and Miranda was not going to answer a tune, so why not?

There was nothing enough to baulk a strong inclination to leave then and visit Miranda. Certainly my commitment to the agency was not a deterrent to stop such an action. An obligation to Kate or Sillitoe and Sillitoe was not even assumed. It was strange, how leaving so abruptly gave an uneasy feeling. In the car I pondered over the whereabouts of Miranda. Would she be in? Would he, Adam be there? What was I going to say?

All doubting questions dissolved as the morning grew older still. A recent rain shower made a wet road that shone as a beacon reflecting sunlight like glass. The now almost bare branches of trees stretched rigidly into the blue sky like hard coral in a shallow green sea. Not one branch conveyed any message but I was there soon enough.

I parked closer than was prudent and the movement brought notice to a few twitching curtains. On the driveway the dinky yellow car announced a definite indication to an impression of residence. A promising confidence began to seep away as I hesitantly knocked upon the door. There was plenty of time to think while waiting. The decision to make a second knock was arrested by progressively louder declaring steps from within and eventual sound of key unlocking. A gap appeared in a tiny movement of the door then by degrees more travel opening in a slow stutter. Three quarters in view before me stood a slight young woman, ski jump nose, dark hair, pale face and ruby lips. "Yes," she said curtly. From her expression, she seemed little pleased at my presence and peculiarly understood exactly who I was. She dropped her eyes, flushed a little, and then walked further inside with the expectation that I should follow her. Still not having uttered a single word, with a gentle push I closed the door which she had conspicuously left ajar. She delayed her walk slightly so that I might follow her at a comfortable pace and distance. She stopped as we entered the lounge and I came to a halt at arm's length. Miranda to my relief could be seen sitting there. On a second look Miranda had different shading to how I remembered with an appearance greyly pensive and pinkly anxious in the silence.

"Mother," said the younger in contemptuous way which daughters often do to their mothers who have transgressed. Miranda rose out from an easy chair next to an occasional table as if the pieces of furniture were reference points to steady herself. She could not disguise a smile of approval at my presence which was much to the disapproval of the daughter.

The daughter could not hide the irritation as the mother said, "Thank you, Patricia." Patricia obligingly left, but not without first fashioning a frown for my benefit and a condescending march to slam the front door for both of us. At the slamming Miranda closed her eyes and shuddered slightly. "I deserve that," Miranda said and looked at me. "She loves me really. She dislikes me at the moment. But loves me all the same," and in an exasperated tone of a parent – "I try to keep my temper."

We both sat. She confined herself to the same chair with the table as a barrier between us. I hugged the nearest possible position on the sofa.

"Hello, Robert."

"Hello, Miranda."

We billed and cooed again. We smiled at each other. Looking from the carpet and up to the nakedness of her flawed toes I knew her loveliness again. Chipped nail varnish seemed to identify her vulnerability which kindled an urge that I could cosset. The legs and ankles were actually thicker than I had held in mind from our lavish intimacy. An oversized pure white dressing gown gave the impression of a virginal bride but betrayed by exposed skin that creased at a makeshift décolletage.

"I know, Robert, do not say a thing." She fumbled in her pocket for something. "I am sorry, things are a bit complicated. I left suddenly the other night, I know. I am sorry. I can explain."

"I've been phoning." I watched as she at last found some cigarettes and placed one precariously to her lips. "I did not know you smoked," I said as a curious spectator knowing quite well she did not.

"No, I don't, I've started again," she ingeniously whispered while mouth clammed the cigarette and efficient fingers struck a match to light.

"I phoned lots of times," I repeated.

"I know, Robert, I am sorry," she repeated. "It's not easy to be me. I went out the other night thinking entirely of myself, swept away by our sudden relationship. When at home, Adam had been feeling ill all day. I thought at first he was faking because – sometimes he is just like a little child – I was going out and he was staying in. He had no idea about where I was going."

"I see," preparing to let go assuming the tale were told.

"No, it wasn't that. I had happily left him there that night. It was that big group of young women at 'The Unicorn'. All half my age, laughing and joking. I had this silly idea they were ridiculing me. Nearly old enough to be your mother – old enough to be theirs. So I left my toy boy at the bar while I rushed off. Could not explain then for some reason. I felt bad about Adam anyway. I did not want to explain and leave or leave then explain – I just left."

She rose to find a couple of glasses and a three-quarter empty half bottle of inexpensive whisky from a hefty antique cabinet. This was done in a comfortable silence apart from the gentle clanking. Her eyes sparkled as I regarded Miranda with a blend of affection and compassion. Returning to her seat she gazed upon me as if looking into my heart. The bottle was emptied, divided into two clumsy measures. "I'm drinking too, for the want of no better resource."

I did not know what she meant by that and it were as if I was temporarily disqualified from the substance of asking. For a minute I felt bound to relate a sighting of a meaningful spectre. By nothing less than a mystery, only the previous day I had persuaded myself of Miranda entering Tesco. Utterly convinced, I followed a woman in high heels, belted raincoat and scarf. Without better knowledge I approached the woman to speak and at the last second was revealed in awkwardness to suffer the strangest look. Similarly, yellow cars flashing down side roads or around sharp junctions had deflected attention. It was the remotest of possibilities to have been Miranda, so much so more likely to have been Noddy. Then at last from inner digression and forgetting the conversation I recovered out of confusion, "I can think of a better resource."

Exhaling smoke she said, "You can forget that. I am not in the mood for sex and Patricia will be back."

Not sure whether it was scraping together certain clues or just a general smack of realisation, but Adam did not appear to be there and a twinge of anguish could be easily be detected in her voice. "Where's Adam?" I said with a surprising note of concern.

"Adam? Well, he is the reason I suppose for this." She tilted her right wrist inclining a hand which pinched a cigarette. Then methodically with the left, raised the glass of neat whisky to her lips. "And this." The kick of the spirit caused an enduring wince on her face as she sourly savoured. "I don't even care for whisky." The coarse refreshment eventually led her to a tranquil demeanour and in the end a lounging posture almost at one with the seat. "Adam was not faking. He was actually feeling ill. Following our pre-theatre curtailed date, in the early hours of the next morning he woke feeling nauseous together with chest pains. Of course I immediately called for an ambulance." As if agitated or hindered by the now empty glass, it was replaced to the table in an expressive pause. "The ambulance arrived promptly. I decided to follow the ambulance to the hospital and drove behind those flashing blue lights with a dull feeling – well I did not feel anything I suppose – just numbness. On arrival, it transpired that during the journey, he had a massive attack. He only survived because of my quick thinking and their medical skill. He was taken to intensive care straight away and has been there ever since. I have spent hour upon hour at the hospital Robert. He really is ill. It makes me laugh, one nurse mentioned how lucky he was and praised my action – 'He is in the best place possible now,' she said. Robert, I wish he just died then. God I hate myself for calling the ambulance. Now he going to die anyway, so what difference does it make? He is so weak. He will never make it. And if he does, what then, what sort of life will he have? What sort of life will I have? The doctor wants to operate. God knows why he is so weak. He will probably just go and die on the table. He has never been strong."

"I'm sorry, Miranda. It must be difficult."

"Clerk is there, he will phone if there is any need. The nurse said I 'should try and get some rest at home'. Rest? Bloody hell! How can I?"

"You cannot rest properly at a time such as this." I filled her empty glass from mine as if the liquid were a magic potion. She was given the greater measure but the remainder taken in one gulp tasted potent without reasoning. "Just try and take it easy, relax if you can." The words were delivered in a tone of energetic sympathy, but as I said them a stab of condescension plagued my head. The conveyance was made warmly or even with an enchanting agility, but there was a distinct lack of original invention – there was something slightly maddening, limiting and frustrating in relation. It were as if I were wired with only coupled expressions in the direction of stock phrases, automatic worn away sentences engaged alongside particular mannerisms for occasions such as this.

A tedious silence followed accompanied by a languid dark colouring of the sky at the window. I reached for and held her soft hand with nothing more than a smile and false confidence. The offering of my skin upon hers was received gratefully as a privileged device to cushion the inescapable inevitability of Adam's fate, the gesture meant much more than the delivery of lines well learned by rote. The silence became comfortable once more, though I still felt helpless. Nothing could be done or said to change things back to their former state. The way we were, albeit not ideal had been infinitely better than at that moment. A solution was impossible, Adam was destined to pass away sooner rather than later and Miranda already weighed down with compounding emotions would be laden further by intense grief.

It is usually so simple for the male, whether he be boy or man to figure out where the fault lies in broken domestic appliances. Generally men know whether it is within their variable capacity to fix something when it has broken. Things do become more complicated, however, when 'it' is beyond a straightforward equation. If X plus Y on the left is equal to theta on the right then 'it' is simple – job well done. The complication arises when there is more than one or a variant value for theta and can occur at both sides of the equals sign. The average male is well and truly flummoxed because for him there does not appear any notion of a workable solution to 'it'. An ultimate solution despite the staunchest of dedication cannot not be found by the man because for him questions of such complexity are impossible to resolve into a complete answer. The answer is no solution because any result will contain a proportion of theta – or to put it another way the answer will always contain at least part of the problem. The female (not so burdened by testosterone as the male) also sees problems which have far from a perfect ending for a resolution. A woman can recognise by virtue of her sex a very different approach compared with the man. Like the rising and falling of oestrogen levels, a woman knows the importance of a perfect delicate balance and can apply it unwittingly to successfully solving an equation. Unlike the male she knows the maturity of compromise and the value of harmony in the world. It was Albert Einstein who produced the theory of relativity but may never have done so if not for his wife. An average man might fix a hairdryer or washing machine but it is the woman who fixes the living of life for livings sake.

"Robert, I cannot relax." She stood and moved with deliberate steps again to the drinks cabinet. Her foot found a loose board which creaked like gloom. The slight movement caused a greater wave to chime bottles and glasses to an uneasy tune. "I cannot relax," she repeated and held each bottle in turn at the poor light of the window to be examined for its contents. "How can I?"

"I know."

A pause persisted as she decided upon a bottle. "What are you thinking?"

It was all right not to answer the first question but the second required a response. "Us," I said quickly.

"Us, can you elaborate?"

"I am sorry; it was very selfish of me to think about where we stand in our relationship right now. Perhaps I ought not to be here."

"Nonsense, I am glad you are here but you can't stay." By now Miranda had filled her glass to the top with sweet sherry and crossed the knees to expose more of an imperfect leg. "Why are you here?"

"Isn't that obvious, it is because I love you," with a sigh. "I love you, Miranda."

"Love you too, but this is ridiculous I cannot do a thing with you at the moment. You must know that. I have things to do and it is better that you are not here under these circumstances. I need you, Robert, but my family needs me and theirs exceeds my own."

"This isn't the end then?"

"For now it is – perhaps next year – you and me – when this over – I have to deal with this now. I have to strike equilibrium, surely you must see that. There are things that must be done."

I sighed again, caught in the frustration of the situation but took comfort and consolation from her words hoping that all was not lost. "It is very clear. I have to accept it." It were as if I had placed myself voluntarily into a sealed envelope which she had wrapped in soft cotton cloth and placed in a box not to be opened until after Christmas.

"What is wrong with you anyway?"

"Eh?"

"Why are you choosing an old hag like me? You should be with someone younger – more your own age. A woman less complicated, without wrinkles and no stretch marks."

The line of questioning puzzled, it was as if she were mocking and yet testing my resolve or checking our love. Confused, I began, "You are not what you said. You are a beautiful woman and very sexy. If you like I will caress your wrinkles and lick your stretch marks. I'd only want a younger woman if that younger woman were you."

"I can't give you babies. A younger woman could. When I am the age of Adam, you will be the age of me now. Maybe you would be in my position in twenty years from now."

I heaved another deep sigh and indulged in these relations. A family with no children and a partner to be old enough to be the grandmother of my non-existent babies – it spread over me like tar. Me fifty-ish, Miranda seventy. I felt a dejected fool. "I cannot help it. You do not choose who you fall in love with, it just happens."

"Robert, listen to me. You cannot love me it's ridiculous. I cannot bear you children." Miranda stopped speaking for a second, she heard herself say something which made no difference. She knew the point was lost on me; Miranda's own words recoiled then coiled around her like a serpent. She made a joke to break the spell, "I can't bear your children and I can't even bear my own."

100

I acknowledged that with a tenuous smile but it was worthy of more laughter albeit inappropriate – though probably just as unsuitable as the caressing stretch marks comment. Again maleness restricted the insight into the woman. What was she saying to me? Did she mean that she could not compete with another woman who was of childbearing age? Was she saying despite the cause and course of nature, somehow it could be profoundly defied and she would compensate by scheme of maturity?

A disconcerting noise of the back door opening in haste and closing with a slam reached us from the kitchen. "That will be Patricia back," Miranda said quietly.

"Mum," came a youthful shout from the kitchen, "where's the hairdryer?"

"In here darling," Miranda returned in a louder voice. "Let's hope she's in a better mood," quietly to me and touching my knee with a possessive hand. "Robert, thank you for coming. I have a difficult few weeks ahead. It is better that you keep away, it will be easier for me this way," her voice tapered away to nothing as Patricia joined us.

The daughter's entrance was vigorous and mildly refreshing as she trudged into the dim room with heavy feet. "It's raining again," illustrating the product by feeling her wet hair and raking it with pointed fingers like a giant comb."

"Could you close it?" Miranda gestured a finger in the direction of the door which Patricia had left wide in her wake. She obeyed compliantly, meanwhile Miranda released my knee. The daughter saw the movement of her mother and quickly sat on the arm of her chair to reclaim her mum.

"You all right, Mum?" Patricia held her mother's hand to comfort and display their attachment."

"Ooo, love, your hands are cold."

"Yes, Mum, it is cold and rainy out."

"Patricia, now that you are in a better mood, this is Robert."

"I know, Mum." Patricia breathed loudly down her nose and moved her eyes upward inside her head as far as humanly possible. Miranda offered an expression of face to explain the whole of adolescence.

"Hi, Patricia."

"Hi, Robert," eyes further into skull.

Miranda gave a youthful effervescent giggle and shook her head, then began. "Robert is going away for a few weeks. He was just about to leave, would you see him out, dear?"

I got to my feet where upon Miranda followed and then did Patricia. Mother and daughter stood together and mother kissed my cheek under the watchful eye of daughter. "Mum, where's the hairdryer?"

"It is in my room, dear, if you would just show Robert out first." It was just part of the conscious polishing in a great balancing act. Miranda continually adjusted the equation with a feminine natural air not to be foiled by the slightest trace of alcohol – it made little difference. I was quite defeated by her blend of gentle steadiness and easy confidence. To my disappointment, I was now polished out, unable to remonstrate for there was knowledge enough to know that that would be useless. I had to trust Miranda to wield her influence to achieve resolution and equilibrium – polish me anew – into view when the time was right for our mutual advantage. It was heartening to know it was part of her nature to be nourished in taste, fancy, aspiration and affection.

A precarious platform of stability which had been expertly manufactured for my departure collapsed at the ring of the telephone. The sound exploded, though it was an ordinary ring it cut through as a dark exclamation. Patricia gave mother a dumb look as mum held out her hand heavy eyed. We each stood as statues at the noise as if waiting for the smell of burning to be acknowledged in reciprocated glances.

"Mum," shouted Patricia while allowing mother to squeeze her hand tightly.

We each saw the neither blue nor green telephone sing loud but still in the corner. We looked with an expectation for some vibration or movement for every note of the ringing hit like a contemptible pain. Paired together by the tone of it Miranda and Patricia froze. Mother and daughter both guessed to know the caller beyond any doubt.

'Are you going to answer that,' I thought I said but actually did not. Miranda looked vacant and shook her head, she read my thoughts. Patricia now held mum tightly and the phone rang and ran. It chased us over and over while we remained motionless. The familiar one, two, three… routine had no purpose, for its use now seemed an exclusive part of the voluntary domain where a virtual world held sway. This was a reality now, almost, not quite absoluteness in the sense of being direct. Indirect for me, but very direct inescapable reality for them, the family – Miranda, Adam and their grown-up children.

A throbbing anxiety accompanied every coupled ring, ten ten, eleven eleven, twelve twelve. "Shall I answer that," I said in the calmest way and she nodded in anguish.

Immediately, "Hello – who's that? Is Miranda there?"

"Hello, it's Robert," I said to the caller. Recognising his distinctive voice, "it's Clerk," to Miranda, but she just looked blank – unmoved. At half arm's length, I offered the receiver to any speaker.

There was the fullest concurrence among us; my placidness was a factor of design which actually disguised hesitant assertiveness, Miranda displayed something near a smile that depicted considerable pain and Patricia remained expressively silent rendering her to the promptest dignity. An interpretive disclosed to one and other by these unspoken features screamed a high probability of bad news – even perhaps the extreme case. Like the reluctance and eagerness one experiences when opening the envelope that houses the utility bill we shied and tensed at the information.

"Give it 'ere," said Patricia cautiously as she approached to take the receiver. She listened to hear Clerk speak as we watched to see her close her eyes as if meditating. A pensive mouth twisted from biting the bottom lip to be presently eased in a sigh of relief.

"Well, what?" thrust Miranda to Patricia as if the whole world depended on it.

"No change, Mum. The doctor is there now. He wants to see you now. He wants discuss 'options'."

"Options?"

"Yeh, you know, it means possibilities. Where we go next? What can be done? That sort of thing."

"Oh we better get ready then," and rhetorically, "why didn't the doctor telephone then?"

Miranda suddenly appeared to sink into contemplation at the prospect of 'possibilities and 'that sort of thing'. From speaking to the doctor previously, she knew exactly what was meant – a bleak outlook.

I first offered, and then insisted that I take them both quickly to the hospital for neither was disposed to drive. Miranda did not argue, immediately seeing the common sense in it and knew I could be safely relied upon to do just that without condition so commenced the process of dressing quickly. A relative impulse to ready with little delay beset deep emotions attached to the serious situation. The tasks substituted the need to think more than necessary. Patricia followed Miranda upstairs amid a considerable silence. The conversation was only sounds of feet on stairs, the opening and closing of bedroom doors, drawers and wardrobes. A noiseless swiftness of action interrupted the audible sounds before the murmur of a hairdryer broke the sequence which had been an intermittent sketch of quietness.

In what seemed less than a couple of minutes Patricia was in the kitchen loading clothes into the washing machine. Water filled the appliance, then by turns and swishes noises in the chore of washing laundry had replaced the sound of a hairdryer drying wet hair to charge the empty space. The movement of water along pipes and filling the cistern commenced a symphony of plumbing. At this, the ladies were reaching the conclusion of their preparations to journey forth, so l found the keys to the dinky yellow car and sat in readiness with engine running. It was the tick over now that presumed avoidant of the silence while I waited patiently.

The gentle rain fell to make limp and streaming rills upon the windscreen. It was noon and unusually dark, which made me shiver momentarily. I opened the window slightly for the heater was making well. Rain became heavier; the increasing volume of raindrops among the evergreens was overtaken by a tremendous pouring which drilled in a sheet of water upon the roof. No longer was I entrenched in thought for Adam but entirely engaged by the thunderstorm rolling up. I listened only to the thunder becoming progressively louder and was taken by the rain washing off the roof which heavily pattered then swam intricate paths zigzagging down plastic cladding of the house.

The car door opened and Patricia quickly took the back seat. In the rear view mirror her hair was wet again and the teeth chattered with cold. I was about to say something probably unsuitable when the door opened again and in sprang Miranda onto the passenger seat. She passed coats behind to Patricia who received them all fingers and thumbs. "Okay, you two, don't panic! Robert, drive safely! It is better to arrive late than not arrive at all!" she said it calmly and collectedly with drops of rainwater trickling down and decorating her lacquered hair. Meanwhile in the back, Patricia savagely combed away rat tails from her own rain-wetted hair. I patted Miranda's knee in reassurance but she took my hand mechanically, up, sideways and put it forcefully upon the gear stick – down. "Drive on, James," she said not realising the particular association of the name.

As I drove carefully forward into the rain, I regarded Miranda with a mingled admiration and compassion. Further on, gutters had broken, pipes had burst, drains had overflowed and roads were underwater. Huge puddles played host to ferociously dancing raindrops upon the turbulent surface. Children celebrated water foolishly, completely soaked, wet through to the skin with feet squelching and squashing in shoes as they cavorted. We all three, incongruously laughed at their amusement as we neared the hospital in an otherwise silent journey.

As is often the case with hospitals, there is seldom anywhere to park, and so it was. Patricia and Miranda scurried out through the fading downpour; the younger proceeded forth with nimble feet while the older laboured in high heels dodging puddles in a broken skip. The rain had slowed to a spit and dark clouds were about to head away. Normal light in a little while resumed as if to refresh the day again. The motorised dash and prompt arrival had reassembled my world to a directionless let down while all around a decisive world purposely busied itself. Having parked the car alone and seeing her retreating figure enter the hospital behind

Patricia without turning back had left me feeling marooned. The locality was unsurprisingly awash with water in varying depths while I was dry to the extreme, untouched by the storm. I sat there, remained in the car for several minutes. People moved about, all around, they were oblivious to me just sitting there watching them. Staff and visitors were talking and walking, some talking, some just walking. People were living their lives selfishly but not without sentiments and sympathies for others. They were nothing to me, yet in a satisfactory manner I saw them as mutual friends.

I stared at the hospital entrance as if it were my own front door. Very bright light lights shone for the general illumination, functional for staff but more of a clinical welcoming for patients and visitors of patients. I was none of these people, so slow but sure I stood for a lengthy and unreasonable time outside. Without so much as a wondering whether the destiny of Adam was good or bad I peered into the throbbing foyer. A man in dark uniform looked out from within, provokingly around, seemingly seeing everything except me. I was invisible behind the glass spattered by raindrops. Perhaps this uniformed security guard's deception was to identify suspicious characters in a conscious act of not appearing to see them. All I had to do was walk in through the wide automatic doors which never seemed to close completely for any time more than split seconds due to the continual in and out of people.

Once inside, the process was simple, just read directions on both posts and plates mounted throughout conspicuously bold for the benefit of the visitor. Coronary Care and Cardiac Wards, second floor. Cardiac Wards, third left. Cardiac Wards 21, 22, 23 and 24. Cardiac Theatre. Cardiac Ward (Intensive Care). Cardiac Ward (High Dependency). Cardiac Care wards 23 and 24. Even the action of moving along the hospital corridor without windows in the brightness which attempted to mimic the sunniest day was strangely daunting. There was no crutch such a hand to hold or a person to speak to who might split any amount of anxiety by sharing it. The corridor became a junction, then again a corridor before terminating by a swelling to a waiting area. There sat Clerk passing the time, deep in thought, placidly looking to an empty chair for guidance. His face was very pale from weariness and no doubt agitation. His hair a lack-lustre shade of grey was disordered from the same cause. No one could blame him for his dishevelled appearance in the enduring vigil.

Miranda and the daughter were probably speaking to the doctor at Adam's bedside. Meanwhile, Clerk scrupulously waited with patience absorbed in his own cogitations. I looked anxiously towards his present place. From the observation and instinctive consciousness, I surmised that he desired not to be disturbed. My ability to probe without speaking soon found its way to him as his thoughts were interrupted. In what seemed to be a delayed perception he floundered before archly asking what business I had to be there. I explained we had travelled together, the reason for travelling together and promptly handed him the car keys. He instantly realised having made an awkward mistake, and then Clerk's eyes met mine so requesting forgiveness without speaking.

I faltered a little before voluntarily proffering a comforting hand to his shoulder and sitting beside him. He spoke dismally, "It is very likely that they will undertake a life-saving operation soon, hours and minutes perhaps. Trouble is it could kill him – the operation. If they do not operate he will just pass away anyway it seems. They are talking with Miranda now. Never before have I seen anyone so ill, so poorly," the final words of his conclusion seemed to be thinking out loud rather than addressing me. I was at a loss to know how to respond, so nodded my head to sooth in a feeble benevolent way. The effort to console was just another feature of helplessness in another uninspired instalment. Beyond obvious empathy, the intense severity of their crisis was for me just a superficial matter. I hated my coiling thoughts working over from which was the winding up – I would be better served by him dying than him living.

Miranda was right; I should go and leave them to deal with things without the complication of my presence. I decided to withdraw immediately and rose to leave only to be pulled back again as Clerk tightly clasped his hand at my elbow. "Sit more," he said, his hair still in disarray. Clerk no doubt saw my comfort to be better than none as he began. "Near or far, blood, water, lies and deceit?"

Even a longer pause and thinking abstractedly did not bring an answer to his incomprehensible question. Clerk looked at me for some time in silence with vacant features of head and body in absolute silence as if waiting for a movement on my blank face to furnish a reply. Eventually, I began not knowing what to say, "Clerk, I'm sorry…"

"Adam," I was pleased at his interruption, "he is a rich man and having money has not brought him pleasure in either spending it or hoarding it." Perhaps Clerk thought that this extra information would help me ruminate better, but was still confused by the words. Clerk spoke like a man possessed. "The truth is, Robert, money has brought him pain and bitterness, and like a ghost it has brought him misery. It still brings him misery as he tries to unburden himself from it. His life has been like that of King Midas turning everything he touched into gold but in doing so sucked the life out of life. You can only know this if you have money – it does not bring you happiness. You can be happy and penniless but you cannot be happy and rich. In life, money has been the source of treachery and deceit – hatred and envy. Money has been the corruption of friends

106

and family. It has not mended feuds but antagonised them and caused them – that is money for you."

Miranda had never related any of what Clerk said to me and Adam never gave that impression either. It certainly seemed very odd that Clerk should tell any of it, so at first I just put it down to his restlessness and his character even though I hardly knew the man. All of it had left me very confused; however, it did occur to me that he may have thought I had a sinister motive. In an attempt to dispel any suspicions that he may have occupied, I countered with, "I hope you do not think I have conspired against him in anyway?"

Clerk appeared not to hear any of it and instead went on. "If Adam were to die today, his estate would be left to Miranda. Wills have been made but the recent succeeds the previous." He spoke these final words with a languid morbidity as if to warn potential inheritors that the money would perpetuate discord like a cursed talisman.

"Clerk, I am sorry, really sorry, but I have to go." Indeed I was sorry and conveyed it sincerely, yet I did not have to go but it was becoming exasperating to stay. The passage out was actually a running away, a drawing to an end but not from an acquaintance to be forgotten.

A number 27, Whitches Central, was the bus ride home that smelled of several wet umbrellas and at least one filthy, rain-soaked, wool jacket. I had established a seat at the rear beside a window covered in condensation. My attention was taken by a hole which one inevitably makes in condensation when travelling on a moving bus. The fleeting houses, fence after wall, wall after fence and each sleeping garden were a diversion distracting to the soporific. A dream awake maybe, not actual sleep gave rise to the noteworthy autumn. With back to the red earth and eyes upward to the black sky stars shone to honour the passing. Leaves fell plentiful once more to accompany a fallen branch that compressed the chest in an oppressive air of sadness. The gloom of the night, the darkened place dwelt as all fell silent. I knew for certain that Adam was soon to die.

Chapter Nine

The dull room offered a polite complement to the morning rather than a substantial hospitality. A soft ray passed through a chink in the heavy curtains, to shine with an ornamental trifle upon the imagination. The unlikely shape of an elongated octagon projected a remarkable plane of light along the floor. It was perhaps better understood as a dissolved rectangle, cast vaguely with finishing touches of practicable shoulders and ambiguous handles. A droll amusement without magical humour defined a disagreeable coffin shape onto the grubby carpet. Such a subtle reminder in that reckoning configuration was a blunt yet incisive inconvenience during the throes of waking. From acknowledging the suggestive sublime spectre I became unable to fall back into slumber. Yes back here again, another Sunday and I resented that time in the morning which defeats sleep by operation of thinking. Conveniently the ingenious bell ringers were silent for some perplexing reason. The absence of the compulsory religious experience associated with every Sunday at that critical hour was the source of yet more wide-awake thoughts. Confounded in the space of an hour, or better more, morning became afternoon. The countdown to the evening had begun.

The uncomfortable unwinding from sleep was characterised by an involuntary summoning up, an inescapable and irritating resume. 'Labour Force', the agency which so eloquently presented itself as 'Labour Force' as being utterly indispensable in the local labour market place, had dispensed with my services. Incredibly, Miss Power Dress following my dismissal had undergone an unnatural transmogrification by thoroughly succumbing to my hidden charms and I was reinstated as a 'Labour Force' employee on condition of never to transgress again. The manoeuvre had taken the doffing of cap, several waves of olive branches and the eating of a particular pie by my humble self. The scheme was franked by an ultimate motive to see Kate again; however, Miss Power Dress despite the metamorphic turnaround still in her wisdom and juggling sent me elsewhere. This of course meant my chances of seeing Kate again were remote if not very slim. Also, Miranda had taken immediate indefinite leave from voluntary work. I learned of the sabbatical from the all-conquering Chris on my latest Friday evening stint.

The afternoon recommenced a disharmony which had a feature of belatedness for it was the first period of inactivity since the rendezvous with Clerk at the scene of the hospital. A space such as this, to take stock and its ramifications were seldom satisfactory in these days. No longer could I reasonably compare myself with Jim. Yes, a beautiful arrangement it had been, when I could contrast his life against mine. I was superior in each category be it mortal or otherwise, physical, mental, social and intellectual – I took inappropriate gratitude from it now with tears in my eyes. He gave and we shared reverence. His acceptance of himself was like a sacred flame, the holiest part of our common nature. With no immediate embodiment of an exemplar lower than myself I wished it would rain. I admired a selfish personal fortitude at not becoming depressed. It was a melancholy gloomy Sunday though extraordinarily comforting for there were others too. People are cold, hungry, without homes, have lost loved ones and lead empty lives – but not me. I claimed to be just one in selfishness of many millions who unconditionally pursue life with an irresistible inclination to visit more.

The dysfunction of absent ringing on Sunday led to contemplations of, could the church tower vibrate again and would each successive Sabbath ever be the same? My lounging and languid laziness for seemingly no reason in particular except for that of arresting acute senses was disturbed by a rattling spirit. It came so inconsiderate from the supposedly empty room which was once the residence of Jim. Now the moment was beheld afresh in a new attention – it was a strange transformation to the day. The noise seemed to stimulate the rain clouds to shift slowly to oppose the dullness they had caused. With enlivened hearing I listened for any suggestion of haunted creeping. There I sat in an imperfect space of my own with closed eyes as if to make detection of movement in nature plausible. I could not hear the grass grow or the ghostly whispers of forgotten lives. Only the silence I could hear, punctuated by the ticking of the usual clock and the feel of heartbeats synchronised like the turning wheels of an old bicycle. A few minutes passed before the barren period of quiet was broken by what appeared to be a noise not dissimilar to malicious banging of a walking stick upon a solid wooden door. More sounds ensued, a scraping revolving of something turning gravely and a clatter too ridiculously disproportionate to be ignored. The sounds announced themselves as far too loud to be anything other than of this world, especially amid the signs of sunlight breaking the clouds. The message communicated was difficult to resist and I pretended to detect a fanciful resemblance to a cry for help from its originator. A natural curiosity is a thing which manifests in us all at times therefore I felt absolutely justified in investigating the cause of these loud embellishments. The peculiar mystery so overwhelmed that I did not consider the hideous possibilities of someone or some persons ravaging the contents of his old room as an act of destruction or theft.

On the landing, I stayed for some minutes to hear the possible ransacker and their moving about inside. I had a few choices; I did not have to go further, I could see it out, return to my room, or venture downstairs and outside. When I had lingered long enough in these deliberations and with a tuned ear for acute observation of sound the decision was made. Without question it was so arrived at, but a gentle knock to the door was unheard within as the noisy rummaging continued. A second knock louder by product of ten caused the person to cease their work, so as no one came on the count of three I determined another though timid tap upon the stained pine.

A tall thin man of about any age between thirty to forty years (that is) opened the door very wide as if not to hide any activity which had gone on within. "Hello," he said jocosely, "you must be Robert from the next room." I answered politely, asked him the nature of his actions and his identity. He introduced himself as Thomas or Tom as his friends called him the brother of the deceased 'James' as he referred. There was no need for further explanation. He received my heartfelt condolences and acknowledged with a vague apposite nod as if to speak just then would bring about tears.

His notes were surprising for one who had recently lost a brother. "Y-y-you are very kind," said Jim's brother in simplicity with Jim's own smile. For what, I did not know exactly and to ask why seemed inappropriate accompaniment in his bereavement. Perhaps he drew strength by regard and hesitation – attaching fragments of survival to a presence still remaining weakened from the death. Tom indicated a disapproval of his late brother's sedentary pursuits and all of his existence there. He threw voices along with various items of clothing and numerous pieces of printed paper of no consequence into a mound into the room centre. The pile was either for burning or imminent disposal. He talked as if on a jolly purpose, while at the very same time embarked upon a mad destruction of Jim's belongings. "You knew him fairly well, did you? Is there anything of his you would like?"

It seemed then that I had known him better than he and we looked at the isolated fishing rod set in three pieces in the corner of the room. It had an exceptional solitary meaning but only for me it seemed. "No, thanks."

"Are you sure?" he said looking about and turning to face me with an exhausted smile.

"Mmm," I nodded, doubting with an unconscious tilt.

"All this is to be thrown out, virtually all of it, there is nothing to salvage – he had nothing. I am just going to save a few personal items that is all."

I occupied a precious space in the doorway peering in retrospectively, witnessing a confidential remnant of his life. "Is there anything I can do, perhaps?"

Tom stopped his sorting and looked at me again. He shook his head and opened his hands to the floor and the mess of it before me. He smiled, "Look at this, Robert, a drink of some kind would be good."

I stood there in a manner embarrassed as if responsible for or had some great obligation after not directing Jim to a better life. There was something very ghastly about this circumstance. On no account was I ever the slightest bit responsible for any part of Jim's way of living, yet guilt seemed to find me. "A drink, yes," removing reluctantly from the doorway.

We sat together in his smelly room. I had the bed to rest on, he had the easy chair to sit upon. We talked of Jim while drinking. He held the coffee mug which had been conscientiously scrubbed beforehand, it had belonged to Jim, a familiar appendage remembered. Tom asked me outright, what I thought, did I believe he killed himself?

"I know the police seem to think so. Near to one hundred percent certain they say. I have my doubts. The last time I saw Jim was when he was going into town. He said, on the way he would have a look at the scene where a number of police cars had gathered. The police had stopped where I had a seen a couple of men running away from something. I have a slender theory which might explain his death in relation to this, but it is a very tentative one indeed. It is much more likely that he fell from viaduct when escaping the oncoming train. I think if he had been hit by the train, it is more likely for the body to have stayed on the viaduct. But Tom, I am sorry, whatever happened I am really, really sorry."

By now Tom had discharged the upfront jolliness for he had not bargained for this. The meaning of the words had produced a characteristic of a loose-skinned dangly face disconnected from the former smile now entirely gone. An expression benign and tranquil was kindled by these other possibilities. "Maybe he did not kill himself after all."

"Tom, I honestly do not know. Tom don't think it was not suicide just because I doubt it, I could be wrong. You know that."

"Tell me about this slender theory of yours."

"Look, perhaps I should not have said anything about that. It is a much less likely scenario than the suicide."

"You have to tell me anyway, please."

"Well, my reason for doubting that he killed himself is based completely on my perception of your brother. He was always the same. A person seeing him only once might venture to consider him as being in a depressed state and would probably see him differently compared to someone who knew him as I did. Tom, your brother was always the same, day in and day out – nothing ever changed for him. Forgive the cruel observation but nothing ever new, remotely exciting or horrendous happened – he was just so. Forgive me, I know his passing was nothing less than horrendous – sorry."

"That's all right, Robert," Tom recognised the sledgehammer error. "Well, maybe that was the reason," he reflected thoughtfully. "Trapped forever in a never-changing world. Nothing to live for!"

I thought about telling Tom about my efforts to try and stimulate Jim by introducing him again to fishing, but with assumed wisdom decided not to. "Maybe," I said not wanting to expand on my guilt and theory.

"So what's the theory, tell me?"

"Jim had lived his life like this for eight years or so. People thought of him as a 'no account'. He bothered no one and kept himself to himself. He saw all, recognised faces and he might have even eavesdropped. He recognised people and said little to anyone. Jim probably knew stuff about particular people in the locality that no one else knew or claimed to know. I really do not know, but what I am getting at is that he may have seen or known something about certain people and this information made him vulnerable."

"Jesus, Robert, are you saying somebody killed him because he possibly knew of something about their illegal activity?"

"I don't know, maybe. In a nutshell, yes!"

"That's so far-fetched – it's ridiculous."

"You are right, it's just my desperate imagination that cannot see the sense anywhere. It is more likely an accident."

Then came an interval during which Tom held the mug tightly in a concentrated frame of mind while gazing at the bothersome heap. The meditation which ensued made it plain that he had no desire to be interrupted. The dialogue between us had been sincere, the manner encouraging but the subject disturbing. At pains to wake him from his thoughtful mood, I did not intervene. In due course, he emerged without a prompt and with a keen brightness in his eye said, "Can you take me there – to the viaduct?"

I was taken aback by his sudden return to an expressive smile and replied that I would. In the moment of saying it realised I had complied to the request with little thought. Looking feebly for an excuse not to go I said, "Daylight will be gone in a few hours."

"We must go now then," he re-joined with a flourishing smile. "I can finish here this evening before I go back." Tom explained that he knew the viaduct, but under the circumstances felt not able to go there alone. Wholly unable to extricate myself from it, the first part of the journey was made in his car. He parked conspicuously half on the grass verge and half off it by the main road. An undulating field of short grass led to the railway line. The winding pathway was marked by dried soil which had covered many blades of grass by great quantities feet in innumerable pairs of boots or shoes. Neither he nor I were particularly good walkers and the trek ahead was a test of our pedestrian powers. I chose not to relate any notion of the previous week's nocturnal excursion along that very same path. The familiar landmarks actually appeared as being unfamiliar in the daylight so observations in sight did not create suspicion in his mind. A second path struck across another field before reaching the railway. We assumed a straight passage along a parallel course to the line with hands in pockets talking freely of his brother. Tom wished he had seen more of James, saying the name with more affection and greater emphasis than any other could. Tom had been so shocked by the news – how it was impossible to know and yet he said he should have known somehow. Any brotherly absence of knowing beforehand haunted Tom as he said, "Like an unstoppable merry-go-round spinning in his head."

The hard discomfort to feet of gravel under my thin-soled shoes was undeniable so we chose to walk on every sleeper with a broken stride. Every deliberate precise step pulled on the calves until finally the vigorous process settled to a stuttered halt as we reached the viaduct. The feeling turned up again unexpectedly as it had done on the last visit, it was a morose and tremendous sensation of finality. For Tom it was a very solemn moment, the realisation had penetrated the depths of his jolly nature. A fearful silence was maintained as wind gusted to crown the end in a time of bitterness. His whole attention was taken at the point on the viaduct from where Jim had fallen. Tom looked down absorbing every part of it, the ghostly information, serenity and dismay. Without fear he looked down to where I could not. By standing back away from him, he was left to his own personal reflections. Meanwhile, I braced against the wind putting hands under armpits and lightly stamping feet useless to defeat the cold air. Tom trained eyes upon the distant landscape, completely focussed and entirely still as if reading a compelling book. The keen wind nipped at flesh, turned cheeks pink and wrapped hair around the face. We saw the tracks of the wind as smooth shadows of clouds across the bleak hills. The flight swept along, rambling fast over field, swift wave upon wave darkening and fading.

At last Tom broke from contemplations then headed brisk and eager back again. I followed, fighting a way against the wind walking quickly then running periodically to keep up. With rapid pace he doggedly strode on. The fierce wind numbed the face and took the breath away. The more forcefully it blew, the better he marched brimful with vigour. On occasion, Tom turned his head to look back reassuring himself that I was still there and then as if to uncoil yet more continued on forward at the same quick pace. For an arduous hour I floundered ten yards behind and never able to make ground until at last we reached the car. Tom hesitated on getting there and after arrival allowed a brief rest where I was able to catch him. Inexplicably, he then left the car and walked more slowly toward the town.

Still by the car I shouted at him through the traffic and whistling wind, "Where are you going?" There was no sensible option except to follow. In a mighty effort, trotting up like a dog, I moved to draw alongside him. Again, "Where are you going?"

"I need a drink," was the exclamation in the tone of a demand that could not be refused.

"Far be it for me to stand between a man and a drink. Okay let's go." The personal preference was to return home; however, the profound necessity of his grief could not be denied, so I considered a drink to be part of altruistic duty. We were on our way anyway.

The comfort of been surrounded by buildings was good on this particular occasion because it gave shelter from the wind and a sense of safety. He took me to or rather he led the way to an old part of town which had been the neighbourhood of his youth. Tom seemed to be in close relationship with native families, bricks and mortar that tended to hem one in. Streets seemed to be absent, it was more of a semblance of old lanes, courtyards and passageways peculiar to the past. You groped a way through such devious mazes that were flanked by iron railings that never became guns or shells. Walls abounded here, there and everywhere into a dead end from who knows when. We travelled round and around. I followed Tom uncomplaining as if there were no sense of direction and certainly no escape. Whatever or wherever our destination it seemed like a secret between the royal postie and himself. Down the thoroughfares so narrow, we went. There were many doorways of ancient origin and doors with layer upon layer of paint, though none became the beginning of our final destination. There was little conversation I just followed like a faithful dog again, assuming that he knew best. Suddenly in a grateful sigh we arrived at the place.

The 'Red Lion' provided a positive haven on that now gloomy winter evening. The wind had ceased its groaning, it had fallen now, or at least it seemed so. Bright windows projected rays of light into the road and inside the very same welcoming. It was a comfortable looking place. The strong cheerful lights cast brightness in all directions. A rousing coal fire blazed red hot with coal stacked high almost climbing into the chimney. A number of tables were strategically placed at a less than sensible distances from the hearth and at them sat several people who had set up camp there. Empty glasses of all configurations had made queues on the tables. A smartly dressed hostess with bright eyes and an enormous smile served and entertained a number of men at the bar. She was a beauty, with curls on her forehead arranged like laid down bottles of beer. I had however, only a selfish concern for my aching limbs and a consideration for flesh was my own which had frozen to the bone. It was no surprise then that I commandeered the closest possible chair and table to the fire. Tom took it upon himself the task of collecting the beer and spreading favourable jolliness at the bar.

"I am sorry," he said coming out of a strange transformation which had possessed him since the viaduct.

"That's all right, forgive my infirmity and if I have a tendency to fall asleep at any moment now, it is your fault."

"Okay – understand." Tom sponged away spilled beer from the tabletop with a sleeve whilst grasping the cuff with his fingertips. "Got to go for a slash."

The conversation between us had returned to a light-hearted good humour. It was as if the atrocious trek had disentangled a knot of angry passion and the ensuing fatigue had brought sense to the hour. I gazed at the fire a while with little thought other than those of that afternoon until my eyes ached, then interrupted by his return after several minutes said, "Are you all right, Tom?" Continuing frankly, "You have been ages at the loo, is it because of Jim's death – would you like to talk about it?"

"No, it's not that. It's more of an individual problem, unique to me."

"Oh all right, do you want to talk about that?"

"No not really it's like a disability but not a severe one. It occurs in certain situations."

"Like now, why?"

"I have never spoken about this to anyone but it is to do with urinating in a public urinal. Or more precisely, not being able to pee in public. Well not a place where it is uncomfortable – it's a psychological thing. Where there are other people around it's impossible. I have been stood in the stall waiting to do it but I cannot the pint has made it worse."

"Tom, I think I know what you are talking about. If I go, I really have to focus on the job. Kind of relax. If there is another person near or anticipated presence of another, it's difficult. Maybe my experience is not exactly the same as yours. Is it a phobia thing with you like fear of spiders or rats, only the object you are afraid of is the proximity of others while you are doing it – or not doing it in your case?"

"Yeah, I think it maybe is a phobia but I thought of it as more of an anxiety thing."

"How long have you had it?"

"Since I was about thirteen, I am thirty-nine now."

"Gosh that's twenty-five years, more even."

"Yeah I know, Robert. I can work it out."

"Sorry, but you ain't had a pee for twenty odd years?"

"Of course I have, you daft bastard, it's just that I cannot go in certain circumstances, like here and now."

"Look I'm sorry, I don't want to take the piss."

"It is not funny, Robert – don't know why I have told you."

"Guess it's a bit like not being able to perform in the bedroom because there is a baby sleeping close by or a cat in the room. Sounds like a self-conscious thing. If your private space is invaded, you feel vulnerable – an ancient built in defence mechanism."

"It feels as if I need to be safe away from others who notice that I am not peeing and are criticising – making me paralysed."

"You can't pee because you need to escape from a Sabre Toothed Tiger instead who might pursue you."

Tom laughed.

"It might be more complex," I returned.

"It is complex."

"Maybe not being able to pee is not the problem."

"Eh."

"Perhaps not being able to do it is a symptom of something else. A deeper problem which just shows itself in this way. Maybe you have insecurities about your body shape. I know it is because you are tall and you were bullied about it at school."

"Don't be daft."

"Okay it's because you have a small penis or an extraordinary large one."

"My cock is a perfectly normal size thanks very much and before you say it I am not circumcised either."

"Well, perhaps that is it. It is because you wish you were circumcised. Or something else much more covert – you are a homosexual."

"No, I am not."

"How does it affect your life?"

"I am not gay."

"No, I mean the problem itself. How does it affect your life?"

"I see. It seems now as if I have always had it. I have just got used to it I suppose. I am always looking out for where and when I can pee and I restrict my fluid intake usually, huh usually. When I am out with people, everything freezes up and I can't go until I get home where there is no pressure from anyone. I just release the pressure and I am all right until the next time. I thought it might have something to do with potty training. If you wet yourself when you are little, you often get chastised, so you quickly learn not to do it again because if you do you might be made to pay. Children want to get the approval of their parents so resist the urge to pee until the right moment when they know they will be praised for doing it. Perhaps the problem started when I was a toddler, was overcome and re-emerged at puberty as a self-conscious thing. Only at thirteen there is no one to help so you just carry on. That is what I am doing – carrying on."

"You know of that American President or somebody who used to overcome his fear of public speaking by imagining his entire audience as being naked. Perhaps you could try a similar strategy to deal with the problem, such as urinating out of your index finger."

"I have tried to imagine peeing from the penis of the man next to me in the urinal and peeing on his shoes. You know like putting myself in the shoes of another person. Another pint? Finish your drink."

A support group for people with dyslexia could not have deciphered the scribbling on the chalkboard mounted high behind the bar. "Difficulty with reading is not a reason to go without food," Tom had remarked reflecting ravenousness that we shared. The hostess informed him of the strict working hours of her kitchen staff, excluding any times between three and seven thirty on from Sunday, Saturday to all other days for that matter. The information had little influence on an empty stomach which had gone almost twenty-four hours without solid sustenance as it was nearly seven o'clock. In desperation which befits two men in their thirties, we resorted to more beer and six packets of crisps restricted to flavours of beef, Worcester sauce and cheese and onion. Tom suggested pork scratchings as they were more filling. I replied something of the notion that such wholesome food would spoil an appetite which was undoubtedly going to be satisfied at a little after seven thirty. In actuality pork scratchings were the object of a tiny phobia which I did not make Tom aware of. A personal experience some years earlier, in possibly 1977 or 1978 the combination of pork scratchings together with a particularly rich lukewarm stout had resulted in projectile vomit and soiled garments.

From the sharing of crisps to nothing and repeatedly quenching with beer our newfound friendship was approved by each. Tom showed himself to be a proper Egyptologist by clever guessing and curious insight. It seemed that he and he alone (except for the obvious inclusion of the beautiful hostess) was the only person present capable of interpreting scrolled hieroglyphics. "Chips," he said smugly with perfect clarity. "It is, it says, basically anything you can imagine with chips," except though in his case because of his tremendous appetite it would be double chips. Any surplus which he could not deal with would be dispatched to the equally hungry mouth of the dustbin – that being myself.

We provided amusement for the hostess and several of her admirers who were definitely transformed by hours of drinking alcohol. These men were crossing the line obscene to the distaste of the lady, yet the more they were humoured by the female, the more they spent. The essence of the fun was mainly attributed to our longing for food in its absence combined with a patience caused by exhaustion and conversation which touched on every conceivable subject that could be covered in the period. Eventually, we were served at a time a little after we had anticipated. The garnish was not unlike a meal in itself, peppery watercress, tomatoes, huge leaves of lettuce and many slices of cucumber. This provided the obscene males with even more material to source and sauce their vulgar palate. The stories so crude and unsuitable for any ears were of no consequence to us as we munched on eating with great gusto. Our attention meanwhile was arrested by the coming in and going out of those who glared back curious to the intense mastication. Tom and I were the greatest possible endorsement for the food served at the Red Lion.

Why Tom should tell of his weakness, I was unsure. His pouring out of this weak point conveyed an extraordinary advantage. A smile of unmistakable charm remained on his face while he chewed. The visage was a display of good faith and singleness of purpose instrumental of the eating. He had the very same genuine expression that Jim had showed in his better moments. Jim could have done no one harm and could be trusted with a life. The difference, well Tom had an expression of profound attention and an interested disposition of all about him. He asked about my life which I related back, avoiding the recent time but running over main points in a concise account of the past. Tom adopted the information accordingly to his comprehension and judgement. His story tied to the history of brothers was given energetically, delivered with colour and without sadness.

"Going to try the loo again," he said formally as if it were a call to the battlefront. I nodded sagely as a shrewd and impartial observer to no infection.

Preoccupied with particular functions, it was reasonable to assume the knowledge of the pattern, that Tom had installed himself there as a general attendant might have done. He had finished wholesale eating and left all but nothing. I toyed with the remaining scraps of a second portion and drank to the bottom of a fourth empty glass. Having recharged the latter to a fifth and a new sixth glass for my strange friend I returned carefully in a public walk negotiating the filling room. On my return, at the table where he had sat in the very same chair was Kate. On seeing her, I had stopped at a short distance, obviously not calculating on the young lady's coming to such an impromptu appearance.

"Hi, hope you don't mind, I have eaten your chips," she announced demurely. There was no hiding my delight I was completely exposed in manner multiplied half a dozen times. She was a perfect fright – stunning – a base temptation. Kate wore lots of make-up which had been applied frank, bold and unnecessary. The painted face had a strengthened nature, full ruby lips formed only for one purpose, unspoiled cheeks, heavy shaded eyes developed for grief and joy.

"Hi, fancy meeting you here," I said foolishly. "Small world innit," foolish enough to sound more ridiculous.

"Had you forgotten about me?"

"No, how could I?"

"Good," she replied with a faint smile and bright eyes. "Is this mine?" Kate cupped both hands around one beer glass by first caressing my knuckles with her fingertips. She then impetuously sipped while engaging her wonderful eyes upwards to mine. "Don't worry about your friend. He is thoroughly occupied. My girlfriend, who is a man-eater by the way, has taken full possession of him in the other room. We – she is out on the pull and I am left all alone. So as chance would have it – you are here Robert." She pulled her chair closer to mine as I sat. "I prefer VAT but this will do for now." Such overt flirting fuelled an impulse to cleave to her, look into her eyes and kiss those lips. However, despite the intense cordiality and mutual physical regard that time was for later. To kiss then would have been inappropriate for the sake of appearances. A greater desirous prospect lay ahead, though it was uncertain how long we could abstain from it. In a careless way, it would be all the better for the waiting.

The tipsy twosome of Kate and I became a very drunken foursome following the return of Tom with his newly found acquaintance. Diana was wild with a blonde bob and cheekbones like symmetry. Kate quite beyond her common senses saw me as vastly superior to Tom or to anyone for that matter. In all considerations, Kate excelled as tigress and angel above her companion in every way.

119

Chapter Ten

Numerous recollections of how Tom said to Diana and what both had said to ourselves became just part of a reminder to a sparkling festival of drinking. Splendid had been Kate wearing stockings and high heels. Thoroughly agreeable indeed was the recent experience with Kate. We, the two of us, that is, now sat at the breakfast table.

Not used to a meal so early in the day, I stabbed a dabbing spoon at the ingredients. Special Muesli, 'a selected blend of cereals', the writing on the box suggested. Credit in italic letters: twenty-eight percent fruits, nine percent nuts and one percent seeds. Not a particular mention of sixty-two percent cereal though. "It's good for you," she said. "Look, almonds, hazelnuts and brazil nuts."

"Mmm," I examined each in turn as an unusual decoration, seeing only bland wheat.

"Dried fruit too, sultanas etcetera." The bowl boasted the very same.

"Not sure about banana. I don't like banana."

"The taste is different. It's not a banana taste. It's sort of biscuity."

"Mmm," selecting an ambiguous flake the consistency of paper, "what's this white stuff?"

"Think that's coconut. Just eat it will you," she said bossily followed by a sigh and then a perfectly natural inquiry. "Do you have a hangover?"

"Kate," a little trait or feeling came out which impressed itself upon her, a kind of loving sympathy perhaps. I cleared my throat. It had seemed ludicrous to excess, "Kate" (the word) my voice, her name upon my breath. Not like a dart to the body pricking, but as a flying caress to the air.

"Are you comprehending?" she put the question comfortably.

I paused in absurd sincerity, knowing or at least thinking I looked physically ridiculous.

"The stubble makes you look sexy," she said.

It was so completely at odds with my knowledge of the moment. Surely this was wholly impossible. "Grotesque maybe."

If there is such a thing as a sensuous smile it was an absolute perspective engendered delicately before me. "Get shaved and come back to bed. I have the cruellest cure for a hangover." She was gorgeously attired, a single article of French fashion covered a suggestion of more gold lace.

In the bathroom, a gaunt feature in the mirror was an expression thereabouts that my eyes saw and the same face belonging gave. The ritual of shaving was now given a purpose beyond the habitual, for meanwhile Kate patiently waited in the bedroom. In that very same space of time, the bathroom mirror misted slightly as I struggled to shave with a blunt blade. A cutting edge that a lady uses to make her legs silky smooth is seldom sharp enough to perform the similar task upon the harsh face of a man. The borrowed razor fit that restriction entirely. A blade that a man discards from exhaustive use of cropping his whiskers can often be the perfect tool for making female legs have a glossy satin finish. It was an endeavour to stand stock still and focus to the mirror. Something could be seen to twitch in the neck and throat as I attempted to avoid my lips with the razor. Contorted was the face, a moveable side seemed to listen to the profile of the other and that very rigid adjacent half received the scraping blade mercifully. A crow, never witnessed before had left its imprints in the corners of my eyes as if to prey upon youth.

The effort was over and I stroked my chin with a sympathetic thumb and fingertip saluting the tedious task which had passed. Now into the bedroom, I approached an adventure, this followed a hovered consideration where there had been a shaking of nerves in anticipation. In I went, only to find that Kate had fallen asleep. A kind of relief it was, and then I remembered by default, after all, still there was the matter of a hangover. The symptoms were inescapable, easily felt and seemingly to be compounded more now than ever. Straightforward with surrender at the overwhelming circumstance I climbed deliberately into bed and pulled the quilt over us like a protective cloak of magical fabric. The mental fidgeting was over for there is something remarkably consoling about snuggling up to a sleeping partner. Kate's head faced the wall, so I faced her hair and gently cupped my arm around her. We were tied together in a fulfilling sleeping embrace. The headache was dulled by the warmth of her body and also through orange juice she had insisted I took as a countering natural remedy.

For the rat race, that morning was conspicuous by our absence and as most things do continued on without us. The world beyond the confines of our togetherness and closed door no doubt ticked on as did the clock within. The hands showed five minutes to ten. I guessed my employer would be furious again and therefore suspected an end to any further work with them. Presumably Kate should also be elsewhere, perhaps filing, typing, answering the telephone or doing whatever secretaries or clerks

121

do. By its own inevitable punctuality the clock on the nearby drawer struck ten in a resounding click. A dire warning to conscience of a dismal prospect ahead of immediate unemployment and even more still of it to come. What will happen will happen. For now, to take advantage of the short-lived feeling, just a simple gratification of our bodies touching side by side. The urge to hold Kate tight was deflected by the certainty of waking her. The strategy was a loose grip as close as possible, touching with feeling, proximity with connectivity – keeping her asleep captured in discretionary silence.

Our bodies were different, mine imperfect, hers perfect, save for the tiny mole slightly offset from centre below the naval to the left. I made a mental note not to tease her about the blemish again following the previous night when she had made an uncharacteristic grasp of my hair at the back of the head. Her skin so smooth and fine, her body both fat and lean in an exemplary configuration of a woman. My itchy fingertips glided delicately across her arm as if self-governing for their own delight. There seemed to be a marked difference in temperature between us. She, much warmer drew me, yet at the point of meeting, the heat almost uncomfortable. Perhaps Kate was processing those female hormones, taking account of them reconfiguring like philosopher and authoress.

I could not sleep knowing that the action of it would produce piggish snoring which would wake her. Besides the moment was one to savour, the captive audience and mind working. It occurred in thought, though after some delay that Kate and oestrogen might actually be feigning sleep. While I expounded on the notion facing her hair, its fragrance while breathing kisses into it, perhaps she was wide-eyed and fully aware. After all, the loving would be half wasted. Little point in being asleep when a man is giving you his undivided attention. The possibility of Kate doing exactly that suddenly dawned. A new line of thinking was borne. Betrayal and corruption. Maybe if she was awake and faking sleep in deception then that would be a betrayal of a sort. If I continued, could I be the corrupter, the purveyor of that very falseness in her. Then, stupid, I thought, she was obviously asleep. How could she possibly be awake all this time and not speak?

This had tapped into a short-sighted prejudice against women that teetered on misogyny. Choosing not to pursue the subject any further by means of negativity, only served to compound the latent questioning acquaintance, disliking women? By not exploring further, I could not suppose to hardly realise the meaning of it. The need was to conclude with any answer. A result was forthcoming from nowhere. How can you hate women if you love them? Not much of an answer to be discovered is it. If a rhetorical question is the conclusion then it is more an impossible riddle!

There was plenty of opportunity for more along these lines. If the roles were reversed and I was pretty well pretending to be asleep – how would it be? To imagine Kate snuggling up instead. To see this position from her perspective but confined by the constraints of masculine intellect. Perhaps in this scenario I might also pretend to sleep. With eyes closed Kate could be monitored by method of contact, measured by how she touched me. How her fingers might lovingly caress my arm, a tender encounter, no less a stimulus than physically making love. Only the device and the mechanics are different. The act of listening to the movement of the other amongst the silence, a more complete effect could not be produced if seen with naked eyes. The temptation to see by sight would be considerable, calling upon fortitude not to open eyes and commence conversation.

Lips touched her hair, nose detected the scent of honeysuckle shampoo and conditioner. A struggle not to sneeze seemed to last for eternal seconds only to be distracted by the clock advance clicking on eleven then the resumption of her slow breathing. To assume her position again, one could not even pretend to wake up unless genuinely asleep in the first place. When the mind wanders in tiredness it is seduced by a need to reach a settlement of conscience and any foolish idea for departure can suffice. The final thought into sleep while still holding notions of sense and nonsense was this, 'I could not possibly place myself in the shoes of Kate because my snoring would wake the other.' Without a chance of solving anything whether be it riddle or otherwise, sleep became easier, instantaneous actually at the new conclusion. Both hands must surely have met on twelve and went their separate ways until the next time.

I woke at mid-afternoon when the day outside was desperately hanging on to light. Thankfully the imperfect dream had been just a dream for in a second of waking I believed I had murdered someone but no one in particular. Where would I be in a week or a fortnight, a month, even a year from now? This was one of those times when a man might ask a question of himself and not get an answer. The question did not unburden the mind. It was the wrong question anyway because the word 'I' needed replacing with the item 'we'. 'Robert and Kate' or better perhaps 'Kate and Robert,' a sure fire tip to be an item at least for a week or two, but not necessarily to be so a year on. It was probable that Kate, whether she had been awake or not, had exited, prompted by snoring in her ear. How I wish I had whispered naughty things of a sexual nature while we lay together. All things in the best possible taste, of course which befits lovers. Also she was gone, but only for a while. It seems Kate had the good sense to go out to work while I wasted another day. Now I felt guilty, the only credit for the Monday had been personal intellectual thought entanglements. Now the conclusion without hangover was a clear witted idea that Robert Oakley was ridiculously sagacious.

Eventually it struck that I had become temporarily in charge of part of her estate. Feeling flattered and trusted all the necessary components were found for making a mug of coffee. Perhaps the phone would ring to acquaint and endorse this new position. Not wishing to disturb her domestic arrangements I selectively ploughed a way through a pile of clothes to be ironed. Sexy underwear and blouses without cotton were a no-no. The phone remained silent throughout the pressing and during the production of the 'spag bol thing'. These very exercises or chores as they may be described in a prouder way gave food for thought. Numerous questions emerged hitherto unconsidered, suppose it must be okay to do so, put them to Kate that is. Not sure, for she had shown a reluctance to answer many things about herself. One does not usually press for explanations, ask for ins and outs if the object of a new intimate relationship is a reluctant respondent. Darn right evasive in fact as if subtly hiding hidden secrets. The only inroads seem to have been made by means of tiny sorties or through like for like tradeoffs. 'I was,' she said, she was in a relationship when we worked together at Sillitoe and Sillitoe. Logic suggested it was over, hence being 'on the pull.'

The temptation to pry into her personal belongings was strong, if only to find out more about Kate. Maybe fooling myself by just confining a search to just casual looking, not delving, not even scraping, and only scanning around with penetrating eyes. There were no obvious signs to indicate a man living there recently. Not unusual, not particularly odd if he had left and it was over. It was not easy to imagine how they had lived there, their lives, their days and night upon night in the flat. Their conversations, the secret conversations and hopes eventually dashed unwilling to reach a point of shared destination. The blow of it, the fear of it broken in its fall. How odd that people arrange their fortunes not to work out. Perhaps a better and different kind of place was near at hand for Kate. It had to involve me. It had to guard against dullness and any melancholy occasion. Sure to have had the worst of it determined to make the best of everything.

Her flat was a spacious contrast to my domain of one room with humble roof. Mine ancient in comparison to the modern style. She had furniture too, perhaps Kate owned it, but paid rent for unfurnished accommodation. Hers was a place to live while mine was a place to languish and tediously construct dreams.

Following the flow gave a nagging sense that something was slipping out of control. Always a fork in the road, not knowing whether to keep left or swing to the right, usually unfailingly staying safe, steering straight and taking protection too far. Would it be a horrifying complication to rattle out occasionally, take the other path and not at all think about what was best? No need to consult the map, for to meditate is to get lost. Guess we had to moralise in the same vein, anything forming a couch of utmost care could be a thing approaching deception.

Darker grew the sky and noisier the streets as faint traffic of the day became a sound of subtle reasoning in the evening. Onto the town of Whitches a speck of brightness shone out from the kitchen window as a word lost in many conversations. The light within such a small kitchen was strong but conveyed to assist only indecisiveness. The oven clock had a vivid gazing face which moved its minute hand in precise periodic starts. Life and living from any given moment has endless possibilities, I had to tell myself this and in that regard neither oven nor refrigerator offered any assistance. The day begins and the day ends, but life is not unlimited or limitless. Looking about, it was pretty much as I remembered it from yesterday, but as night fell the kitchen light seemed to brighten to receive me.

Kate wore an unfashionable yet stylish three-quarter length coat, all black, bobbles and bulky – it could have been 1940s. "Thank god it's you," she said this while negotiating the door, bags, lock and key. "The lights on and everything. How come you are still here?"

"Oh," I replied economically and a little embarrassed.

Kate gaped bafflement and looked almost condemning in the confusion. "I just assumed you'd be gone, that's all." She shook her head then smiled as if to realise eventually the possibility that our relationship could extend beyond a one-night fling.

Still a little puzzled, "I'm sorry." I cleared my throat to buy time to think. "Perhaps I should go," as a gentleman might suggest in order to salvage some respect out of the situation. We both knew well that she could not possibly condone my immediate departure for there was so much to lose in doing so.

Kate produced a perky smile and showed she was wearing a blackish lipstick which for the first time struck as cheap. She unbuttoned her coat to reveal a white blouse and figure-hugging skirt. She lifted on her toes to kiss my lips with a peck. "Stay. What have you made?"

A blend of enthusiasm and fatigue was not an unreasonable way of being on returning home from work. It made me feel more than a little guilty and uncomfortable. Without offering any observation I tried to be immediately amenable and establish an indication of presence which extended beyond the temporary. By now Kate had removed shoes and coat then flung them in the corner. She lay flat on the sofa with back to the ceiling and head inclined towards me. "My back aches again."

The automatic thing to say is 'sorry', but again I felt loathed to say it despite every part wanting to announce the word. Instead I sat down cross-legged upon the carpet as if on the pavement to the admiration of bystanders. At a respectful distance I lifted my hand transacting the business of body language by placing a warm palm to along her back with a little friction. By throwing myself luxuriously into the action of support the impulse to say the word was nullified.

"I am afflicted with a bad back forever." She looked in a way that resembled a hopeless wreck. "Resigned, resigned," making double the observation and eyes cast down to the carpet. A long pause developed as I looked curiously to the carpet with her.

Coming to the rescue I said, "Sorry," then in the pleasantest manner, "can I get you anything?"

Miracle tablets under the heading of those which are anti-inflammatory in nature provided a little relief. The drugs were easily found for they were handily placed in the kitchen and had the notoriety of having had frequent use. Kate sat upright, ate food and tablets together. Spaghetti bolognaise is just the meal to eat beginning at a tray from the knees, the distance there is always greater than the tabletop. Higher is the possibility of spilling sauce somewhere, spoiling clothes, splashing here and there without concern for care. "This isn't bad really." It was an inadvertent jewel, a female not criticising the cooking done by a man. It is just the way of a lady, for you to take them into your head. "It is nice but this portion is far too big for me Robert. Open a door sufficient enough to get through and close it carefully as before." Profound or what! While we ate, the discussion came around to the back. "The main thing is fluid, or absence of it. To get fluid into the discs you have to dance upon it. The pain is there anyway and there is really no way to escape it. You can dull or dampen the pain that's all. Like a ballet dancer on tiptoes – always painful. You have to dance into the pain to reap the benefit. Grace isn't the same has relief though, although the principle is sound."

Sure there must be powerful reasoning to every word, though it seemed to be overreaching an understanding of sense. Kate had described the human body as a three-dimensional perfectly balanced labyrinth, yet littered with drilling, digging and patching. Cracked streets, potholes and the spine itself as an ailing super conduit between mind and body. "I am not quite with you. It is not that I don't doubt any of what you are saying…"

"Okay, think of it this way. The body has an amazing capacity to heal itself. The body is doing it all the time – every second in fact. Everything is connected, actually a toe is an ear in some ways, they are made of similar stuff and are connected as Whitches is to London. Not the best

126

example perhaps. But it is all about balance. A crude way of putting it –
if someone trained exclusively with weights and then after sometime of
doing that went to play football – you can guess at the outcome! The result
would be that he would be racked in pain afterwards, body tight, jarred,
pulling both this way and that. The solution is simple, the training should
involve a combination of exercises, strength, anaerobic and especially
bending/stretching for suppleness. The result would be better fitness,
reduced fatigue and quicker recovery. Balance is the key, as a balanced
diet keeps you healthier, so simple good health stimulates the process of
healing and the same processes promote good health. A complicated cycle
put simply. Oh, thanks Robert but I cannot eat anymore."

The idea of self-deceit was a sort of negligent tactic which formed to
convince myself that I did understand what Kate was saying. A more
considered, perhaps better-informed view which took into account our
newness and the lack of time we had spent together meant something else.
It mattered not whether either of us had understood what she had said.
Kate had given a pardon and cleverly decided to speak, for I had nothing
to say except to comprehend by return and listen. These thoughts must
have given me away. "You needn't trouble your head about me," she said
it in the midst of calculation. I put my tongue into my cheek as if to display
a pensive full accordance. I really wanted to shrug my shoulders and
remark 'I really don't get it'. Maybe it does not follow that one more
talkative becomes more agreeable to the other. Perhaps the merits of near
silence were to good advantage and her philosophical knowledge was
engaging to my taste. "Perhaps I could trouble you to stand on my back
again and dig your feet into some stubborn tissue."

"Kate, I would be glad to. Have you had an excessive quota of
painkillers to dull the pain? I do not want to hurt you. If it helps," I lost
my thread for it seemed grotesquely sexual. "Well, I want to give you
particular satisfaction," resuming in a tangle. The concept of standing on
the back of a lover bringing pain to alleviate pain was a strange one. Not
so much frightened now by the probability of a flawed therapy but
comforted by the foreknowledge. How she could express a demeanour of
perfect confidence for the act was beyond thinking about.

The main living area was small and cramped with more furniture than
necessary but despite this we avoided tumbling over each other while
preparing a space. Kate did not remove any more clothes, and then
dexterously assumed a position there to that of a hedgehog. A ball, limbs
tucked inward out of sight and head down almost underneath somehow.
Kate's muffled voice found a way out to give precise commands. My
reaction was to brace for the particular instructions. Just as Kate suggested
I knelt down with knees to where her head should have been, hands gently

on shoulders. Her hair had been adorned by a ribbon, pink, but it could have been any colour, such was her complexion. Her youthfulness was both appealing and unsettling. She took such perfect skin for granted for I was bewildered by her overuse of make-up. Miranda had used cosmetics sensibly to enhance the attraction, whereas Kate in comparison seemed to just daub it on for the sake of it. For a moment I wished I were with Miranda fingering aged bumps and cellulite.

Kate could not remember The Beatles, how could she? I barely did, just the tail end and the songs on a transistor radio when they were current. Apparently the best aid to memory is the sense of smell. Not sure about that, but the smell of her hair was exactly like some 1968 perfume worn by the mother of a childhood friend. His mother was a hairdresser who had a cat named Ringo – peculiar that. Also the pattern of our lives, peculiar, it seems as if I made Miranda up now. Miranda could remember The Beatles, Buddy Holly and even Billie Holiday.

Kate's neck was as smooth as a new laid egg, she murmured more than once giving mild encouragement to continue. The fortunate situation led to affectionate words of soothing kindness. As a way of discouraging competitors I asked outright about her former partner. Kate was reluctant to answer and through soft murmuration was not quite so intelligible as might have been. The reply was given with such feminine authority to satisfy honour both in her head and in my heart. I asked, "Do you have a cat?"

Despite feline purring, no cat existed except the religious avoidance of such creatures. By now Kate had already been tempted further than intended to go due to stimulating curiosity. "I am allergic to cats – get a rash," she said lifting her head and stretching arms – fingers like claws. "This isn't comfortable Robert – you are not supposed to turn me on." I felt flattered. Disinterested stimuli is always flattering, especially in the case of sinking affection. Mysteriously Kate shook her head and pursed her lips. "All things considered this is pleasant enough but confusing. The combination of touching and pressure – two different things. The mingling of them both is a muddle. For correctness I need pressure without touching." Kate sat up completely with arms folded, eyes wide open and knees tightly together. "Why are you still here? Why didn't you leave before I came home? What do you want, Robert?"

I had a sudden feeling of dislocation. I had envisioned something different. Scorned, I descended into *Eastenders'* script teenager mode. "Kate, I really like you. I want to be with you. Thought we could spend some time together – you know. What was last night all about, eh?" It sounded so pathetic showing immaturity beyond comprehension.

"Robert, are you mad?"

"Mad?"

"Are you mad at me?"

"No, why? It's me."

"No it's me. I have just broken up with him. He got his marching orders and he is not coming back. I saw Diana this afternoon. She is coming round here tonight. It is going to be a girls' night in you know. No men allowed. Chocolate cake, ice cream, pizza and if we are lucky pizza delivery man. Look, phone in a few days. I need to know if I miss you. You need to know if you want me. I know what you think. I know what you are thinking. A rebound thing – anybody in trousers. My bloody back is killing me. Diana can do the pressure thing. She doesn't get me excited. Phone me in a couple of days and fuck off before I shag you."

Chapter Eleven

In a bleak December where the nights were long and days cold it was dawn again and only eleven shopping days left. Jim was lucky to miss Christmas this year. The big build up, less than a fortnight now and forever compressing as the days shorten still. Not a concern for him though in a matter which touched my own interests as part of a gloomy envy. Why presume all of us should be seriously privileged to be here and living comfortably?

It was the day of Jim's funeral. I hated it and hated to say it. He was dead. A number of complications had meant delay upon delay, but finally the day had arrived. I wondered what would happen. Just a handful of people there I imagined; the deceased, Tom, me, and the vicar – Eleanor Rigby! Really just family and I maybe. Kate had offered to hold my hand because 'that is what couples do' she said 'support the other'. That did not seem right though, she never knew him, anyway, Tom could hold my hand. 'The subject of the funeral is best avoided,' Kate had said. I wished to be able to avoid the funeral altogether, Jim would have understood in his way. Hey, no big deal just a funeral. I would make my way to the church; arrive early, see it out, give condolences afterwards, leave quickly and wait. Loiter in readiness for that pleasant kind of sorrow to hit like comforting melancholy, glorious, sad and disappointing – one great homogeneous contradictory counterpoint. The grieving would then be over, swept away to nothing and soon it would be Saturday.

It never happens as planned, the time came, the service had begun and I was a late arrival. The oak doors creaked loudly then I hastened to a rear pew. Excluding the bearers, there was an assembled company of a little more than half a dozen; Tom, his brother perhaps, three middle aged women together, two more standing apart, then my landlord and his wife. It seems that black would not suit me or any of the others in our greys and browns. If ever it was the case for the working classes, all black funerals went out with flat caps and Sunday best. Death shone shadowy upon stained glass like heavy eyes glaring through tinted spectacles and for life sepulchral candles had been lit which showed everything continued no matter what.

An inclination to congratulate oneself for enduring the service and being an absolute brick to the brothers was short lived. With no other immediate business at hand it seemed appropriate to slip out or die. Notwithstanding the extreme idea the onus eventually fell away into reasonable common sense. Tom and his brother suggested we repair to the reserved function room of the 'Cock and Bottle.' None of us could refuse such an implored invitation particularly as the numbers were so few that any fraction of the whole to fall away would be an absence greater than a tenth. The energy at which we all agreed to go there was borne from decency at the cost of dispersing our separate self-persuasion to flee. It lacked a certain decorum perhaps because the 'function' by nature of it involved a feast. Perhaps that word 'feast' was an exaggeration if it was associated with banquet or celebration – it was neither. Actually there were too many sandwiches and of course a comparable amount of alcohol which was in relation excessive. Tom's brother Nick convinced any doubters that Jim would have approved of the drinking even though he seldom drank. Nick had already removed a black tie to his pocket, perhaps this was a subtle signal giving permission for the few of us to relax. We adjusted for a moment and I vaguely remember being slightly angry at God during the prayer. Life goes on but these were faces of other people.

A feature of Tom's face was the addition of a frequent handkerchief regulating tears. Nick had a composed rigidity modulated self-styled and inflexible – he talked. "God, he refuses to prove his existence. For proof denies faith and without faith God is nothing." No one was really listening and I am not sure whether the vicar approved of the preaching Nick. Lots of beer had been consumed so Nick could have been excused the profound sermon which bordered on blasphemy. The landlord, not the 'Cock and Bottle' one but mine (as evidenced by my arrears) did not seem to approve so he and his wife gave more condolences, excuses and left. The vicar had flown too which left two knots, the ladies huddle and a group of Tom, Nick and I.

The singularly amiable ghost, the feature of Jim played upon the whimsical visage of Tom. A slight shadow from the diamond latticed window was caught on the face of Nick attaching a curious epitaph as if were a tranquillising influence. The words were tapped out with gentle delivery but as bold as letters etched upon a tombstone. "Jim was my brother," he gave a brotherly look at Tom and corrected, "our brother. Jim was shy and awkward by no fault of his own. He was no less a person than another – better than most. His life here was unhappy and the world wronged him. I shall live on contented, not forgetting Jim, but believing his particular aversion to living as he did was better for his passing." He raised his glass, "To Jim – we will miss you."

The little speech left the small party confused, it had a displeasing boldness and strange aloofness. An obvious presumption in Nick that we all would feel a familial pang missed and left us all a little embarrassed. Moreover the curious question which surrounded the circumstances of his death still lingered. It was necessary for him to be respected and the delicate moments for his memory to not to be ill remembered. We steadfastly avoided any word in that direction which may have compromised his esteem in the eyes of Tom and Nick. Jim for all his good ways in life and blessing a death had become the instrument of hurt to his brothers. For all his smiling face and quiet tongue he had been caught in the cruellest snare. The weaker Tom had abandoned himself to tears in an overwhelming sense of shame and grief. Any sight of distress in the stronger Nick were as sobs and tears in the heart like arrows from Tom. They had comforted each other in praise of Jim relating high gratification to no less of a man than he was. Nick composed, had impressed upon us that very thing – no lesser man than Jim. He gave a comfort, one to remember what Jim used to be, but in doing so rekindled anguish by recollecting what he never was. The wickedness of the world had worked its discerning way upon him.

Word after word, phrase on phrase Nick spoke and Tom recovered himself. Though I felt sympathy for their misfortune there was no reconciling agitation which had become a legacy of his passing. I wished he had given an excuse to hate him, but not a thing could explain a restless state of mind not like the mourning of a friend. I told myself over and over, 'not cross, not moody, but grieved – sorely grieved'. The strong emotions dissipated more, then still more with the alcohol until all the grief was swallowed into a stout heart. Jim had gone out of the world as if he had never been in it and life carried on much the same without him.

It was Nick who said it, 'Jim as a young adolescent could fit twenty-five Maltesers in his mouth without swallowing one'. It was Tom that decided, 'Jim nearly choked because he must have tried twenty-eight'. Nick asked Tom if he could do the same with 'wagon wheels'. Tom replied to the affirmative, but declared it was very unlikely because he disliked them so. They talked of their mother who was in the throes of advanced dementia and agreed that her state was the best state to be in for then and forever. The onset of dementia was first regarded as a problem when she stood around a lot apparently. Tom told of how their mother would stand at a bus stop for hours and as each bus pulled up she would tell the driver to 'piss off'. She would stand in the corner of a room in urine-splashed stockings, armed to the false teeth, complete with imaginary gun and tranquillising darts disabling visitors. The lady would never nudge into anyone, but just barge with the living daylights.

132

Tom let Nick know that personally he thought Nick was fortunate for living in the south. Nick thought this too (even though he worked away for half each year, but realised Tom had attached a different meaning to the remark as he first understood it. "What do you mean?"

Tom answered in a detectable tone of northern prejudice. "Better standard of living, more money, better weather – better life entirely."

Nick looked slightly dislocated by the remark before returning to counter the words of his brother, "You are right," he said cruel and smart. "Absolutely right, generally life is much easier down there. Even the women are better looking." He did not realise at first that in saying this he had inadvertently insulted the few women close by who overheard every word of the dialogue. Nick then tried to make amends by a misconceived apology of the poorest quality. First he wound himself up in tense expression like winding clockwork, then ran down by releasing air from his lungs and then uttering the words. "Your resilience to insults is very commendable."

The middle-aged ladies who had resolutely attached a benevolent function to proceedings were rendered speechless momentarily and their articulation was impeded by the remark. Then one by one they took up a position by presenting themselves to Tom and departing with their final condolences before leaving together as one. The ladies whispered to each other with little further hesitation as if they were going to begin a great speech of considerable chatter. In the next half minute, when outside and beyond our ears that must certainly have been the case. Now only the three of us remained, Tom, Nick and I.

"Women – hey – hey, Robert," Nick ejaculated the words. "Let them carry on with their washing and knitting." He gave me a determined laborious look as if to gain an answer through a confidence. My reply was no words, only a sexist smile which was summoned in part by the alcohol, but nevertheless left me feeling loathsome of myself. "Be thankful you are not Napoleon Solo fighting thrush," he said and paused before changing the subject. "Did you know, if you shave the fur off a tiger, the skin underneath is striped?"

"Is that right?" Tom interjected with an unaccountable voice which had a sardonic charm about it.

There was a quiet few seconds of fascination while we attended to the idea of a bald tiger. The long morning and afternoon had led us to a surreal state of contentment like some inevitable force to dissolve the funeral. It would require more than a hairless feline to take away the motionless cloud which had so enveloped us. An invisible voice at my shoulder understood the phenomenon as an easy note of succession to leave. The tone was an assertive whisper, so deep inside the ear to be an absolute

133

command. Despite this, my mouth overrode the need to depart and held me there. "Where do tigers live?" The words came out like an idiot folly weighed against any simple notion of wisdom.

"I think tigers live in zoos and are very rare. There maybe a few wild ones I think. Perhaps tigers live in India in the Indian jungle," Nick said the latter part with strong emphasis on 'Indian', as if he had adopted the mocking theme from Tom.

Tom re-joined, "Yes, tigers live in India and lions live in Africa. You never hear of a clash between them. Different territories you see. One in Africa the other in India."

"What about the Asian lion?" replied Nick.

"Eh?" I said confused.

"The Asian lion, the Romans fed the Christians to the lions. Not lions from Africa, but lions from Asia."

"Eh?" repeating.

"There is more than one type of lion. You might think immediately of the African lion, but the Asian lion is more solitary than its African relative – well the males are. The male Asian lion has a less flamboyant mane or collar – or whatever they call it – less fur – not shaved obviously."

"Oh," instead of 'eh'.

Tom unbolted, "Yer but lions and tigers still don't live on the same patch. Maybe the Asian lions hang around China and the tigers prowl India."

"Lions in China! I just thought they had Pandas," I said.

"Yes, of course," re-joined Nick.

"What do you know about China?" replied Tom.

"Loads, they invented gunpowder," replied Nick.

"Discovered," Tom.

"Paper," me.

"The Egyptians had papyrus – papyrus's didn't they?" Tom announced rhetorically.

Nick began again. "The Chinese invented the breast-strap harness. This made horsepower more efficient at a stroke. Much greater loads could be pulled by horses fitted with the breast-strap harness, utilising their power through the chest and shoulders."

"Big deal, Nick," ventured Tom.

"Yes well the Ancient Greeks just used ropes wrapped and tied around the horse's neck. When the Romans were not feeding Christians to the lions, they had chariots attached with dubious tack to horses which gave limited pulling power. No one had invented the breast-strap harness. Today that basic principle of tapping into the strength of a horse this way seems simple and fundamental. Imagine a man for instance, pulling

134

something by dragging it by a rope around the neck – it seems so ridiculous."

"Mmm, ridiculous," commented Tom who was not entirely absorbed by Nick's lesson.

"And the horse-collar," said Nick enthusiastically.

"Horse-collar?" said Tom becoming more objectionable but evidently intrigued by such a device he had never before thought about.

"A further advance on the breast-strap was a horse-collar which was developed about a thousand years ago. By using horses for farming, instead of oxen, had several advantages. Horses are much quicker and can walk a few miles before starting work. Farmers, peasants could suddenly plough more, be more productive and as a result lived together in larger settlements. This led to a transformation, sowing seeds to medieval economic revolution in Europe."

By now, Tom had sat in the corner with his glass resting on his knee, while leaning back yawned and addressed words back to Nick in an incomprehensible mutter. Indeed, there was something about Nick's subject knowledge of China and corrupted by references to Europe which especially bored. More clearly, he continued. "You thick bastards that could not do languages at school, you did European studies instead of French or German. We were talking about China. What about gunpowder?"

Nick observed the brother with half a mind to a smile, but did not take his eyes and returned the question, "Gunpowder?"

"Yes gunpowder," said Tom, spreading himself in the corner with no hesitation. "Everybody thinks about gunpowder when ancient China is mentioned. How did the Chinese know it could even exist before they made it?"

Nick began smugly almost overlapping Tom's voice in enthusiasm. "Obviously it must have been an accident – like discovering LSD. They probably stumbled upon the greatest single thing for killing people by weapons. The irony is that they were trying to make an 'elixir of life'. Obviously it was an accident."

"Obviously," Tom joked at Nick's overuse of the word.

"The Chinese tried to subdue potassium nitrate into a medicine you could take. Various experiments led to adding honey, saltpetre, sulphur into a mix and evaporating it into a volcano. Hey presto, gunpowder for the use of... *BOOM BOOM*." Both Tom and myself were impressed by its profound retrospective prognostication. "Imagine gunpowder in Europe before the Battle of Hastings and the impact it must have had in a time of valour, knights in armour and castles. It is assumed that the Chinese used gunpowder for fireworks and in Europe it was used as a weapon. Think again! The fact is there were many more fighting factions in Europe than in China which led to an advancing arms trade and quick improvement of weapons development. Obviously!"

"Obviously, obviously," Tom again.

Hopelessly lost I said, "So are you saying the Chinese were more civilised than Europeans because Europe found a more destructive application for gunpowder than the Chinese?"

Nick was quick enough to take my question into account, but the answer seemed to require contemplation, he gave it with full weight and a piece of pantomime. His arms spread in and out by many gestures now which were not dissimilar to those of an Italian. "The answer is no," shaking his head and arms akimbo. "No, only that medieval China was far more advanced than Europe. A huge amount of rice was grown, it had irrigation, ceramics, a vast internal economy and external economy with Japan. It had silk, silk production, printing and books everywhere. The Chinese had paper since the second century BC. There was toilet paper, wallpaper and bureaucracy. Medicine was far more advanced than in Europe. There was a fundamental structure of success – a model of self-efficiency. It even had banknotes in an economy which was almost too successful for its own good because it led to complacency."

Nick had also used the impacting word 'complacency' to ascertain that neither Tom nor I had fallen asleep. My state of mind suggested that we had to figure out what he had intended to mean by 'complacency'. Or had Nick assumed that somehow we had knowledge enough to understand? Or were we supposed to enquire just what he meant just to prove that we were actually awake all of the time? Perhaps it was best to leave him to take his own way and in the meantime I was left to consider a reply. By some wearisome repetition of thought I arrived at a recollection to excuse partial ignorance. It was in the form of a question which I put to myself rather than an answer to the complacency conundrum. Had I heard somewhere that the downfall of ancient China which is referred to here as 'complacency' was actually attributed to the majority of the population succumbing to the influence of opium? Nick did not insist on an answer, so why should we give him one if it could serve to show our own ignorance? Besides it was better to preserve his good humour by not interrupting. Reflection was comparatively harmless and was broken into brightly by Tom.

To me he said, "He sleeps with books. He does not read them." Now directed at the both of us, "You put books under your pillow at night don't you Nick? All the knowledge from every page seeps into your brain while you are asleep. 'The Complete History of Europe' volumes one to twenty-seven by A T Cher. Also, 'The Concise History and Culture of Ancient China' according to Nick Butler."

Nick was only slightly amused by Tom's peculiar description of acquiring knowledge the easy way and looked as restive as a horse might before continuing. He came up with something equally absurd. "Tom you must not play with your navel. You know quite well that if you undo your belly button, then your guts will fall out." The very thought gave rise to an unnatural image that made me curl like hot paper, only to straighten out again at the impossibility of it. Tom was more thoughtful now than sorrowful, as Nick and Tom had developed a kind of urinating banter exclusive to themselves as brothers.

Tom involved me again. "Robert, what do you think started the French Revolution? How did it begin do you think?"

"The French Revolution! I don't know. I would guess something to do with the realisation that the French aristocracy were no better than anybody else and people rebelled against the unjust hierarchy."

"You have drunk too much," replied Tom. "Tell him, Nick."

Nick was lifting beer to his mouth, he changed his mind and put it down again. He shook his head with a little laugh of recognition. "The French Revolution, well it's like this. European missionaries went into China and found a well-ordered society which they felt was due to ideals passed down through the generations. News filtered back to the people in Europe who were amazed by the Chinese Bureaucratic Imperial State. To the surprise of Europeans, they found that positions of the Chinese in society had been determined through their own talents, by becoming top and passing a rigorous system of exams. The Chinese had not bought their positions or had them passed down by the aristocracy such as what happened in Europe. The modern-day civil service is built on the Chinese model. You could say the Chinese experience underlay the ideas of the French Revolution. It was seen as a model for the future anyway. So there was more to China than just gunpowder."

Still half-curious I asked, "What about the complacency you spoke of?"

"Well, it was not so much complacency as a clash of culture. It was not all one-way traffic. The West took maths, astronomy and mapping to China. Although the Chinese may have been impressed by Europeans who could accurately predict an eclipse, they did not really understand mathematics or the modern nature of science. The Chinese had never undergone the experience of the European renaissance. In the eighteenth century the Chinese rejected western technology because they were happy as they were. Protestant missionaries saw the Chinese as heathen. The Chinese in the nineteenth century chose to reject religion with anti-propaganda – anti western science. The West viewed Chinese science as insignificant. It was said the Chinese lacked abstract thinking or at least had thinking of a different type at least. Things tend to happen more quickly when there is intense competition as in Europe. In China the large unified state did not have the same pressure to stay ahead in the technological race. Politically they had no desire to embrace technology."

The opportunity to discuss the subject further was dispatched and lost as we gave a wandering observation to the absence of Tom. We both together learned by our own separate deductions that he had taken off during Nick's mini lecture.

"I know where he is. It is not unlike Tom to disappear sometimes for a few moments without giving prior excuse. It is almost as if it is expected at some point of my brother."

Presently Tom came hurrying back with a dazzling fiery faced blush from his expedition. "I am sorry," he said, "I have been and could not go. It is so uncomfortable. I have to leave immediately. I am sorry. You understand?"

"Yes, that is perfectly all right, Tom – no sweat." I said this with a hidden sense of relief. It was the best time for us all to go on our individual paths again. We said our hasty but fond goodbyes and Nick left with Tom. Following a final acknowledgement to the bar staff and sip for Jim, I left alone.

I thought that my sympathy for Jim's brothers could not have been more acceptable or delicately placed. I confidently took bold steps to steer a straight line upon the pavement towards Kate's place. She would be glad to see me I thought, but the pleasure of having a woman to cherish and comfort was all mine. She had a touch so gentle and easy that enabled a man to deal with anything. The temptation of Kate could not have been more magnificent or ingenious. It was a snug and comfortable feeling to have at last a partner to return home to. Kate had endeavoured to instil a flattering confidence in our relationship which was adorning and charming like old furniture. I in the same vein had a similar and connected interest. However, I knew, she knew, we knew that there comes a time when furniture becomes familiar and out of style. That period was surely for later because for now our drawers ran smoothly and polish gleamed.

I knew that I had drank more than enough, not only by the irrefutable evidence, but also by seeing the looks on the advancing faces of others that shared the pavement. A trembling half smile here, an almost speaking look of derision there and glances of all sorts from annoyance to utter irritation. It occurred to me that in the best interests of new relationship, things would continue on a good footing if I returned home sober.

It was the sight of the moon in the encroaching twilight which stirred the surface of my sluggish thoughts. Then I gazed at the artificial Christmas tree sparkling in the window of a café. The day was becoming a blur and perhaps a jug of cold water thrown over the head would have brought me back the usual senses. In giddiness I began to feel as an addle-headed fool might. With tie already removed the loosening of the collar was a feeble resource to prevail upon. That done, it was necessary to maintain a posture akin to standing without falling over. The frame of the café window was a friendly stabiliser. It took some minutes to overcome the uneasiness of limbs and body. When recovered sufficiently to move on again there was little inclination to do so. The inviting smells and lights from within pervaded the entrance as a welcome bosom might give to a grieving man at a funeral. The staff inside were judges to take account of my position, but they behaved with impartiality to this drunken fool who had every intention of returning himself to a sober being. Black coffee and vegetable lasagne was the order, to which they accepted and then made available to my surprise. Even a place was prepared for and either by accident or design it was done with contented delight of the staff.

It was busy inside, it was busy out on the street, but remote in the sky was the moon. By looking intently at the moon above the town through the window there was a distinct feeling of security like a confidence that it would never abandon my world. No such thing as green cheese, so how could the man in the moon be made of it? There were layers of coloured green cheese pasta in the vegetable lasagne. The moon did not smell of green cheese, it smelled of nothing but gunpowder. The lasagne did not smell of green cheese it had only the nose of lasagne. The plate looked as if someone had unbuttoned their navel and emptied the contents. I ate with rapacity unlike a hungry man, but one determined to do it.

Chapter Twelve

He shaped his course along the major road going east. On soon reaching the determined spot he came off that busy road, stopped at the hedge, and then found a suitable place to clamber through. He turned himself around, looking all about before hastily bulldozing a sparsely grown place to the other side. Following the noisy breaking of twigs with scarcely a scratch he quickly recommenced the walk, but now over countryside at an absolute right angle to the road.

The living world around him continued down its very own path, virtually oblivious to his passage through nature via field and hedge. Fishes still swam nearby in the cold shallow stream. Birds continued all the same flitting in the branches from there to there. Standing cattle gave him examination with perusal of gape and stare while his course negotiated their ground. Each stirring blade of grass kept a quiet fastened watch upon his progress in the softly chilling wind. All about these elegant guardians of the world could not make him stray from the purpose in his journey. There was no abandonment, for the design and plan could not be changed by the natural flow of nature's scrutiny.

There was a little anxiety to be observed concerning his dress, for he was ill equipped in such a purpose as a march over muddy fields against a wind that chilled. Such apprehension was outstripped by a truly set direction rushing down an interminable perspective which he fearfully surveyed. Already mapped out ahead, it was indeed a direful day to happen. During the setting of the sun he kept looking back in slight starts of fear at the knowledge of the dreadful deed to come. The sun was small comfort, but was welcome enough in some way as it represented life and motion from an active day. It was the dark, wakeful, silent, watchful night, all of that away from the bustling town which scared him.

It was becoming dusk and suddenly this was like the instant of yearning for madness. From the observation of his being one could make out, perhaps hear a whisper of vengeful dreaded wicked thoughts. Eventually he came to a stop by finding one and most convenient of several giant circular straw bales. He sheltered here to wait, while still the evening fell muttering at his conscience. Even more it stabbed now as the shadowy veil of night did drop all around him.

It was not in any shape or means entertainment, though it had been a dream that was vivid, extravagant in detail and becoming evermore fragmented. Little by little I became alert and fully aware of the present again. The dark, the cold and the noise of the road outside – each piece brought me increasingly back to reality. A lucid communication at the window shone in from the streetlights and then back out again. An intelligence, up from the polished surface of the coffee table, shining and reflecting like the vision of that same man. Sheltering, waiting, with his shrouded expression over a sunburnt face against the night. The man was not I, for I was not there in the dream. It was only I who had seen him again and again from above by looking down upon the scene. He was a potential criminal by the motive given to him without reasonable choice. The information supplied by virtue of the deliberate mistake for which I should have known and would eventually realise the identity of would be mine. For a future responsibility I knew it would be easy to reconcile the deed and the mistake by manner of that very vague dream. Prophetic sub-conscientious was only a recollection, and cut short too – so how could I be blamed for his deed? If any power of mercy lay within, it would occur because of ignorance rather than weakness. It was for me alone to decide by taking account of the circumstance, but whether or not to affect it would be something for only him to judge upon. The influence upon the matter came down to a simplistic though albeit far reaching dilemma – to tell him or not.

The desire to conveniently forget was appealing, but something so important and consequential could never be kept out of mind. At best the information could only be laid aside until the moment arrived as a natural course. Alternatively, the anticipated moment may never occur, in which case it would fester and haunt me forever. Perhaps it was expedient to tell him as soon as possible for the sake of wisdom and let it be decided for himself. Time advanced more still and having approximated a solution, it now seemed sensible to turn on the light as it was difficult to see otherwise.

There it was, at that moment easier to discern by brightness, better now as a mental picture, the face of the man in the dream sharpened and I knew him. The encouraging development had made my head shake somewhat involuntarily with the circumstances of the realisation. The person I must tell, I knew the name of, and equally I was fully aware of the same – the man in the dream. Those considerations found me reclining in a thoughtful manner of gratification. The clock had moved on only three hours from my dining at the café. I began to recount every word of the funeral as if performing a short series of anecdotes like a calming therapy.

The sofa belonging to Kate was something of an uncomplicated comfort as the upholstery simpered agreeably. Late night shopping I surmised, that is where she would be, maybe buying my Christmas present at the very moment. In a dilatory way I gave a little groan and counted up to a dozen seconds as I looked intently from floor to clock. The little arm or hand of the clock pointed directly to eight. The hands sectioned out the face precisely into one third and two thirds as if it were a direct command to signify a move or to disengage. The dividing of the pointed hands, one straight up and the down to my left spanned the face in a gesture. They were not open arms of sympathy, but more irritable like an incomprehensible Lilliputian semaphore signal. The third hand which is better understood as the second hand mapped out every minute of a degree and did the same for each degree of the minute. The hand counted similar circles at sixty times an hour in a perpetual start, stop, start and all powered remarkably by just one solitary AA battery.

There is a sort of jesting which is also serious and staid – I call it Christmas. The annual impetuosity headlong and sombre with little thought for baby Jesus is hideous to endure. Encouragement, endeavour to be everything and anything that is good. Smiling through it and all that friendly office is such a chore. The instance of the tide now is clear with festive patronage which has gradually encroached upon since October. In the near future I will no doubt adopt the courteous demeanour to everyone quite regardless of the moment. 'Have a merry Christmas and don't drink too much,' all pronounced and conveyed in a fashion that in nothing else but jocular.

Evidence so Christmassy abounds as the room gives way to ocular inspection. A plastic tree of artificial colour and seasonal decorations testify to the time of year. Yes those inescapable cards overshadowing the former centrepiece; that is her picture, the print of Renoir 'The Boating Party'. Christmas cards have multiplied like hobgoblins: the daubed snowman, baubles, three Christmas trees, a Christmas parcel, another bauble, Santa, Santa and his reindeers, and Christmas tree singular. Christmas cards announce cheerful sparkle with a slight tingle of miserable nausea. Only one card with a star and another with carol singers allude to the true meaning of Christmas. 'To Kate and Robert from Andrea and family with kisses'. 'To Katy and Rob, Merry Christmas from Clare and Ian (no kisses). 'To Kate and Robert, wishing you a Happy New Year, all the best to you have a lovely Xmas from Elaine and Rich (no kisses either, but very smart with a Marks and Spencer motif). Who are these people I wonder?

It was clear. Kate and Robert. Gosh that is Kate and I – a couple. There is a card here with meaning which is easier to relate. Only an empty sleigh and footprints upon a snowy rooftop, but inside it clicks, 'Merry Christmas and Happy New Year, best wishes from Diana and Tom'. Kate and Robert, Diana and Tom – two couples and I am half of one of them. There must have been a grin which accompanied these thoughts, but perhaps the advantage was not to see this and to passively accept the sacrifice of it.

A noise at the door served to detract from the particular train of thought. *Knock knock* was heard accompanied by the reaction of a hasty step together with a combination of curiosity and mild excitement. On my opening the door to an incautious wideness there was a stranger to behold on the doorstep. There stood a man perhaps in his late sixties with a healthy sheaf of hair for his years. He adjusted his collar and tie to perfection. He was very much abashed, but looked as if he had something of great importance to communicate. His shoes were so shiny that they appeared to be impossible on such an unassuming fellow. I believe I did enough to have given a slight nod, not a contemptuous one for the intrusion, but passively maybe for interrupting the lamentation.

He began, "I beg your pardon for knocking at your door." His hand moved to the right pocket of the large checked sports jacket which he wore in a terrible display. A white envelope was drawn deliberately and held firm by both hands. "I received this Christmas card from yourselves this morning." The man paused as if to steady himself for a gallant speech. He spoke with a little shake in his voice at first before regaining a precise composure. "I am a widower of two years on Christmas day and I do not send Christmas cards. I thank you for your card though."

While he spoke, I pieced together who he was. Kate had described a certain time recently when she recalled a short conversation with an old man one morning. That moment was then followed by subsequent greetings on consecutive days by the same man almost leaping out to waylay as she left for work from the front door. Kate, filled with season's greetings and goodwill to all men must have delivered a card to his house. On being a little stumped at how to respond I returned with, "Sorry to hear that. There is no need for you to apologise." A short interval elapsed before either one of us had the fortitude enough to continue the conversation.

Not knowing quiet how to continue, while seeing his look of melancholy, I asked him inside for a Christmas drink. I half hoped he might refuse the invitation. To my surprise either by politeness or some strange impellent to engage with another human being at Christmas time he accepted. An instantaneous appeal or considered pride in our nature as human beings could only partially explain the situation and the unpiloted stranger. We sat apart but faced the fire which gave a welcome smile and relief from the cold outside.

"My name is Robert."

"Pleased to meet you, Robert. George is my name."

"Is the whisky all right, George?"

"Yes thank you, but I prefer malt, Robert."

"Oh yes, don't we all, George, don't we all. This is bargain booze from Tesco." I refrained from making a stupid joke about vinegar in the kitchen.

"Mmm."

"My girlfriend's name is Kate."

"Yes, I know."

"Oh she's probably out late night shopping."

"Mmm, yes."

The strange manifestation of the situation continued like a dancing step extremely difficult to achieve – there were only uncomfortable dubious movements. Gradually, the conversation lubricated by the whisky which he drank and I only sipped progressed to his times with his late wife. As with the drink, I partook sparingly, short sentences and rationed words. He spoke of her with a unique fondness and of their love. Through all the sympathy he seemed like a broken man, miserable and never able to recover from the loss of his spouse. It was clear that he was toiling through a great solitude and I was naturally affected by the dialogue. At beyond tolerance point, I straightened myself in a surprising effort and stood to my feet. George gazed upward into my face and I returned a look ineffectual. I wondered how he was, what were they like as a couple. I wondered what the point of marriage and death was for it to make him so heartbroken. His tears gave way to a half smile, helpless, feeble and melancholy almost to sickliness. He reflected again, turned his head and shook it. George, a helpless stranger, inclined attention away, this moved me a little more. I was grateful for the distance, but still uncomfortable by the proximity.

I wished Kate would return for I had served a very attentive turn listening to George. A woman such as Kate could perhaps talk humour into him. Make him feel better. Make me feel better. Kate could talk. Keep him quiet. Talk about shopping, Christmas, anything, but do it better than I. Still hearing every word and every sound I listened on. To see immense loss was difficult to fully contemplate through his eyes. So much for empathy, my inwardly mocking uselessness. I witnessed his glimpses and words which gave despair, yet his demeanour remained tender.

As if to anticipate the presence of a saviour there was a timely knock at the door. On hearing it, George softly muttered some words as if prepare

144

to leave, but stayed as if confined by his longing. It was not Kate at the door (to my disappointment) for she could have absorbed the heat by presenting herself to George. No, it was Tom. Tom had changed into casual clothes, while in contrast I was still partly dressed in funeral attire. Tom entered. I introduced one to another. George rose acknowledging as if he were stronger now and greater for the conversation. He had mastered courage to carry on that bit longer. Life was still precious to him, if only for the memories. Tom had a soothing touch about him and a sympathetic tenderness that detected George's despair. I merely saw it as a promising means to pacify the old man, or just a speedy device to lead George away towards the door. George took the hint and could not have left quicker if he had gone through the window.

With George discharged in a subtle haze of casual haste it was necessary to explain. "He doesn't send Christmas cards and he lost his wife a couple of years ago." That was sufficient enough, but I added more. "He doesn't know about the funeral." Tom nodded and I asked, "How are you anyway?"

"What do you think, Robert?"

"Sorry, silly question."

"No, I'm sorry I need to talk."

A burden and flattery all to me in a mix. Yes, it is slightly unnerving to finally realise that you are the one that other people are naturally drawn to. People, for whatever misguided reason seemed to spill the beans or confide in good old Robert. Tom was glad of a chair back to support himself, a little comfort, it was clear that nothing could repair for the loss of a brother. My attention was on the window as if glancing between it and Tom would somehow spread the weight or suppress the unveiling of the truth which I would soon reveal. Tom now seated put middle finger and forefinger to his temple as if the head throbbed. For a moment the tongue would not move. His eyes rested upon mine from a quizzical look at the same window. He did not have to ask, for really I knew intuitively his question.

The answer was bound in the recent knowledge, only a few hours old now. How could so much be ascertained, it was chance, pure fluke that a happening should express itself with such insight. Under the influence perhaps, but not so out of it to deny obvious logic. That was my state, suspicion, plainly an inner quarrel at first, but later the realisation. The discernment being the discovery of the perpetrator and his deplorable act. Bit by bit my slow thinking had led to the ferreting out of the circumstances. It was the calling contained within even a little drunken patience that found a particular picture to be intelligible.

The anticipated question, "…Tell me again how you think Jim died. I know it was not suicide despite the evidence, the weak evidence to suggest that it was. Could it, was it more likely an accident, Robert?"

"Perhaps your brother ought to hear what I am going to say also," I said stalling. "Where is he?"

"I am sorry about my brother ranting on about Chinese and European history. He has gone back home. I waved goodbye to him at the station before coming here."

The arcane haunted me like a danger now, too wild and ungovernable by keeping it alone. Now was the time. I had struggled with the triumph of piecing together the clues and cowardice of unloading the knowledge that would bring the inevitable shock. I had been maddened and hardened by conscious reasoning. The moment of detestable exultation had arrived. I could hear it, *murder, murder it was murder.*

"Tom, I am sorry," it escaped, the coded truth announcing between visceral heartbeats.

Tom knew and stayed motionless as if manacled to the chair. "You know much more than I do, don't you Robert." He was not declaring me as a candidate for general omniscience. Tom had recognised a hidden message in the sorrowful apology.

"Yes I know more than you Tom. I think I know, well almost all that anyone such as I could know. More here than the police anyway and that is something at least." Tom remained quiet in anticipation of the next words to be uttered. I searched for an explanation, a vocal application that would not easily inflame sensitivities or revengeful passions which still lay benign within. His stillness unnerved as if a dormant animal preparing to thrash out suddenly into a fiery fight.

Slowly on, step by step in order to be precise I determined, however, against it the primitive instinct in me felt ready to turn and run quickly in fright. With the mind unsettled I continued faltering in the reality of the dreadful. The room in a blink appeared mournful, I wanted it to disappear and the street to explode into the wandering. People to shout and the noise could echo from brick to brick. The loud cries which were never in the room died away. There was just the hum of traffic from outside and the stumbling matter of my words continuing. "The, the, I, I." He listened intently as I managed to return better the information in a measured steadiness. "The police had chased two guys, big lads, through town. That was the last time I saw Jim. I had told him what had occurred and he went off I think to see for himself. Now here in Whitches we have a drug problem. Old dealers, new dealers moving in all the time. Lots of kids with lots of money. This is an affluent area. I feel strongly now that his death was drug related. He did not do drugs. He did not deal I'm certain of it, yet I know. Jim may well have known something deadly about those guys I saw – more than I know certainly. They must be dealers. Equally he may have known nothing, but they may not have known it. Really, he got everywhere – saw everything."

His response came roaring and disbelieving. "He was just stupid, stupid! You could be wrong!"

"Could be, but I'm not. Tom, Jim wasn't stupid. Slow yes, feeble minded maybe."

"Fuck off, he was my brother."

I flinched at his loud cry, then there was silence, we shared perfectly blank faces. He did not seem to have the least desire to pursue the conversation further. "You need not speak so loudly I am not deaf," was the spoken exchange. "Nor am I blind," giving myself a cue.

A minute passed, perhaps more before Tom was recovered enough to quiz and acknowledge the appeal. "I'm sorry, Robert, how come you changed your tune? Are you telling me now that someone killed my brother?"

This hit to head and heart, I could not say it. "Listen, Tom. This isn't easy. After the funeral I called in at Edison Café. The very same guys that I mentioned were there and they were near enough for me to observe them closely. I noticed that one of them was wearing that distinctive watch. The personalised divers watch complete with initials. He had won it in the Lakes fishing competition before the motor bike thing."

"So what are you saying? They killed him because he knew something. Then stole his watch. For god's sake. They took him to the top of the bridge, took the watch, left the wallet and pushed him off?"

"Yes, exactly."

"Why should he allow himself to be taken to the viaduct?"

"They forced him, not necessarily by brute force, but with a knife, a gun – whatever. He had a broken neck. Must have been headfirst. He died at the bottom. According to the police he had no other injuries. They say he killed himself. I know different – we know different."

"Okay, say you are right, do we tell the police?"

"Tell them what, Tom? The police are bloody useless. You know that. They are apathetic, underfunded – fucking incompetent."

I gave little thought for what now was in store for us and also reluctance to congratulate myself on inspiring Tom with the information. An impressive observation of Tom and the realisation of it between us meant we were at pains still to repress the grief. There still was a rendering occurrence for Tom and me to accustom ourselves to. By our faults, revenge be it moral or not, we might lose sight of it knowingly but we had to avail ourselves of the possibility. The final remark, 'incompetent', eliminated any confusion and it was undoubtedly sold to Tom. An appropriate silence ensued. There was no dispute as to the position and no ridiculous excuses ventured in the face of the rational. We were committed to the suggestion unsaid by looking at each other in silent recognition. Momentarily perhaps we felt a mood in the ascendancy as if we were compiling a plan of action to balance the wrongdoing. If we were to suddenly make a start then the character of our conviction would be possessed with uncertainty. No, the planning required caution and forethought to ensure the desired outcome. We were not to do anything in uncalculated haste. The solution was to remain in a state of vacancy, to be supplied eventually through careful considerations. Tom looked thoughtfully now at me and seemed to have perfect understanding of the meaning. We both appeared enlightened by the unspoken as if it were an emphatic comment. The moment of awakening by words had to wait for the influence, with the action to come. We had to formulate a plan to be carried out without mistakes, otherwise either one of us could be caught up in danger. Eventually, we each would realise in our own way that we needed participation of the other and constructive ideas in a workable alliance. There was no doubt about it, I was convinced we were on the threshold of something. With the exception of however the very something to be arrested by a return of harmony.

The harmony was Kate personified, she had returned in high spirits with Diana and indeed they had been Christmas shopping. Their arrival was a very convenient advantageous circumstance, for suddenly I was moved, feeling Tom and I could temporarily dismiss the notion of entertaining revenge – or maybe even my involvement in it might just melt away gradually to nothing. I secretly hoped that the concept of retribution here might be discharged as been overly romantic and unlikely. Maybe the unusual emotions in us would subside and give way to misgivings. Perhaps the resolution of it might be best served by not pursuing it further in some sort of cowardly denial. I wondered whether we could separate our thirst for retribution from our own justice in a natural way leaving only a dim shadow to remain.

"Hi you guys, we have had a great time shopping tonight. I got the lot for Christmas – well almost everything – still one or two bits to get though – no hurry. Hey Tom, what are you doing here? How did the funeral go? Robert, we are starving. Can you go to Chico's? Pizza all around – hey Di? You stay here Tom – it is cold out – no need for you both to go. Diana has told me all about you, so come on and open this bottle of wine."

Unable to exclude things from my mind, still I remembered the vague dream. I had stood as if on a bank looking down, a spectator upon imperfect shapes but with a thorough meaning. I also remembered that murderer in the café, a disagreeable character indeed – the knowledge of him still alive an aversion to me. Mixed feelings, yes, but on the whole I distrusted myself, for now I doubted our motive for retribution as concerns would become dire consequences. Contrasting moralities were indifferent to the conclusion for I could not reconcile.

"Go on, Robert, off you go now."

With a transport of coercion I made it out alone. For once I was pleased to be the one out in the cold. The frosty pavement sparkled in the light, but I was dull inside. Kate had unwittingly handed me the opportunity to escape for a while. It was the perfect stratagem, not to be accompanied by Tom and thus not to be burdened with the immediate prospect of considering unholy revenge for his death. It was a relief too to be unburdened from the knowledge by sharing it – what I had discovered – there was to be no secrets – well perhaps a few little ones.

Tom is the walking, talking, living paradox. Despite the bashful bladder tag, he is a rambling gambling man. The proof, at the drop of a hat he moved in with Diana, Tom moved house, moved town and moved job. Diana with cheekbones and head of symmetry is completely taken by the lopsided oaf. Yes, and Tom is my new friend whom is more sophisticated than Jim. He replaces Jim, as Kate replaces Miranda. However, Kate is necessary and lovely – Tom is neither.

Chapter Thirteen

Each day ends the beginning of that very same day and this is a stark reality of time. Life goes on, first comes day upon day, then week upon week and year upon year. All of us have a marvellous capacity to forget our dead, this is how we merge the past sympathetically with the future. Perhaps the process is some sort of instinctive thing, where we constantly look forward with a guarded relish and only look back to remember out of needy necessity. People soon forget, handle guilt about feelings and they always remember in the end. Our very own small worlds take precedence over the great big wide world outside our immediate sphere. The same conception of thought lets us realise that in the big world people die all the while one after another – time upon time. Maybe it is good this way after all, it is hard to check ourselves, but losing someone occasionally is better than a constant stream of bereavements. What do any of us know really? We live on until it is our turn to die.

'Jim, hey', said his former landlord, 'who would have thought it, Jim so quiet-tempered too.' 'Exactly like a dream,' I had said it, only that was not the least bit like a dream – only a nightmare. Actually it was not a literal nightmare at all, just a suggestion or a projection alluding to one. Tom had said, 'it is beyond belief,' we all echoed that, all agreed and then eventually the subject was slowly worn away.

The mourning was wearing thin, moving towards an end or a comfortable point of acceptability. Dust had settled now, following the initial maelstrom. How easy it was to continue. I could go forward these days without thinking of Jim. Now instead the substitute, parts of every day were occupied with the thought of Tom. It was not Tom exactly, but contemplations of the scheme he would doubtless be brewing to avenge. I guess we both knew the rudiments of a plan or were acquainted with the extent of it anyway. It was only a matter of time before he would approach me. For now, he must be coming to terms with it all by trying to quell a searing destructive passion into a formulation that is a meticulous cold-blooded strategy. Tom is more of a man of mystery than I, so like a scattered picture made from scraps, he only made known his past in little pieces. He had been in the army and for all that any of us knew he could have killed. Tom had not spoken of killing; however, such experiences of extermination could prove particularly useful for carrying out the plot.

I had considered joining the navy, the air force or the army all quite recently only to discover a wonderful commiseration that I really was too old. I had resolved to resist any foolish and possibly absurd notion to join the army in the seventies when there had been an unrelenting campaign to recruit. The prospect of killing someone and getting shot at did not appeal to me as a wet behind the ears yet sensible adolescent. Now the stakes were higher, lose everything or win and gain nothing.

Kate wants me to tell her I love her. She is determined to make me say it.

"I love you."

"You only said it because I asked you to. You do not mean it. You never say it with feeling."

"I looove you."

"There is no need to be sarcastic – Pratt."

"I love you in the morning and I love you in the night. I love you in the evening when the stars are shining bright."

"Bastard – you always have to make a joke out of it."

I tell her I love her all the time at night in bed. Kate says that in bed it is just sexual, so that does not count for anything. Why do I not say 'I love you' when she brushes her hair so vainly or, 'Kate, I really do love you when you speak to me like that,' or, 'I love you when you pee with the door open so that I cannot miss a word.'

"I love you."

"You never tell me."

"I love you."

"Do you?"

"I just said so, this bastard loves you."

Kate looked impatient by seeing at first there was no way out of the cogent assertion. However, not to be outdone and by now a little tearful, whimpered, "Robert," then introduced a deliberate pause to collect herself. "Robert, love is not supposed automatically. You have to be distinct about it by telling me. I expect this of you. Keep telling me that you love me. I don't know if you don't tell me, do I?"

I was not so clever as to understand the reasoning, it seemed like backwards logic. I assume she knows that I love her; it just seems unnecessary to tell her that I love her when she already knows it. That is male logic, I suppose it is ridiculous. At a loss to be eloquent enough to reply with any form of sense to her crushing argument I could not speak at all. Kate saved any further cogitation by repeating it with tears on her eyelashes. "Love is not to be supposed." This was a prompt that rescued my voice because we began to kiss spontaneously. The little prior episode had been instantly consigned to the past like an impounded pet that bites. At the caressing of the teeth and lips I recognised, for real and for the first time that I did love Kate after all.

"Do you still love her?"

"I thought I did."

"And you love me now and all that is over." Kate was telling me what to say and that perhaps is the thing she wanted to hear. "What happened between the two of you? Why did it end?"

"The usual I suppose. It never really began. She was married – I know you know – it was never ever going to work out – she was much older." The gentle kisses continued to the noise of our mouths together before she pushed my chest slightly inwards with her soft palms. "I have to go or I will be late."

Though be it only temporary, all alone again, accustomed as I was to reading at where my life had been assigned. An important transaction had just occurred between us as if it were delicately engineered or (in contrast) entirely a profound accident. I really could not decide either way. Fate, I hoped, yes that is what it was, a 'happenstance'. They have such a word in the USA, although perhaps more frequently applied than ever necessary. As silly as the word sounds it seemed to fit into a thing that happens by chance combined with a circumstance. A pragmatic trade off perhaps, establishing the facts of the case arriving at a sort of truth by both evasive and explicit. There was a kind of deceitful honesty or mutual understanding between us. I think Kate realised the diplomatic role in my part of it which involved lying by emission – it was not telling the whole story about the affair with Miranda (even the mention of her name was absent). Moreover I could not deny or conceal the serendipitous moment which had fully exposed the realisation of it – being in love with Kate. Incredulous though it was, could a person such as I, be so entrenched in the epitome of corruption in human nature. It seemed practically inconceivable that I, endowed with so much low self-esteem could be simultaneously be in love with Miranda and Kate in equal measure. Maybe it was possible to delude oneself into loving both, yet in actuality love neither because I loved the other. Certainly, I had thought of Miranda in the early relationship with Kate. I had thought only of Kate or only of Miranda (never the consideration of them both until now). Amid these permutations selfishness was to continue from the root of these loves. It would surely be easier to retain the fruit of affections in the short term than reject them. The constant intensity of these feelings would serve to be important for my own greatness to counter the nagging poor impression of myself. Strangely the influence began to replace anxiety with a sense of arrogance manifested as wandering speculation into the near future. Ideas gave way to imaginings as a scheme to have both Miranda and Kate in an impossible fantasy.

The phone rang as if to testily interrupt an improper subject. "You have that interview at eleven thirty – thought I'd remind you. And we are having Christmas dinner at Diana's tomorrow – remember it is Christmas day tomorrow. I will be home early with a bit of luck. Good luck, I love you, kissy kiss."

Oh yes, the interview. It was not that I had forgotten, only it was the last thing on my mind – a temporary weakness in the system. Then Christmas, better not think about that until tomorrow. Diana and Tom, definitely do not even think about him until tomorrow.

What about Miranda? Miranda and our little affair? The strong brief infusion that we shared, the spicy romance and marvellous loving was all washed away on that day diluted in the heavy rain. Back then it was, now just a cherished memory and weakened by the experience of meeting Kate. Far from forgetting our agreeable arrangement, though never perfect, I took it fondly into account. Maybe it is best to try and not think about Miranda at all.

The job involves selling both spurious and genuine car parts (sales assistant) apparently. Long hours and low pay. I do not really want to work there, so I am bound to get the job. This is the way it works and anyway we need the money. 'It is not to be supposed,' I heard as my fantasy had dissolved away. Smart casual dress I thought would be fine for the interview (social worker style rather than big noise salesman). More or less anyone will do for them I suppose for they are so desperate for staff. I better not say when asked if I can do the job (best not to be a smart ass), 'well it is not quantum mechanics is it – I am very capable – able to do the job standing on my head – with one hand tied behind my back – you want to think yourself bloody lucky that I'm here at all considering the poor wages you're paying.' I got the job. It must be my charm. I was to start on the day after Boxing Day apparently, so I explained Boxing Day is on Saturday so Monday will suffice okay – they agreed. Time to celebrate. Congratulations were in order, and then perhaps on second thoughts none of that at all for this was really a mild catastrophe. Hampered a little, like sustaining an injury, was how it seemed.

The curious thing, by being so engrossed in one's own thoughts, I had walked, retraced a familiar path and all to the exclusion of observing surrounding buildings. I had failed to notice where I was going and arrived immediately at the door of the café as if I had been beamed there by Scotty. It was almost one o'clock and incredibly busy as one might expect on such a day. An hour had passed since the interview; it became apparent and alarmingly clear that I must have behaved in a nonsensical way for some time. The journey from there to here should have been just less than a ten-minute walk. Funny that!

As if to dismiss the lost time, I was suddenly consumed by a pang of hunger at the greasy laden scents emanating at the door of Edison Café. This is undoubtedly a place to be when the constitution requires warm nourishment. The brain must have been assembling a picture supplied by the aroma. I recalled the lasagne which so filled a gap previously and felt quite confounded by this grotesque attraction to food which seemed to saturate the whole body. Duly captivated I entered the crowded café to indulge, to eat heartily and the excuse offered for gluttony was obviously the new job. It was so unusual for me to allow the voice of the stomach to directly influence the act of living from one moment to the next in such a peculiar way.

There was not one empty table for any newcomer to sit at, only a limited number of solitary chairs which had the inconvenience of been uncomfortably close to a person, any person. On another day I may have surveyed the situation using a selective eye and promptly left to find a more appropriate place with space. On this day I asked the man seated opposite my standing position, 'if by chance anyone was sitting at the chair before him.'

He had a well-polished bald head that reflected light intriguingly. His bristled moustache defied belief, particularly as cod, chips and mushy peas disappeared below it as if on a conveyer belt. The shiny pink cheeks were overwhelmed by stick out prawn eyes. Between mouthfuls the lips took the form of an expanded grin not unlike that of Jack Nicholson. The chin was very double and I wondered how one could conceivably shave inside the crease. He was little and wide or perhaps big, short and wide. Seemingly he was poured into his brown suit so tight. The man was sat but I imagined his legs to be thick and extraordinarily bowed designed especially for carrying potatoes. Like an appendage the afters were before him which appeared to be treacle sponge pudding and custard. I found the possibility of that combination (fish and custard) distasteful, even nauseating and thus had a sudden loss of appetite. My meal was instantly restricted to coffee, a wizardry livener perhaps to explain those movements of the escaped time.

Very determined I was to give hidden memory a chance to recollect those missing minutes, I closed my eyes to unlock my mind. There was only an elongated nothing, so I opened them again, seeing before me the chewing face of the stout gentleman. Perhaps amid the café hustle and bustle he had found this strange behaviour entertaining. Certainly, interest was caught as his eyes blinked and chins twitched. The pinkness upon his face now gleamed like his head, ill defined, excited, suspicious and something else.

I had inadvertently given him cause to be curious. His unusual glow unnerved, so therefore I refrained from the notion of producing anything from incantation or otherwise. My eyes were kept open without as much as a blink. It was a relief that he did not speak, but I remained tormented by the persistent mastication and gaze. After a lapse of many seconds which seemed like an immense time, his eyes surveyed more. The looking was ever more mysterious, and I was quite sure nothing could be gleaned from behind the prawn pupils. Beneath the table a wave of kelp and hand of cod grasped my knee like a lobster. Then the man spoke in a higher voice than anticipated. "I am glad you came. I have stodgy pudding here or do you prefer an even sweeter dessert, such as…?" I did not wait for a full stop, with modesty completely at an end there and accounting for the obvious difference in visage the liquid meal was promptly terminated.

I headed quickly to the doorway before the bald-headed man attained full height. While passing out at the exit, my hand remained upon the handle with door ajar, while stood irresolutely for a moment. The reason, a surge of humiliation and hint of defeat. The solution, to dispense of the bristling feeling by returning swiftly to kick him good and sharp upon the nose. The instant resolution was not realised as I became flushed again with common sense from experience. It was not easy to walk away because the only consolation was to save embarrassment. Spurning him with my heel seemed little punishment compared to a punitive toe in the face.

The incident is probably best recalled as an inconsequent jotting to be rubbed away as soon as one developed the means to forget it. A good strategy is to fill the head with other 'stuff' which should be of no obvious value. Load the mind with rubbish or pathetically useless trivia, such the process of memorising the kings and queens of England or prime ministers. This uses up lots of space. Doing this is not easy because you have to consolidate the process then recall with the efficiency approaching that of a computer. One might ask the question – why do we learn all this 'stuff' at all when as intelligent beings all we need to do is record it, then retrieve it using a computer, books or just simply a humble pen and paper? The brain, apparently we only use a fraction of it and somehow all the surplus capacity is laid to waste because in our advanced humility we have not learned to use it yet. The actual reason as to why not is debatable, but could it be because we are wasting time memorising the kings and queens of England. Maybe we ought to invest more in each other. Yes, you guessed it, relationships, oh yes and other things. Things…. I wonder if at the foundation, the nature of it is higher abstract thinking perhaps – 'big stuff' and 'bigger stuff' not even conceived of yet. And because we have not understood 'big stuff' as yet, then this could be 'super abstract' beyond our perception like a fourth dimension.

Afternoon light was gradually disappearing while starting homeward. Before me a bright ribbon of coloured electric lights exaggerated the onset of evening as I picked a way through late Christmas shoppers. The frequency of Christmas trees and associated decorations had become a commonplace blur now. The murmuring tide of people hurled themselves at numerous vendors who were still selling gifts for Christmas before it was too late. Then there was no need to rattle and chop anymore, with shoppers at my back. Soon the coming away was good and quiet. The distance home materially lessened as my stride gained more at the prospect of home (our home together now).

Kate had not yet arrived, she was probably still detained at the tipsy festive lunch. The day outside was solemn, legible by the smoky clouds written upon the sky against a page of darkening grey. I was keen to tell her of the new job and relate the unexpectedly interesting personage to our news so that I could begin to forget it. The question of the missing minutes was of particular concern and I decided to tell no one of it. I presumed, however, that although 'it' or the 'gap' was so mysterious, an explanation would be eventually forthcoming.

With feet elevated upon the sofa and armed with a mug of coffee I was determined to unravel 'it.' The scene was set, room in shadows, curtains not drawn and only the light from the street. The matter of the 'gap' asserted itself as a form of excited phenomena. All the circumstance of the dark, relative silence and relaxing ease seemed to work. It was a method I did not comprehend, but it transpired that a symptom of the process was assembling pictures in the imagination. Perhaps another piece of brain was been used that seldom had exercise. Sparks fizzing around an otherwise empty head, that was it, may be using a few extra areas of that grey jelly. Paradoxically it seemed unimaginative; one can usually divert the course of a dream to some extent by imposing a positive or negative imagination upon it, in this case, however, the visions ran away with me. The only control I had was to simply stop the sequence by opening eyes to see the ordinary world once again, doing this dispersed all the images of the pattern back to the dark room with only an after taste of them remaining.

The content did not relate directly to any type of literal possibility that could be explained. No familiar landmarks or distinguishing objects could be seen or applied to give tangible meaning. The sequence did not fit the 'gap' as a key might unlock a door. However, I think I knew instinctively that it was the 'gap' which was responsible for the sequence.

The beats of my heart could be easily counted while eyes were open. The beating was then overtaken on the closing eyes by a presentation of a shaky vision as if transmitted from a wobbly camera. There was a start stop start element to it, moving slowly then quickly, both to high and then to low resolution. There was an obscure impression of light giving an almost monochrome vista conveying the onset of a storm. At first the picture presented itself fading in as what could have been fields and hedges. The vagueness of it was further tainted by intermittent scratches of diagonal lines that were possibly light rain. On this very first bleak stage no figure could be seen. Then, in the distance, a bobbing dark grey figure appeared. It began as a stationary object and then a moment more, it was realised to be a blurry small shape of a man. The shape was running, then clambering over what could have been hedges, while all the time stopping for a few seconds to eagerly look back. At this point I instantly opened my eyes to feel my heart pounding within. Everything in the room was as it had been before. Little by little heartbeats returned to their normal pace. I breathed deliberately slowly to try and relax.

With the need to know more I closed my eyes once again to see the frame return and the same figure. The man continued forward. The nearer he came, the more anxious he appeared to be. The closer he came, the more terribly frightened he looked. His stride progressively became slower as each successive obstacle caused him more difficulty than the last. His face could not be distinguished being all one shade of grey. I could not determine anything about him except the obvious exhaustion for he was clearly reaching the end of his strength. At the last hedge (nearest to my view) he approached half climbing, half throwing himself over it and collapsed into a heap once beyond it. The figure managed to adopt a final position that appeared to be of painful crouching which throbbed in wait and anxiety fearful of a possible pursuer. Then the picture went blank as if part of a reel of aged celluloid had melted and therefore may be some minutes would elapse before resumption.

Now on seeing the room again my heart seemed to be beating normally and as I placed a hand to chest this was confirmed. It was cooler now and the sound of the clock was reassuring once again, though its hands could not be seen clearly in the twilight. I breathed a sigh of temporary relief and looked about retracing familiar objects that still gave an impression of convention, all in their usual places. There was no reason whatever or particular cause to fear the figure jumping out from the scene to disturb the furniture. The logical reassurance enabled a continuation of the process.

The last frame had now become the first of more, only the further images became ever startling. Fading in from the top of the panorama could be seen a progressively darkening figure which zigzagged then juddered to and fro. Then swift movements sideways again, then forwards and backwards gave this new figure a pulsing irregularity. All the while the first figure remained frozen in the foreground, hidden to the new figure by the final hedge. It became apparent from the twitching changes of the new black figure that it was searching for the first. No discernible shape could be identified from within the blurred changing motion of the figure. Ill-defined it was, terrifying, the transit suggested it was intent on killing, exulting hate with a thirst to destroy life. Rapidly the distance reduced between the two. Soon the moment came when the black figure was almost upon the grey. Now at close quarters the black pursuer was recognisable as a man, yet nothing as to his identity could be made separable from another. Two men, the grey tormented by the black. Suddenly the grey rose from hiding with arms raised in defence from the hovering black. Then the black figure was taken hastily backwards in surprise and in that very movement his face was revealed to be that of someone not unlike Tom. Instantly, I sprung up while finding clothes drenched in a sweat and myself entirely bound in a resolution to keep eyes open, unwilling to see more.

I was bewildered, terrified and then intensely fraught by hard breathing. The feeling of horror was so extreme to physically freeze. The sight so close at hand, still vividly remembered and mentally profound. After a frozen interval, the electric light had to go on to break the darkness and eventually bring back a restoration to dignified composure. That bulb now had a stronger latent expression about it which was influenced by the switching moment as if spoken and then shouted, 'Tom, Tom it was Tom.'

I sought to reassure myself. This was home now, it had to be. I was intimate with the wallpaper, spherical things that could have been floating were gently printed on the bright white background. Pastel shades, green, lilac, yellow and pink were all drifting bubbles unequal in size. Back to normal again, yet all this, despite the staring contemplations at the full feature memory still close. Kate had tinselled the walls with decorous calculation to harmonise Christmas and home. I really did love her for it and I was unafraid now because of it. The curtains should not be drawn yet, streetlights were shining in as a comforting reminder of the world outside mine. Peaceful stars beyond and my friend the moon made good too.

The passing seconds turned into minutes and the evening grew darker. Status quo had returned. I was calm and relaxed now. Though not timid for completion of the scene, this was easier said than done, for I was all alone there, yet the moment had to be it. More curious and not scared at all as these eager eyes closed once more. To see and to know, was more important than being afraid. The picture presented as the very same scene without either figure there. The simplistic hedges and fields were as they were, only no rain at all this time. Clearer was the view now and greater was the contrast. The hedges were featureless, but undulating to the contours of the land and as bold as jet. The fields were a fuzzy grey and suggestive enough to have a sparse covering of vegetation. No figure though yet, just again a static scene of fields and the very black hedges dividing it. Looking with eyes closed was as if gazing through a solitary window into a black and white film of years ago. It was not to the past, but to the future. Not miles and miles away either. No, it was near here as close as yesterday or tomorrow, I thought abstractedly that both were absent, but instead were as one. I felt the night and the day together merged like an alloy. Without absolute focus, a representation of a human body appeared ahead, it moved enough to make out slow moving steps downward through the scene. The figure became observable as a man casually walking forward and negotiating each hedge in turn. The scene was hushed as I listened while looking on. I realised the figure to be myself in some future state, slowly walking around on a voyage to a place where my destination lay. The scene contrasted markedly to the former. Now it was a plodding picture easily reflected upon from minute to minute. The images must have meaning. The challenge was to apply a kind of thought to interpret and arrive at a reasonable endpoint of sense. Something precious was to be found in the meaning, for now it was to remain indistinct and seemed unattainable.

Chapter Fourteen

Under current circumstances and also because it is Christmas day this might seem to be a strange thing of concern. Apparently, the overuse of that very word. I say the word a lot and use it even more frequently while thinking. It is usually unnecessary to include this extra word, that same superfluous word and then at other times it is important to use it. All the time almost, using 'apparently' with more frequency than is sensibly required seems ridiculous. Apparently, lots and lots of 'apparently' used so often has become a habit. Apparently I am good at sex, well at least Kate says so. Who am I to argue?

"Last night in bed was fantastic and you felt really big inside me," apparently.

All the practice which we have had lately, variety and development of technique is not necessarily the definitive explanation or indeed the larger chunk of the reason. Maybe it is something to do with the long period of abstinence coming to an end recently on my part. Well actually (not apparently), the absolute secret revealed as a man of the world, the important part of sexual prowess is mainly down to foreplay. The three 'f's; foreplay, foreplay and foreplay. It has to seem like hours and hours of it. Most men, by the time they reach their thirties know the importance of foreplay. You can read about it in books and have the experience, but there is no substitute for every unique moment of making love. If you love someone, foreplay should be continually renewed and consolidated. A combination of planned desire, spontaneity, lust and responsiveness are apparently the main parts of foreplay according to big Robert. Yes, and the emotion – Kate says sometimes during orgasm she sees pictures. Apparently last night it was coach and horses rolling through the countryside in olden times. I wonder if she was thinking of Darcy in overly tight jodhpurs rather than Robert inside in bed. I worry that Kate thinks I am thinking of Miranda rather than Kate.

It feels like a Sunday morning, we cannot hear any traffic from outside. From where we are it seems as though the whole world except ourselves has gone to sleep. We sit up in bed and exchange our Christmas presents. Mine is wrapped expertly in holly berry red paper with crinkly icicles and giant snowflakes. I had encased the ring box with thick silver paper using clumsy fingers into a shape defying irregular ball. The watch which she gave had a splashy looking face without anything ostentatious, exactly to my taste. Really it was just another watch to replace the old one, whatever it had been I would cherish it for it was chosen and given by Kate. 'Just what I wanted, it is lovely,' we echoed to each other. The ring was a tasteful display of a diamond and sapphires. It was obviously much more than I could afford, but I may well have spent hundreds more because I loved her.

Her charming eyes were nailed upon mine as if she had been won over body and soul. I was devoted as before, yielding and reined up in a similar attendance. Kate smiled a satisfactory air, comfortable of mind and easy of manner. Here she was affable and luxurious as a woman could be. I basked in it. We coiled together snugly. Her toes scratched my shins. Knees, hard and knobbly were a humorous velvet touch. We could have held it all together, just there until spring, applied ourselves to each other and the divan. In this delicious space, the warmest ever at Christmas, we were giants in leisure. With the fondest of imagination, the rustling of sheets and shuffling of feet was a magic place in a story. I wanted to dig right down into the floor beneath us, placing posts just there and with staples attach barbed wire. Capture ourselves in wire so we could not run away.

"I don't want to get up."

"I don't want to get up either."

"Me neither."

Kate got out of bed first, this was only fair because she is younger with a superior body to mine. Kate likes to be watched and be lusted after. I like to watch and lust after. She knows it and loves it. I wonder if it is normal to be so gorgeous and know it and show it. She walks around naked in a one-minute detour to the bathroom. Her spine looks perfect, a wonderful curve to her bottom, how could Kate possibly ever have backache.

We are both out of bed eventually, but I only leave it when hearing the shower switch off. She returns to the bedroom wearing only a pure white dressing gown which she is so fond of. Her head is tied about the hair by a faded pink towel in a wondrous arrangement in a wrap beyond the skills of any man. The breakfast is light, just toast and coffee. The conversation relaxed, just her and me.

Nowhere to dash off to so quickly today. It could be Sunday morning, only it is not and the pealing bells are absent. Christmas day is only a short day – good! If you are not a child or do not have children, then Christmas day feels like a Sunday. Christmas is not white either, it is grey or just

161

dark. We have the house lights on to brighten the day, but these half extinguish the day, while the day extinguishes the lights. Gloominess prevails on Christmas day.

Festive as usual, Kate conjures seemingly from nowhere three broad but squat candles of indeterminate uniform colour. Neither red nor wax of gold but somewhere betwixt. That miscellaneous drawer, a wonder forever still, Kate's bits and pieces are in there – all such wonderful things. With lights off, Kate strategically placed all three candles here and there. When lit in an enthusiastic skip, the candle flames and the image of the candle flames upon the dark grey window pane make it just like Christmas after all. The candles flickered of their own accord, the flame twisted then righted itself again and again as we moved around the room.

Mulled wine perhaps or even mince pies, it was a seasonal dreamy scent which pervaded from the candles. "Oh how very festive my dear," we joked with an old-world slant of Christmas past. My lap was a table for her ankles and feet as we lounged candlelit upon the sofa. The television was on now too which sort of spoiled the atmosphere. The program, however, put an edge on Christmas. There was little choice, lots of cartoons, 'Lassie' or sickly children receiving Christmas presents in hospital. The presenter from the hospital kept going for the emotional hit and kept repeating the notion of this time of year being the time for families to get together.

I said, "Tell me about your mother and father?"

"There is nothing to tell. They are dead, that's all. Tell me about yours?"

"They are dead too. I do not want to talk about them if you don't talk about yours."

"Okay," replied Kate in a singing voice of almost victory.

"You are too young to have dead parents," I said, half-joking and disbelieving.

"My parents were old parents. What about yours?"

"Oh mine must have been even older than yours. What about your brother and sister? Tell me about them?"

"I don't see them. I don't talk to them. It's just me and you, everyone else can fuck off."

"Come on Kate, it's Christmas, couldn't you phone them or something. You haven't got one card from a relative."

"Neither have you."

"Yeh, but they don't know where I live and I don't send cards anyway."

"Exactly."

"A girl without hair of about five years of age opened a parcel covered in silver paper to reveal a large doll and I tried to stem my emotion."

"Do girls still get dolls for Christmas then, Robert?"

"Apparently," and overcome I said, "perhaps we could have a baby."

"I think we should turn this off if this is the sort of thing you are going to talk about." She prodded my groin with a playful foot. "I'm too young to have a baby and what about my poor back? Nine months before and nine months plus after."

"You are not too young, you are just about right at your baby producing peak."

"Forget it, I am not thirty yet. There is plenty of time for me yet."

"You may not be thirty yet, but I'm past it."

"Robert you are not past it. You will be shooting sperm right into your seventies."

"No, I mean past thirty, narna. Just come off the pill and see what happens."

"Yes, we know what happens; I get pregnant. How do you know I'm on it? Typical man leaving all that stuff to the woman. How do you know there isn't anything wrong with your sperm? Maybe your sperm is not normal."

"Normal, I hope it's better than normal. Don't you want to have children?"

"Yes, but not yet. I have only known you five minutes. What's the matter with you? Anything could happen, it's too early."

"What if Diana gets pregnant?"

"Robert, god forbid, Diana will have an abortion. Anyway how can she get pregnant? Tom cannot even piss!"

"How do you know that?"

"God you're so naïve. Diana told me of course. Do you boys ever realise that we girls cannot keep a secret? Women talk more to each other than to their partners. Why do you think women are smarter than you and men are a laughing stock? It's because women talk to each other. All men talk about, to each other, between grunts is football and women."

"Does she know what a big lad I am?"

"Robert, I am not going to tell her that am I? Anyway you are not a big lad; you just think you are."

"You said it felt big inside."

"That isn't the same; it's not what you got it's the way that you do it, and that's what gets results," breaking into song.

"So are you saying I'm not a big lad?"

Laughing she replied, "You'll do. How many erect cocks have you seen, apart from your own everyday?"

163

"None."

Still laughing, "Well, that's a relief. You should measure it."

"You can measure it if you like."

"It's okay, that won't be necessary, really. It is enough to know what I know."

As if to bring an end to the subject, the man in the hospital said, "There is more to Christmas than 'The Snowman' and Rudolf the red nosed reindeer." It was a visible and audible sign to take note of, outwardly conveyed then taken inwardly as a spiritual clutch. Nothing more to be said, the conflation of his words and Kate's seemed to be full of meaning. Thus this juncture appeared mildly satisfactory, yet I looked at her for something more. Kate added nothing to it, her reply was a bridling smile. I just sat entranced in its contemplation. This disposition was short lived as the phone rang and broke it.

The thoughts were abandoned with the interruption, it was Diana to say we could go over as soon as we wished, only she kept Kate talking for a long time. Meanwhile I was left yawning and cast my eyes around with a renewed ascertain. The vivid images which I had some way conjured up yesterday in the very same space seemed somehow supernatural now. Then and now were like unrelated worlds. It was her place still. A bookshelf, her own, books slumped sideways or laid flat. They were all fiction, looked new and not read. No photographs anywhere but lots of small mirrors scattered about with evidence of make-up upon them. The kitchen even had a wall mirror. Cupboards reached the ceiling, they were over and over painted the colour of magnolia. Inside they were crammed with numerous plastic boxes with ill-fitting lids just chucked in at the side. Cereal in polythene bags and condiments were stored in the same space. Pasta, rice, teabags and various paint emulsions were easily accessible from the same shelf. A drawer also thickly coated with convenient magnolia housed every conceivable kitchen utensil. Another drawer kept cutlery which had been thrown in without any consideration for easy selection. A large cupboard on the floor the size of a washing machine, kept seldom used saucepans by the side of tinned food. Nothing especially unusual about any of it, except that it all seemed alien because I had never had a kitchen and lounge to share since childhood.

Kate set a cup of coffee in front of me. "Diana says we should go over there now. What do you think?"

"Isn't it a little early?"

"Have you got the presies sorted and the wine?"

"Should I wear this stupid sweater?"

"Do I look too tarty in this dress and does my bum look big in it?"

164

"You look absolutely wonderful in it. You have the perfect figure and it shows off your legs."

"Do you think I should wear the blue one instead, it's plainer, more conservative, and less tarty?"

"You look good in anything."

Over an hour later, we were on our way. It was afternoon, mild and the path in front slightly at an incline. Her hand felt soft and small in mine as we walked each with a carrier bag in our other hand. The rows of houses watched us, all those trees in the windows with coloured bulbs for eyes split like tiny stars looking out. It was unusually quiet for midday. There just softened in the stillness was a murmur of the distant main road. A group of people, that is all, not us but a proper family strung out along the pavement. Grandma and granddad in front then mum and dad while at the back were daughter and son on their new bicycles. On reaching the street corner we swerved a kicked football which was quickly followed by three boys all wearing new kit. We talked only a little, one subject, prominent though was the anticipation of the meal ahead for our stomachs felt empty.

A black dog wagged its tail and crossed the road towards us before following. It had body and tail like a Labrador with legs of a corgi. "Maybe it knows something we don't," said Kate prophetically.

"I think it likes your perfume," the dog attended close while panting and looking expectant. "Maybe if we run a little we could lose it," I said optimistically.

"If we go any faster, I will lose it, my breath that is. I think we better stop," Kate concluded. We came to a halt and Kate wheeled around to stamp a foot. The dog faltered and stopped only to begin wagging its tail again. I made a pretence of rushing at it which had the unnerving force of causing it to cower. I felt guilty and took up her hand again in a masterful hold. As we progressed forward quickly, the dog appeared to lose heart and gave up allowing itself a sympathetic whine.

We jingled in at Diana's. Tom had a brace of full wine glasses in his hands for us as we arrived and he wished Kate and me a happy Christmas. Then on meeting his eyes, I saw, rather him actually saying it, 'I want a word with you.' Diana's glass was recharged as she dispatched the perfectly cooked roast potatoes into the microwave oven for convenient storage before lunch. Kate talked as the perfect guest always does, observing all the niceties of a top socialite and involving all of us.

Tom had an awful purpose beneath his own silly sweater that caused fearfulness in me, enough to be a mortal dread. The very slight intonation of his voice was laced sufficiently to make me tremble at the possible idea of killing someone. Although I was charming, placid and mild on the surface, beneath I suffered terrible twinges of conscience. With the affectedness of the knowledge I almost took on a desperate determination to run away. I only stayed by resolution of honourable commitment and the foolishness that would be attached to the notion of possibly deserting them.

Despite the initial clandestine announcement from Tom, I managed to keep up appearances nevertheless. It was done terribly well at first and I hardly used the protective presence of Diana and Kate. For an hour or two before lunch the conversation was handled impeccably by all of us. All four, being very careful as not to mention Jim, his funeral nor the conclusion as to his death. We seemed to lull ourselves quite gently into mild festive oblivion and contrary merriment. I took the situation to be an advantage of obvious fortification against Tom's impending approaches.

Amongst other things, Kate much more than a lover now, she was a wonderful social resource. Although our party just consisted we two couples, Kate proved over again that she had great social qualifications. I felt humbled in comparison, with guilt too as I subtly used her congenial personality to deflect attention and shield me from my own conscience.

Throughout the turkey dinner, my input to the conversation was minimal, yet behind my contracting brow the meditations were large. Perhaps I kept my face in perfect control while listening to the chatter. The expression had a smile, then no smile as I mulled over the knowledge of what Tom and I were harbouring (the condemning secret from Diana and Kate). While pondering more intently, then moving fork to mouth, I fell into a strong and grim profounder silence. Then still practising a smile and eating simultaneously I was brought to order by Kate. "Didn't he, Robert?" Now awakened from a relapse I nodded and with a wrinkle kept smiling on.

It was Tom's turn to talk, he had taken some derisory comments from us all with regard to how he was dressed. He pointed out with uncharacteristic stiffness that, "The sweater did look a bit ludicrous after all." He was right when he said, "It's informal and it is Christmas anyway, so what?" As friends we conceded, yet expressed a sense of difference. Any form of misconstruction in our banter was either flattering or had the good propensity to be unaccountable. It was of course Christmas and therefore it should be good will to all etcetera. It seemed so very necessary to emphasise this point at every opportunity.

Kate looked at me with a slight inclination of the head as Tom carried on speaking. There was an unspoken recognition of each other as her eye rested on me for a moment. In one instant it was a searching glance of suspicion. It seemed too, as if she had observed my unusual manner sooner. A secret look had given something away, she realised that I was actually more uncomfortable than I normally would be. When Tom's words had finished for the moment, Kate politely interrupted and said, "Are you all right, darling?" It was not really a question of concern, but more one of her distrust and the enquiry of course was not without foundation.

"Yes, of course, dear. It seems to have become hot suddenly. I think it must because of this big meal."

"Yes, you are right, Robert," said Diana, unwittingly coming to my rescue. "Open a window, will you, Tom." Tom obediently opened the window with haste and then at the table again recharged our wine glasses without a word. In turn, I then gave Kate an approving survey through my replenished glass as if to rub out the moment. She was looking sharp after me, yet with no real reason to complain, so said nothing and returned to the current conversation which was still the likely subject of Christmas.

The final straw which left us bloated was the eating of the plum pudding. We then arranged ourselves about the furniture in respective couples like swollen pythons. Kate thanked Diana for such a wonderful meal and Tom conveniently fell asleep. We were keen enough to laze away the short day. Diana remarked that the hours of daylight were actually becoming longer and I was pleased at this for the darkness of winter made one prone to be depressed. The ladies were well settled each snuggled to their partner, equipped with plenty of wine and before the television watching *Eastenders*. Once again my lap had become a comfortable resting place for Kate's luscious legs. I managed though, in this circumstance, to quell the carnal instinct. While Diana and Kate were gripped by the television, I dismissed the soap and reflected upon the weird happenings of the previous day.

It is strange how sometimes the influence of alcohol on the person not only clouds the process of clear thinking but also produces an alternative take on reality. This was just one of those times when the slightly changed perception produced by wine had made a definite difference. Alcohol seemed to break down barriers which I had obviously placed unconsciously to shield myself somehow from the anticipated intent of murder; not by me, but by Tom. However, if Tom were to murder the killer of Jim I would doubtless be an accomplice to that very murder. Only I could identify Jim's killer. Simply, if I did not cooperate with Tom and his plan then he could not commit that murder. If I did lead Tom to Jim's killer and then Tom killed the killer, I would have blood on my hands. I hated the fact that his killer had got away with it. I hated the real possibility of Tom acting out an exacting revenge.

As Tom was now asleep, the girls were tuned into *Eastenders*, I took on the responsibility of refilling the glasses. The pouring was done in silence, only the television and the noise of the liquid disturbed the thinking. I remembered all the peculiar events of yesterday and looked deeply to their meaning. I ventured that there could possibly be a third way. An alternative to break the dilemma and bring about a possible solution. I had convinced myself that the missing time of yesterday was accounted for somehow by the source of the strange visions. What if, these were just visual ideas that used up minutes thus in themselves being responsible for missing time? Or neither of these were the case, the two were not at all linked and part or all of it was relevant to the solution.

I was pretty sure now that the visions were a metaphor, in part like and unlike a dream. Also literal, in as much as the killer was being pursued by Tom and Tom was pursued by me. Maybe the visions were merely an expression of a possible solution which I had already and unconsciously begun working upon. There was of course, the matter of the vivid dream which seemed much like a remnant now. In that dream it was Tom who I thought I saw making that journey and then hiding away in wait for the arrival of Jim's murderer.

Diana and Kate clung at their soap opera as if to a honey sticky heart. I opened another bottle of chardonnay and shared the contents accordingly. Tom still slept a noiseless sleep. I knew him well enough by now to predict his advance. He would seize the first opportunity to speak to me alone. There would be no beating about the bush. He would cut straight to the chase, as they say in the movies these days. No small talk or subtlety, it would be up front and no nonsense. 'Robert,' he would say, 'you are right. My brother was murdered. We are not going to the police, because they are, as you say useless. You are going to find the guy. It will not be difficult. Tell me who he is and I am going to kill him. No messing about.' The distinct possibility to me soon and the combination of the wine became an obvious fillip. The incentive to recall the content of yesterday's 'gap' was quite enough. The stimulus worked perfectly as I began to recollect the detail. The time space continuum in question was the nature and content of the period between leaving the interview and finding myself at the door of Edison Café. It seems that I took a detour of purpose, arrived at the library and set about finding a solution. The problem was the solution, to find a third way. I probably did not know what I was doing, only that I was driven somehow by an unseen force.

As if guided by another hand I came upon a book which had been left on its own on one of the many tables. The large book had a hard cover, was deep with many pages which were crisp, glossy and smelled of new banknotes. It was heavy, looked to be cut into a perfect wedge as if it had never been opened. The title, 'Psychology, The Science of Mind and Behaviour'. I flicked through the pages. If you open any book at random to reveal a particular page, it is not unusual to find that place exposed to be a well-used one. A picture, photograph, particular passage or even just a juicy sentence might easily be revealed to the reader, simply because in a previous viewing of that same book a page had been opened at a point of interest. In this case the book fell open, despite the extreme newness and the previous flicking. On the very page, there to guide me and declare the third way. Weird, uncanny, beyond understanding, it did not seem to matter for there it was before my eyes.

Persuasive communication, by all means not a foreign concept, but the art of being smooth tongued to good effect is something that evades the majority of us. Indeed, why should we waste our time being persuasive when we have our own lives to live? A parent naturally teaches a child and often uses persuasive strategies. However, seldom does an adult persuade another to bring about a change in attitude. Persuasive techniques are used extensively in sales, some religions and politics. They are seldom used effectively otherwise, because life is just not worth the effort and the incentive is just not worth the investment. It would be nice to have a device that on the flick of a switch could change a persons attitude for the better. The 'persuasive machine' would doubtless sell well, but such a device is fanciful notion.

The book identified four major factors involved in persuasive communication. The implication was that no matter how skilful or persuasive a person could be it did not mean they could miraculously bring about change in the views of another. I was clearly up against difficulties if I were to change Tom's attitude.

The first factor to be identified was the source. I was the source, essentially my role was to convince Tom that to kill Jim's murderer was not a good idea and plainly wrong. I had to appear to have status and credibility. I had already convinced Tom by evaluation of the evidence in the case of Jim as to the more likely conclusion and the fortunate consequence of this had elevated my status above that of the police. I really needed to appear more attractive too, for this is seen to be more persuasive than an unattractive source. This is why so many politicians strive to adopt personal appeal to entice voters by the process of creating a media style. Tom may adopt a contrary view to that being advocated if I was seen to be unattractive or not liked. It is important therefore that I am seen as being presentable at least by adopting a pleasant manner perhaps by being humorous and charming. It is important for Tom to know that I do not have any ulterior motive, so I have to be genuine and sincere. Non-verbal behaviour is also important to consider for attitude change, over familiarity, or conversely being too distant are seen as negatives, I have to find a happy medium.

The message is probably the most important factor, so it is absolutely imperative to get this part right. Surprisingly delivering the message with confidence has been shown to be over and above more significant as an influence for attitude change than the content in some cases. Also, the non-verbal aspects are just as much a part of the source as the message. So when I try to argue (in the softest sense of the word) that killing someone is not a good idea, I have to do it convincingly with a confident delivery whilst being aware of non-verbal influences. There are other things to consider within the message, such as the explicit and implicit. This simply means, should the argument be spelled out to Tom or not and which of the two is more effective? Should Tom be virtually given a conclusion (explicit) or left to work it out (implicit)? It has been found that generally implicit messages are more effective. So in this case it is best not to tell Tom that murder is fundamentally and morally wrong. He should be left to work it out for himself. The level of emotional appeal is important, it is claimed that people can be frightened into changing their minds. It has been shown that attitude change is highest when moderate fear is applied and lowest when very low fear or very high fear is applied. So it is maybe best not to play the fear card with regard to the consequences if found out for murder. While attending to the message it is important to consider whether to pursue a one-sided argument or a two-sided argument. Better educated people are more influenced by two-sided arguments, so by bringing the pros and cons to the fore would perhaps make it easier to sway Tom towards my argument given that mine is a better alternative.

The third factor of persuasive communication identifies the recipient (Tom) as an individual, who has concerned himself with his very own specific motives which are both conscious and unconscious. His motives are governed by functions of attitudes, these provide a ready basis for interpreting the world, processing new information and also a way of gaining and maintaining social identification. This apparently forms part of the reason for Tom's decision to kill the murderer. Functions of attitudes operate at different levels in different people which make incorporating counter measures in persuasive communication difficult. Formulating a counter argument, no matter how convincing can be contradictory, because when counter arguments are available, this is when the recipient's resistance to persuasion is strongest. Also, the greater the gulf between the view held and the opposing view, then there is less likelihood for change. Of course Tom is unique with his very own level of persuade ability. It was not going to be easy to change his mind. Let us not forget the final factor which is situational context, where the consensus here is generally that informal approaches are more successful than formal ones. That is all right then because any conversation between Tom and I just had to be informal.

Eastenders had come to an end and the television still on hosted the enchanting *Wizard of Oz*. Follow the yellow brick road, follow the yellow brick road. None of us watched and no one had the inclination to switch over or turn it off. Tom woke up just as Dorothy was given the ruby slippers, Diana gave him a look of disapproval. Quite enthusiastically Diana and Kate decided to clear the dinner things. "You boys can watch *The Wizard of Oz*. It is quite all right," said Kate both whimsical and condescending. The girls confined themselves contentedly to work and chatter.

At last here was the moment I had been dreading. Tom and I were left alone and he was galvanised back to life with even more wine. "Robert," he said.

"Yes, comrade."

"Robert, there is no easy way to say this. I want to kill the guy who killed Jim. Show me who he is and I will kill him."

171

Chapter Fifteen

For some days my head had run high on a painful theme, it was not a euphoric or sharp feeling, but one of profound uneasiness. Tom had visited to talk again following our first discussion of the matter on Christmas day. There was nothing mysterious in the encounter, apart from the content which was confidential of course to ourselves; however, he had adopted a manner which was becoming ever more sinister. The confidence which he had assumed between him and me on the subject left me especially worried. I believed I was vulnerable, there was little he was not capable of, given the incentive. His newfound assertiveness seemed to envelope me like a mildly restraining power of authority. It was as if there were no means of repelling it except to refuse completely and the obvious consequence of that would be to sever our friendship. In all honesty I really only had Kate and Tom now.

There was just one that I could sensibly seek advice from and indeed another single person alone I should complain to – Kate and Tom respectively. Neither option seemed practicable. It was as if an inevitable brace was gradually winding around me and the only way to extricate myself from it without causing damage would require more art than I was capable of. The knowledge which Tom had come to know, being that I actually had a hidden need to avenge Jim's death, was an insidious part of the theme which left me further troubled. Despite all the best efforts inspired by the psychology that was found so imaginatively at the library, I had failed to convince Tom not to formulate a plan to kill the murderer.

Tom's assertive conduct had become particularly uncomfortable and I considered my awkwardness around him to be more than just a disconcerting fascination. I wondered why I went along with his scheme at all when I knew it was fundamentally wrong, we could get caught or even worse be killed. I thought about his voice and his whole manner together – it had changed markedly since our first meeting. I ventured to think that his character was askew, just temporarily altered perhaps, until the deed was carried out to the end. I surmised that only at that point would Tom return to his former self, but of course he may not be able to if unhinged by horror of the deed completed.

Tom was strange in these days, always smiling and serene. On the surface there was no dislike or animosity shown about a thing. No, it was all hidden behind a covert frown or a vague impression which reduced his human faculties as if possessed by some cold devil. I wondered if part of crime is an expression of rage against humiliation. I have to admit to recognising something obscenely sensational when considering Tom's motive to commit murder. He is absorbed emotionally against morality and I wonder at the causal process which is spirited chaos wrapped in the apprehension of vengeance. I think about shoplifters and vandals who delight in their own deviance; the process of committing these crimes is so exciting like running the gauntlet by risking utter shame at their arrest. The young men who are linked to gangs strut down the street like symbols of evil and take pride in their bad reputation. Muggers play games with their victims and opportunist robbers gamble as a way of life with their own vices. I think about the few evil men who seek a distinct power or notoriety in a modern world through defilement and senseless murder.

Of course I excused Tom for his behaviour. He had a reason to do as he was doing. In pursuit of the strong purpose I was just an unavoidable component or spanner in the works to him. Tom had a seemingly unshakable resolution, belief in mind and commitment in body.

In the exercise of the project, entirely devised by Tom, I had spent a deal of time and money at Edison Café. The purpose of this was to identify the perpetrator of the crime who would then become the victim of another crime. Tom's own enquires had found him in name only as 'Edmund', also known on 'the street' as 'Spider'. The instructions given to me were to alert Tom when Edmund had been found in the café and from my phone call Tom would arrive as soon as possible. Sometimes Tom was also there at the café, this left me a little anxious for I knew his reactions to be unpredictable. Either he or I would sit waiting for the other to arrive and then wait together in hope for Edmund to appear.

The plan was flawed in this beginning, for it depended almost entirely upon Edmund turning up when I was there or him being there already if I just stuck my head in. Pure chance was poor probability. Tom might go there alone sometimes in the peculiar possibly that someone fitting his description may materialise. In this unusual case Tom should contact me by phone, and then the onus was placed on me to whiz around quickly in order to determine whether the hailing was justified. Time upon time I visited Edison's (as it became better known) with greater frequency of snacks and drinks. Breakfast, lunch, tea and evening were all the times, these different occasions at Edison Café which I tried to attend. In the beginning I went there three times per day, juggling it with home and the new job. By mid-February the visits had reduced significantly to half a dozen times per week. Eventually I decided we were actually wasting our time trying to find Edmund this way. I assumed that he must have left the locality.

"Robert, just because you have not seen him in nearly two months, it does not mean that he is not here in Whitches." I had thought recently that Tom was relaxing his resolve, but this showed how wrong I was. He continued, "We will have to try elsewhere in town, widen our search. Behave less like amateurs and more as if we know what we are doing. Let us go to where all the druggies hang out."

"Wouldn't it be easier to just to put a few feelers out, ask a few people here and there. You have already found out who he is. We have a sort of idea about what he gets up to. He is a drug dealer, surely it can't be difficult."

"We have to be careful if these so-called people point us in the right direction. Remember although it is with good reason that we are assuming it was Edmund, he probably had accomplices. These same people are going to smell a rat when we kill him."

"You mean when you kill him," I said protesting.

"Okay, when I kill him, but you have got to identify him."

"Tom, you don't need me for this. Half the scum in Whitches are at hand. You can find him without me. I have played along long enough. You can do it on your own. You alone, it halves the risk. If two of us try, there is more chance of mistakes being made. If one of us gets found out then the other gets found out too. The less I am involved in the process, the less likely it is that anybody is going to be found out."

"You mean you and me. You want out."

"Tom, for fuck's sake, I was never in. I have told you what you are planning is wrong – you don't need telling. Jesus, I am not going to tell anyone you did it. I am not going to go running to the police."

"It is not the police I'm worried about. It's the other guys."

"You know the risk Tom. It's become an obsession almost." I found myself drifting off, I could see the causal process of Tom committing the crime. Maybe I was acting too forceful and needed to cool down. Obsession was the right word to use, I was sure of it. In the eighteen thirties, a twenty-year-old Normandy peasant killed his pregnant mother, a sister and a brother. He then wrote scores of pages to explain his reasons for committing the crime. He killed his mother to protect his father from her constant cruelty, and the siblings because they sided with her in family quarrels. He also wrote that by killing his young brother (who the father loved dearly), it would turn the father against him, therefore making it less burdensome for the father when he came to be executed for his crimes. His written composition was in the form of a contemporaneous journal.

He wrote about the background to the crime, the writing was meticulous and emotionally compelling. He made only a small reference to how he butchered his mother with many axe-like blows, or to the details of the obvious fatal violence to his siblings. Instead he focussed almost exclusively on the family biography. The narrative was elaborate in style, had a kind of sophisticated rationality. Drifting back in from the just a moments delay, equipped with this knowledge I said, "Give it up, just drop it Tom. It's not worth it. How are you going to feel when you have killed the bastard?"

The French peasant's account stimulated much interest from scholars who engaged with the various views expressed by professionals such as the priest, lawyers and doctors. It had doubtless been a homicidal event, yet this had been glossed over by his narrative that credited a moral power which was almost exculpating. The consensus among interpreters and the State followed his lead. After the fact, many rationalised the event as being a logical outcome of an ongoing family injustice – a form of madness or mental illness.

"I will feel good, Robert, feel good, it's the last thing I can do for Jim."

This encounter with Tom and the implication that he could now legitimately murder Edmund without compunction was very unsettling; it seemed to be obsession, not unlike that which caused that ill labelled 'righteous' slaughter all those years ago, almost justified as sensible by the murdering, French peasant. I struggled at first to find a reply which did not betray my feelings. I settled on this compromise which was far from perfect, but assertive enough by saying, "Okay, wrong question, but Jim would not want that. I do not want to be part of this anymore. If you cannot do it alone, why don't you get Nick to help you? He was his brother too."

"He wouldn't do it. Nick is not even convinced that he was murdered and he believes in the law anyway. Perhaps you could tell him. Tell him what you really think happened, you convinced me."

"Hell, Tom, he is your brother. There is nothing I can tell him that you cannot. If I speak to Nick he is going to know that I am involved too and that will increase the chances of us been found out even more. You have got three options. First option, let it lay, try and forget about it. Second option, kill him yourself and count me out. Third option, count me out and involve your brother instead."

"Fuck off, Robert."

I was left trembling, yet infinitely less distraught than I supposed I would be in this case. Without any further hesitation, I rose to leave, striving so hard with emotion to remain silent. I was out without looking back and actually pleased at Tom's outburst. The tipping point was reached. It had burst in like a fresh little stream, a caress of reality again. It was an overwhelming reminder back to sense. Tom had yielded to the departure, the interchange between us seemed to be the final one – happy and sorry – foolish and wise. Our friendship was over, the poles, steps and platforms fell inwards. All the scaffolding which we had built from the memory of Jim came tumbling down. Planks, beams, bricks and mortar were piled high blocking the doorway as Tom told me to, "Fuck off." But I was pleased by it and relieved. Alleviated, I could step down from the ladder, clamber over the rubble and jump out through the gaping window. Demolished and over forever. All that psychology nonsense of the source, message, recipient and the situational context was dissolved. It did not matter anymore. A cloud must have passed over Tom's face, for he understood. I was free of it. No more worrying. I could just let go and leave Tom to his own labyrinth searching with his head tied up.

There was a sudden awareness of other people around me as I felt like running. I was in a crowd, but alone and confined to a particular movement. The others seemed to pulse by inflating and deflating to my heartbeats. I struggled for a moment sensing others at my shoulder. I was breathing with difficulty again and had a tendency to fix my eyes in stare, the mind seemed to fail as hardly a thing was seen as it was. There was an odour, quite indistinct, not pleasing nor unpleasant, something near to furniture polish. Not music, but a noise in the ears, like irritating bells being played around the corner. Ready to sink in the confusion and feeling nauseous now. So conveniently, I made for a vacant town bench, directing feet in a waver to be straight as possible. After a few long minutes taken to recover came the clear realisation of wounding, Tom was lost as a friend. On returning to a peaceful frame of mind, the body was restored to normality. Then the greatest coincidence and without mistake there was a tiny pang of excitement as Edmund could be seen with two others disappearing into the crowd.

The non-appearance of Edmund had lulled the previous days into a kind of fortified retreat. Now the surprised sighting after so long was understood as an alarm at first. However, with more consideration, the probability was recognised as fortunate for it served to endorse the disconnection between Tom and me. Knowing that Edmund was in the vicinity held me back from any foolish notion of contacting Tom. The knowledge of the easy possibility of Edmund being found again was to be kept hidden away as I tried to forget about the whole business.

A couple of weeks passed, yet the suspicion of being pounced upon by Tom did not leave the mind, the possibility of holding further communication seemed to grow greater as each day came. The gloomy picture of seeing him again presented itself as I cogitated Diana's association with Kate. In fact by the end of February Tom did phone. Our conversation was civil, though a little stilted and he did not offer an apology. The reason for the call was to arrange a meeting in March between the three of us, the other person was of course Nick. I agreed to the meeting on condition that is was held at Kate's (my place). Having the meeting here meant that by taking the moral position in the likelihood of an argument, it would be easier for me to ask them to leave if necessary. In this case it would reduce the possibility of bad feelings between us afterwards.

March came and the appointed day arrived. We had dispatched of the small talk within twenty minutes. There was no male bonding or moments of brandy and cigars. It was frank discussion with a plot worthy of ill fortune, accompanying were coffee and biscuits. Beforehand the meeting had been given little thought, except to my dread of it. Indifference was a view of mine along with the stubborn determination to continue washing my hands appropriately. Tom on the other hand seemed to have rehearsed the very fabric extensively, it concerned all of what he was going to say in order to persuade me to cooperate. On realising his preparation, I made it clear from the earliest point that any practical involvement by me was completely out of the question. However, by way of compromise I allowed Tom to use a limited amount of guile, without a countering negative reaction. His inveiglement was taken as a subtle influence and I began with caution – just enough to satisfy Tom and Nick alike. Tom had me explain again as to the assumed construction of how Jim had met his end and to conclude somehow that it required a response. I was pleased to be interrupted as Tom dismissed all possible counter arguments to this conclusion (the conclusion that I never quite arrived at due to Tom's intervention). Nick remained sceptical, but agreed that the police appeared to be useless. Tom went on to endorse the notion that Edmund (plus at least one other) were the murderers, as I had convinced him of the same. Nick appeared pensive and quiet, absorbing the information. Digestion was employed with his usual look of scepticism.

When Tom had finished speaking, a long silence followed. He waited for a reply from Nick, but there was none forthcoming. I felt a moral duty to acknowledge the emotional significance and rational instinct held by Tom. As if seeing my thoughts Nick looked in my direction as if to prompt an input. He was not disappointed, for he succeeded in finding a response.

"Revenge is a natural kind of need in men, but generally it cannot succeed on cost benefit grounds because you would be left with chaotic inner questions about yourself. It is not rational either, even though it may feel that it is. Revenge is actually irrational, if you kill or if you just attempt to kill Edmund (or anyone), you run the risk of being found out and facing danger yourself. Exacting revenge may feel good in the short term, leading up to and past the act. In the long term it is bound to gnaw away at you and moreover the whole thing is impractical because the risk is so great."

The little speech seemed to make Nick think more deeply. For Tom those words inflamed his passion more as his face flushed red. Tom was about to speak his mind, but I interrupted him by stating the obvious. "You are angry, Tom. Are you angry, Tom?"

Clearly he was but the clever question had served to halt his line of thought and he was compelled to answer with particular venom. "Of course I am angry! Did you expect me not to be?"

"I don't know, Tom. I really don't know what to expect of you anymore." This seemed to have a certain form to stifle his earlier argument (whatever it was), but it was Nick that came to the rescue immediately.

"Tom, aside from losing our brother, we have both been left with this odd feeling of humiliation which leaves us angry. It is as if death has betrayed us and it is life that is left which is laughing now. It is like a sort of raging thirst that needs to be quenched. The anger is against part of the world like bitterness."

"Jesus," said Tom exasperated. "You are as bad as Robert. Am I supposed to let Edmund and cronies off the hook? He was murdered. We have an issue Nick, it's a good issue. Okay it is vengeance and it is steeped in anxiety and rage. So what Nick? So fucking what?"

"Tom, you have the right to feel this way. God knows, (I don't know), I would probably feel the same. Don't you see, revenge will only make it worse?" I said this believing and pleading. It was having no influence, except to draw abuse.

"Fuck off, Robert." Again, I did not like it. This time it's my own home, so I spare him the reasoning.

Silence ensued before Nick broke it with perfect timing. "Let's calm down. This is not getting us anywhere. We need to think this through Tom. Maybe Robert is right. We may end up worse off or even dead. The powerlessness does make me feel anger, but trying to do something about it would just leave to more trouble. Take the case of Bernhard Goetz."

"Who?" interrupted Tom with disbelief at this tack.

"He is the 'subway vigilante' who shot four young men in the confined space on a subway train in New York City. He was aggressively accosted and cornered by these men who demanded money. Goetz who had been assaulted and mugged twice in the past, pulled out a gun on the unarmed men, then shot them. Many people saw him as a hero because he stood up to his attackers and defended himself. Like here, the police were well known to be increasingly ineffective; they were failing to combat crime.

The four men had set a trap for him, but when he produced the gun the situation was reversed for they were trapped instead. Goetz had used gratuitous violence in the context of the situation by shooting at defenceless men. Showing them the gun should surely have been enough to stop their advances. I believe because he felt ridiculed by them, his action was borne out of anger into rage. He had demonstrated rational irrationality of violence, and you Tom are planning to do the same. Revenge is sweet only for a moment. You seek revenge as a means of gratification against humiliation which you and I both feel. Violence as you propose to kill him, will only be countered by even more violence. Here, what seems rational at first is actually irrational." Nick finished the sermon and we all fell quiet following the account.

"What happened to Goetz and his attackers?" I asked to satisfy a curiosity and hoping that there might be some moral justice or appropriate comeuppance.

"The guys who were shot were not killed, but one was made permanently paralysed. Two years later, one was convicted of raping, beating and robbing a pregnant woman. Another committed further muggings. As for Goetz, he was acquitted of all but weapons charges and served eight months of a prison sentence. The common thought was that he had overreacted, but considering all the circumstances a reasonable person in his place would have believed their self to be in danger. So I think the moral here is that nobody wins. He obviously went too far, ended up in prison and one guy became paraplegic."

The general mood had definitely become calmer and Nick was very much onside against Tom. I felt it incumbent to relate the story of the nineteenth century, French peasant, to tie it in with Goetz's experience and Tom's desire for revenge. The relationship between the three was tentative, yet subtle enough to make more than one argument and those were both explicit and implicit. They had both listened to my story with interest. I hoped the message might filter the negative stuff from his head.

Nick attempted to further consolidate our argument against revenge by pointing out the seduction and repulsion of a kind of 'national legitimised crime' in the wider world. "Take the United States," he said as if to begin another speech. "The powerful States of the West, for whatever their reasons, they find themselves in one dubious militarised situation after another. They promote wars that cannot be won and enter battles which they lose for winning. All they achieve is domestic emotional support and notoriety in national history. Not using violence would signal a loss of meaning for they are seduced by their own myth of omnipotence. Hundreds, sometimes thousands are killed before the inevitable retreat arrives. That is rage against humiliation. When people die because of our actions, maybe we should not flatter ourselves to be able to judge so well what is right and wrong."

Nick's lesson had brought finality to our discussion. It was difficult to tell whether our efforts had managed to swing Tom in the other direction. Tom now had a complexion and rather a pensive look about him which conveyed a kind of equilibrium. We had devoured a family pack of assorted cream biscuits and each drank to the bottom of a coffee mug twice. An hour had passed, it seemed shorter. This was the end of it. Only Tom knew what he would do.

There had been no apology from Tom, so I had not asked him how he was. Instead, "How is Diana, Tom?"

"The last time I saw her was a week ago. Apart from the shouting and the swearing she seemed fine. We had a big bust up and I left. I'm staying with Nick for a while."

With a resigned sigh I said, "I am genuinely sorry. I had no idea."

"Yeh, I know, I'm sorry too Robert. The thing is, she says she has a job lined up in India. It is with the Red Cross or something. She has an uncle out there, so that is where she is going. Also, Diana has asked Kate to go with her and Kate said yes. I'm sorry too, Robert."

I found myself speaking without thinking. "Go away for a while and come back again with an alternative."

"Very well, Robert," he replied with a casual smugness, but all the same allowing something.

My crumbling exactness of stern face presented as a token of satisfaction for Tom. Despite his recent ill fortune I imagined that he took a certain amount of sickly glee from my unrelenting fate. His was a feint to be virtuous. The proof to me was his undeniable brightened spirit venturing over his resignation, while all the while my imitation smile was as convincing as a false clock.

Without Diana, Tom could arrive safely at his recent temporary home, fall into an ordinary routine of his new life and have Nick to lean on. Without Kate, I unlike Tom would gradually fade back into misery. Any amount of direct alarm or slight encounter with normal living would make little difference to my daily existence. Nick I think at some level recognised some of this and maybe felt a degree of pity or embarrassment for me. However, as men so often do on these occasions, he adopted a gallant heart showing a rough manner by saying, 'goodbye' like a battle cry and slapping shoulders like a warrior. Nick was sympathetic in a promising deceit. The eventual exit of both was a disappearance in a wave of bravado.

Chapter Sixteen

The mirror in the kitchen, ours, but it really belonged to Kate. She had bought the mirror, I had hung it there in the kitchen of all places, for her request had been my privilege to complete. The repellent face was my own, it was only eighteen inches away, this being familiar, craggy, dented and lopsided. The distortion? Well, overcome by its fiery grip, this was from emotion coursing through the head. Seemingly to be free of dire sensation, I would have to die, the furious headache was not enough to do the killing. Inescapable here and confined there, this was not the ordeal I wanted to address.

Kate glided into the kitchen letting the door close gently behind her. She found me at the sink washing plates from yesterday. As ever Kate was beautiful, light reflected from her hair, cheeks had a warm glow, lashes full with mascara, eyes outlined and shaded to perfection. The bright pupils stared out like those of a puppy but were filled with a plot. Her knuckles danced lightly upon my wrist, "Hi," she said. "How did it go? Are you and Tom mates now?"

"Kate, I do think we will see Tom again. In a similar way, and not at all intimate, Diana will not be seeing him either. But of course you know that bit already."

"Oh, he told you, I thought he might."

"Well, yes of course he did Kate." My voice was raised. "When we men are not talking about football – it is about women." I hated my own ridiculous self-mockery. "Why did you not tell me they had split up? No do not answer that, because I know the answer." There was a pause and I just added some more to fill in the space. "It was hardly a match to last." This sounded like a compromise to half excuse her deceit.

"Diana is going to India. She has got a job there. She is staying with her uncle for a while." Kate glanced away guiltily biting her top lip as nostrils dilated and breathing became deeper. "I have always dreamed of seeing the world. This is just really the first step. She asked me to go with her, so why not?"

"What about us Kate? What about me? What about your job? What about money?" As I said these questions rather than asked them, they seemed a pointless irrelevance. I was selfishly resentful. I scarcely dared to consider the knowledge that Kate had chosen Diana and India over the two of us or the whole scheme set against simple impulses of affection towards me. Now I knew it was fiction, to believe that our mutual love to actually be equal.

"Robert, I have had enough. It is not because of you. It is just here, I get bored easily. There is more around the corner, opportunities, possibilities to unfold, something new, something untried and things I do not even know about yet. I will write to you if you like. If you want, when I settle you can come over. I have handed my notice and there is money saved. I won't need money anyway, everything is so cheap there. Don't worry about me, Diana knows the ropes, we are worldly wise. I'm not stupid, I will not come to any harm." She paused to think and find more courage. "You can keep the flat on, maybe get someone to share and help pay the rent."

"Don't go, stay." I heard my own words whine and knew it was an empty appeal for her mind was set.

"Life has become so predictable, nothing changes anymore. I need adventure. It is too comfortable here. I want to shake my memory loose, become dislocated for a while, it's good for the soul. I want to plummet into somewhere and half begin again. It won't be at all bad, Diana's uncle is well placed there and very comfortable. The weather is better, well warmer anyway."

"Kate, it is stiflingly hot there, then the weather breaks and it pisses it down. It is a better climate here."

"Robert, if you prefer it here in your temperate zone, then stay."

"Oh so I am invited, am I?"

"No, not really, you would just mess it up. You have to want to make it work you know."

"So you and I are not working, is that it? Because you don't want this, you and I anymore."

"I have told you already. It is not because of you. It is because of me. You know it would not work, the three of us – you and Diana would be alternating gooseberry. Me in the middle satisfying your sex drive and saving Diana from herself. You can meet other people now Robert, be single again. Wear stout shoes and keep sensibly away from the edge."

"And what's that supposed to mean? Are you saying I'm boring?"

"No, you make me laugh. I love you, but I don't need you. You are only boring in a Ken Barlow sort of way, just stodgy sometimes when I want to fly."

"So I am boring." I kissed the pulse in her neck to try and prove otherwise.

"No, I have just said it. You are not boring, I am just bored. I have got to do something. What do you want to do, Robert?"

"I want to carry on just as we are and have a baby."

"Carrying on is not an option anymore, not like this. Having a baby, that is something else. Carrying on here with a baby, no way. We have discussed this before. You know that. No, Robert, No!"

My predicament was not something fully engaged in, despite a determination for concern. There was not enough attention given to the subject of a baby. She dismissed the idea as not worth consideration for years yet, or simply inconvenient and superficial. A baby, perhaps the thought of it just emerged as a desperate possibility to stop Kate moving to India. A baby was a mythical product as a mere mental exercise to stand in the way of Kate's adventure. I was imposing my own separation from Kate by not cooperating, a no compromise manifested as male pig headedness. She had offered a plain ultimatum, either I should stay or follow under her terms. To go would be to absorb the change in a kind of social delusion, complete with culture shock. Could I carry on without Kate and in doing so throw away a yearning towards her intimate allurement? In her absence would I withdraw from the worthy world into reclusion like a freaky religious devout in a cave? Would I fall into isolation indefinitely, waiting for Kate to return some day and profess her unending love for me? Should I stick around just to see, all summer long, then elapse and disappear beyond into succeeding years?

Maybe the preferred alternative ought to be becoming an unwanted passenger on an expedition to India bound to fail. Playing gooseberry apparently, or at least half of one with seeds and juicy fruit exposed turning rapidly into a prune or something. Being someone still, who drifts from one crappy job to the next, perhaps I could become a char wallah or a brush wallah. With an imagination maybe I could string along with the minimum of pain and entangle myself in a profound expectation.

Meanwhile Kate would surely embrace India in a trick of living that was borne from her own unique intensity and find sustenance in people. Like an intimate secret unwound, she could do that, skilfully unravelling more and more. Kate could distract you from yourself and boost any almost absent feeling. The more that I had been drawn out by Kate, the finer I had become like wire. It was a gushing forward, an eagerness to please, an opening up bearing your soul and exposing your own being to her. You could find yourself getting deeper, saying too much and explaining all in an overexcited way. Then you wake up from courtship, into over involvement, dive too deep and realise that you really are in love.

A separation of some distance had become a likely possibility. Being not fully engaged to the mounting, facts I wondered if splitting up was contagious. Kate ran fingers through her hair, playing with it as if to flirt, only that was not it, maybe I was supposed to understand this subliminal message. She poured two glasses of red wine. The hair thing was a smoothing of the waves, except this was a messy sticky ocean. She was twisting hair now into coiled strands and lacing it behind her ear. "Obviously you have a problem with this. Soon I will start packing my suitcase and eventually will go. This is not going to be easy for either of us. I know you are dead against this. I could say if you loved me enough you would come with me. If I said just that to you, you would say (because I know you), you would say if you loved me then you would stay. You know what I mean anyway. It sounds a bit muddled like a riddle, but it is not. The best thing for us both is for me to go and you to stay. If you want you can follow me there, but later, you need to think about it. Sort your passport out," Kate said all this so soothingly as if she had been rehearsing it for days. "Life is full of these little damp moments of gloom. Things only happen if you make them."

"This is hardly a little damp moment, is it, Kate? Things happen to me without moving."

"Come on, you are a big boy, I bet you have had worse days than this – I have. Think about tomorrow, it will be different then. In a few weeks we will laugh at this. Nothing is as hard as you think it's going to be," Kate said it as tellingly as she could without seeming unkind and all the while selfishly pursuing her own needs and hopes. This (the option) seemed so strange to me, I could accompany her which was my decision and her concession to allow it.

My role in Kate's life had become unfairly diminished by the effect of Diana's sudden single status. For me, not going to India was actually a rash step, one of resignation where the crazy short-term consideration did not serve the long-term interest. Her pursuit of India seemed like a degrading assault, an ultimate injustice to erode our relationship to nothing. Unable to shield Kate from the temptation of India or further encroachment of Diana on her life, I drew back by reining myself in defeated. By stifling an urge to lash out, I had failed. Being unsuccessful was not using the primitive feeling from inside and directing it outwards to good advantage. To fight with Kate would be against all common sense because I loved her and it would drive us further apart. It would have been conveniently easy to blame our catastrophe on Diana, but doing so by attacking could not work for this only deprives us of dignity. Maybe I should have been proactive or provocative instead of trying to deny feeling by suppressing the emotions. Their scheme unloading on me like this really deserved a counter reaction, one more hostile than a matter of fact attention which I had given it and gave them.

I was incapable of concealing the pain, despite best efforts not to show it. Only fighting the feeling kept me from coming apart. Unable to prevent a tainted emotion upon my voice, it was unsurprisingly shaky. "I'm begging you not to go. Is there anything I can do or say to stop you Kate?"

"Look, it's all planned, there is no turning back. No changing of mind. That is it."

"So, who had the idea? Was it yours or Diana's?"

"It was Di's naturally. She has been before. She is the one with the job out there."

"Why do you have to go?"

"Robert, I have already said. I don't have to go at all. I have decided that it is the best thing for me at this time. I'm bored here in Whitches. Don't you see, something has got to change for me. I'm still young. I'm not super career woman or a convenient receptacle to carry your baby."

"Our baby."

"No baby, no baby," she cut the air with an open palm as she stared emptily at the open suitcase on the bed. "Give me five years yet. Besides it looks as though I will be doing without sex for a while. It will give my fanny a rest."

"Well, that's consolation for me at least. I thought you and Diana had something going there for a moment."

"Ha, don't be ridiculous, Robert. You know me. Diana is man mad. You know that too. She is over Tom already, there is no stopping her."

"So what happened there? Tom and Diana, how come he has moved out?"

"Have we had this conversation before? Did he not tell you? Did you not talk about it with him?"

"Tom has gone to live with his brother for a while until he gets sorted out. And besides we are not on the best of terms. He left here under a cloud. I don't think we, I mean, I don't think I will see him again. So what happened?"

"It seems that he can't get it up. And you know Diana. He is hung up about his dead brother. He claims the police have got it all wrong and he reckons that Jim was actually murdered. Oh yes, and he is stoned half the time. He is fucked up big style."

"Tom will be okay, that lefty brother of his will look after him. Nick said, none of us really know for certain what happened to Jim. And because we do not know, we guess and think we know. As shocking as the event of his death was, the uncertainties actually define our sense of authority on the subject. The motive, the consequence, the whole meaning of it come together to stun and stagger us. It seems hard to believe that we don't know anything for certain. The confounding thing is that not being able to know is what passes for knowing."

"Well, whatever, but it seems to me like Tom is not the same guy that we met at Christmas. Diana is better off without him and so are you – we all are."

Tolerant detachment, I felt this, like slipping into it to escape, for Kate had a knack of speaking pointedly and pointlessly all at once. Now I was bracing for her move, rather than embracing, it was Kate surging onward stepping out with forward optimism. All new for her at first, though a day would arrive eventually, postponed momentarily, then gradually every day over and over again – realisation would come softly in the heat. Bit by bit there would be a wilting and a growing out. Perhaps Kate would become homesick, not here necessarily, just England instead of India. This was a hope of mine as I pictured her wearing a cotton sari, only partly hiding those luscious curves. Her voice might carry some special weight there, like a curved texture or a buoyant mellow bubble distinct from the crowded tumult of exotic India. If only Kate would pause, allow me to catch up and let a new stage develop. No, she had declared herself to go, making a nuisance sauntering off, travelling under my haze and drifting away. Dancing out, her feet could not keep quiet like her knack of speaking. Boring wisdom dictated to me, 'do not do anything' take measure and surrender to Kate.

Evidence of a prearranged visit transpired as a knocking at our door. Kate instantly knew who it was before the opening. In came Diana, that yearning for her friend had brought her here. The magnetism of Kate was a force I knew as familiar, yet as an unspecified allure, this was something she had in abundance. It was imminent, when she was to suddenly go this would strike me down. I knew this, for soon I would plunge into a storm. For now I had to share Kate's warmth with Diana and suffer Diana's irritation. Diana was still dealing with something inside, yet she had an unsavoury superiority in her suffering. A piece of Diana was missing Tom, or something else. Diana was unreadable, almost a blank to me. Yet she was established here in our home, in our niche to prise us apart with artful purpose. This was something which I was powerless to prevent. Indeed I was party to it, setting myself up to be torn away.

When confronting negative consequences to my life I develop personal mannerisms which become irritating to others. This I know because Diana told me. "Your arguments are so tedious Robert. The same thing over and over. Going round in circles. And stop scratching yourself so. It is a waste of time you cannot stop us. We are going. We are not running away. And don't patronise me either. Why must you trivialise this?"

186

"Diana you are both running away to nothing. There are more prospects here, you have potential, you both just need to tap into available opportunities here." The argument was not going anywhere, all it was doing was providing a temporary steadying for me. I could not stop them or change their minds. The more I argued, the more Diana and Kate proved themselves right. Being proved wrong and outnumbered too was painfully debilitating. Kate kept quiet now because she knew Diana could speak on her behalf with assertive conviction. I had been uncertain to begin with but had tried every possibility. Diana was hurtful with her words. At least when Kate beat me down, she did it without ridicule. Kate did not browbeat or insult, no she nurtured in her winning. 'More opportunities here,' who was I kidding, it sounded ridiculous as I said it and even more so afterwards. If this was the best I could come up with, it had to be the final word. Diana might flagrantly masquerade as an unaffected and unconcerned former lover of Tom. However, she secretly took enough ruthless enjoyment by lowering me, imagined as being his dumb effigy. While Diana was revenging herself on me instead of Tom, Kate was silent leaving me defenceless.

The subtle viciousness of Diana with such swift sentences was telling enough to succeed. My complete understanding was clear, I was so dreadfully disadvantaged. There was not a single thing to be done to stop them, Kate and Diana were definitely going to India. Absolutely nothing could be done and nothing could be said to change this. It was as if I were offered a natural proposal of no difference. It was another ultimatum, only this time an extraordinary ultimatum 'take it or leave it'. Either 'take' their notion to go to India with natural acceptance or 'leave' them to travel off as proposed with (or without) my own approval. It did not really matter whichever way, because the result was always the same.

An almost whispered conversation continued between the two of them. Their voices seemed unusually low, distinct and passionless. The sound of the words which slightly rose and fell embraced a tone tagged with respiration. I uttered not one word, questioning nothing, nothing to answer, like a spider on the wall waiting for nothing. Occasionally Diana looked strangely at me and I could not help but look strangely back at Diana. It was a gentle sort of 'face off', a truce where the only consequence was that it meant nothing any more. Like a spider I was left waiting for a tug on a spoke of a web; something to gain possession of which would give a minute sustenance to my life.

The ten days passed quickly towards their eventual departure. We slept together still, but I could not help thinking that Kate might prefer to do the sleeping bit with Diana. Kate seemed to remove herself from everything and this growing away left me distant. A dismayed longing in myself became a serene and cavernous bemusement. In a mood celestially mild and accepting, Kate was slipping through manly fingers unnoticed before my eyes. This said, my thoughts were not absent, I dug them up into the space of reality, only to plough them under again for false comfort. The process continued as if looking at someone else's life, out through an open window with curtains fluttering in the breeze. There were dark Indian arms beckoning for Kate and Diana in the moonlight. That mysterious and invisible country far away muttering in the night had become the bane these last days.

I would see Kate in a quiet moment, shaded in a sadly trodden pensive look. I wondered at her thoughts beyond the murmur of India and the hopes that would unfold. She was leaving a once happy home (one of life for me), into a parting excuse of absence, leaving a solitary flat of grief. Was there a tender melancholy pleasure inside her head remembering the good times we had? I faintly understand her, but cannot reconcile it. There was a time when we were together, silly sensible and loving. The moment now was saying something about the passing of time that sometimes erodes the path to satisfaction. At last I was relieved of an assumed responsibility of keeping Kate happy. I was good for a little while, but maybe now laughed at. I feared that being dull and stupid in the present meant no happy future. It was only blind courage which prevented tears rising to my eyes.

My offer to drive them directly to the airport was rejected. Kate reasoned that a compromise would be more appropriate to make it emotionally easier for everyone. Kate's practicality observed too many hours and minutes meant an extended farewell which would be more painful than a shorter one. Diana would feel less awkward if I took them to the train station and left. No long goodbye, it was easier that way, apparently. "Just dump Diana and I at the station. Diana will allow us a few minutes at the end," it was so final. "Then you have to turn away and drive back home. Think about what you are going to do when I'm not there anymore. Make your mind up Robert. Sort out your passport. It's better for us this way. And Diana will not have the chance to get embarrassed by our extended parting. No stretched out feelings this way. This way is easier. Station, taxi and plane."

They appeared with deliberate yet hesitant steps coming slowly into the road. The subdued simplicity of the journey to the station restrained any protest. The unchangeable reality was an expression etched upon their faces. Anxious anticipation, a combination worthy of indifferent aspiration, careful and yet careless future. Suitcases crammed in the boot, hand luggage beside me, Kate and Diana silent behind. I was both being used and flattered to be doing the honours. Proud and humble, taking the pretty young women towards their immediate ambition. Kate was no longer a lover, now only a friend fading away. Our relationship was already old as I drove mutely through the streets waiting to kiss Kate goodbye.

We soon reached the moment and the place. The drop off point was swollen and blocked by stationary cars. I drove on a little further, only finding a precarious stopping place. Kate and Diana leapt out. Vehicles dodged us as I suddenly became aware of a weakness which possessed my violent heaving of suitcases. The action brought a drawing of emotion and I was frozen to the spot as if injured. Diana grabbed her luggage and pecked my cheek before moving away to leave Kate and I together. We hugged a while like bound fragments of a whole before releasing. Her eyes were now unfathomable. She kissed me quickly before thrusting her diamond and sapphire ring into my palm. Kate then grabbed her suitcase and bag. She then shot into the road just narrowly avoiding a van, unscathed thankfully, but I struggled to instantly interpret the action and decipher the unusual emotion. I wrestled with the wrench and the meaning of her frank transaction dispensing with the ring. The impulse to follow her was immediately killed by the prospect of being completely rejected. Instantly I was wounded and quite resigned to a low condition. Leaving her at the station and resuming the road home was an endeavour for the harshness of the moment stabbed at the heart.

***

When home it was desolation, cloistered in, bleak and alone again in the now dreary flat. The decorated walls seem blank and stare down in monotony as I know day will succeed another day as I live companionless once more. Here is no longer that magical dwelling place where hearts were together. This place is deserted except for within there is the stone vacant person that I have suddenly become. Grim is the possessing reality of myself housed behind the dark windows which lower down on to the street in the sadness. I keep a neglected appearance in the scanty brightness of the day which frowns heartlessly upon dark night isolation.

I am wronged somehow and thus imprisoned by my own fruition to shut the outside world away. Behind the door, beyond the gate, down the street and out of mind. Yes, the door, I could draw a portrait on every one to enchant a spell upon it so I could see her still, an image of Kate. A monstrous comforting fantasy, made of lines furling, curling and twisting into shape. The make believe would be only a petrification, to see her love, keep her here after she has gone. To no avail our love is extinguished, past gate and street she is gone - just the echo of Kate remains. Ghosts on the walls, a vision of Kate upon the sofa, she has shunned me and this hopeless place. The shadow still remains, yet she has driven herself off of her own accord.

The loneliness asserts itself, throbbing like a bad tooth, yet the desolation is manifest as passive. Not quite like veils, but curtains hang heavy and droop insensitive. Shadows and furniture shrink this inner world forgotten into loss that only I am the victim of. The colourful carpet seems grey and faded into nothing as if to reflect my soul. Those many mirrors so personal to Kate are dim as if stained by an unlikely film of make-up so faint and perplexing. Floorboards creak that never did and pictures secrete themselves seemingly into the walls which all of a sudden are damp. Already dust has begun to accumulate making a ready meal for insects to come. The air is laden with moisture, then so beginning its work soon to produce stains damp, then mildew and decay. The clock might never give the correct time again, the face tells it wrong now and only by chance of a better mood could it be wound right. I am but a gentle figure moping through the gloom, moving in the solitude with a fragment of life which keeps my being from turning into stone.

Spore, scatter, might fungi bloom, sprout on the window sill. Grass grow upon the roof or in the gutter? I expect it would happen eventually if I did not snap out of it. Damp, cold, will the walls turn to yellow, then go to black before the plaster cracks, crumble and the pieces fall away? I expect it would occur in the end. New books become old and wallpaper peels away on its own like it always does - like me. Only the television for company and the telephone seldom rings.

Season would succeed season, memories of Kate will fade, but sometimes there will be a pricking or jogging back to exasperate in recount of reflections causing pain for her absence. For now this place, a wilderness doubling as a home. I would be haunted by our once shared thoughts and pursuits - yet nothing could harm me now. I can sit anywhere, but at the moment I nestle near a chair and think of her. For now I suffer the memory by comforting melancholy, so unexceptional and natural without fear. Kate's objects surround as such a mark of her presence gone and now they are only tokens of our obsolete relationship. I would go out, but dread coming home and hate the return knowing she would not be there.

To sleep away to forget and then to wake at night to see her head upon the pillow could only be a cruel dream. In the morning before dawn a kind of twilight filled the bedroom. As the day was waking there was only a little noise from outside, but more light from the curtained window than before. I would imagine how life could be if Kate had not left, despite the dismantled room without her. I would love her and believe she loved me too. We would share a common hope at least. I could see her bearing our child. Kate would have been a potential mother with a doubtless constancy of purpose. Beyond the solemn wandering of mind, conscious of commiseration, I would cling foolishly to a soothing consolation of the knowledge that Kate was somewhere with our baby. Being pregnant with our child would now form the immediate purpose of her life. Filled with tears, a swollen belly and a developing mother heart she would return to renew a love. We would spend our lives together forever. I would love her and we would pretend she loved me.

Chapter Seventeen

This stupid thing within and outside me perplexes. To let Kate go to India like that defies a rational explanation. The supposed justification to not follow Kate and dream of her instead, appals the very sense of understanding. Against my human impulse to be with Kate, I have an elemental imperfection like a blot disparaging self-interest. I have a seemingly natural contrary feeling which considers it all ludicrous or bizarre with no reason to suppose this should be so. Practically speaking, I guess I am a man who does not know how to act it. 'It', also seems to be a kind of strange voice which I have invented that excuses responsibility and absolves the essence of life without a care. If I say 'it' out loud, there is no person here to hear and therefore no one to care. This is not a cry for help, 'it' is a voice made up so I can wallow in self-pity. The reason for this is unknown, I do not know for it is beyond my comprehension. There is no point whatsoever in martyrdom for oneself.

Two hundred and ninety-five pounds, this was given as an expensive ring – did Kate forget that? Too narrow, too small, what can a man do with a diamond and sapphire ring? Play with it perhaps. Try to squeeze it on the little finger. Drop it in disregard upon the floor because it is not wanted. Stamp the ring into the carpet and break it out of anger like a broken heart. Pick it up for examination and to see it unbroken. Touch it, feel it, taste it, crunch it, remove it from the mouth covered in spit and throw it against the wall to fall somewhere unseen to be enveloped in dust. That is what a foolish and heartbroken man does with an unwanted ring. Thrown away, two hundred and ninety-five pounds down the drain.

I really think I am suffering now. No big deal I suppose, feels like it is the worst thing in the world that ever happened. Nobody cares, who cares about Robert? Answer, nobody. Why should anyone care about Robert? Answer, no reason. If nobody cares about me, why should I care? Losing a girlfriend this way is nothing and no big deal. Losing a brother to death, now that is something. Jim who died as young as he did was something, it is definitely something to Tom and Nick. Losing your children, that is everything, that is a big deal, that must be every pain on earth.

Profound this last substantial thought, it may have been the particular one which transformed me latterly into the outer man. It was not an immediate transition, but this was a slow process of separating the miserable conscience into a higher esteem of worthiness. It had begun, a new subtle presentation, as if the softened sky at sunrise were blending into a new day. Now I was taken into the wearing of a soberly demure air towards self-satisfaction. Regardless of inner feelings that can serve to pull a man down, I disembarrassed my own self from them. I came to it gradually with a triumphant manner, by route of my very own brazen confidence hitherto unseen. With eyes roundly wide and crooked teeth gleaming white, here was the falsest smile that I could muster. Yet behind the obedient face that smiled, submitting to the outer world was still a trembling inner self. This was a new presentation which only hid away the usual doubts.

It took weeks and months, but the falseness brought me into a sizzling state of inner power and authority. If necessary I could easily shout at people in supermarkets and not fear the consequences. The false strength helped me cope with the never received letter from Kate. Where was she? Well, in India of course, it is in the eastern hemisphere! She is going to write soon, so that I can write back you will see, you see! It was fancy in the mind and taxing on the brain after so long; this kept me from quaking more through my weakest spells. I had these secret thoughts appearing to be read out copiously from expression, yet still locked inside, in a state of mental suspension that no one who looked could fathom. Little did I know that no individual wanted to make this out or form an impression of inside my head. It was ignorance of oneself and the outside world which kept every part of me engrossed in life only for surviving. I had not informed myself sensibly to yield to the influence of the world. With the false face I made an unwritten bargain to hurry on through the experience of being here without absorbing better living.

Remaining faithful to the imagined deal between the world and I was not at all difficult. Living this way was easy. Leading life with no expectations was very numbing, only occasional desire made it disconcerting. Only the emergence of an unexpected event or a possible disturbing eventuality (once hidden away for reasons of comfort) could shake the equilibrium. So it happened on a night in early December as if the world had conspired to unfix the status quo.

The phone rang. A voice from the past, once buried but now dug up again. The words, although laden with emotion were easily recognised to be those of Tom.

"How, are you, Tom? What are you doing now? Where are you?" All these civil questions blurted out as if I were pleased to hear from him again. Here was the very false face again, with feelings energetic and controlled. This a contrived process of reaching out to consolidate the broken pieces like an explosion in reverse. The device of automatically listening kicked in against my will to reject him and put the phone down. I kept telling myself I did not need this, for Tom and I were finished. Why should I be so righteous? I was supposed to be on a second six-month sabbatical from those secular and non-secular sanctimonious 'do-gooders'.

Tom began in a strange fashion, "I don't know where I am, I forget. I am not in Northern Ireland anymore. I came out of the army having done not one, but two tours of Northern Ireland. People did not recognise me anymore when I came out, they were afraid of me. I'd changed, my character had changed. I was not the same person."

"Tom, try to calm down, it's okay. Where are you?"

"I'm here, Robert. I thought I might as well go back, but the army would not let me. I had gone for that sergeant with a knife. You serve your queen and country and that is how they repay you. Everybody looked at me like I was scum. They had no appreciation of what I went through there. I did not expect to be treated as a hero, only to be accepted. On coming home again I just felt hopeless. One minute I was on patrol in Northern Ireland living on the fucking edge. The next minute I was walking the streets of Liverpool without a fucking job. Anyway, I gradually over years adjusted back to life in Civvy Street and got my personality back. It was hard, but I did not get aggressive anymore at loud noises or the drop of a hat. Fitting back into civilian life was not easy but I made it."

"You did well getting there, Tom. You have done well."

"I was making it. I made it for years until recently. It started I think, only a little at first with the death of Jim, but I could fight it. I could handle it. Then I lost Diana, took to dope and booze. The bitch, I guess she has good reason. Woke up one night and I was choking her, but she is no angel either. Diana rightly threw me out and says she is going off to India. Took Kate with her. We did not love each other anyway. Bollocks!"

"Where are you, Tom?"

"I don't know, I tell you. I am not in Northern Ireland. I did not know they had walked into it, the line of fire. The sergeant should have known the Mick set up. Shaker and Spud got shot up because of his neglect. It was that asshole. He blamed the Mick, but he should have known about the shooter."

The wind blew harder and the rain patted more on the window. He stopped talking, his breathing was heavier. Assuming I said, "What are you drinking?"

194

"What is it to you?"

"Tom, have you taken anything?"

"Yes, just some tabs and booze. Nothing serious. Plenty, no more than I have had before."

"What tabs, Tom? How many?"

"Christ I don't know. Any old shit, all sorts of shapes and colours. A bloody broken rainbow. Don't worry I'm okay, I can handle it. No big deal!"

"Shall I come and get you? Where are you?"

"The army train you to be a soldier and then let you get shot up like Shaker and Spud. It could have been me that was killed, should have been that fucking sergeant. Hey maybe it should have been me too, why not? Ask me why I did not kill anyone while I was in the army. They show you how to kill, then won't let you do it. I should have done the sergeant, stuck him right through and cut his fat belly open."

"Where are you, Tom?"

His voice kept fading away and back again with a surge willing himself to carry on against drink and drugs. "I cannot remember when I last had a good night of sleep. I wake up and it's like Northern Ireland again. Bombs going off, unable to fire back, enduring the endless drizzle, the rain, taking abuse, squaddies screaming, Shaker and Spud shot to pieces. What happened there every day and what failed to happen every day? Something and nothing, that's what. No emotion, just numb, the mind and life sucked out of you. I should have died there. I wake up crying, trembling, sweating, try to scream but can't. Can't, can't."

Tom had given good cause for me to dislike him. Now he was executing a trust at my feet, to lay a pressure as if I were his confidential agent. A situation of devoted judgement was presented before me, an outstretched hand informing of errors in his life. This was a sacrifice offering up considerations of his past never admitted to or volunteered for scrutiny. Out of respect for his novel speech should I be privileged into humble duty or converted back to dignity and reject his immediate need? There was no appetite within me, it was just condescended words which struggled to form. My own voice kicked in as if stumbling forward over stones. "Stay awake, Tom. Where are you?" His disclosure began and finished as an indecipherable mutter that faded to only loud breathing. A distinct clunking of phone to floor resounded down the line. I imagined Tom in a stooping position. I wanted to picture him lying prostrate with blood oozing from a temple and rats arriving one after another to dispose of Tom. I wanted him to have fractured leg in the desert, next to a standing camel he could not mount.

There was no urge to shout, no feeling to do it, for this would be pointless. A surreal scenario, deep breathing Tom asleep, my voice screeching 'wake up, wake up', for anyone to hear except Tom who could not. Why should I lower myself? For what reason, other than a selfish one, did Tom have to share his burden? His anxiety became mine while he slept soundly. The worry of thinking Tom is on the verge of suicide, yet knowing always too completely this was just not so, became painful. Having no such idea at all makes me both thick headed and thoughtless. Yet he found himself unburdened until the next time.

I have no longer any kind of sympathy for Tom, despite the evaluation that concludes this unfairness, the pulse still races while hearing his breathing. A finger is placed reluctantly on the telephone receiver rest to cancel, to save his bill and my anxiety. The feeling has not gone, only now it is overlaid with guilt due to the action. I telephone Nick now and heave gently to contain stress while waiting. No answer, maybe he is not there. It is late so perhaps Nick has gone to bed. The ringing continues. The pulse and heart plunges more as each second realises that there is no reply. It rings and rings. No one there! All that can be heard is the rain still bouncing on the window, a telling signal possibly to give it up and put down the telephone.

There it is, over with, perhaps forever or just until the next time. All I want to do is sleep. Shut it out, to close the world down without this reminder of the past and marker to the future. Be gone Tom, good riddance or bad riddance, either way, without him being there as a tag to remember past days of Kate would be fine. While laid in bed, the very thought of being proud to wish the demise of Tom was disturbing. The strangeness of the concept unreal, like a character outside of me, and no reconciling any part with having phoned Nick. It made me think deeply about our short history and all since the death of Jim. On this very point came welcome sleep right through until morning.

On waking, the realisation of Tom's phone call still agitated. It would distort the day ahead. As usual there was no breakfast. By being unable to stay still long enough to drink coffee, I decided to walk early for work. Then came a thinking nursing illusion that something could be done which seemed as sensible as anything else that came to mind. Will an end to it. Try and dispose of the feeling. I was prepared to imagine him dead, but the mistrusting disgust at the thought of this brought more uneasiness. All that the overdose had done was simply knock him into restful sleep. Tom was an otherwise strong and healthy man. And what of Nick? Not answering the phone in the early hours is not inexplicable, so no answer had revealed nothing. In order to slip back into ordinary life I was motivated towards an inclination not to know. Just forget the whole thing and to endorse this I should exercise absolute restraint from speaking to anyone about it. No point in phoning Nick again for there is far from a need to get involved. The phone call, all sundry information held by me alone, completely in the strictest confidence, to be thrown away conveniently. In the event of a catastrophe happening I would pretend not to know a thing.

Summer had passed and nothing of significance happened, not even a holiday, that is usual now, plenty of work and no play. Enough rest to be protected from being hurt by no holiday or each time there was a birthday. The seer is sleep itself. At the end of each day the brain is reset to keep one sane. The more one rests the less crazy one is. The mind switches off the body relaxes. To be safer from madness one must sleep enough to allow forgotten dreams to disentangle the memory of the waking hours. No dreams though now. An overnight recharging in preparation for the day leaves the mind at the face blank. All the slightly deranged and unbalanced stuff should be dumped with relief into the recycle bin during the night of dreamful sleep. Dreams are unremembered in black nights, where together with blank days there is nothing, and nothing and nothing makes nothing. This was no plot or design. This was just how the time passed, sufficiently crafted to be a regular feature, yet only remotely cruel to oneself.

I took the liberty of giving the world a warm reception now, while feeling sure to receive a cold one. Occasions were conducted to have a willingness of face and form that was not for faltering. Whatever came at me, I was soon recovered, hurt sometimes, but never in danger. The truth of loneliness had its own courage forever presenting a secret battle within me which was resilient and solemnly assured. The world was a picture in the morning. In the day I would seek to wrestle the answers from short hours of light. At night, the only possible attention could be given to one's own comfort and ease. On arriving home in the evening, lights would be kept bright with heating switched on to a tolerable assurance of artificial affection. At a suitable juncture, usually when being overcome by convenient tiredness, I would convey to the bedroom and then be safe into bed. The next day would follow just as indistinct as the last, then slowly and quickly into satisfactory night again.

Perpetual time became lighter to bear as observations roused little sorrow, if at all. The woodenness was sawn from estrangement between my little world within to the greater world outside as it widened more and more. It was not hard not to have affection or not to give it. As each day had passed creeping with little notice there was only deepened knowledge. Anticipation or optimism had been compelled into forlorn hope, then transformed into black of night and blank days.

Here it was again. Christmas had approached with extra efficient stealth this year. Only a few days to go now. Nothing on the horizon, just plastic reindeers. About one year on, one year older and nothing happened. Today is no different from yesterday or tomorrow.

It was Friday, Christmas Eve 1993 and being not quite ready for anything I watched television. Only a picture to look into, to keep from a solitary existence. Alone and isolated I am with unnatural stubbornness wasting away the hours. This was exquisite unhappiness. There was nothing on the television or the characters upon it to tell of anything of the world. I tediously absorbed all of it for nothing but presence of false company and much exasperation. Pins and needles below the knee of the left leg were testimony to this peculiar discourse. The television was an old and tested companion when I have no one. I was its humble friend, or rather it was mine as it served to mollify pride and passion by means of sharp perception.

I had a very private opinion that I chose to silently ignore and draw away from, yet it was clear that if I left this view alone for long enough, something would be bound to happen. So I waited with patience and withered hope that time would eventually produce a flow of life from the tardy hours. Something will turn up. I no longer had the weird experiences of inexplicable visions, those that had been much more than ordinary daydreams. Plenty of deep sleep in recent months seemed to have erased any possibility of the phenomenon repeating. It was good sleep which had saved peace of mind like being wrapped in a blanket, cosy within and only looking out at others. Other lives, other people, moving both forward and backward while mine remained there arrested on the spot. The kind of equilibrium for mind and body gave me reason to think beyond certain confines. The timid, yet willing eyes of sleep and the darkness behind them had led me foolishly perhaps to imagine I could predict the future. To foretell precisely an event beyond the present is of course a doubtful concept. Yet to envisage that some indeterminate event would happen somewhere soon and close to home could easily please any sceptic on the balance of probability. If things do not stay the same they will change, is a safe prediction and there is nothing prophetic in that. I could then perhaps forgive myself for thinking that I knew something important was going to occur very soon and as fate would have it happen on Christmas tide.

It came as a disturbing intuitive mood, somehow from the calm tranquil night or the pulsing television. A clouded moon was there outside. As I looked out, the streetlights appeared cold and foreboding. The antipathy of light and gloom just then made me shiver. I checked the lock on the door as if to prevent the feeling, this seemed to do the trick as imagined beckoning fingers faded. Gradually the strange moment softened as if trodden by some sympathetic foot. I chose to switch off the nonsense program that had not held any attention and fell quickly into gentle slumber.

The telephone woke me. While opening eyes I corrected distorted vision by plunging probing fingers into screwed up sockets. The noise seemed to become louder like bells in a steeple, the noise drilling into my head. I stood up with more than the occasional twitch by moving with expressive determination. The telephone ringing in the early hours brought utmost vigilance of mettle. On realising the dozing off in the chair, a glance at the clock revealed one twenty-seven, Christmas Day! While simultaneously eyeing the telephone and hearing the ring, I partly expected it to speak announcing a ghostly Christmas visitation. It kept repeating of course, not words as might have been a ridiculous presumption, but astonishingly loud tones which cut through the silent night. I guessed correctly at the preparatory utterance from the caller by instinctively knowing the origin. It was Tom as I confidently assumed. "I'm coming in. Give me five minutes." The phone went dead, no explanation necessary it seemed. Nothing to be gleaned from his intonation. Not quite, but almost slightly stamping a foot I wondered what he had meant. 'I'm coming in,' was probably some battle cry of retreat. And would that 'five minutes' be to allow for his arrival or was it merely five minutes of time to spend in his company. He sounded fairly calm, yet irregular enough to justify or allow his imminent intrusion. As one does when a little perplexed and expecting an untimely visitor at such a moment – I switched the kettle on. A kind of scratchy knock at the door was heard apprehensively before boiling point had given time enough to contemplate contaminative baggage.

Tom had seen better days, yet his expressive gaze of satisfaction and intelligence gave a contrary air. His face glowed undignified giving off a loathsome indifference procured by a dreadful deed. I curtly said, "You have killed him, haven't you?" His returned look offered nothing but a stare which was not consciously connected to my words. He had killed him. I knew for sure as confirmed absolutely by the vivid intensity on his face. "You better drink this you idiot." He took the hot tea. I must have looked the image of despair. "You have blood on your hands." A quick inspection revealed more blood soaked into his coat. Backs of my fingers instinctively felt the clammy dampness as if resigned to approve the act of murder. I conducted him to the kitchen and sat him down. "Take off your shoes." Enthroned upon the stool, hardened by fatigue and softened by the business – he stared now bewildered. "Take off your shoes," I repeated. He was oblivious to all instruction in that state. I bent neck and knees to heave away his muddy shoes. "Stand up," I demanded, "stand up, you idiot." I proceeded to unfasten his coat while he remained seated. I gave up for a moment to breathe and waited in that surreal space of the early hours. The kitchen with its clean surfaces, Tom stunned in the middle as solid as a statue and now myself again pulling hard at his sleeve. The main zip had broken but one button stayed fast, so I tugged savagely until the coat broke open. I shoe horned his rigid arm from the sleeve at the elbow. On a twist and a final wrench I fell back against the table complete with coat in arms. Tom recoiled, then took tea again.

The collar of the coat was matted and felt greasy as I held it tightly examining the pockets. A heavy object swung against my leg as I rummaged. "Not exactly army issue," I said. It was what looked like a cowboy gun which was ever so gently placed in the sink. Another pocket had pen and paper with a map sketched upon it. The next had a bloody handkerchief, deeper was a thick wad of banknotes, all fivers on scrutiny. "There must be five hundred pounds here."

"Six," he corrected with his first words.

"Oh, it speaks."

The contents from the pockets were deposited into the sink. The cold tap dripped just once as if to emphasise that each item was part of the same story. I piled shoes and coat together in the corner for disposal at the convenient time. Tom stared vacantly at the pile while shivering a little. In the bedroom was found the seldom worn coat and a new pair of shoes which were too big for me anyway. The clothing was received with good grace by Tom who was beginning to come around at last. I refreshed his mug of tea as if it were some bizarre remedy to purge the soul.

It was almost two o'clock and stillness outside was broken momentarily below the window as late drinkers celebrated Christmas. The night cast its shadow upon Tom who was spotlighted beneath the bulb. The sound of the bin bag rustling was almost enough to pierce eardrums as I put dirty shoes and coat into it, "There." Removing the contents of the sink to the table before I could wash my hands made him wince as realisation hit him again. "I don't know about guns Tom, but that looks like it should belong to 'Dirty Harry'. How come you have a gun?"

"It was his." I emptied his pockets. "Found that. I don't really know why I took it. It has not been fired, as far as I know, at least not tonight. I stabbed him a few times, four or five maybe."

"Is that all," sarcastically. "Only five, that's all right then. So you had a knife and he had a gun. You won?"

"I took him by surprise. It was so easy. I thought about it for months. The dread and fear of it – all that planning – all over now. When the moment came it was easy. I found what seemed like superhuman strength.

Both hands, one almighty thrust. I felt the knife hit bone as it sunk in. I pulled it out real quick with a big wiggle. I did it again and again until he was dead. Once was probably enough. I was possessed in that one second. There was blood everywhere, squirting, pumping and that look on his face. He was dead and the feet really do twitch like on those war films."

"Where's the knife? What did you do with the knife?" In the quiet he calmly drank more tea. "Tom," I said slowly, "where is the knife?"

Tom's blank face was not about indicate any sign of hurrying. A gradual disagreeable impression surrounded him as he contemptuously said, "Don't worry, I got rid of it. And, before you ask, I wiped it clean of prints. They cannot link it to me that way."

"Yes, the police, not immediately, what about anyone else?"

"Robert, trust me. I have been planning this for months. No thanks to you by the way. No one can make a connection back to me. Coming here now was part of plan 'B'. Killing someone for the first time is fairly stressful. I could not make it back straight away you see. I know you would help me out at this time."

"Thanks for the complement compliment, I guess this makes me an accessory."

"That's why you are not going to tell anyone. Just you and Nick need to know."

"Does Nick approve?"

"He does not know yet. What Nick does not know cannot harm him, or me, or you. Trust me, Robert, it has all gone smoothly."

"Why did you take his gun?"

"I did not expect him to be carrying a gun. Perhaps I should have left it with the stuff."

"What stuff?"

"Well, he had some coke of course. I had to leave it to show the police that his murder was drug related to distract them."

"You dope, that will lead them to suspect that the opposite is true. Don't you see, if it was drug related the murderer (you that is) would take all the stuff? He will be known to the police anyway, you idiot, as a known dealer. Still you took his money I see."

"Yeah, I don't want it. You can have it. Think of it as hush money."
"Cheers."

"He had a wallet too, I dumped that with the knife."

"Great, so they find the knife and the wallet together. That's smart. At least they won't charge you with wasting police time."

"Okay, maybe that was not a smart move, but that should work for me. The police might just assume that it was a robbery that went wrong. If they come to find him with coke, a gun, identification and cash they might just assume it was a hit. This way they are confused."

"So what happens now? In the morning when the happy families are going on their Christmas walks with new bikes, dogs old and new. They find a dead body, in a hollow, somewhere in the woods I suppose, covered in leaves and branches!"

"Something like that. It may take a while for the body to be found by anybody. I hid it very well. A few days perhaps. Kids are not likely to find it. I have thought this all out. Give me credit Robert. I picked the best time of year, all perfect like the D Day landings."

Chapter Eighteen

That great day in nineteen hundred and forty-four! The beginnings of summer, perfect day, a window in time, armed to the teeth and ideal weather for such an operation. It was do or die. All in, no looking back or nothing worthwhile for tomorrow. Those soldiers who ran up the beaches, they risked their lives for future generations. We the grateful successive generations, salute those brave men. All who marched triumphantly into France and the others who died for us – every one of them a hero. The violent collision was far from perfect, though proud are we all of this imperfection.

There was hidden within me, a conceit at Tom's malicious relish and I had a restrained repulsion towards the vulgar comparison which he made. Tom had put together an unworthy association with his own foul deed and that great military operation which saved us. Tom saw it as planned well, being carefully constructed in advance, a fine meticulous strategy to an operation requiring precision. This was stealth, weapon, trial, deed, triumph, but not necessarily in that order. These are the extreme thoughts that occupied my head, gradually waking on that which was another Christmas morning. The only kind of perfection was formed indifference, accordingly asymmetric in a makeup of feelings and knowledge – directed at Tom. The bizarre relationship between he and I meant nothing now. The recent murder had left a stain, but was merely another hopeless consequence which had unwound to the end.

I sat up in bed and recalled drop by drop that my demeanour towards Tom in the early hours had in the end been far from agreeable. Without actually coming to blows, or at all threatening, I had suggested something of conflicting hospitality. 'You can sleep on the sofa for a few hours, but make sure you have gone off out by breakfast.' Now in the bedroom, past the space that should have been breakfast time, I was still alive. Tom had not added me to his murdered list during the night. Or maybe, I questioned, he was just deferring, for there was plenty of opportunity to do it? Again, indifference, this is how I felt, without possession of happiness. Of course, instinctively, I would defend myself if attacked and would not be keen on being stabbed several times and left alive to die.

Gone was the immediate habit of the day, no stretching. Just a sharp ear of extraordinary application to detect any sound of movement. All was silent, except for the always-active refrigerator which under normal circumstances would not be heard. The acuteness of rabbit ears could not have sensed any sign of Tom, so with nerves settled I creaked the door open. The sofa had only two cushions upon it. I said 'Tom' out loud for him to reply if present. The measured volume was just enough to be heard in every part of the silent flat. My special attention decreased as I plonked down on the sofa relieved. He had left the bag of blooded clothes for my disposal. A knot had been tied at the neck, very precise and tight as if to depict a punishment for his sin. Tom was not usually neat in anything observable, yet here it was, all squared in the keenest of his powers avenging the death of Jim. This now done meant the arrival at his destination. The only obstacle now in Tom's way was his very own disaster. He was on his own now, much more than I could ever imagine being. His wrath and vengeance had worked a wicked way. Now he must deal with the future and maybe suffering is not enough.

Perhaps Tom had already begun the process, he had recovered the watch which once belonged to Jim. The watch was there, centred on the kitchen table. He had left it for me. Perhaps leaving it there was the beginning of it, now with the obsession to kill extinguished. The strap was very shabby, though watch itself obviously expensive. It had belonged to Jim, but still worthless to me. The blood, the watch and Tom's confession was surely enough circumstance to prove that he had killed. It was pointless to entertain any doubt of the crime, for it had been executed, proved sufficient, beyond any further question.

During the second coffee of the morning, a disturbing thought occurred to mind. There it was, the obvious notion of the possibility which had evaded all sensible thinking until then. Perhaps leaving the blooded clothes and the watch here was a trap. Had Tom as part of his operation (not unlike a military exercise) set me up in a frame for the murder? All he had to do was anonymously phone the police and point them towards me. Could the police, at any moment burst in and find the evidence – plus a further capping clue of a wad of notes with cocaine traces?

Things may have a habit of always flying back in your face when you least expect it, but I was never one for clichés. Tom had crossed the line, but there was honour in his vindictiveness, he would not cheat, not to the extent of blaming me, not by proxy or otherwise for the murder. At the touch of a straw, Tom might very easily collapse and go running to the police. He might mumble at the mouth, rather than shout it, 'I have made myself disgraceful', he would croak. 'What?' Police would answer with a question. Tom might garnish the words with delight, letting them see eventually that he was the one who did it. At first he might toy with them in an insane way of his, putting his face close to the main officer. Tom could pucker his features into a malevolent grin, then blabber out with crying or a laugh and give an unearthly shriek. It could be a way of business, as part of another perfect plan to convince them of a madness that was part of him. Tom could do passion.

For this crime of murder to be convincing as a kind of passion it must be opened up to various interpretations such as moral justice. Revenge as a means of gratification against humiliation was more of a poor excuse rather than a sympathetic defence. Mitigating circumstance was actually weak, there was no escaping from the facts as I saw them. This crime was committed with malice aforethought, they would call it Murder One in the USA. Tom was guilty of it, in every piece of the process. It was premeditated because he formulated a plan to kill him. He deliberated over it, weighed up the pros and cons. Nick and I tried in our futile way. We explored the consequences together, attempted to stop Tom. We could not prevent his intent. Tom steeped in his very own will, ignoring our plea, carried out his plan with the greatest of intention and succeeded. I told him murder would be madness. Maybe Tom was mad. Murder certainly seemed like madness, maybe this could be his mitigating circumstance to diminish the crime into a partial exoneration for Tom.

The police would ask Tom questions that he would decline to answer. They might say, 'while you are helping us with our enquires, stubborn silence is not helping your case.' More likely he would speak, tell them all of it. Eventually they would throw him out. They would say, 'the man is a nutter. He claims he has killed someone and cannot remember where he dumped the body'. Or if the body has been found, say, 'the man is a nutter. He must have read it in the newspaper, he has not told us anything that is not already public knowledge'. Meanwhile as Tom may have been turned away, he is a rueful picture of despair, aimless and unfulfilled. Actually vengeance had not done it for him after all. Life goes on without Jim and for Tom the life of the living goes on without him.

Back to my little sofa in a quaint compact square of a lounge, it is like sitting on a park bench on a dull day. Just passing away the morning and wishing to be carried away on a magic carpet – was as usual confounded. Very own personality reined in the self. Sometimes you know that just by sitting tight, it cannot destroy your prospects. Doing nothing cannot justify a decent future, one really has to think ahead. Living as I was is a feeble imitation of life. Apt was the great escape, switching on the television to discover that very film *The Great Escape*. Steve McQueen, what a perfect name for an actor. His casual underplay makes one warm to the screen, the acting so cool and natural makes a person want to know him. Paul

Newman, too, that same kind of charm. I want to be like them, have that graceful appeal and that indefinable something that makes women adore them. I have envious hate for timeless McQueen and Newman, so endearing. There is nothing I can do to be anything like them. I have to tell myself, each of us is unique and we all have good qualities. These qualities are perhaps things that we do not recognise in ourselves, yet others see it, others can maybe even love us for it. That is what I really want on Christmas day in nineteen hundred and ninety-three, I want someone to love me for part of me that is me. The over used word, 'love'. I want to love them for loving me and I want them to love me for loving them. I blame Tom, for it is he who has made me feel this way. Because I hate him. Tom can fuck off. I want nothing to do with him ever again. He is the ultimate bad penny.

This is me, I am not Steve McQueen in The Great Escape, I am not Paul Newman in The Sting, I am Robert Oakley in Whitches. This was not comfort, this was hobbling along in misery. Drizzle, dull, Christmas day and a bag over my shoulder like rejected Santa. Street by deserted street I ventured, looking for a suitable place to dump the incriminating clothes. In the festive gloom I imagined people having a wonderful time, all hemmed into their houses like caged birds. They have to be so nice to their relatives, some against their will. They want to scream, though choosing instead to drown themselves in alcohol. To endure the period, they might peck at the walls, tear out their feathers. A net curtain would twitch, there could be flapping wings and a beak scratching out at the window.

I would quake momentarily, thinking of the consequences of getting caught. It was taxing, keeping a serene innocent face. There was no darkly threatening action to worry about while limping down an empty street in broad daylight complete with bag, careless, neither subtle nor cautious. It was an extreme case of foolishness, any mischance could see me up to my neck, yet I did not care. Boldness was blessed by fortune as I found a perfect place for disposal. There was a suitable corridor, little more than an alleyway, between the backs of shops and houses, where bin bags were piled at various intervals. I took this route which was empty of life, save for a tabby cat. The place became host to my bag, this was relief, for no longer was it dangerous and repellent upon my back. Now unburdened I could return home again and drop the watch into a street grate. It was over, the gentle despatched splash confirmed it.

Despite the monstrous distraction of murder, the essence of passing time was still the softener of anger and consoler of affliction. Circumstances which once blazed away would smoulder and then eventually extinguish. Yet, exasperation and passion will always be a characteristic of world and life. To be a slave to living seemed as natural as a prisoner who is a willing captive. Being caged like a bird stifles a person useless and clips the wings of a free mind. To comprehend the truth so honestly is to know that there is nothing so unnatural and yet being so seems most natural. To judge oneself so harshly does little for esteem. I wish I were a doctor or something, nothing as righteous as a clergyman, but at least a family man with commitments and goals. Not any of this, I am Robert Oakley, just a reflection of my own life or a manifestation of circumstance. I am the foot that treads the path. I am the wheel that meets the road. I am everything that follows and what has been. I lament at future possibilities as a simple plant might enter into spring. Nothing to do but push leaves into light, at night sleep for morning and in daylight wait for dark.

Now is nineteen hundred and ninety-four. As far as I am concerned, Tom has disappeared into a void. I keep an eye and an ear tuned to every scrap of local news. A forty-seven-year-old man has been jailed for five years. He pleaded guilty to threatening staff at a post office with a fake gun. It seems that this amounts to a bungled armed robbery, where cash was taken. The culprit was caught soon afterwards and the cash was completely recovered. An independent inquiry has been confirmed to investigate how seven patients died at The County Hospital. A mystery illness, apparently, it only came to light retrospectively as up to forty former patients had complained. Police had found the body of an elderly woman at a gravesite in woods. There is speculation that the body is that of Joanne Spencer, who has been missing from her home for several months.

Nick would have been quick to make a critique of the news. He would be selective of course, homing in on everything involving police incompetence as a positive factor to summing up. 'The good plod have succeeded in locking up a harmless middle-aged man for up to five years for holding up a post office with a toy pistol. The cost to the taxpayer is immaterial. Further, as a bonus they captured all the missing loot, without one penny of it going missing – remarkable. Meanwhile, other officers acting on information accumulated over half a year, stumble upon a long deceased missing person – brilliant.'

It was good to know that the two-week-old corpse had not been discovered. The chances of Tom getting away with it were increasing day on day. Remote possibility indeed, perhaps the police were not even looking for a missing person.

A dreary impression of a new January was an especial contradictory feature of bright morning sunshine. Blue sky and airy clouds implored a vigorous freshness to one's struggle in life. The message, sublime as it was, conquered the day and provided refuge for the night. Waking each day before dawn was the hardest thing, a sickly wound from the peculiar event of that Christmas. Dread of this feeling repeatedly stamped the murder indelible. Impossible to bury and not forgetting would always make it an injury to tolerate. The sickliness was understood as a mental symptom of condemning and condoning hypocrisy.

Notwithstanding the agitation or nausea of mind and body, I walked on. To move along the straight street thus, was the only way ahead and be absolutely resolved to the town. Quietly acknowledge the little, raindrops, shadows on the pavement, simply see the world about, this is the faithful reality which I am bound. The ground beneath my feet is the path into tomorrow. The direction of the day to wherever, endeavouring is the key, get up as one with life and advance into the morning. The strengthening sunshine cast upon the town accompanies a mood of optimism. Good morning Whitches and good day to people in Whitches. Breathe it, drink it, fresh air and exercise of walking never did a person any harm. This was the moment, just there all around, it meant yet another point where a move towards something better and perfectly restorative could begin. It seemed that the sun reflecting upon windows of successive houses had lit many lights just for me. A number of endless possibilities were hinting out for me and to the world as the sun shone. The shining made an appeal, a kind of confidence made from light as if it were a signal, a pointer of unspoken hopefulness. The extended moments of walking and the passing of people appeared to convey a conviction into mind. It was moving, listening and watching that made me wonder eventually. Well that and the sight of a woman.

Falling visually to the attractive persuasion of the female was a snare to which I easily became entangled that morning. The not uncommon sight of a woman's legs exposed from knee to ankle was nothing unusual, yet this ordinary spectacle of the day was given to my stare. These were the most perfect pair of legs ever to be seen. Sheathed in burgundy fishnet they gave rise to the most compromising imaginings. Sheer lust had rekindled a dormant virility and as such I was less expert at controlling a particular body part than a thirteen-year-old schoolboy. Despite the impromptu embarrassment, there was no one near enough to witness this change of state. The not so obvious thing to do is to think of a constructive counter measure, an incomparable vivid memory, such as school cabbage, the funeral of a friend or a murder for a friend.

The legs were not as shapely as Kate's, overly straight perhaps, but delectably adorned. Leaner than Miranda's, but the consensus is that thin legs are better than fat ones. The woman, older than Kate and younger than Miranda had these legs. I wondered had she seen this licentious look,

208

perhaps she had not noticed, maybe unaware, probably unconcerned and preoccupied with things to do. Being noticed so, is likely to be just a symptom of dressing smartly and stylish. Or do women dress to encourage the attention of men? Do they like being objects of desire? I do not suppose this woman wants men such as me lusting, imagining her wearing suspenders. Or maybe being watched by a younger man such as I is a turn on, nothing so sexy as to be the object of desire? Women do not dress to please men, they dress to please themselves. I want to ask her if this is true, but it seems there is nothing more ridiculous than approaching and asking, "Do you know you are driving me crazy, oh and by the way could you answer me this?"

The comfort of undertaking such a walk indicated that I had not lost all heed of space and time. I should have been at work hours ago, yet this diversion was just a blip. In all considerations it was a pervy expedition, I conveniently labelled it as a handsome dream which had fused together reality and impossibility into a dubious kind of balance. Of course dreaming with eyes open and wandering aimlessly with direction seemed to be as faulty as it was particularly contradictory. Nevertheless, for a while, faculty of thought gave an impression which was temporarily caught in the power of obsession. Feminine aesthetic was favourably influenced by a configuration of footwear where the height of the heel determined the appeal. My eyes delighted at numerous legs in various shapes, forms from darn right ugly to absolute perfection. The well-turned ankle is especially under-appreciated these days. In olden times, the rare sight of a of a stark ankle was regarded as risqué enough to set the male pulse racing, meanwhile, exposed breasts with cleavage was commonplace and humdrum.

I struggled to arrest this great theme and wondered with serious caution if thinking this way was at all normal. The worry that I might be turning into a weirdo was becoming real. The images of women's legs from toe to knee adorned with shoe and stocking was the cause of this. The symptom of this very thing was to not look above the knee for fear of disappointment. An unlikely source for the apprehension of these thoughts was the beach, not an actual shore with sand, but an unreal one. A beach, scores of miles from the sea, not inland but in my head. This was the strategy deployed to overcome the emerging fetish and it worked by using sensible control.

Now with the device successfully in place, if every one of us is represented as a single fragment, the many pebbles offered numerous possibilities. The lashing sea pounds, knocks us about in similar directions, yet our individualities enable alternative movements. Take a pebble, there are many and I am just one. As the sea erodes the rock, the waves of life wear away at a person. Abrasive is the process, grinding, smoothing, then one huge event cuts away, breaking hard rock like a chisel. The pieces are sharp, have jagged edges, yet only the sea of life can make them blunt again, by filing away, gradually smoothing, soothing with harsh caresses. Perfectly rounded is the goal, yet the cast of it is the litter of sand. Life and the purpose of living results in erosion. So what, life is a grind, we know it, this is taken for granted. All so similar, all so unique, we are like pebbles upon the shore and by living we throw our grains onto the beach of sand. Like pebbles we are different, colour, shape, texture, harder, softer, old, new, hove down and pleasant to touch.

The very spirit of weirdness became weak as if faint hearted, then arid as I found the oasis of Edison Café again. Still blasé, only this was no longer Edison Café. The venue was the same, it was the name, prices and food that had changed. Décor and furniture were exactly as they were since the last time. There was not a sign of the cod faced, prawn eyed, bald apple headed man who had caused me to rush out with a hasty retreat. The reuniting with this place known now as 'The Coffee Pot' also gave rise to the reminder of Edmund. I found myself a little flushed besmeared with sweat. There was a little credit in being red and out of breath for it confirmed that I was against any doubt human after all. However, the recall of this memory acted as a psychological cue to mental suffering and possible danger. The feelings were more pronounced now, than during the time months ago when there was good reason to believe a dire prospect. Obviously the passage of time had not had sufficient duration to complete the work of allaying anxiety. The Coffee Pot was not recognised as charmed ground, so the application of common sense worked a way for about five minutes until I felt sufficiently easy of mind again. It became clear that moments like these were ones which I would have to endure on and off indefinitely. Nothing was so easy as to purpose as disposing of a meaningful diver watch down a drain.

A 'pot' of coffee was indeed my opium, it was both loving cup and poisoned chalice. Coffee made life bright bushy tailed and dull as night. Another drink with further sips, taste of habit and a habit of taste. Moreover, coffee tuned my life into focus, let things happen, allowed my existence under pep. Drink coffee in, nothing so potent keeping me awake, then falling later into rapid sleep. Shaking my head as it aches, due to coffee. It does little for any amount of sense. This was where I was in the world, full of vitality and all out of vigour.

Chapter Nineteen

An unseasonable mild January night and occasional noise from the street allowed me only to doze uneasily, but never sleep. As each hour passed I became more exhausted of mind and body. Always present was the light from the street which shone through the shaded window. The delicate glare pervaded all rest like a dull sorrow or a half-lulled sense of pain. I thought of Jim and the last time I saw his face. When I sleep there is seldom a dream to be had, yet with these eyes and this night I could have dreamt it.

Jim came to sit beside me. He was younger than any memory to be recalled. He said, he was better known as James, and smarter now too. I said, if you are so clever, how come you are naked? He said, there is no need for clothes in heaven and he was more normal now like before the accident which had made him weak of mind. I asked James, how did he die? He said, he did not remember, but that did not matter, he only knew that he was dead, (and I believed him). I said to James, what is it like to be dead? He said, being dead is like nothing that can be told (he had convinced me).

Jim (I mean James) was a good man, Jim was so honest, to see him here again assured the truth. I felt emotion of joy and pain, but no longer did I pity him. He said, he was sorry that Kate had left me and added that the bonds of grief are the greatest bonds that bind us. He said that, Thomas, Nicholas and himself were not for talking about. About me he said, sympathy is not up for discussion, it is just that things have happened to you. Misfortune is actually a gift from god which gives a man courage towards constancy into tomorrow. Today will become yesterday and tomorrow will become today. I did not reply but asked him eventually, what of Miranda? He said that he does not know who Miranda is, or how she lives, therefore he has no opinion about her. He only knows from the emotion, tone and tremble in my voice when I say her name that I have feelings for her. He said, because he was dead, whatever I do will not make a difference to him. Further, he told me that whatever I do will make a difference to me, it is that one makes fate and not fate makes one. He said, think always that he is left in the grave so he can stay forever with his kind. He then said, I should never dream of him again. A noisy car passed by to indicate an alliance with reality and then I fell into a dreamless sleep until just before noon.

Within the mirror frame, a shadow had fallen upon my face, the dreary meaning of it was more expressive than if I had groaned out loud. The reflection told a story which acknowledged both the presence and absence of Jim. The darkness upon his face had become deeper as he turned away and momentarily there was increased comprehension as the glance wandered back again. If he was here at this place of dwelling, then we were in silent company together. It was early in the night and late in the day to be haunted, if indeed that was the case. I found a shrewdly expectant intelligence, yet it was still absurd and valueless. In the anxious anticipation there was no supernatural expression, only natural disappointment in the incredulity. Not a movement, sound, vision or any form of connectedness could be detected. There was only the ghost of some remembrance which had inspired enlightenment. The information that had been given now seemed vague in my forgetful state. Recalling what I thought he may have said weakened the very process of reasonable thinking. Through the jumble to an end, I became impatient to conclude with any rational assumptions. Despite serious scepticism and indistinct remembering, I may have been caught somewhere. Perhaps it was a half world where there was some kind of echo of something which I believed to be him. In that very place I was offered, rather than given particular messages. Why this happened and what it conveyed seemed really unimportant. The important thing appeared to be that an event which could have been other worldly had occurred and this either had a point or it did not. Whichever way it was, my interpretation was the same. A voice said, do not chew over that which is eating upon your mind, for this is negative, do what is positive by leaving the past to itself.

Mild air confirmed the sun was burning freely behind grey clouds. The sky was faded enough to be melancholy, yet sufficiently bright for optimism. This provided good encouragement. Control was the key to my new journey, a mission which had materialised as if it were a command. Simple apprehension of purpose that should have been obvious, struck as it was, for this had sunk in eventually. No preparation, just a directive through streets, thoughtful and confident. This was the means to which I was bound, completely focussed on the one thing. My footsteps were hurried, but restrained enough to be only walking, though towards it on and on. Little attention was given to the taking in of surroundings during the quick conveyance. Instead, energy and emphasis was offered to alternative examinations. Preoccupied with the various possibilities ahead, the head raced and my heart thudded on.

I stopped a short distance from my intended destination. While waiting for some minutes, I began to absorb all that was around. This was a kind of needy observation, very familiar and the memory not tainted. A little had changed perhaps, but essentially all was as remembered. The gate was closed, the house at the end of the path and driveway appeared empty. This was a poor clue, for every house in the vicinity looked empty and surely not all of these could be unoccupied. In the exceptional stillness, there was a silence as if I were the only person left in the world. The presence of a black and white cat on a neighbouring lawn explained the absence of birds. A collapsed spider web hung from a damp evergreen as if to tell something. Could this be signalling a mysterious message, or just a simple notion that I should give up perhaps by turning around and heading back?

A tiny squeak of rusty hinges cut into the afternoon as the gate gently vibrated through my hands. The attempt to close with as little noise as possible made me question again, why? To spring this mine upon myself shivered and tested resolve of self-reliance. A small anxious fever encroached which could have easily swollen into panic. I stood still, clinging inside the garden, not letting go of the metal on the gate. Perhaps the iron served to send anxiety to earth somehow as I managed in the successive minutes to master that feeling. The encounter with the very near future was blind, regardless of risk, this could only happen if made to. An unexpected rendezvous, a brave meeting, face to face, it would trigger a momentary shock, emotions induced for both of us.

Like an imagined electric shock or the trembling of the ground, a knock upon the door meant absolutely no escape. When no one came, I shrank there as if to let the air go by in a sweep of breeze. Then rising courage again, I knocked hard as if in confidence, almost knowing there would be no answer. Surprisingly, unintelligible sounds could be heard by listening very carefully, neither their nature nor origin could be determined. I suddenly felt strangely remote and unprotected as if exposed to any terror. The very instant was short lived as now I heard a female voice speaking to another within. There came the turning of the key in the lock and lifting of the latch on the door. Too late! No time to run now! Suddenly as the door began to open, I felt so alone amid the unravelling plan. Stood before and looking down to my lower level was a young woman who could at first sight have been mistaken for my former girlfriend. The expression upon her face was both of great surprise and astonished recognition. She closed the door in one slow movement as if caught in a protective second of indecision. I remained frozen in that bewildering moment, rapidly trying to interpret. A surge of fear hit me together with an empathic sympathy to explain her action. Perhaps I had a dormant wayward scheme which was as yet unknown or understood. During this contemplation, the door was opened again, only this time swung wide and inviting. The same woman stood before me. I first understood her to be Kate, against all sensible probability. Her eyes and hair looked like those of Kate. She was of similar height, but thinner and much younger than Kate. This woman was a teenager. This teenager was a girl. This girl was a young woman. A very short skirt, ostentatious cheap jewellery of plastic beads and bangles disguised the woman beneath. First I saw her adorable long legs, principle focus being from ankle to knee. A drifting vision to above the knee left me doubting personal morality. Direction of eyes switched quickly to her head. The nose was not retroussé anymore and other facial features had grown pleasantly into those of a woman. Breasts had developed accordingly, but the hips still required more time.

"Hello, Patricia. Is your mother in?"

Patricia could easily remember who I was as the voice reaffirmed and consolidated the appearance there. She either chose not to answer or was actively flummoxed by the situation. "Come in," she said in an accepting tone of surprise. She held the door back as I stepped inside. I stood waiting as Patricia closed the door. She swaggered ahead, her body summoning me deeper inside. The lounge was empty except for the furniture. Sofa and chairs had a resonance, an affectionate reminder of Miranda. A peculiar light from the mirror and fire gave off a subtle echo pertaining to Adam. "Sit down, please." Patricia pointed to a particular chair.

I gave a nervous cough before sitting. "Thank you, is your mother in?"

Patricia was stood as I sat, then she stepped towards me. With arms folded, she placed weight on one leg, while the other formed a large 'D' against it. The seemingly provocative exercise had caused her tight skirt to ride higher upon her hips. Patricia's bare thighs were uncomfortably close at eye level. "Yes, she is upstairs. Mum will be down soon. Mum knows that you are here." My eyes falsely looked away, always despising a lust which was then the uppermost theme. A lurking desire for this young woman was a distinct contradiction which pervaded each thought. The constant idea that Patricia had a misshapen scheme of retaliation about her, foxed the life out of me. This was clearly a woman who had recently gained the awareness that she could infect a man's behaviour. I was sure Patricia could artfully entrap men, for her crude display against my will was not completely ineffectual. "Shall I put the kettle on," she suggested while lifting the hem of her skirt slightly then stroking a thigh with long nails.

"That would be nice," I replied as she moved into view again. There was a point of potent virility while adjusting my seat in the chair. Patricia smiled again, now perhaps she was content with her own knavery and a little abashed at the accomplished feminine device. We heard an announcing cough from Miranda, whose presence had been obscured behind Patricia. The daughter turned around quickly and in doing so seemed to separate one subject from another.

"Tea would be nice for all of us, Patricia," this accompanied a motherly look of discordance to daughter. Mother and daughter seemed to merge momentarily in passing, Miranda within to the lounge and Patricia out and away into the kitchen. Miranda saved me the awkward embarrassment of standing by gesturing a polite apprehension to stay seated as I was shuffling forward in the chair. Miranda crossed her legs at the knees, the jeans were black, socks and slippers pink. "You have to excuse my daughter and her sexy legs. She has recently found out, we women have sexual power over men and how to play it upon your weakness for our strength. However, she has yet to refine her prowess, as you have discovered, 'in your face' is not very subtle or ladylike."

I could not hide the creeping laughter. "I am so pleased that you turned up when you did. Who knows what could have happened."

Miranda smirked, "Yes, that worries me a bit. I know Patricia well enough, she feels absolutely safe while I'm here to protect her from herself. Patricia was actually teasing herself, not you," Miranda paused as if to register my reaction in her mind.

"Oh?"

Miranda laughed, "Robert you are practically salivating! Do not flatter yourself. Her real targets are to provoke handsome boys who fantasise uncontrollably with swollen pants. Thankfully, Patricia does not know your value. For her an older man is a challenge. She is unwittingly honing a craft, all the time learning and developing a way to manipulate your race. There is much more to being a woman than you can ever imagine."

"You are a constant amazement to me."

"Thank you. So how are you? What is your life like these days? What brings you here today?"

I want to say that I seem fine, but really I am not. Life is a long road stretching out, away to the horizon which is always receding and never gained. I want to tell her that some facsimile of Jim burgeoned me into coming here. I want to tell Miranda that I came here panting, filled with battered optimism and am throwing myself at her cosy pink feet. "I am fine, life is okay and I was just passing."

Patricia entered, legs the same and breaking the barrier with a tea tray. Miranda quickly found a space on the coffee table to place it. "Are you not joining us, Patricia?" Miranda questioned the obvious whilst observing two cups to one teapot.

215

"Mum, I'm going out. And before you ask I am going to see Wendy. You have lots to talk about I'm sure. Best that I'm not here, so see you later."

"Don't be silly darling. At least stay a while talk to Robert with me."

"Muumm!"

"Oh really, Patricia," resigned. "What about Lauren?"

"Mum, I am sure you can cope." Patricia kissed her mother on the forehead. "See you, Rob," she swaggered away.

"See you, Trish," in a reply neutrally defined. Soon the door banged behind her.

"Shall I be Mum?" Miranda poured the tea. "So?"

"You look well, Miranda." She had lost weight and looked older, more than by the months that had passed since we were lovers. I picked up the cup.

"Adam died," her eyes moved as she spoke as if unable to look at me directly.

"Yes, I guessed, I'm sorry. Was it then at the hospital when I last saw you?"

"I'll never forget the rain, that day." Her eyes were welling with tears. "Yes, it was then." She pressed a cuffed wrist hard to each socket to absorb and only able to say these few words without crying. I was easily taken into infectious emotion, being overwhelmed by a togetherness feeling of compassion and regret. Furniture appeared to be so unlike anything resembling its function. Table and chairs suddenly seemed obsolete. At the spur of this moment, the sofa was awkward like one giant obstacle and I was rapidly overcome. By Miranda's feet I knelt, to be tender and protective, I reached out for her hand. She composed herself a little, clasping my hand, touching my hair and confessing a tiny laugh against red eyes. "I saw you through the window. I saw the condition you were in. At first, I could not believe you were here. I felt the nervous apprehension that you gave off at the gate. I thought I would never see you again. I tried to erase you by attaching a hate to our brief love somehow. Obviously it did not work. Look at me. Look at us. Oh Robert, why are you here? Things have happened, it isn't like it was. I mean the situation. Oh god, what's the matter with me?"

The question was taken as rhetorical and I had no idea of the answer anyway. "Miranda, there is nothing the matter. Everything will be fine," this sounded weak and unconvincing. "I did not want to leave you then, but I did as you asked," I said, now proud of the words and able to look into her eyes again with confidence.

"I did not want that, you know it. It was for appearance sake, you know it. Then you never called until now?"

216

"Miranda, I have thought of you –"

She interrupted, pushing my head away, "Do you like my breasts?"

"What? Yes I suppose so, yes I always did. What do you mean?" I was left confused by the strange digression.

"You appear to have a special interest in them, you keep looking like longing."

Perhaps some of my vision had fallen there. I was lost to explain. I searched for a compromise to simultaneously confess and excuse. "Have you had surgery – a boob job – mastectomy?"

"No," she said half teasing, half-serious and definitely confusing me.

"They look different."

"Oh, how?"

I noticed her bright red cardigan of fine fabric, tied with coloured buttons like boiled sweets. "They are swollen, fuller and your nipples are pointy through the wool."

"So how have you thought of me, naked perhaps? Is that it?"

I was becoming lost in the questioning and was not quite sure where all this was going. I tried to get back on track. "I have thought of you. I was overtaken by events. I met someone soon after we were last together." Saying these words together like this seemed wrong despite the truth of it all. I did not want to tell Miranda anything about Kate. "She left me, but that is not why I'm here."

"So why are you here?"

"I honestly do not know. I have been on my own a good while now. We loved each other didn't we? Maybe we could again. See how it goes."

Miranda stood up, moved to the window and looked out. She left me waiting for her reply which then came energetically. "What should I think Robert? This expedition of yours to see me, as if you have nothing else to do. Just passing indeed. Do you think I'm stupid? Why don't you just fuck me now and fuck off again? Or maybe you just want to fuck my daughter instead. Perhaps it is money you're after! Which is it Robert? What do you want? Do you think I am stupid or what?"

Her questioning stunned enough to leave a moment of no means of replying. I assessed 'which,' it was none of these. 'What,' I honestly did not know. 'Stupid,' certainly not. Perhaps I was the stupid one, being not able to know personal motive. "I – I'm sorry," seemed the only thing to say. "Let me try and explain somehow." This gave me more time to think and incorporate her points. There was a stammer with the, with the, inner articulation, coming backwards and forwards rapidly. I felt unworthy of Miranda and unable to convey anything confidently that could entirely be understood. It was difficult enough to conceive answers, let alone discuss them. Of course there was no one to speak for me and no one better acquainted than myself to communicate. I could have turned away in cowardice, but that would have served neither of us. I began despite the inner conflict. "I do not know what you think, only you can know that. It seems silly, but I know how it is because I don't know what I should think either." It all sounded like sophisticated gobbledygook, but I still kept on. "I know what I don't want you to think. I am not sure why you should assume that my motives are anything of what you just said. Okay, I may want to make love to you, but that is part of something else – you and me – you know that don't you – you remember that don't you? The unfounded insulting remark about me, me with your daughter, well I cannot believe you said it. I would not dream of it. You know that, you also know that you are the one I want. And okay, I know about the money, it had to be assumed and Clerk confirmed it. That's another story, all I can say is that it is your money. I don't know what to say except that money means nothing. I'm here because of you and I'm here because of me."

With emphatic quietness of feet, Miranda moved back to the sofa. She settled noiselessly among the cushions, her reddened eyes now imploring conciliatoriness. "I remember you," she began, "all too well, I tried not to. I have not grown tougher with age," Miranda pondered on this then continued, "only weaker and softer. I'm sorry, Robert." She looked away now, into an empty space as if to find her words again and sniffed a little more. "I have fallen into sorrow, kept going out of necessity and positively numbed by it to keep on. Never to be raised up again properly, or so I thought until today, until now. I want to hate you, so it can help me forget." She dabbed the corners of her eyes with a crumpled tissue. "I want to blame someone to bring about a something else and stop this empty feeling. I cannot blame you, especially not you." She turned her head to see me again. "I cannot blame anyone anymore. There is no one to burden upon. This feeling, I don't know what it is. It isn't guilt or grief, it is neither, it is numbness, like adversity, like pain and like comfort."

Miranda stopped speaking suddenly to listen. A small unidentifiable sound could be heard from outside, before the bursting open of the front door. There was more than a twinge of disquiet to my senses from this combination of events. An explaining voice was uttered, "Forgot my bag, Mum," this faded away into an abrupt door slam in her trail.

I waited a second before saying, "Do you think she...?" Miranda shook her head, curtailing the question. The movement ceased and we sat together immobile.

The moment was not prolonged as Miranda seemed to fix on something specific, and hastily left the room without imparting information. "Back in a minute," Miranda shouted unseen from behind the door.

Here I was alone again, in the room where once waiting for Adam, all of those months ago. The tardy length of time since I last saw her had finally come to an end. Miranda and me? Well, it was going to be different now. The path ahead still seemed unclear. This very short period together had already gained altitude, dipped, then high again, while all the while there was a returning to stability. Small talk had quickly been dispensed of. I had imposed upon Miranda with a statement which was a combination of virtue and selfishness. Incomplete solicitude in a mixture of ordinary concern and the desire to love again seemed like a sustainable question to be postured again for our destiny. Optimism declared itself like an appointment, yet it appeared to be a kind of guilty confession. It was as if I did not deserve a happier life or that I should be confined forever to my own lonely misery.

With Miranda having been gone some minutes, my mind was set wondering. Had she gone off in pursuit of Patricia or was she hatching a plan? When our desire for each other had been fresh, I might have imagined Miranda naked in bed awaiting my arrival. It seemed sensible now not to fling myself at the staircase in eager anticipation. For now we were just tip toeing, not ready for something so extravagant. Her mood and mine with all the volatility seemed nothing more than feeling our way back in with straightforward honesty. Perhaps Miranda was carrying something else, it was a thing that I could not possibly guess upon. At this early stage, I dared not ask what this could be, for it might spoil our progress so far. There might be nothing of course, I had been wrong before. She may object to the asking. Miranda would tell in her own time if she saw fit. I had to be available and support her. I had to be what I did not know I could be anymore.

In the light from window were bright flowers, kissed by the sun and presented through a sweet homely touch of a woman. Six daffodils, delicate, fresh, simple nature without fault. It was salutation, perceptibly captured in a discrete vase of welcoming. There were photographs too, a subtle display depicted an exclusive personal history of family. Part of the unostentatious arrangement was a six by four portrait of mother and daughter together. This photograph boasted such a perfect familial pose demonstrating the epitome of their attachment. Both showed loving smiles, Miranda looked youthful, though perhaps flattered by a few extra pounds. The daughter was definitely a youth, skinny, shapeless, but pretty just like her mother.

I felt relief that the interval was coming to an end as Miranda's footsteps could be heard again. I stood up, keen to resume the rekindling. Miranda's singing voice flavoured the air as she approached. "Poor little love, you was lonely wasn't you." My very curious attention to the application of her voice was both satisfied and astonished as she entered the room. As Miranda carefully walked towards me with the biggest ever smile, she cradled a baby. Miranda's full white breast was exposed as the infant suckled contentedly. "This is Lauren," she said, not looking at me anymore, but nodding in mutual gazing with Lauren. Their relationship immediately superseded any of mine. I was strangely stunned as I seemed to be able to do nothing except observe blue veins under the pale skin of her breast. During the pause, Miranda afforded me a smile and sat down while nursing Lauren. "You look surprised, Robert. Say hello to Lauren."

"I'm speechless," I said, now able to recover a little for the shock. Boldly my hand reached out as if possessed by its very own feeling. The baby's head beneath the fine hair felt softer than velvet. I tried to tame a masculine voice, "Hello, Lauren." Lauren's bright blue eyes looked sideways at me, though not entirely distracted from the feeding, then she saw Miranda again and disregarded me.

"She likes you," Miranda said, always soothing as if the suckling had the effect of reducing all earlier anxiety. I was profoundly overcome by emotion which determined that I kissed the baby's forehead. It was more than a velvety touch to the lips as Miranda simultaneously stroked my hair. "I'm thirsty, Robert, would you mind getting me a glass of water and help yourself to a drink?"

"All right, do you mean from the kitchen?"

"Yes of course," half-smiling with a smirk. We were tuned in again at last.

The kitchen should perhaps have provided a sanctuary to clear my muddled head, furnishing a platform to explain this unforeseen circumstance. Had Miranda had a baby? Surely, she was too old to become pregnant, by that token too past feeding, as it was, it should have been impossible. If by some miracle of medical science, Miranda was the mother, then who was the father? A grasp of maths dictated the news that it could not be me. Explanations, despite the influence of the empty kitchen, were not becoming evident. The brave visit had developed into a mystery which detracted from the original purpose. It was gradually becoming apparent however, in all the desperate months before this day I had actually always loved her.

"Breastfeeding is thirsty work, thanks," she received the glass with unusual relish. "It is also very convenient, oh and cheaper too. If I keep hydrated, Lauren gets all she needs and I lose weight. Yes, a bonus for a mum – a woman. There is reduced risk of breast cancer and less the possibility of arthritis in later life. Of course it is good for Lauren too, I burn an extra five hundred calories a day and she gets the benefit. Lauren feeds when she is hungry, but also when she feels frightened or is in pain or even just lonely."

"Oh and the fuller shape and pointy nipples." For now I had to be content with her touch via homely daffodils.

"This isn't funny, Robert. But I'm glad you like them anyway. For now these breasts belong to Lauren, they are very much part of the maternal bond that a man can never understand properly."

"There is a lot I do not understand." I keep thinking to myself, I do not understand this. "Whatever you tell me, Miranda, it will not change a thing or anything."

"Robert, I think we could be talking forever at cross purposes. Of course it changes 'a thing or anything' as you put it. Let's not think, let us just be so. Let me just tell you about benefits to baby, greater immunity as protection against disease, less chance of having eczema or developing diabetes, higher intelligence, superior…"

"Miranda," I shouted, "sorry," I spoke, "I didn't mean to shout."

"You will frighten Lauren, don't do that."

"I'm sorry, but are you going to tell me?"

"It is not easy for me to just blurt it all out like it is oh so simple. I've had to deal with things, difficult things in my world. I have not known your world lately, have I? Forgetting you, maybe was the easy part. Do not think for a moment, if you had been here that it would have made any difference. No, god knows what you must be thinking. Lauren is and isn't my child. I am far too old to be the mother of a nine-week-old baby. Lauren is not my daughter, she is my granddaughter. Patricia has been a brick. It was hard for Patricia too. We have supported each other, only my need has been the greater and there is natural limit as to how much a teenager can support a needy middle-aged woman – even if she is my daughter and I her mother. It does not work completely, not for me, I have to give much more than I have permission to take. This is where Lauren comes in, this tiny thing, this little human being, this exquisite buddle of love – she has saved me, Robert."

"I think the buddle of love is falling asleep, perhaps you better get her wind up."

"Do you mean you know about babies?"

"Not really, it is just paternal instinct. And I do not understand how you can wet nurse."

"Well, for your curious information, adoptive breastfeeding isn't so unusual, even for menopausal women. This might be a rare occurrence for Whitches, but within the realms of possibility as you have understood." Miranda adjusted herself inside the red cardigan and rubbed Lauren's back while putting her to the shoulder. "Lactation can be induced by constant stimulation like through the suckling infant. At first, the flow was only drops and then with regular feeding, I eventually produced enough milk for Lauren. Oh, and there would be little difference between my milk and mum's." Lauren obliged with a mighty burp and we laughed. "We are not supposed to laugh for baby's sake. So Robert, you learn something every day. Any more questions?"

"So why doesn't Patricia feed Lauren?"

Miranda laughed a little again and even more when she recognised my surprise at her amusement. "I think we have got our wires crossed here or at least you have. Patricia isn't the mother, thank god. No, it is a long story which is difficult to relate and telling it is not easy." She adjusted her clothing accordingly while putting Lauren to the other breast.

"You don't have to tell me a thing about anything if you don't want to."

"I want to tell you things. I need to tell you things. This is where Lauren helps me by comfort." Miranda continued in a matter of fact way. "I breast fed all my children. I always tried my best for them. Adam and I had one boy and two girls. Our son lives in New York. He would not even come home for his father's funeral. He and Adam had a big falling out over money and other things. Adam had lent him thousands to invest in stocks which plummeted. Our son then asked for more to invest in shares which subsequently took off, only he could not buy on the second time because Adam would not lend him money again. Our son never spoke to Adam after that. Patricia is here with me, but my other daughter met this much older guy and asked Adam for a fraction of the amount of money which our son had lost. Adam disapproved of the boyfriend and chose not to let her have a penny. Our daughter left us, disappeared with her boyfriend. In each case I trusted Adam's wisdom, I thought it was the right thing to do at the time. I called it tough love, but the result was losing my son and daughter. My son, well, we are speaking again, Patricia, Lauren and I are going over to visit. For my daughter it is too late. My daughter's girlfriend phoned me just before Christmas. The girlfriend told me I was the grandmother of Lauren and in the same breath informed that my daughter had been killed in a road accident. She has been very supportive, the girlfriend I mean. In fact, she said she might drop in, see if I'm okay and check Lauren out. She calls herself Lauren's fairy godmother." Miranda gazed at Lauren, "I'm your mum now."

"Miranda, I'm very sorry, I really had no idea."

"Yes, well, hopefully the worst is over. I'm living again, I still have a son, a daughter and Lauren don't forget. Patricia is looking forward to meeting her brother again. It has been hard for Patricia too, losing her father and her sister."

"Do you think about your other daughter?"

"Of course, I wish we had been on speaking terms. I wish I'd been better able to influence Adam. I wish I'd taken their side against Adam. That is my daughter and I in the photograph next to those daffodils."

"So that isn't Patricia, your other daughter had a look of Patricia and you look younger there."

"I was younger. She wasn't at all like Patricia, Kate was determined, single-minded and quietly stubborn." Her train of thought was interrupted by a loud knock at the door which broke the moment. "That will be Diana, now hold on to Lauren for me while I answer the door." In a tearful condition of incredulity, I cautiously offered my arms to accept the exquisite buddle of love.